Quest of Eight Part Five: Release of the Demons

Richard Reda

Quest of Eight Part Five: Release of the Demons

Richard Reda

The Quest of Eight

Part five: Release of the Demons

Quest of Eight Part Five: Release of the Demons

Richard Reda

The Quest of Eight

Part five: Release of the Demons

By

Richard Reda

Quest of Eight Part Five: Release of the Demons

Richard Reda

Published 2012

ISBN-13:
978-0988365605

ISBN-10:
098836560X

This book is dedicated to our first eight Grandchildren

Summer

Lochen

Solveig

Sean

Natalie

Stella

Quinn

Liam

With a special thanks to my wife for her support and her editing and to Jill Fox and Melanie Simon for their editing. And a special thanks to Quinn for the names of many of the characters.

Quest of Eight Part Five: Release of the Demons

Richard Reda

Quest of Eight Part Five: Release of the Demons

Richard Reda

Quest of Eight Part Five: Release of the Demons

Richard Reda

The Quest of Eight

Part five: Release of the Demons

Chapter one

The image of the troll as he lowered himself to the ground and fell into his final sleep weighed heavily on the minds of each of them. Ever since they had left the towers at Virkio, the skies had been a gun-metal gray, which did nothing to lighten their mood. Now faced with the knowledge that someone, who appeared to be a Rebbercand, had beaten them to the locations of both of the remaining pieces of the pendant, a feeling of desperation settled in.

They had also lost any sense of time. They couldn't recall if it had been night or day when the towers were destroyed, or when the dragon flew them untold miles to deposit them with the sentinel, Sarnanok. It was probably close to evening and they should probably be seeking shelter of some kind. Each was lost in his or her own thoughts. No one wanted to make a decision. Finally, Liam decided for them.

"We need to stop for the night," he said. "We're close to the end of this forest and will reach open fields tomorrow. After that it's another two or three days to the Swamp – maybe more. We need to find

11

some food, gather materials for a fire and to build a bit of shelter, and find some things we can use as weapons."

"Are you expecting danger?" asked Natalie.

"Not around here," he answered. "But once we get into the Swamp, that's another story. I almost never went out without some kind of armament, and never on foot. Right now, we'll be doing both."

"Wait a minute," interjected Sean. "Are we going to pretend we didn't see what we saw back there? We're acting like nothing weird just happened. We just saw a troll curl up and turn into a pile of dust."

"I don't think we're unmindful of what occurred," said Lochen. "I wonder if we fully understand it."

"Oh, I understand it all right," Sean replied. "A giant troll, which none of us thought even existed, told us he doesn't eat people anymore – anymore? Are you kidding? And then he tells us to go to the Swamp, but doesn't tell us where. And then, as if all that isn't weird enough, he drops to the ground, looks like he's going to take a nap and turns to dust. I understand that perfectly."

"That's not what he meant," said Solveig in defense of her brother. "Why was he so old to begin with? Why was he chosen as a sentinel? Is what happened to him going to happen to all the sentinels we meet? If so, then it must have happened to Beebee, and who knows who else? And if that's true, then why?"

"Actually," interrupted Lochen, "I think the answer to those questions should be relatively obvious."

"Not to me," said Sean.

"Me, either," added Quinn.

"I think I know – at least some of the answers," said Stella. "They – the sentinels – were chosen by the Alchemist. I'm not sure why, or when, but I would guess that he did that when the Kelpies were rebelling. He must have cast a spell to slow their aging down to almost nothing, which is why they all seem so old."

"And what breaks that spell?" asked Natalie.

"The spell is broken when they've served their purpose," said Lochen. "Maybe even sooner than that."

"And what exactly is their purpose?" asked Sean.

"To provide us with something – information, guidance, perhaps a defense of some kind against what we are facing," continued Lochen.

"And then what?" asked Summer. "They die and turn to dust?"

"So it seems," answered Stella.

"Who would volunteer to do that?" asked Sean. "That's crazy. I know you couldn't get me to volunteer."

"Sarnanok said they didn't volunteer; that they were chosen," pointed out Solveig.

"What did the old woman – what was her name? Beebee? What did she say about being chosen?" asked Liam.

"She didn't make much sense of anything," said Solveig. "I don't remember her saying anything about it. But to be honest, once I saw that she had turned me blue, I wasn't really paying any attention to anything she said."

"OK," said Sean. "They didn't volunteer, they were chosen. And they were chosen by whom? By the Alchemist? Why?"

No one answered immediately. Lochen looked deep in thought. He believed he knew the answer, but it was only speculation at this point. He thought it better to keep his opinion on this to himself, at least for the time being.

"And if they die once they talk to us," Quinn said when no one answered Sean's question, "why would they want to talk to us? Seriously. If it was me, I'd run the other way. Why wouldn't they?"

"I imagine their extremely long life is not as appealing towards the end as it would appear at the beginning," offered Lochen.

Before anyone could ask what he meant, they came to the end of the forest and upon a vista of tall grass and rolling hills that stretched as far as they could see. Even with an overcast sky, the view was a pleasant change from what they had been faced with for the last several days, maybe even weeks.

"Wow," said Summer. "I forgot what wide open spaces were like."

She flew out ahead of the others and did a few loop-the-loops before returning.

"That's what I was worried about," said Liam.

"You're worried about wide open spaces?" asked Summer. "Really? I know it's still not a bright sunny day, but these wide open spaces have to be an improvement."

"It will be easier walking," he told her, "but there's no shelter. We'll be exposed with no place to hide. We need to camp here until morning."

They found an area at the edge of the woods where a clump of trees provided a small barrier behind them and opened up to the fields in front of them. Quinn and Natalie went in search of firewood, while

Sean and Solveig looked for food. Liam and Summer hunted around for sticks that could be sharpened and used as spears.

Lochen and Stella agreed to construct some modest shelters, but they argued that there was little need for defenses, at least for now. They had told the others that since they were beyond the Alchemist's spells, which protected the towers, their own powers should be sufficient defense. However, Liam pointed out that there was no way for them to tell when those powers could be compromised by some other kinds of spells.

"With all due respect," he said. "I'd feel safer if I wasn't the only one with some old fashioned weapons. And I think we need to post a guard during the night."

"If you insist," said Lochen. "I won't require any sleep. I will be glad to stand watch while you all get some rest."

Quinn and Natalie returned with their arms filled with kindling and logs – enough to keep a good sized blaze going throughout the night. Quinn had a huge bundle of sticks under one arm and several good sized logs under the other.

Sean and Solveig returned shortly after Natalie and Quinn. Solveig had a wide assortment of fruits and nuts. Sean had some items that Solveig told the others it was better not to ask about. Solveig was able to carry a large supply in the several pockets she discovered in her cloak, and Sean had his arms full of a wide assortment of roots and tubers and things Solveig didn't want to think about.

Liam and Summer returned with Liam carrying most of the items, and Summer pulling several strands of honeysuckle vine. He had found a few sticks that could be sharpened to spears, and some larger pieces to which he could tie rocks with the vines to fashion some clubs.

"Who do you expect to run into?" asked Sean. "An army?"

15

Quest of Eight Part Five: Release of the Demons

Richard Reda

"Didn't you get a good look at the images on that troll?" Liam asked. "There were a lot of what looked like hobgoblins following that guy that looked like a Rebbercand. We could be running into a lot more trouble than we know."

"I thought they looked like gargoyles," said.

"No," answered Liam. "Gargoyles are smaller. And they're not as smart or well-trained as hobgoblins."

Lochen started a fire while the others finished building some lean-tos. Sean went about wrapping the food he had found inside some large leaves. When he was done, he placed them along the edge of the flames to heat them up. In a few minutes smoke and steam began to rise from the wrappings.

"What's burning?" asked Quinn, wrinkling his nose. "It smells like walrus fat gone bad."

"It's <u>not</u> walrus fat," answered Sean. "It's an old family recipe and you're going to love it. And how could walrus fat <u>go</u> bad? Doesn't it start off that way?"

"It smells more like you're burning some old family members, instead of a family recipe," remarked Quinn.

By the time everyone had finished whatever they were doing, Sean pulled the rolled leaves from the edge of the fire and passed them around. When they were opened, the substance inside looked like a gray paste, smelled like worms and had the consistency of leather. It tasted even worse, except to Sean who dug in heartily. Or more specifically, it would have tasted worse if any of the others had gathered the courage to try.

"What's the matter?" he asked when he was no one else was eating. "Aren't you hungry? This stuff is great!"

Quest of Eight Part Five: Release of the Demons

Richard Reda

The others looked from one to the next, each waiting for someone else to start in. Lochen took a deep breath and muttered something about whatever didn't kill him would only make him stronger, and scooped up some of the glop onto two of his fingers. He hesitated as he brought it towards his mouth, closed his eyes and shoved it in.

"Maybe I was wrong about it not killing me," he mumbled, swallowing hard and smiling feebly, trying hard not to choke.

"Good, isn't it?" asked Sean, wolfing down another mouthful.

"Mmmm," responded Lochen, trying hard not to grimace.

He winced in spite of his best efforts, shifting the portion he couldn't force down his throat from one side of his mouth to the other. One by one the others took tentative tastes and when Sean wasn't looking, flung it into the woods behind them.

"Here," he said, noticing that Quinn's food was all gone. "Have some more."

"Oh," said Quinn. "I couldn't. Really. I'm stuffed. I've had too much already. Liam, you can have it."

He passed the offered leaf and what Sean claimed was food to Liam, who only glared at Quinn and reluctantly accepted. As soon as Sean was distracted, it was flung into the woods with all the other helpings. Seven empty stomachs crawled under the lean-tos immediately afterward and hoped that the morning meal would be a little more palatable.

The fire did a lot to dispel their worries about the unknown and the darkness, but none of them was able to get much sleep. They all did their best to muffle the sounds of their grumbling stomachs.

Aside from still being hungry – except for Sean, who was wolfing down his meal – were troubled by what they had recently encountered.

Quest of Eight Part Five: Release of the Demons

Richard Reda

What little sleep they were able to get was filled with recurring images of Rebbercands, hobgoblins, trolls and dragons chasing them through the dark – things nightmares are made of.

The new day arrived looking much like the previous one – gray and depressing. The sky was dull and flat, but at least it didn't look like it was going to rain. Stella was the first to awaken and found Lochen sitting near the fire, poking it with a stick, lost in thought.

"They're too far ahead of us, aren't they?" she asked, reading his mind.

She sat down next to him, picked up a nearby stick and added it to the fire.

"Yes," he answered. "I believe they are."

He added his stick to the fire.

"But I haven't given up hope," he added. "At least not yet. We have two advantages. First, I don't think they know the exact location of the Kelpie, which will slow them down, and second, they don't have someone with them who is intimately familiar with the Swamp."

"I'll grant the second advantage," Stella answered. "Having Liam with us clearly gives us an edge. But I don't know if we have any more information than they do about the exact location. Even with the map as I'm able to envision it, I can't see precisely where we need to go. I don't think I know enough to tell Liam where we're going. As well as he knows the Swamp, it's still a large area."

"Ah, I think you underestimate us," Lochen said with a smile.

He turned to face her.

"Do you recall the markings on the cave or whatever that room was when we first met Quinn?" he asked.

"Yes. The symbols he was certain referred to us. You don't believe that, do you? They couldn't really represent any of us, could they?"

"Let's just say that for right now, I don't <u>disbelieve</u> it," he said.

"Those were ancient folk tales," she objected. "And those markings were made long before any of us were born – long before any of our parents, grandparents, or great grandparents were born. They couldn't possibly be connected to any of us."

"Do you recall the markings on the band that Summer wrested from Ena Ray?" he continued, ignoring her objection.

She thought for a minute, trying to remember what she saw. After a few seconds, she shook her head.

"Honestly, no," she finally said. "It all happened so fast, and it was so dark in there. I remember the band flying across that cavern and then hanging in the air in front of us. It seemed to expand in size, didn't it? And then we all held on to it. What happened then is all a blur."

She seemed to be concentrating on the event. It was like trying to remember parts of a dream. Lochen watched, letting the memories come back on their own.

"Except I remember being somewhere underground," she continued, "and that the band sealed some kind of portal, and then...nothing. I don't remember anything after that; and I don't have a really clear memory of what I actually do recall. It was like a dream."

"Well then," he said sitting up a bit straighter. "I suppose it's a good thing that I have a better recollection."

"Of course you do," she said sarcastically. "Why am I not surprised?"

He smoothed the dirt with his foot and then used the stick with which he had been poking the fire to draw a large circle. Then he drew a larger one around that. Satisfied that they were relatively even, he started making marks between the two circles at regular intervals, partitioning it into eight equal segments. He backed up slightly to view his handiwork, and then he began to make markings inside the segments.

"I can't remember the precise order," he said. "But I don't think that's critical."

He continued until there was a mark in each of the eight segments.

"There were eight symbols," he continued. "Quinn noted that three of them included a triangle, which he said signified a person of rank or position – or something like that. They were related to the air, the land, and the sea and had those types of symbols below them. Something like these here."

He pointed to the three symbols that included triangles.

"Yes," said Stella, as the memories slowly returned. "He said those represented Summer, Solveig and Natalie – the three princesses."

"Exactly. Then there was the symbol that appeared to be a flame, which I believe he said, represented you."

"That's right," Stella replied. "And there were the small circles that were the stars and planets that represented you."

"Hmmm. Stars and planets. I suppose that's one option," he answered, shaking his head. "Although I'm not convinced that's quite accurate."

He seemed to be thinking, but didn't expand on what he thought was inaccurate.

"However," he continued, "there was also the symbol that looked like trees, and the one that he mistook for an ice shelf, but we persuaded him represented his position as a Guardian of the Ice Kingdom."

"I remember now. He didn't agree with that interpretation. He argued that he wasn't special, that he was just ordinary, and, therefore, he couldn't be represented by one of the symbols."

"That's correct," Lochen said. "Which leaves this last one."

He moved the stick in the dirt drawing the image of an arrow head, the shaft and lines representing feathers.

"The directional arrow. Of course — the symbol Quinn said was connected with Liam," said Stella.

"Which is what we thought at the time," answered Lochen. "I'm not so sure, though, that their meaning is limited to what Quinn expressed. I think these symbols — not just the arrow symbol, but all of them — mean more than what we first understood them to be."

"I don't follow you," said Stella. "What else could they mean?"

"Close your eyes and tell me what you see."

She did as he asked. At first the images from the map that had been seared into her mind's eye were all she could see. She concentrated on trying to move them or diminish their prominence, but they persisted in remaining in the forefront of her vision.

"I'm sorry," she said after several seconds. "All I can see are the images from that wall or whatever it was that appeared. The thing that none of you saw."

"You said it contained markings that you somehow knew depicted the locations of the Kelpies," he reminded her. "Don't fight those images.

Quest of Eight Part Five: Release of the Demons

Richard Reda

Let them come forward. Close your eyes again and describe what you see."

Once more she closed her eyes. Her brow was furrowed in concentration. Beneath her lids, her eyes moved back and forth. As her internal vision became clearer, Lochen could see the expression on her face change.

"I can still see all the markings," she said, "but they're fuzzy – all but one. It's the one I think we're closest to – the location in the Swamp where we're heading. It's getting clearer and clearer. It's...it's that arrow!"

Her eyes popped open in surprise until she realized that when she did that, the vision disappeared. She quickly closed her eyes again.

"That's it exactly," she said. "It's the same arrow as on the cave wall. Wow. It's really gotten sharper. It's more visible than it was before. It looks just like the one you drew in the dirt – well, almost."

She concentrated for a few seconds, trying to memorize the vision. Then she opened her eyes again and took the stick from Lochen's hand. She smoothed the dirt at her feet and began to draw.

She started with a straight horizontal line. To the right she drew a triangle with the base line parallel to the horizontal line, another line perpendicular to the left side and then the downward line connecting the two, slanting to the right. Several inches to the left of the triangle, she drew four lines, parallel to each other and angling slightly away from the direction of the triangle. Then she stopped and looked at Lochen.

"That's the symbol," she announced, smiling at him.

"I thought you said it was an arrow," he said as she stared at him, still smiling. "That's not an arrow."

"This is the half that's above the ground," she answered and continued to draw.

"Are you saying that the other half is underground?" Lochen asked. "I'm not sure I understand."

"No," she said.

She finished the drawing, mirroring the first part immediately below. It now looked like a completed arrow.

"Not underground," she continued. "Reflected in water."

Lochen looked more closely, nodding.

"So what we're looking for is a series of trees near some kind of triangular object."

"We're looking for four identical trees near a large triangular object along a body of water," she corrected.

Lochen straightened up and turned towards her. A slight smile began to creep across his face.

"See," he said. "Our second advantage has just gotten stronger. We have more specific information. I'm confident that Liam will know with a high degree of certainty precisely where this location exists."

"What location?" asked Liam.

He was rubbing the sleep from his eyes as he walked up to where the two were crouched over some markings in the dirt.

"I heard my name being mentioned," he said, yawning. "Have you discovered something? I hope it's a better family recipe than what Sean forced on us last night. Anything would be better – well almost anything."

"Yes," said Stella. "We have discovered something. Not about the recipe, though, but about where we're going."

"Possibly," said Lochen.

"Possibly?" asked Stella. "What are you talking about? You just said you were sure he'd know where this was...is."

"That's correct," replied Lochen. "I am sure he knows where this location is, but I'm less confident that we have discovered much more than that."

"What more do we need to know?" asked Stella.

"A lot," answered Lochen. "We don't know how close we are to this location, or how much closer our adversaries are. Even if we reach it before they do, we don't know what to do when we arrive. And if we arrive at the same time, how we will be able to stop them from doing whatever it is they plan to do. There are far too many variables to be certain of much."

"You're a real buzz kill, you know that?" said Stella.

"Wait a minute," said Liam. "You're sure I'd know where what is?"

He turned his head in different directions trying to understand what he was looking at, and ignoring their banter. He saw the circles Lochen had drawn, and then looked to the image that Stella had drawn.

"Does this look at all familiar?" Stella asked him, pointing to the arrow she had scratched in the dirt.

She pointed first to the drawing of the trees, and then to the triangle and finally to the reflection.

"Yeah," he said. "It's an arrow. Do I win a prize?"

"Besides that," said Stella.

She rolled her eyes and ignored his question about a prize.

"Do you recall seeing anything like this in the Swamp?" she asked.

He studied the drawing a bit more closely, squatting down to get a better look. He raised one hand to block out the bottom half which Stella had added to represent the reflection in the water. He scratched his head and wrinkled his face. Then he moved his hand to reveal the entire sketch, and stood up.

"Yes, I do," he said, nodding his head. "It's on the far side near the edge — I guess from where we are that would be more like the near edge. It's at the southwest tip of the Swamp. I've only been there a few times, and I never looked at it from this direction, but, yes, it does look familiar. Why?"

"We think this is where one of the Kelpies was hidden," answered Lochen.

"Can you find it?" asked Stella.

"Of course I can," he replied. "But do you really want me to? It's one of the worst places in the Swamp, and that's saying a lot."

"In spite of my trepidation, I'm afraid we can't afford not for you to find it" said Lochen. "Powerful forces are about to be unleashed; forces that have been hidden for centuries. If our combined efforts are insufficient to stop one of these Kelpies, we will certainly never be able to stop more of them."

"More of them? How many are there?" asked Liam.

"I believe there are eight," Lochen replied.

He turned to Stella and asked, "Do you agree?"

Stella thought about it for a few seconds, looked at the drawing Lochen had made, and then answered, "Yes. There were eight symbols on the map that appeared to me and that is now burned into my memory."

"And there were eight symbols on the band that we removed from Ena Ray's possession in the Crystal Citadel," added Lochen.

"I'll have to take your word for that," said Liam. "I don't remember much about the Citadel, Ena Ray or that band."

He looked down at the drawings in the dirt.

"Is that what all this is?" he asked, waving his hand at the figures in the dirt.

Lochen and Stella looked at the markings, then at each other and then to Liam.

"Yes," Stella answered. "It all seems to be connected. These symbols seem to have something to do with the location of the Kelpies. My vision is clearest of the one that's closest."

"I would assume that when we get closer to the other locations, those will get clearer, too," added Lochen.

"If we know where they are," said Liam, "then it should be easy to get to these places, but what are we supposed to do then? Do we hide them better? Is there some way to destroy them? And in any case, what's the rush? If we have a map, aren't we the only ones who know where they are?"

"Those are all good questions," said Lochen. "I'm not sure I can answer all of them."

"I can answer the last one," said Stella. "No. We're not the only ones who know where they are. When that vision appeared to me..."

"That invisible wall thing?" asked Liam.

"Yes," said Stella, looking a little defensively at the two of them. "That invisible wall thing. When that...thing appeared to me, I could feel that it was happening somewhere else at the same time."

"How could you know that?" asked Liam.

"The same way I knew that the piece of the pendant that was hidden at Virkio was gone before we even got there," she answered. "I can't explain it. Something about this stone," she reached up and touched the pieces imbedded in her headband, "makes me able to feel...I don't know...some kind of connection between the pieces and anything connected with them."

Lochen could see the confusion and disbelief in Liam's face.

"I have a similar connection with Solveig," he tried to explain. "A bond exists between us that allows us to feel when the other is in danger."

"And I have the same kind of connection with Natalie," added Stella. "Every Enchantress is linked with a soul-mate from the time of her birth. It's that kind of connection that exists between the pieces of this pendant. I knew the last piece had been found and fused to the other one the instant it happened.

"I think that's also when the vision appeared. I have to believe that same vision appeared to whoever now possesses the other pieces of the pendant. If I'm right, then that person knows where the Kelpies are hidden, too."

"Maybe it's the Alchemist," said Liam. "Or someone like him."

"That may be possible," said Lochen, "But I believe it to be highly unlikely. Consider that Virkio was the fortress of the Alchemist and guarded by a dragon. If the other pieces of the pendant were in the possession of the Alchemist or one of his supporters, why would that person have killed the dragon? Why were we set upon by hobgoblins?"

"And don't forget the images in the Troll's tattoos," added Stella. "More and more, I'm sure that those were accurate. We're chasing some Rebbercand and a small army of hobgoblins. And we have no time to lose."

"Then you probably want to take the most direct route, don't you?" asked Liam, slowly shaking his head.

"That would seem to make the most sense," answered Lochen. "But I sense some hesitation on your part."

"You sense correctly," said Liam. "The most direct route will take us across some open fields, which should present no problems. However, I would have preferred skirting around the Navedis Forest."

"We've been in some strange and dangerous places before," said Stella. "What makes this one any worse than any of them?"

"The Navedi," said Liam.

"What's that?" asked Stella. "Some kind of creature?"

"It's a who," said Liam, "not a what. They're a tribe that lives in the woods near the Swamp. I've never seen them myself, and I admit that my knowledge of them is limited to stories told to me when I was a child, but trust me, the stories were pretty scary. If half of what I remember is true, we need to be very careful."

"I take it they're dangerous," said Stella.

"If the stories I was told are any indication, no one who ever ventured into their territory ever returned," he responded.

"I'm not sure I understand," interjected Lochen. "If no one ever returned, who told the stories about these people?"

Liam thought about that a minute.

"I suppose you've got a point."

"If you have never seen them, then it's possible that these people no longer inhabit the region. Isn't it?" asked Lochen. "That is, if they ever really existed in the first place."

"I suppose," said Liam. "The few times I traveled in that area, I never saw any signs of them, but then, I wasn't really looking, either."

"Well," concluded Lochen, "it's appropriate that we remain vigilant, whether the Navedi are real or not. We shouldn't run headlong towards this location in any regard. Rebbercands, hobgoblins and Kelpies are sufficiently treacherous for us to keep our guard."

"What should we tell the others?" asked Stella.

"It might be best if we limit our discussion to what we know, and what they already believe: that we are in pursuit of a Rebbercand and a small group of hobgoblins; and that we're all converging on a location where a Kelpie has been imprisoned for about two thousand years."

"That should be enough to make them edgy," said Liam.

"That and the thought of having to eat another one of Sean's home cooked meals," said Stella.

Chapter two

When B'nair led his party from Virkio, he had more than a dozen followers. By the time he had departed the fortress of the Thumpers, he was down to ten. He chose not to wait for the additional men he had directed meet him at the drawbridge to the walled city that had long ago been devastated by some kind of plague. He knew he was being followed and that he had to take advantage of whatever lead he currently had. He had underestimated these people before in the mines of the Trepans, assuming they were the same ones. He wouldn't make that mistake again.

He knew he was headed for the Venomous Swamp and would probably lose a few more of his men, but that couldn't be helped. In his earlier travels when he was searching for a new home for his people, he had come upon the Swamp on more than one occasion. He was well aware of the hazards in that area of the world – severe enough to prevent his people from ever trying to settle there, regardless of how short a time that may have been. No matter what they did, they would never be able to make that place even minimally hospitable.

In spite of the potential dangers ahead, he had set off from the drawbridge at a run and hadn't stopped. It was now near nightfall, and he was well out of the forest, into the open fields. He had to admire the handful of men that was following him. It was clear they were well-trained and well-disciplined. No one had complained about the pace he had set. They probably knew better.

When he finally stopped, he sent some in search of food and others to set up guard stations in a circle around their encampment.

"Whatever you find to eat," he said, "be prepared to eat uncooked. We'll have no campfire tonight."

He expected some grumbling at that, but got none. His own Rebbercand soldiers would have made some noise about eating raw meat. Maybe he had underestimated the hobgoblins. When the hunting forays had returned and the encampment was in place, he announced to everyone that he was appointing Vardelos as his second in command.

"You do me too much honor, sir," Vardelos had said.

"I don't think so," B'nair responded. "I need someone I can trust, and you've proven to be that person. Besides, a time will come when I will need certain skills, or difficult decisions will have to be made. You know your people better than I. I will call on you to help me make those decisions."

Vardelos was on the verge of asking what kind of choices would be expected, but then thought better of it. The less he knew, the better he felt. He wasn't sure how much he could trust this Rebbercand. He worried that he already knew too much as it was, and that having too much information could make him a threat. He had seen B'nair acting strangely after the second piece of the pendant had been found.

He expected they would try to search for the remaining pieces, but instead B'nair had announced that they were going to find a Kelpie. He thought that perhaps the other pieces were in yet another location, or, quite possibly, in the possession of the Kelpie. He had never seen a Kelpie before, but he was aware of the stories told about them. They were not individuals to be trifled with.

When everyone had settled in for the night and the guards were posted, B'nair found Vardelos and pulled him off to the side, away from the others.

"Are you familiar with this area?" he asked.

"The area we are in now, or the one to which we are headed?"

"The one through which we will have to pass."

"Only by its reputation," Vardelos answered.

"Explain," ordered B'nair.

"Ahead of us, before we reach the Venomous Swamp, is the Navedis Forest. It follows a long river to the west and then to the north, curling around the westernmost edge of the Swamp. It would be more advisable to avoid this Forest."

"What do you know of it?"

"It is a place from which few return," said Vardelos. "I have never been there myself, but I have heard stories of the inhabitants. They are most unfriendly and exceedingly treacherous. It is difficult to subdue an enemy in his own home, but the Navedi have never been conquered. They are far too cunning and elusive."

B'nair nodded as Vardelos provided his commentary. His knowledge of the Forest was the same.

"The place we are seeking," explained B'nair "is on the other side of this Forest. As you have said, to bypass it will add another day, at least, to our quest. There are others who are following us who would do whatever it takes to keep us from our goal. I believe they will risk passing through the Forest in order to narrow the gap between us."

"Are these the same who followed us to the Towers?" Vardelos asked.

As soon as the words passed his lips, he wished that he could take them back. This Rebbercand was very powerful and very treacherous. He was also very unpredictable. Vardelos was not ignorant of how easily and quickly B'nair had usurped the leadership of this band of hobgoblins. He would have to be more careful about asking questions and seeking information. This new leader was not like his predecessor. It was not evident that questions were welcome. B'nair, however, didn't seem upset or concerned by the hobgoblin's curiosity.

"Yes," he said. "They are."

"I don't understand," said Vardelos. "How can that be?"

"It can be," answered B'nair, "because they defeated more than a dozen hobgoblins and escaped from those Towers. Unless you are telling me that your friends deserted their posts and allowed these strangers to leave the Towers unchallenged. Could that have happened?"

"No, sir," Vardelos answered after giving the question consideration. "They were too well trained. They would have stayed until the task was done or until someone relieved them or directed them elsewhere. Your assessment is correct. If the strangers escaped, they defeated my comrades."

Quest of Eight Part Five: Release of the Demons

Richard Reda

B'nair stared at the hobgoblin for several seconds, considering his answer. Vardelos struggled to maintain eye contact, but held B'nair's piercing gaze.

"I believe you," B'nair finally said. "If your comrades had been outnumbered, I might disagree, but the reverse was true. I think you're right. They stayed and were beaten – somehow – which only proves my point. These strangers are not to be underestimated."

"What do you propose?" Vardelos asked, once again chastising himself for being so impertinent.

B'nair studied the hobgoblin, weighing his options. He decided it was time to put his new second in command to the test.

"Which of your men is the most disposable?" he asked.

Vardelos wasn't particularly happy about the way the question was put, but this time he held his tongue. He wondered if this was the kind of difficult decision the Rebbercand had been talking about earlier. He gave some thought before responding, carefully considering the qualities of each of the remaining hobgoblins. He was certain that whoever he offered would not remain with them for much longer.

"Gazzien," he answered.

"And which one is he?" B'nair asked.

Vardelos discreetly pointed him out. B'nair studied the candidate and nodded his agreement. Gazzien was posted at one of the guard positions and was gazing at the stars instead of surveying the area in front of him. The Rebbercand surmised that this Gazzien would probably be adequate in an attack, but would not likely be missed if he were not to return from the assignment he had planned.

"He should do," said B'nair.

B'nair put his good arm around Vardelos' shoulders and leaned in close to discuss his plan. Vardelos had a hard time concentrating on the words being spoken to him. Being held this close to the Rebbercand was unsettling to him. He put his fears aside with great difficulty and focused on the instructions.

"Do you understand?" B'nair asked.

"Perfectly," Vardelos answered.

"Can you give such an order?"

"Yes, sir," the hobgoblin answered. "I can."

"And are you comfortable in doing so?"

"Comfortable?" Vardelos asked. "No. But it is necessary to ensure the safety of the rest of us and the success of our mission."

B'nair studied the hobgoblin and wondered if he was expressing what he truly thought or merely spouting a rhetoric he believed B'nair wanted to hear. In the end he decided it didn't really matter. Any delay this Gazzien person could create would put B'nair and his men at a greater advantage.

At first light Vardelos pulled Gazzien aside out of earshot of all the others. When they were alone, he instructed him to quietly split off from the rest of the group and make his way into the Navedis Forest. Once he entered the Forest, he was not to be inconspicuous. On the contrary, he was to attract attention. Once he made contact with the Navedi, he was to attack and injure or kill as many as he could, creating as much havoc as he could to enrage them into battle. Gazzien stepped back from Vardelos and looked closely at him.

"Is this a suicide mission?" he asked.

Vardelos knew that it in all likelihood it was, but he tried to shift the focus.

"It's a diversion," he answered. "Don't linger after your initial attack. Strike and then run. Is that clear?"

Gazzien continued to look at Vardelos. The only thing that was clear to him was that his chances of survival were little more than non-existent. He held Vardelos' gaze waiting for more of an explanation. Vardelos was waiting for Gazzien to answer his question. When he didn't respond, Vardelos became uncomfortable, and continued.

"You are not expected to defeat them," he said. "You are only to engage them so that they follow you. After you launch your attack, run back the way we all came. Lead them in the opposite direction of where we actually are. There are others following us. We believe these others will venture through the Forest. You are to lead the Navedi to them. You are NOT to get yourself killed."

"We?" asked Gazzien. "Now you and this Rebbercand are one person?"

"What does it matter?" Vardelos snapped back.

He could tell that Gazzien knew his chances of success were minimal. He could tell that Gazzien knew he was expendable. This knowledge was making this decision even more difficult than he had initially expected.

"It is the Rebbercand's plan," he tried to explain. "But I agree with it. We need for the Navedi to attack these others and either destroy them or at the very least delay them."

"And if I escape?" he asked. "What then?"

"No," said Vardelos, emphatically. "WHEN you escape, not IF you escape! When you escape, pick up our trail and meet us at the edge of the Swamp. We will be circling around the southeastern side of the Forest towards the river."

"The Swamp is very large," Gazzien said. "How do you expect me to find you?"

He thought Vardelos was being far too insistent about his ability to escape. He was convinced that Vardelos didn't believe what he, himself, was saying.

"I will leave sentries. One will be at the river where we leave the fields; another will be at the point where we enter the Swamp; and another will be along the trail we take once inside the Swamp. They will each wait and lead you to the rest of us."

Even as he said the words, Vardelos knew they were lies. He was sacrificing his friend and there was no way to describe it otherwise. Gazzien knew these were all lies, too. No sentries would be posted. No one would wait for him. No one would lead him to the others.

Without any further words, Gazzien picked up a bow and a quiver of arrows, added a pair of daggers and a sword to his belt, and departed. He made no farewells and didn't once look back over his shoulder as Vardelos watched him go.

Vardelos, on the other hand, watched him until he vanished from sight. He was still watching when B'nair came up beside him. He could feel the Rebbercand's presence, but made no move to acknowledge it.

"Get used to it," B'nair said.

He came up behind Vardelos, having watched the exchange between the two hobgoblins.

"Being a leader requires making hard decisions – decisions that affect the lives of others. It's all for the greater good – just as you said."

37

Quest of Eight Part Five: Release of the Demons

Richard Reda

Vardelos wasn't convinced any of this was for a greater good. It was only for the Rebbercand's good; but he kept silent.

"Let's get moving," B'nair said.

He turned and headed back to the encampment to get everyone assembled and ready to leave. A few seconds later, Vardelos silently wished his friend good luck and then turned to join the others.

The main group veered off to the right, giving a wide berth to the far edges of the Forest. They were still in open fields as the end of the day approached and they needed to make camp. The next day was much like the one before — wide open fields with no sign of any other living being. High in the sky a mass of black birds flew in perfect formation overhead, changing direction randomly, but in complete unison. They were heading for the Forest, but none of them came down far enough to be noticed by the travelers.

The hobgoblins were not particular about what they ate, and managed to get their fill by eating grass and some of the shrubbery that they passed along the way. B'nair's diet, however, had previously consisted of more traditional meals. After two days of not eating, even the grass and bushes were beginning to look good to him. Fortunately for him, however, a Blue Falcon decided to get a closer look at the small group that had been running across the fields for more than two days.

It had been following the swarm of black birds, waiting for a straggler to separate itself from the larger group and provide him with a tasty snack. No such straggler appeared, though, and the Falcon was easily distracted by the creatures on the ground.

It swooped down low enough to get a closer look, and became a target of one of the more attentive hobgoblins. The hobgoblin quickly and accurately fired an arrow that brought the creature down. He had originally intended to eat the bird himself, but Vardelos convinced him otherwise. He reluctantly offered the feast to their leader. In keeping with his own order of no campfires, B'nair ate the Falcon raw – meat, feathers, claws and bones.

The next day they began to encounter signs that the Swamp was near. There were marshy areas that appeared scattered throughout the grass. A few trees grew, but more had fallen – their roots rotted and poisoned by the toxins in the water. As they neared the river that separated the main body of the Swamp from the fields, Vardelos ignored his better judgment and offered a suggestion to B'nair.

"It might be good to use some of these trees to make a raft or two, and travel through the tributaries to the main body of water," he said.

B'nair looked around at the foliage, surveyed the path ahead and looked at the ground under his feet, which was already soggy. He hadn't thought much about how they would navigate the marshy areas of the Swamp. He had been too focused on their goal.

"I agree," he said. "Gather a few men to assemble the logs and send some others to find vines to tie them together. If you can find enough to make three rafts, do so. And include some kind of bulwark – enough to create a small edge all the way around the surface of the rafts."

Vardelos understood completely and set about the task. B'nair watched as he directed the other hobgoblins. Among the Rebbercands, too much independence and initiative would have been perceived as a threat to his leadership. He didn't feel that threat with Vardelos, though. At least not yet. It seemed as if the hobgoblin merely wanted to be of as much service as possible. Still, thought B'nair, he needed to be watched carefully.

Once the construction was completed – and Vardelos had managed to build three small rafts – they were pushed to the water's edge and launched. The hobgoblin had noted that there was nothing with which to make sails. Instead he found a number of long, narrow, but sturdy branches.

Quest of Eight Part Five: Release of the Demons

Richard Reda

"What are these for?" asked B'nair when he saw them being loaded onto the rafts.

"I thought that if we stayed close to the shore, where the water wasn't as deep, we could use these to push off the river bed in case we had to sail opposite the direction of the current. If that meets with your approval, that is."

B'nair looked from the poles to Vardelos and a smile crept across his face. Vardelos could barely distinguish the expression from a grimace, and was once again worried that he had gone too far.

"You're cleverer than I had given you credit for," murmured B'nair.

Vardelos wasn't sure if it was a compliment or a warning, and wasn't sure how to respond. He was still having a hard time understanding the Rebbercand.

"Thank you, sir," he said weakly when B'nair failed to say anything more.

He only hoped his response was appropriate. The Rebbercand continued to look at him for a few more seconds, only making him more uncomfortable.

"Yes. It meets with my approval. Besides we will have to travel against the current," B'nair eventually said. "These poles will help us do that. But I'm not too sure how close we want to stay to the shore. The last time I was in this cursed place, the so-called shore wasn't any safer than the pollution and poison that passes for water."

Vardelos had never been in or even near the Swamp before. The stories told by the hobgoblins painted a picture of a very forbidding place. B'nair's comments only reinforced that picture. He was aware that gargoyles – a distant cousin to the hobgoblins – inhabited the underground caverns that existed beneath the Swamp. However, some kind of feud had erupted between the gargoyles and the hobgoblins. He wasn't sure what the origin had been, but only knew that any information the gargoyles had about the Swamp they had kept to themselves.

The more he thought about this place, the less he liked it. He would be glad when they found whatever it was they were looking for and could leave. Right now, though, he hoped B'nair would decide to wait for morning before venturing out onto the water. There were still a few hours left before nightfall, but the thought of navigating these marshes in the dark did not appeal to him.

B'nair looked to the sky, and then back the way they had recently come. He wondered if Gazzien had been successful in creating the diversion he hoped for, or if the hobgoblin had realized what his fate was going to be and merely ran home. He assumed he would find out soon enough. He then looked towards the Swamp and the narrow, winding tributary where the rafts sat.

"Get on board," he shouted. "We'll stay close to the shore and stop before dark."

Vardelos swallowed hard, but kept his expression neutral. He turned to the others and started issuing instructions. He divided the group up, assuming B'nair would be in the lead raft. He chose three men to ride with the leader. He picked three more to board the second raft with him and left the remaining four to board the last one.

"Vardelos," shouted B'nair. "You're with me."

The hobgoblin quickly pulled one of the three he had chosen to be on the lead raft and motioned for him to go on the second one instead.

"I'm putting you in charge of this craft," Vardelos said to the one he had taken from the first raft and sent to the second. "Stay close and tell the last raft to do the same. If we get separated, it's not likely anyone will come looking for you."

Richard Reda

"Understood," came the reply.

When B'nair stepped over the low side and onto the raft, he noticed that several large leaves had been spread out on the deck. He saw that they were several layers thick and covered the entire deck.

"What are these for?" he asked.

"I thought they would keep the water from seeping through the logs. They'll keep our feet from getting wet," Vardelos answered nervously. "I can remove them if you think that's better. I should have asked you first. I'm sorry."

B'nair looked at Vardelos blankly. He looked down at the leaves and then back at the hobgoblin. Vardelos expected him to chastise him, but instead, he began to laugh.

"To keep our feet from getting wet," he said.

He laughed harder as he said the words, and shook his head.

"That's a good one," he said through the laughter. "We're headed into the gates of hell and you're worried about getting your feet wet. I'll have to remember that. If nothing else, Vardelos, you keep me amused."

- - - - - - - - - - - - - - - - - *** - - - - - - - - - - - - - - - - -

Gazzien marched off without another word. He was under no illusion that he would ever see his friend again. Some friend, he thought. Vardelos didn't even have the courage to be honest with him. He had half a mind to forget about all of them and find his way back home. That's probably what Vardelos and that Rebbercand expected, he muttered to himself.

Quest of Eight Part Five: Release of the Demons

Richard Reda

"Well, I won't give them that satisfaction," he said out loud. "I have the others to think of. If they need a diversion, I'll do it for them, but not for Vardelos!"

He walked for several hours as the distance between him and the rest of his party widened. Late in the day, he decided he had gone far enough and made camp for the night. Since he was alone and no longer subject to the silly rules of B'nair, he gathered up some small twigs and scrub and made a fire. He hadn't seen any signs of life for several days, and he doubted there was anyone who would see his camp. He was wrong.

The next day, he was still miles from the Navedi Forest and decided to slow his pace a bit. He surveyed the surrounding area and could see the first signs of the Forest on the distant horizon. He looked up at the overcast sky, hoping it wouldn't rain. That was when he noticed a single Blue Falcon floating high above. He knew they usually traveled in larger flocks and at least in pairs. Seeing one was unusual.

What he didn't know was that one of his comrades had shot down the Falcon's mate. This one was searching for it. The pair had been following a large swarm of black birds and then, unexpectedly its mate had disappeared. Like its partner, this one made the same mistake of swooping down too far to get a better look at the lone figure crossing the plains. That night Gazzien roasted a large Blue Falcon over his camp fire.

Like the previous night, his campfire, and now the aroma of the cooking, was observed. The pair of eyes that had noticed him earlier was now joined by several others. They watched intently as he made his way towards their home. Word of his pending arrival traveled fast. Soon more pairs of eyes were watching the moves of this intruder.

By early afternoon of the next day, Gazzien entered the Forest. As instructed, he made no secret of his arrival. He whistled and then attempted to sing. In the end, he resorted to talking to himself.

Quest of Eight Part Five: Release of the Demons

Richard Reda

The trees weren't thick in this Forest, but their branches extended great distances, like very long fingers stretching out from very long arms. The trunks were wide and covered with bark that was black as night; the long black limbs and thin black branches were dense with leaves that were also black. The muted light that penetrated the gray sky also filtered through the network of branches providing just enough light to see – but not very far.

Eventually, the gray clouds above were obscured and replaced by a greenish fog that rolled across the ground and rose up to the black leaves. Gazzien slowed his pace even further, trying to see through the trees. Before he knew it, a person appeared before him – about twenty feet ahead. He looked around but saw no one else.

"And just where did you come from?" he asked.

He looked around again and still saw no one else. He had been expecting to see more of the Navedi, but he was secretly relieved to see there was only the one. Maybe he could scare him and get away from here after all. He slowly removed an arrow from his quiver and placed it in his bow. Taking his time, he pulled the bow string back as far as he could and took careful aim. His target didn't even bother to move. He showed no sign of fear.

"I have a little present for you," he said as he released the arrow.

The shaft shot across the expanse between the two of them and at the last second, the Navedi stepped sideways, reached up, and grabbed the arrow in midflight. The smile quickly vanished from Gazzien's face.

He thought about shooting another arrow, but decided his target would merely do the same thing – grab it in midflight. He was so fast that Gazzien realized he couldn't fire faster than the Navedi could grab the arrows. Instead, he hung the bow on the quiver on his back, and pulled the short sword from a scabbard on his belt.

"Let's see if you can catch this," he said as menacingly as he could.

Gazzien walked slowly, shifting the sword from one hand to the other and back again. He was crouched down and varied the speed of his approach. He was hoping to provoke some kind of reaction so that he would know how to better make his attack. He had been trained to use his sword with either hand, and found it more effective if his opponent wasn't sure from which side the attacks would come.

The Navedi didn't appear to be intimidated. He simply stared at Gazzien as the distance between them closed, cocking his head to the side and watching. When it had been reduced by half, he began to slowly step backwards, moving away from Gazzien's approach. Gazzien smiled – confident that his foe was frightened. He would make this as quick and painless as he could – well, maybe not as painless as he could.

"I thought you Navedi were supposed to be brave warriors," he said, taunting the single hunter. "Not back peddlers."

The Navedi continued to walk backwards, his eyes fixed on Gazzien. It was apparent he was very familiar with these woods, since he didn't seem to need to see where he was going. Gazzien shifted his approach slightly in the hopes of forcing the Navedi to back into a tree. Instead, the Navedi sidestepped the closest obstacle and backed up even further, moving stealthily through the woods.

Gazzien's smile faltered only briefly. He can see better in these woods moving backwards than I can moving forward, he thought. He quickened his pace slightly to try to close the distance between them. As soon as he did that, the Navedi stopped. The sudden change caught Gazzien by surprise and he, too, stopped. He stood upright rather than in the crouched attack position in which he previously had been.

The silence was shattered by a tremendous screeching sound. Gazzien looked upward in the direction of the noise. The dense leaves were moving. He realized they weren't leaves at all, but thousands of black

Grackles. Something had spooked the birds. They took flight, baring the limbs on which they had perched and filling the air with their shrieking.

When Gazzien realized he had been distracted, he took two or three quick defensive steps backward and raised his sword. He looked towards where the Navedi had been standing, expecting to see that he had moved. He hadn't. Instead there were now three of them. Two more had joined the first, lone Navedi. Where had they come from, Gazzien wondered.

This changed things. Although the odds were not in his favor any more, and his confidence had dropped, he knew he had been trained well. That training included facing multiple opponents at the same time. He looked closely and could see that the three facing him didn't appear to be armed, except for a stick that each of them carried. The stick was straight and smooth and about three or four feet long.

Gazzien was certain he could easily cut through those sticks, disarming each of them. Even with three of them to face, he believed he was better skilled and better armed. By now the Grackles had settled back to their perches, seemingly to serve as spectators to the impending battle. Their squawking noise died down, and the ensuing quiet worried Gazzien. It was too quiet. He sensed a presence behind him.

He kept his sword pointed forward and shifted his body sideways before sneaking a glance behind him. He jerked his head back and then as quickly returned his focus forward, pulling a dagger from his belt with his other hand in the same instant. In the split second he looked back, he was able to discern shapes he was sure had not been there before. He took another look, snapping his head back to the area behind him.

He had been right. There were new, different shapes: four more Navedi. He was surrounded. Where did they come from, he asked himself. He had been extremely vigilant, studying his surroundings from the moment he entered the Forest. There was no way they could have snuck up from behind him. It was as if they appeared from thin air.

These four looked like the three in front of him – armed only with the same kind of sticks as the others. Seven of them! This would be more difficult than before. He would have to inflict wounds and try to make his escape.

He decided to focus his attack on the four behind him. He threw his sword and dagger downward, sticking them into the dirt. He pulled the bow from over his shoulder and an arrow from his quiver. He readied his bow. If he could wound one or two and distract the others, he could make a break in the confusion, running back the way he had come.

Attacking the three that were in front of him would be easier, but once he got past them, he'd only be deeper in the Forest – deeper in territory that was their home, and completely unfamiliar to him. He would have to take his chances with the four behind him.

He pulled two more arrows from the quiver and stuck them in the ground at his feet, next to his sword and dagger. Here they would be closer at hand and he'd be able to fire them in rapid succession. He thought if he could hit at least two of them, he'd then quickly retrieve his two blades and charge the remaining two.

He pulled the arrow back, but before releasing it, he felt a sting at the back of his neck. It must have been some kind of insect. At first he ignored it, and again pulled the arrow back. Once more, before he could release it, he felt another sting. This time it was near the top of his shoulder.

He spun around, looking for the source. All he saw were the Navedi behind him. One of them had the stick he had been carrying raised to his mouth. What was he doing, wondered Gazzien. Then he felt

47

another sting. This one was in the middle of his back. Where was this coming from?

He turned back towards the four behind him. None of them had moved any closer, but one of them had his stick held up to his mouth – exactly like one of the ones behind him. Then he saw the Navedi in front of him jerk his head. He could barely see the tiny dart as it shot forward, striking him in the chest.

They were shooting darts at him. How foolish was that, he thought. They think their tiny little darts are a match for arrows and swords? He reset his arrow in the bowstring and started pulling back. He'd show them what real force was.

But his arms wouldn't cooperate. He pulled with all his might, but the bow and the string barely moved. Then his hands failed him. He lost his grip on the bow and the arrow. They fell to the ground as he felt another sting. This one was in his chest, close to the other one. He reached up to pull them out, but his hands wouldn't close.

He lifted his hand closer to his face and stared at it. He tried wiggling his fingers, but nothing happened. Why aren't you working, he mumbled out loud. The sound of his voice startled him. It wasn't his voice he heard. His words were slurred. He couldn't feel his tongue.

He began to panic. Get out of here, he told himself. Run as fast as you can. He lifted one foot, but he couldn't feel his legs. His foot slapped against the ground and he staggered first to the right, and then to the left. Another sting – in his thigh. He looked dumbly down at the little dart.

By now each of the darts was burning his flesh. He tried to pull them out, but his hands wouldn't close on them. As quickly as the burning sensation spread, it disappeared. He poked his chest where the first dart had planted. He couldn't feel his chest either. His skin was numb. His muscles were numb. He fell forward onto his face.

Quest of Eight Part Five: Release of the Demons

Richard Reda

He had closed his eyes as the ground seemed to rise to meet him. He tried to raise his arms to break his fall, but they dropped and hung uselessly at his sides. His face smacked the dirt as it hit, but he felt nothing. He could hear the leaves on the ground rustling, so he knew he was still awake.

He opened his eyes. One was blocked by the ground, but the other could see the floor of the Forest and the bottoms of the trees. Then he saw a pair of feet approach. He tried to say something but he couldn't form any words.

He could see one of the Navedi push his shoulder with the stick he was carrying, but he couldn't feel anything. The next thing he saw was the Forest roll past him. He was looking at the tree tops and the faces of several Navedi staring down at him. He was completely motionless, but his eyes were wide open.

He wondered if this was some kind of dream. He tried to call out, but nothing happened, other than some unintelligible noise. His level of panic rose when he realized that noise was coming from him. He could see and hear everything, but he could move nothing.

Two of the Navedi disappeared for a few seconds. When they came back, they had a long pole which they dropped on top of him. The pole landed on his chest and smacked him on the face, but he didn't feel anything.

He saw one of the Navedi raise his arms while another tied his hands around the pole. Still he felt nothing. He couldn't see it, but he was sure others were securing his feet to the pole as well. Then he saw the pole rise up into the air and his head dropped back –downwards toward the ground – changing his view.

The Forest was now upside down and he could see that he was being carried. The Navedi had captured him and were now taking him to their encampment. Gazzien knew he would not be escaping. He knew

49

he would not be rejoining his comrades. He knew he had not been successful in his mission.

While he didn't know what was going to happen to him, he knew it was not going to be good.

Chapter three

The three rafts were eased into the tributary and pushed through the reeds towards the main channel of water. The going was very slow at first. It was difficult to determine how deep the stream ran or where it actually flowed. Sometimes it seemed to disappear altogether. Having decided to embark before dark, B'nair felt committed now to continue, although he was afraid they would still be in this marsh by the time it was so dark they would have to stop.

Vardelos watched the two crafts that followed the one he was in. There was only enough room for one person to use the long poles to push the rafts along. The one with that task started at the front of the raft, along the side; sunk the pole to the bottom of the water and then, pushing down on it, walked towards the back of the raft. Once he reached the end, he pulled the pole free of the muddy bottom, carried it back to the front and repeated the process.

Quest of Eight Part Five: Release of the Demons

Richard Reda

If this had been any place other than the Venomous Swamp, one of the others would have climbed into the water to push or pull the craft until it reached deeper water. However, no one was willing to volunteer for that assignment. He couldn't blame them, and hoped that the Rebbercand wouldn't think of this himself.

The large leaves he had placed on the floor of each of the rafts, while keeping the water away from them, made the walking more difficult. If the pole got stuck, or the raft got caught up on undergrowth, the leaves proved to be too slippery for the pusher to get a good foothold. The hobgoblins in the last raft decided they were far enough away to flaunt Vardelos' efforts and threw the leaves overboard.

They were able to get a better footing and able to propel their raft a bit more steadily. As a result, they often bumped into the middle raft, pushing it ahead, keeping all three rafts in close proximity to one another.

To Vardelos' relief – and to B'nair's, although he would never admit it – they broke through a cluster of razor grass and into the main stream shortly after the last daylight faded away.

"Stop here," shouted B'nair. "Shove your pole into the mud as deeply as you can. Tie off the raft and use the pole as an anchor."

The lead raft stopped close to the shore line opposite the Swamp and the others butted up against it. One after the other, the poles were driven into the mire and the rafts were tied snugly to them. B'nair ordered a guard posted in the first and third rafts and then everyone settled in for the night.

It was difficult to sleep. Throughout the night there were odd sounds coming from the reeds on one side of them and even odder sounds coming from deep within the Swamp on the other side of them. To make matters worse, there were several insects buzzing around them all night. Vardelos, in spite of his efforts to get some rest, stayed awake the entire time.

Quest of Eight Part Five: Release of the Demons

Richard Reda

During the night, well below the bottoms of the rafts, a nest of Niekumites were alerted to a change on the surface of the marsh. Niekumites were tiny amphibian creatures – scavengers. They attached themselves to plants and animals that fell victim to other predators in the waterways of the Swamp – or to anything that stayed in one place for too long.

They were so small that individually, they were almost impossible to see. However, they never appeared individually. They appeared in the thousands – hundreds of thousands, in fact. At first they seemed to look like some kind of mold, clumping in a black fuzz-like cluster on dead vegetation or carcasses. But then the "mold" would grow and infest its host, devouring it from within.

They burrowed their way deep inside and began to eat their way outward, destroying whatever they were attached to. On rare occasions, they came upon a living source to infest. But once they did, the infestation happened with amazing speed; and once infested, the host would almost never be able to get rid of them.

This particular nest of Niekumites was disturbed when the pole from the third raft sunk into the mud to anchor the craft for the night. The pole had been driven deep into the nest and then stayed there. The closest Niekumites latched on while others inched their way over and upward.

Throughout the night, the blanket of mold crept up the pole and then to the underside of the raft. It spread across the logs, looking for an opening upward. They found several in the spaces between the logs. They oozed through the spaces and up to the floor of the raft.

Almost as a single entity, the horde of Niekumites stopped once it reached the night air. Hundreds of scouts probed in each direction until a food source was found. Less than a foot away was another opening. It was pressed against one of the logs and looked like a large tunnel lined with ridges and thin strands of foliage. They moved silently and relentlessly onward – deeper into the tunnel.

The hobgoblin on guard on the third raft was near the end of his shift. He scanned the horizon that was just beginning to lighten. Aside from the strange noises, which by now he had gotten used to, there had been no signs of danger. He wondered how soon their leader would want to continue moving, hoping he would be able to get a few hours sleep.

He looked down at the three who were asleep on the deck and bent over to awaken the one closest, who was supposed to relieve him and stand guard until morning. He shook his comrade's shoulder, trying to be careful not to awaken the other two. Sensing no response, he bent down closer to whisper in his ear.

"Wake up," he said. "It's your shift for guard duty."

The sleeping hobgoblin wrinkled his face, but was otherwise unresponsive. The guard gave him another shake. When he rolled onto his back and turned his head upward, the guard noticed something strange. There was some kind of odd shadow covering the sleeper's ear – the one that had been pressed to the floor of the raft. It seemed to be moving.

The guard leaned even closer to get a better look. There was some kind of mold covering his entire ear. It was on the floor where he had rested his head and was coming up through the crack between the logs.

"What's going on?" he muttered. "What is this stuff?"

He reached down with his finger, and then thought better of it. He looked around for something he could use to scrape the mold away from his comrades face. Finding nothing, he picked up a nearby spear and turned it so that he could use the handle. He turned back to the sleeping hobgoblin.

Quest of Eight Part Five: Release of the Demons

Richard Reda

As the morning light tried feebly to illuminate the gray sky, he could see more clearly. The mold not only covered that one ear, it seemed to be coming out of his nose, too. He moved the handle of the spear closer and tried to brush the mold from the sleeper's cheek. When he did so, the entire side of his head caved in.

The guard jumped into the air screaming and backing away. The sleeper's head crumbled and the mold poured out of his mouth, through his eyes and out of his other ear. The guard's shouts woke the others.

"Help," shouted the guard. "Save me."

He climbed up onto the edge of the raft's wall and jumped over to the next raft, still screaming. The other two hobgoblins, still on the third raft woke up with a start only to find a strange black fuzz had engulfed the man next to them. They looked down and saw it squeezing through the gaps in the logs immediately beneath them.

They jumped up, rubbing their arms, legs and feet as their friend's body flattened to the raft's floor, the Niekumites having spread throughout his interior, devouring his organs, his tissue and his blood. Now that the first host was nearly gone, they had moved on to the next ones. The two hobgoblins still on the third raft could see traces of the black mold on their feet.

One of them wiped the substance away with a part of his shirt and then threw the shirt into the water before jumping to the second raft. The other one tried brushing the tiny creatures off with his hand, only to find them stuck to that skin and burrowing into his pores. He was too stunned to react. He stood there watching as they drove deeper and deeper into his skin and then into his blood stream.

B'nair awoke instantly when he heard the first scream. He looked for the source of the attack, but seeing none, he turned his attention to the screaming guard. He turned just in time to see him jump from the third raft to the second. In a few seconds, a second hobgoblin jumped onto the second raft.

He reached across and grabbed the nearest man on the second raft and pulled him to the first one.

"Move," he shouted. "Get out of the way."

Once he got the nearest man off the second raft, he jumped over into his place and pushed his way to the rear to get closer to the end raft.

"What's going on?" he shouted.

The guard could only point to the mold that was spreading at an alarming rate. The first body was completely covered. The mass of black fuzz was moving. It was covering the feet of the man who could only stand and watch as he was being devoured. He turned and looked back at B'nair.

"Help me," he pleaded.

B'nair looked down at the floor of the raft. The mold was still seeping through the gaps between the logs. He looked down at the floor of the raft on which he was standing, but nothing was there. In a quick motion, he swung his axe downward and cut the line that secured the third raft to the second.

"Push off," he ordered.

Everyone stared at him in shock.

"NOW!" he shouted even louder.

When no one moved, Vardelos pulled the anchor pole from the mud and pushed it into the hands of the nearest man on the lead raft. He reached up and turned the man's head to face him.

"Push," he said in a calm voice.

Then he pulled another man from the second raft to the first one and took his place. He pulled the anchor pole for that raft from the mud and pushed off. The two rafts slowly pulled away into the center of the river, leaving the third raft behind.

The stranded hobgoblin watched as his comrades deserted him. After less than a minute, it no longer mattered. The Niekumites had worked their way through his blood stream, into his internal organs and quickly to his brain. Before the other two rafts were fifty feet away, he collapsed. His fears and worries evaporated like a mist, as did his consciousness.

B'nair watched him as he dropped to the bottom of the raft as his bones and muscle disintegrated.

"Where did it come from?" he asked in a voice slightly above a whisper.

"It came up through the gaps between the logs," said the guard, who finally was able to find his voice.

B'nair spun his head around to face the guard, and then looked down at his feet. The floor was covered with the large leaves Vardelos had gathered to keep their feet dry. He jerked his head towards Vardelos, who was still pushing the raft with the pole.

"How did you know?" B'nair asked.

"I didn't know, sir," answered the hobgoblin. "Honestly. I put them down to keep the water from getting us wet."

What none of them knew was that the leaves were from a Banchu tree, and they were a natural barrier to the Niekumites. Something in the fiber of the leaves acted as a poison to the tiny creatures, but didn't seem to affect anyone or anything else.

57

Quest of Eight Part Five: Release of the Demons

Richard Reda

B'nair hesitated a minute, and then lifted the edge of one of the leaves, half expecting to see the ominous black mold. Nothing was there. He put the leaf back in place, and flattened it securely with his hand. He straightened up and looked again at Vardelos.

"I don't suppose I will be laughing at your choices in the future."

He then reached over and pulled the pole from Vardelos' hand and passed it to one of the others.

"You're a leader," he said. "This should be done by others."

He moved Vardelos closer to him and bent in close to speak to him in a low voice.

"I owe you a debt of gratitude," he said.

"That's not necessary, sir," the hobgoblin answered. "It is my role to serve you."

B'nair looked him in the eye. He had never experienced this level of loyalty from any of the Rebbercands. Instead, his instincts told him to be wary of treachery. Now he wasn't so sure he should trust those instincts. At least not with this one.

"Your former leader, Ercon, spoke to me of Kelpies. Do you know of this?" he asked.

"Ercon shared very little with us," Vardelos answered. "But I know about Kelpies."

"We're going to a place where one is supposed to be hidden," continued B'nair. "I intend to release it. Does this concern you?"

"No, sir. My people have searched for centuries for them. But our searches were haphazard. We had no way of knowing where they were hidden. There was a legend about a stone – a pendant that had been shattered, but nothing more than that – until you arrived. Now it appears you possess parts of that stone."

"I do," answered B'nair. "And the locations of the Kelpies."

Vardelos' eyes widened at that comment.

"All of them?" he asked. "Not just the one we seek now?"

"All of them," B'nair confirmed.

"How do you know this, if I may ask?"

B'nair explained how, when he found the second piece of the pendant in the glass shop in the village of the Thumpers, a vision appeared to him. He could recall this vision in complete clarity whenever he needed to. In the vision there were symbols that designated the locations of the Kelpies. The closer they were to any of these locations, the clearer the vision of that particular symbol became.

He didn't know the relevance of the symbols, but each one was distinct. Three of them included an additional marking of some kind. At this point he couldn't be sure what that marking was – it appeared to be a triangle or an arrow head – not the same as the arrow head associated with the symbol they were now following.

"What importance is the stone?" asked Vardelos.

"I don't know exactly," B'nair answered. "At least not yet. I can feel a certain power when it's in my grasp, but it doesn't seem to give me any special abilities. I have to assume that it may be more valuable to the Kelpies than to me."

"Do you fear that the Kelpie, once released, will want to take the stone from you?"

Quest of Eight Part Five: Release of the Demons

Richard Reda

"He may," said B'nair. "But I am convinced that without the stone in my possession, the map to the other Kelpies will vanish. That can't happen."

Vardelos had almost forgotten how treacherous the Rebbercands could be. He realized he had been much too inquisitive and B'nair had been much too open. He began to worry.

"Why are you telling me this?" he asked nervously.

B'nair allowed a faint smile to show. He understood the question and the reason behind the question. The hobgoblin was concerned that he might be the next one sent on a mission from which return was unlikely.

"You have demonstrated your loyalty," B'nair answered. "You have earned my trust."

"Thank you, sir. I will not let you down."

"I know you won't," B'nair said – a bit too ominously for Vardelos.

The rafts were pushed for several hours along a winding river. In some places the passage widened out and the current was almost non-existent, making the chore of moving the small boats a little easier. Other times, the passage narrowed and the current became much stronger. In those instances progress was slow.

They had to stop several times to rest. They were all hungry and thirsty, but none of them was willing to leave the rafts in search of relief. The land to their left, where the Navedis Forest was located, began to rise high above them. Eventually, it disappeared from sight, and by the time the cliff side leveled out and became a shore again, all signs of the Forest were gone.

Everyone wondered what had happened to Gazzien, but no one asked. As the afternoon wore on, they started to see changes in the terrain on the Swamp side of the river. Large trees appeared sporadically. Most of them were dead or covered with vines. Large rocks also began to appear.

It looked as if some giant had thrown the boulders down into the muck at random intervals. The rocks varied in size and shape, but they were all large. There were no mountains in the area and, except for the rocks, the ground was soft and marshy. The boulders looked very much out of place.

The trees were equally strange. Most often there was only one standing by itself, nowhere near any others. Most of them appeared to be tall palm trees, except the palm fronds were missing. Instead of the palms, there were a few long, gnarled branches shooting out from the tops, and nothing else.

The hobgoblins continued to push the rafts with their long poles, staying close to the side of the waterway furthest from the Swamp. Each of them had heard stories about the plant-life and the creatures that lived in the Swamp. What made their journey even more exhausting was the anticipation of encountering some disaster. But nothing happened; aside from the attack by the Niekumites.

B'nair kept focused on the far shore. He could feel they were getting closer. In fact, they almost passed the spot before he recognized the four trees. They were nearly identical, reaching up more than twenty feet. Their top branches had broken off and the trees were slightly bent, all in the same direction.

As soon as he saw the trees, B'nair shifted his focus to the rock that was half buried in the mire about twenty feet to the right of the trees. It was so covered with moss that he had missed it.

"Turn back," he shouted, pointing towards the rock. "Turn back and push us to the other side."

Quest of Eight Part Five: Release of the Demons

Richard Reda

The rafts made a wide arc, crossing from one side to the other and turning back the way they had come. The razor grass that grew along the shore line obscured whatever land there may have been. As the rafts eased into the grass, the long blades whipped across the hands and faces of the hobgoblins. The edges of the grass were so sharp that the cuts they made went unnoticed at first.

Soon, they all noticed that they were bleeding. Each of them had several cuts and each cut was deep. They started pushing the rafts away from the grass and back out into the river.

"No," shouted B'nair. "Stop moving away from the rock."

"We can't," one of them shouted back. "We're getting cut."

Vardelos looked around for something that would deflect the grass. He bent down and picked up one of the large Banchu leaves and wrapped it around his hand. Then he pulled his sword from his belt, and moved to the front of the raft.

"Move ahead of the other raft and then proceed slowly," he ordered the hobgoblin with the pole.

The raft carrying him and B'nair slid to the front and then inched forward through the reeds, which reduced the whipping of the long grass. As the blades came within reach, Vardelos hacked at them with his sword. The Banchu leaves deflected the cuts from the razor grass and he was able to cut a path closer to the large rock.

It was a bit clumsy trying to hold the sword in a hand covered with the leaves, but he somehow managed. Before long the nose of the raft slid into a muddy shore line a few feet from the front tip of the rock.

"Well done, Vardelos," said B'nair.

He moved to the front of the raft and stood next to the hobgoblin.

"Anchor the raft," he ordered.

The driver shoved the pole into the mud and tied it to the raft. No one moved. B'nair stayed in the raft, studying the rock and the ground surrounding it. After a few minutes, he turned to Vardelos.

"Now what?" he asked.

Vardelos was shocked. He had never been asked his opinion before and he never believed the Rebbercand would be in a position where he didn't know what to do. The problem was, neither did he. He had no answer for the question.

"I...I..." he stammered. "I don't know."

"No," chuckled B'nair. "I don't suppose you do."

"Does the rock mark the location of the Kelpie," Vardelos asked. "Or is it the trees?"

"It's not the trees," B'nair answered. "They only pointed the direction. The Kelpie is inside the rock. The question is, how do we get him out?"

B'nair carefully bent over the side of the raft. He readied himself in the event something jumped up out of the water, but he needed to see where the land began and how firm it was. He moved from the side, around the front and to the other side of the raft.

"Move us more towards the front of the rock," he ordered.

The pole was removed from the mud and the driver tried to push the raft further. They were as close as they were able to get.

"As I thought," B'nair said. "Anchor the raft again."

Quest of Eight Part Five: Release of the Demons

Richard Reda

Once the raft was secured, B'nair climbed over the front edge of the raft. Vardelos was so stunned by the sudden action, that he was unable to do anything to stop him. Instead of sinking into the muck, he appeared to end up on solid land.

B'nair gave a gentle swipe of his axe and cut away the brush and grass that covered what he was standing on. Unlike all the other surroundings, which were natural, at least in appearance, B'nair stood on a perfectly square piece of granite.

He turned around and cut away at more of the undergrowth. In a few minutes he had uncovered what appeared to be a kind of walk-way. Eight identical stone squares were revealed. Three were lined up across the front of the large arrow-head shaped stone where B'nair believed the Kelpie was buried.

In front of those three squares were two more and in front of them were three single blocks, all of which resembled the letter "Y." B'nair walked on the stones up to the larger rock and used his axe to scrape away some of the moss. Underneath the growth, the dirt and the debris, he found the same granite as the blocks.

The burial rock was not any more natural than the stepping stones. The centuries that had passed since the imprisonment of the Kelpie had disguised it to look like all the other ordinary, albeit unusual, boulders that were scattered along the shore.

"This was hidden in plain sight," B'nair said to no one in particular.

He stepped to the left of the tomb and then to the right. The entire rock was covered. He turned back to the watching hobgoblins.

"Get out here and start cutting away the covering. I want this stone stripped to its surface."

One by one, the hobgoblins slowly and carefully climbed out of the rafts and onto the squares of granite. They started clearing along the edge of the larger stone. They were able to cut away the vegetation that surrounded the rock, but found nothing but mud and earth on the other three sides.

Once they had cleared the ground, they began to scrape the surface. They chipped away at the hardened coating, eventually getting down to the granite. When they were done, they had revealed a block of pure white granite. The front edge rose only a few inches above the ground and was about four feet wide. The sides extended ten feet to the back, which rose six feet into the air.

The front surface of the block was unmarked except for an engraving near the center. It was the same mark that appeared in the vision: an arrow. There was no sign of any seams or other ways to open the rock.

"Maybe it must be raised," suggested Vardelos.

B'nair ordered one of the hobgoblins to bring over one of the long poles they had used to propel the rafts. He stuck it under the front edge of the large rock but was unable to move it.

"We need a fulcrum," he said. "Find a large rock."

"What about one of these stepping stones?" asked one of the hobgoblins.

Without waiting for an answer, he turned to the one furthest from the tomb and grabbed the edges. He pulled upward, trying to free it from the mud. He pulled with all his strength until he felt it finally begin to shift. He lifted it several inches, but when he tried to turn, he couldn't move.

"It's not all the way out of the ground," one of the others called to him.

"Help me with it," he grunted.

65

Two others ran over to assist. They grabbed the edges and pulled. It rose slowly. Soon they were standing straight up, the top of the stone at chest level, but it was still not free of the ground.

They shifted their grip, moving their arms downward towards the ground and lifted again. Once more, the stone slid slowly upward. They pulled it as high as they could. The top was now almost ten feet above the ground, but it was still stretching downward into the ground.

"Forget it," said B'nair. "This is the work of the Alchemist. For all we know, these stepping stones reach all the way to the core of the planet. Find something else."

They had all been working along the shoreline of the Swamp for several hours. So far, nothing had happened to them. They had become so absorbed in their tasks they had forgotten where they were and about all the stories they had heard of the dangers of this environment. They had grown careless.

A few of them began digging into the ground around the tomb with their fingers and their swords, trying to reach underneath the stone. Others ventured further into shore in search of a rock or a log that could be used to pry the stone open. Two of them, Sangka and Kumas, wandered off towards an area of thick vegetation, looking for a log.

They found a few broken branches, but nothing wide enough or solid enough to be of much use. Their finds, however, encouraged them to go deeper into the jungle. Sangka looked back towards the way they had come. He was worried about going too far, but he could still see the others. He thought they were still all right.

Kumas found some other pieces of tree trunks. He didn't think it was odd that he saw no signs of any trees, though. What he did think was odd was the ground. It was covered with strange looking leaves. They were a mottled brown and green and carpeted the ground. Where did these come from, he wondered.

He bent down to pick one up only to find that it was attached to the others. He pulled harder, but it wouldn't come loose. He stood up straight and turned around to call to Sangka. The leaves behind him had moved. They had risen into the air and were silently moving towards him. That's strange, he thought.

Before he could react, the wall of leaves slammed down on top of him. The weight was incredible. He could feel the breath being squeezed out of him at the same time he could feel himself being wrapped from head to toe in the blanket of leaves.

He struggled to free his arm, but they were both pinned to his body. He moved his hand enough to pull a dagger from his belt. He tried to cut into the leaves, but he could barely move his wrist. He tried calling out, but his voice was smothered.

Shortly after being engulfed by the leaves, Sangka became aware that his partner had disappeared. At first he was angry at having been deserted, but then he heard a rustling sound not far away from him.

"Kumas," he shouted. "This is not the time for playing tricks. Where are you?"

He listened for the rustling sound and when he heard it again, he turned and headed in that direction. In a few steps, he saw what looked like a mound of leaves rolling up into a ball. He drew his sword and moved forward. He was within a few steps of the quivering pile of leaves.

He reached out to pull them away from whatever was underneath to discover that they were all connected. He pulled harder, tearing one of them loose. As soon as he did that, a mammoth plant stalk rose up and engulfed the leaves, pulling them and the mound beneath them inside.

Quest of Eight Part Five: Release of the Demons

Richard Reda

The plant rose up more than twenty feet into the air, wavered, angled downward and then shot forward, apparently aiming for Sangka. He moved just in time as the top of the stalk opened up and crashed into the ground like a giant plunger. Sangka fell backwards, skittering across the ground as the stalk rose up again. It seemed to sense where he was and shot down at him. He rolled out of the way at the last instant, got to his feet and ran blindly back to the others.

"Help," he yelled. "It ate Kumas. Help. Save me. It ate Kumas."

He ran for his life, stomping across the foliage as he went. The plant that had eaten Kumas had a taste for more. It snapped and dove like the head of a serpent, trying to capture Sangka. It pulled its roots from the ground and moved forward like a four legged animal, replanting itself with each step.

"Arm yourselves," ordered Vardelos.

"Get back here, you fools," shouted B'nair to Sangka and the others who had wandered off.

The rest of the hobgoblins quickly formed defensive ranks, ready for an attack. They didn't yet realize they were being attacked by a plant. Sangka ran, tripped, got up, and ran some more. He had drawn his sword and was flailing it blindly. The giant stalk was gaining on him, pulling up its roots and lunging forward to replant them.

B'nair looked at the approaching threat and then looked at the stone tomb. He was certain that if he could release the Kelpie, the ancient sorcerer would have the power to save or protect them. However, he had no idea how to open the crypt. He pulled the pieces of stone from his inside pocket and held them in his hand. Looking at the engraving on the rock, he pressed the stone against it. Nothing happened. He moved the pendant stone across the surface of the tomb. Still nothing.

Quest of Eight Part Five: Release of the Demons

Richard Reda

"Why would you lead me here without the knowledge of how to set you free," he shouted in frustration at the buried Kelpie.

The agitation of the plant that was chasing Sangka had awakened other creatures in the Swamp. Dybuks appeared in the razor grass close to the water's edge and began to creep towards the hobgoblins. Vines began moving and slithering across the marshy ground, springing up and wrapping around the legs of those closest. Tentacles rose up out of the water, cutting off any retreat in that direction.

B'nair stepped forward and cut a long vine tendril from Vardelos' ankles before the hobgoblin was dragged into the bog. Swords were swinging ineffectively. Vines and other plants were hacked down, only to be replaced immediately. The Swamp was gaining the advantage.

The hobgoblins were crowded around the large rock, their backs pressed against the granite, cutting and stabbing. When one of them was caught and dragged to his feet, another would lunge forward to cut him free and pull him back to the circle. There appeared to be no escape and no lessening of the attack.

The large stalk that had chased Sangka was now towering over them all. B'nair readied his axe and waited for the plant to strike. It smashed down towards the Rebbercand, who sidestepped at the last second. The plant crashed into the surface of the crypt, having missed its target by inches.

At that precise moment, before the plant could rise up, B'nair swung and drove his blade into the top of the stalk. The axe sliced through easily and struck the granite beneath with a resounding clang. The blade of the axe met the stone in the center of the engraved arrow and imbedded itself.

B'nair pulled back, trying to free it. It was stuck. He jerked it up and down, in near panic, trying to free it. His movement widened the gash he had cut, cracking the surface. The crack spider-webbed down the front and up towards the back end.

69

Quest of Eight Part Five: Release of the Demons

Richard Reda

A dull green mist spewed out of the break, and was accompanied by an overpowering odor of decay. Instantly, the attacking plants and creatures pulled back. Unaware of their retreat, B'nair kept moving the axe back and forth in an effort to work it loose. As he did, the crack widened.

Suddenly, the axe was out and the stone crypt fell open. The fog poured out of the split and covered the surrounding ground. The hobgoblins reacted to the stench and moved away to the front of the tomb, cowering behind B'nair. Two of the hobgoblins closest were enveloped in the fog and began choking. They fell to the ground, were covered with vines and sucked into the marsh surrounding the tomb.

The rest of them immediately stepped back and out of the way of the mist as it rolled out and dissipated. B'nair watched, expecting he, too, would start choking on the poisonous gas. Instead, he felt an electrical charge form around him. He touched his vest and felt the stone inside his pocket. Some ancient magic was protecting him from the poison.

Through the cloud and up through the fissure in the stone, a figure appeared. It floated upward into an upright position and hung above the ground. Then it moved effortlessly forward and out of the tomb.

The mist slowly faded away, revealing a head covered with long matted hair that hung in thick strands. It was the same dull green and gray as the fog. It framed a face that was long and gaunt, wrinkled like a prune and as gray as the slime of the river bed. His lips were thin as was his nose and the rest of his face. He opened his narrow and close set eyes to reveal a pair of bright green orbs that surveyed his surroundings.

He lowered himself to the ground as the last vestiges of the stale air and enveloping fog faded away. His body, long and thin as his face, was draped in ragged and stringy clothing that looked more like the moss and thin vines that hung from the trees deep inside the Swamp. It dragged along the ground in strings as he stepped out of the mausoleum. It looked as filthy as the most grotesque parts of the forbidding environment in which he had been hidden.

He was only feet away from B'nair and the hobgoblins. They could move no further away and were cowering close together. He stood over them by more than a foot. Looking down, he fixed on B'nair, and raised his arm to point in his direction. He extended a long, thin arm. His hands were old and skeletal and as gray as the skin on a corpse. His fingers looked like the dead branches of a dead tree. His nails were black and cracked. When he opened his mouth to speak, the stench of death was on his breath. His voice was thin and reedy, the sound piercing the ears of all who could hear him.

"I am Pantano Izaki. I am the Kelpie of the Swamp. Who are you?"

Chapter four

From the time they left the fortress of the Thumpers, Liam had been leading the way, although because of Stella's vision of the location of the Kelpies, she could just as easily have led the way. She had to admit, though, she wasn't as aware as Liam was of the potential dangers that might crop up. As they progressed across the open fields, they had kept a fast pace, but in a loose group. Now that they were approaching the Navedis Forest, they closed ranks.

As they finally reached the outer edge of the Forest, Liam stopped walking. He looked up at the sky and then at the field around them immediately adjacent to the Forest. He thought it might be best to make camp there and proceed at first light.

Richard Reda

"But we still have a lot of daylight left," said Stella.

"I agree," said Lochen. "We are losing time. It's quite possible those ahead of us bypassed this Forest. If so, then we may be able to reach the location of the Kelpie before them. Camping here loses whatever advantage we've gained."

"I understand all that," answered Liam. "But I don't think it's wise to be in this Forest at night. It'll be bad enough in the daylight. Trust me."

"I'm all right with making camp here," said Sean. "I can find all sorts of stuff to cook. Let's get things set up."

While the others rolled their eyes, Liam mouthed a silent, "I'm sorry."

"I'm in favor of camping here, too," said Quinn. "Those trees are spooky. I'd just as soon not have to try to sleep in there."

They all looked in the direction Quinn was facing. Two very large and very old trees stood out from the rest – almost as sentries, guarding the entryway. Branches extended outward from both of them more than twenty feet, and drooped to the ground like they were blocking the way. They blended into the low lying scrub brush that would have been hard to climb through. The access to the Forest was clearly through these two large guardian trees.

More branches extended upward, but not very far. It looked as if the weight of the limbs stunted their upward growth. Between the two trees, their branches intermingled and created an archway that was inviting and threatening at the same time. Together they created an image of a gaping mouth, extending an invitation: "come in for a taste."

A shiver ran up the spine of each of them.

Quest of Eight Part Five: Release of the Demons

Richard Reda

"I suppose you're right," acknowledged Lochen, whose acquiescence was immediately echoed by the others.

Without any prompting, they broke into teams and foraged for fire wood, materials for lean-tos, and food. Solveig had nearly depleted the supply she had stored in her cloak, and that had been enough to keep them going after the last meal Sean had prepared. Now, however, it seemed as if their luck had run out. He was preparing to cook again.

"We better find something else," Solveig whispered Natalie, "or we're all going to bed hungry again tonight."

"Go with him," suggested Natalie. "Maybe you can distract him from digging up roots or grubs or whatever it was he found the last time."

Solveig joined Sean in seeking a source of food, as the others went about their self-assigned tasks. Lochen found a small creek that appeared to provide a clean supply of water. Along the edge of the water, he found some mint leaves. He picked a few of the leaves. Then he waved his hand and conjured up a small pot to collect the water.

"It might be nice to heat this up for some tea," he told Stella, who had joined him.

"Or if Solveig finds something good, maybe we can make a stew," she added.

They all returned to the clearing several yards from the two trees that marked the passage into the Forest. Quinn found enough to construct some lean-tos, and Liam had a nice camp fire burning. He had put a large flat rock in the center of the fire in the hopes that someone had found something with which to make a hot meal.

Lochen proudly produced the pot he had conjured filled with the fresh stream water. He placed it on the rock to let the water heat up. A few seconds later, Solveig and Sean returned. Sean was in the lead with a wide grin on his face. Behind him Solveig was looking dejected and making a face that implied something none of the others immediately understood.

"We're in luck," shouted Sean as he approached the camp site.

Solveig, a few feet behind Sean, was shaking her head vehemently to the contrary.

"I found the ingredients to make my famous Varmint Stew!"

He held up a pair of large, bug-eyed rodent-like creatures with long white tails, waving them back and forth.

"If we only had a pot to cook them in, and a few roots for seasoning, we'd be all set."

Lochen immediately turned back to the campfire, snapped his fingers, and the pot disappeared, water and all.

"What a shame," he said, turning back towards Sean and the others. "I was so looking forward to...what was it you said? Varmint Stew? A pity we'll have to miss out on that."

"That's OK," Sean said, undaunted. "I'll just save them. Maybe something will turn up. Besides, they get better when they've aged a little."

"We'll just have to eat the fruit I found," said Solveig.

Sighs of relief ran through the group. They sat around the fire and enjoyed Solveig's find, commiserating with Sean about being denied an opportunity to sample his culinary talents. The gray skies they had traveled under the entire day continued into the night, making the air cool and damp. Once again Lochen agreed to stand watch, still not needing sleep. Everyone else was happy to let him do so, and turned in for the night.

When he was sure they were all asleep, he conjured up the pot again and quietly crept back to the stream for some water. He placed the pot in the campfire when he returned and pulled from his pocket the mint leaves he had stuffed in there earlier. He conjured up a cup, poured the hot water over the leaves and settled back to enjoy his tea.

He spent the night staring at the clouded sky, recalling from memory the locations of the planets and the stars above him. Another part of his thoughts focused on the recent events and their current journey. He thought about the symbols Quinn had shown them – how long ago was that? It seemed like years.

He was puzzled that these same symbols had appeared on the band that Summer had wrested from Ena Ray's possession and which had transported them to some unidentified underground location, and then secured the doors to some unidentified portal. What did it all mean? Why would those symbols appear in two such different places?

And if all that wasn't puzzling enough, now those same symbols appeared in a vision to Stella, depicting the locations of a group of sorcerers who had – what? Abused their power? Formed a kind of evil alliance? Whatever it was, it was sufficient for the Alchemist and the Enchantress to have cast powerful spells on them, banishing and imprisoning them. So it seemed that in addition to appearing on an ancient wall in the Ice Kingdom, and on the band possessed at one time by Ena Ray, the symbols were also connected to these Kelpies.

He understood that the release of the Kelpies had to be avoided, but he wasn't sure why. He also understood that somehow he and his seven friends had been tasked to stop such a release, but he wasn't sure why – why them? What was their connection to all this, or to each other for that matter. He and Solveig were siblings, and there was a similar bond between Stella and Natalie, but the others – what about them?

Summer's people and Sean's had been long time enemies. Liam's people had all vanished. Quinn's were so far to the north that they were isolated from everyone else. Lochen thought back to how they had all come together. At the time it had seemed somewhat random. Now he wasn't as certain.

"I suppose it will all be revealed in time," he said aloud.

"All what will be revealed?" asked Liam.

"I'm sorry," said Lochen. "I wasn't aware that I was speaking out loud. I didn't mean to awaken you."

"You didn't," said Liam. "I couldn't sleep. It's too quiet. That's what woke me up."

"I don't understand," said Lochen. "How can it be too quiet to sleep?"

"We're near a forest," he answered. "There should be all sorts of sounds, but there's nothing. That makes me nervous. When I'm nervous, I can't sleep. Don't you find the lack of noise the least bit disturbing?"

"I see," said Lochen. "About not being able to sleep due to the quiet, that is. I've never given much thought to the lack of noise, I'm afraid."

"It will be dawn soon," said Liam. "We might as well wake the others and get started. The sooner we get through that place, the better I'll feel."

"And then you'll be able to sleep," added Lochen. "Of course, assuming the night is filled with noise."

77

Quest of Eight Part Five: Release of the Demons

Richard Reda

Liam looked at him to see if he was being sarcastic. Lochen looked at him as he stood up, and smiled. Liam still couldn't tell.

"Right," he finally said.

They woke the others up and all of them finished off the food that Solveig had gathered. Lochen remembered to make the pot and the remaining water vanish before Sean rose. Liam had noticed the container on the fire and the cup of tea that Lochen had been drinking, before it vanished, but kept this to himself.

They were as ready as they were ever going to be, shortly before sunrise. There was a thick fog that covered the ground as they passed through the two large trees guarding the entryway. No one recalled seeing it before, but they kept their concerns to themselves. Liam was in the lead, with the others clustered closely together behind him. Sean had his slingshot out and at the ready, although he could barely see more than ten feet in any direction.

As the first of the two suns rose, its light seeped through the gray clouds that still lingered in the sky. The filtered light gave the fog a greenish cast. Deeper into the Forest, the fog thinned out, but didn't disappear. It hung around the trees and the long thin branches that seemed to reach in every direction except along the path they were walking.

About an hour after they had passed into the Forest, Liam slowed down and then stopped. Lochen was close behind him to his right. Summer was still riding in his hood, sitting on top of the folds, peering over his left shoulder. Natalie and Solveig were behind and to Liam's left. Sean and Quinn followed directly behind Liam and Stella was watching the rear. As with the night, there wasn't a single sound to be heard.

"What is it?" asked Lochen in a low whisper.

"I think we walked into a trap," Liam whispered back.

Quest of Eight Part Five: Release of the Demons

Richard Reda

"Why do you think that?"

"Do you see those sticks in the dirt up ahead?" Liam asked.

He pointed to three sticks about fifteen feet ahead of the group, and spaced evenly about eight or nine feet apart. They stood about two and a half to three feet straight up from the ground. It was clear that they weren't trees or bushes or limbs from any nearby plants. In fact, there were no plants nearby. They appeared to be in the middle of what seemed to be for a path. They were straight and bare, less than an inch in diameter.

"They do seem to be out of place," answered Lochen. "What do you suppose they are?"

"I don't know. I saw four of them several feet back," he said. "At the time, I didn't think anything about them. I should have. When I saw those ahead I realized my mistake. I think they're breathing tubes."

"Breathing tubes?" asked Lochen, a stunned look on his face. "I'm not sure I understand. Breathing tubes for what?"

Before Liam could answer his question, the ground around each of the sticks began to move. One by one, three bodies rose up from under a shallow covering of dirt that fell to the sides. They removed the breathing tubes from their mouths as they rose and held them loosely in their hands.

Stella had stopped when the others had, but kept her focus behind them – the way they had come.

"Hey, guys," Stella whispered. "We're not alone."

"No kidding," whispered Natalie.

Stella hadn't seen the three people rise up from the dirt to their front. Instead, she watched as a similar event occurred behind them. Four

79

bodies rose from the ground, their positions marked by the same sticks Liam had noticed.

Natalie turned at the sound of Stella's voice and saw the four people behind them.

"Neither are they," she whispered into Stella's ear.

She tugged on Stella's sleeve, turning her around and pointing to the three in front. The seven Navedi all looked similar. They were as tall as Quinn, and were thin and muscular. The hair on their heads was cropped close, with patterns or designs cut down to the scalp. Their skin was a deep tan, which was hard to see, as they were covered in dirt. Some of them had bones or small sharpened sticks piercing their ears and noses. They all had necklaces made up of bones and teeth.

Their eyes were black under heavy brows. On their chests were welts or scars that formed designs or words in letters that were unknown to those they had surrounded. Their feet were bare; the soles calloused and hardened.

Without breaking eye contact with the one in the center, Liam whispered out of the side of his mouth.

"Don't anyone try casting spells. They probably won't work, and even if they did, the ones behind us would attack before we could disable all of them. And Sean, please put your slingshot away. We don't want to appear as a threat to them. Keep still. Nobody do anything to provoke them."

"What are they?" whispered Quinn, leaning as furtively as he could towards Sean.

"I think they're carnivals," Sean whispered back.

Summer turned around to look at the two of them.

"I think you mean…" she started to whisper.

"No," interrupted Quinn. "Not carnivals. You mean carnivores."

Summer rolled her eyes and tried to say, "They're not…"

"No," Sean whispered, cutting her off. "I'm pretty sure they're carnivals,"

"They're not carnivals," she interjected, getting frustrated. "They're…"

"I don't think that's right," Quinn interrupted. "It doesn't sound right. They must be carnivores."

"That's not right either…" whispered Summer a little more loudly, now standing on Lochen's shoulder with her hands on her hips.

"Yes, I'm right about this," whispered Sean, once again cutting her off. "I've heard about them. They're carnivals. I know it."

"They're cannibals!" Summer shouted. "They're cannibals! Not carnivals; not carnivores. They're cannibals."

Everyone and everything was silent. All heads turned towards her. The eyes of seven Navedi shifted in her direction. She ducked her head and raised her shoulders, looking embarrassed at all the faces staring at her.

"I'm just saying," she said.

When no one said anything and all eyes were still on her, she slunk off Lochen's shoulder and crawled back into the folds of his hood.

"I'm done talking now," she announced.

Quest of Eight Part Five: Release of the Demons

Richard Reda

As this was happening, the Navedi in the center of the three to the front had approached and was standing in front of Liam. In spite of the interruption, Liam had not taken his eyes off the advancing native. He watched until the Navedi was standing immediately in front of him. He was looking Liam up and down, periodically sniffing the air around him.

"You are a Pathfinder," he finally said.

"Yes," answered Liam. "I am."

The Navedi stood up straighter and looked at him defiantly.

"Your people are not our friends," he declared, his voice tinged with anger.

"My people are all gone," said Liam. "I am the last of my kind."

Solveig stepped forward and stood immediately next to Liam.

"We are his people," she said in a clear firm voice. "And we are not your enemy."

The Navedi took a stunned step backwards. He quickly regained his composure and stepped over directly in front of her. He looked at her closely from side to side, and sniffed the air the same way he did with Liam. After a few seconds he straightened up and made a slight nodding movement.

"You were blue," he said definitively.

Solveig's eyes shot down to her hands. She rubbed them together and turned them over, searching them.

"That was supposed to have gone away," she said. She looked towards Liam and repeated to him excitedly, "That was supposed to have gone away. You all told me it was gone. Isn't it all gone?"

Liam leaned over towards her and said, "It's gone."

She looked into his eyes. He nodded his head, signaling that it had. There were no traces of blue in her skin.

Relieved, she turned back to the Navedi. "You guessed," she said and demanded, "How did you know?"

The Navedi turned his head slightly and said, "The odor lingers."

"Odor?" exclaimed Solveig. "Odor? There's an ODOR? Do I smell?"

She turned back to Liam and pulled on his sleeve.

"Do I smell? Please tell me. I bathed. I shouldn't smell. How can I smell? Is it bad?"

"It was barely noticeable," said Liam, trying to calm her concerns.

The Navedi moved past Solveig and stood before Natalie. He studied her.

"You are Sea Sprite," he stated.

"Yes," she answered. "And if you tell me you can smell me, I'm going to knock your block off."

The Navedi either didn't understand her or chose to ignore the threat. He walked around the group to Stella. He looked at her and then noticed the headband and the stone still imbedded there. The expression on his face changed imperceptibly. He said nothing to her and continued to circle the small group.

He stopped at Sean and nodded silently. He motioned wordlessly to the slingshot. Sean looked at it and then at the extended hand. He wasn't sure if the Navedi wanted to look at it or was demanding that it be surrendered. He looked at Liam for some guidance. Liam shrugged. Sean handed the slingshot to the Navedi, who turned it around in his hand, studying it. He snapped the firing band, and then he gave it back.

He moved next to Quinn and studied him for a few seconds. Once more he sniffed the air around him. Something different about Quinn caused him to take a step back. He looked Quinn in the eye and started to say something, but then stopped. He took another step away, giving him a wide berth and then stood next to Lochen. He noticed Summer inside his hood.

"A pixie?" he asked Summer.

"Absolutely NOT," she answered trying to stand up, but losing her balance in the material and falling back on her butt.

"I'm a princess of the faeries," she continued, still struggling to stand. "We are nothing like pixies. They're disagreeable, irritating, untrustworthy, and...and...and deceitful!"

She got to her feet, folded her arms across her chest in a defiant gesture, but lost her balance and fell back on her butt again. The Navedi bent closer to look down into the hood to see where she had gone.

"Pixies are our friends," he said to her.

"Oh," she answered meekly.

"Way to go," muttered Sean. "You keep saying things to make them mad."

The Navedi moved around to face Lochen. Lochen raised his eyebrows and smiled. His gaze moved to the bone that pierced the Navedi's nose. It was sharpened to a point at both ends and was about six inches long. It went through the septal cartilage between the nostrils. Lochen was so mesmerized by it that he reached up to touch it.

"Did it hurt very much to drive this bone..." he started to say.

As Lochen reached up to touch the bone, his hand was instantly grabbed by the Navedi in a vise-like grip.

"Oh," he said. "I meant no disrespect. I was just curious."

The Navedi waved his other arm to his comrades. Then he released Lochen's hand and turned back to Liam.

"You will come with us."

He didn't bother to make sure they were following. He turned and joined the other two who had been in the front and began walking deeper and deeper into the forest.

"We can probably jump them," whispered Sean. "They don't have any weapons except for those little sticks."

"Those sticks are blowguns," said Liam. "They shoot poisonous darts, and they're very accurate. We wouldn't get three steps before we'd all be hit."

"Look who's talking about getting them mad," Summer said, shooting a dirty look at Sean.

"I don't sense we are in danger," said Lochen. "Well – I mean any more danger than we were earlier."

"I agree," said Stella. "If they wanted to do us harm, they could have done that before now."

In a few minutes, they were aware that they had begun a slow climb upward. The Forest hadn't changed, but they were definitely going uphill.

Quest of Eight Part Five: Release of the Demons

Richard Reda

"I know where we are," said Liam after a few minutes. "I've seen this from the Swamp side of the river."

After a while they came upon a village of sorts. There were more people around, and low stone bunkers appeared. Most of them were covered with dirt or brush of some kind, and the openings led into the ground. It was clear they could be quickly and easily hidden from view, if necessary.

Off to one side of these mounds Liam noticed a figure staked out on the ground. He and the others were moved passed this figure rather quickly, and Liam wasn't sure if anyone else had noticed. He wasn't sure of what he saw, himself. The figure looked similar to the hobgoblins that they had fought at Virkio, but there was only one.

He was spread-eagled and his hands and feet were tied to stakes on the ground. What was he doing here, wondered Liam. There must have been others. Where are they? Why is he staked out like that? The figure turned his head and looked towards Liam and the others, but made no sound.

They were led past the hobgoblin and the huts to a dark area nestled between very large and very old trees. As they got closer, they could see an opening between the trees. Behind the opening was a mound that rose a few feet up, but blended into the surroundings. It was much larger than the mounds that seemed to be the homes they had passed, but it, too, could quickly and easily be hidden from view.

Two Navedi were standing on either side of the opening, as if guarding it. What wasn't clear was if they were keeping people out or keeping someone in. The lead Navedi passed the guard and went into the opening, which turned out to be stonework steps about four feet across. The chamber into which the steps led was half above and half below ground level, but camouflaged with dirt and brush like the other structures.

Inside, the chamber widened out only slightly. There were small oil pots on the ground at a number of places along the wall in which low fires were burning. This provided some light to the otherwise dim room, but it also made the air hot and stifling. Once inside, their guide gestured to a figure on a pallet against the far wall, and then departed.

"Where's he going?" asked Quinn.

"He's going about his business," the figure on the pallet answered.

His voice was weak and wheezing. Everyone turned towards the sound and saw a very old Navedi under a pile of pelts. His skin was wrinkled and gray; his hair, cut closely like the others, was white. No designs or patterns were evident, and he wore no bones in his ears or nose, and no necklace.

"And what business would that be?" asked Lochen as he stepped closer.

"He is... about to gather... more bones and teeth... to decorate his body," the figure wheezed.

They all looked at one another, and the figure coughed a brief laugh.

"Not from you," he added, gasping for breath between each phrase. "From that hobgoblin...you may have seen...outside."

"Is he going to eat the hobgoblin?" asked Sean.

"No," came the answer. "We don't... eat hobgoblins."

"That's good to know," mumbled Quinn.

"They're too bitter," said the old Navedi.

"Why are we here?" Liam asked, trying to get the image of the hobgoblin out of his mind.

"Because...you're them," he answered.

"What does that mean?" asked Lochen. "We keep getting told that, but we don't understand."

"That's not...for me...to say. That's...for another...time."

"Who are you?" asked Solveig.

"I am...Nevarnik. I am...a sentinel. And you...are here...to release me."

"I thought we were supposed to be finding some hidden Kelpie," said Natalie. "One that is somewhere in the Swamp. We don't know anything about releasing you. Release you from what?"

"You're too late," said Nevarnik. "The Kelpie has... been released. You...must find...the next one."

"How do you know this?" asked Stella.

"I know...that's all...that is...important. Those...who you follow...have gotten...there first."

"You said we're here to release you," said Liam. "Are you a prisoner? Are you being held against your will?"

"You are...wasting time...My time...is short. I...am not...important."

Nevarnik started coughing and gasping for breath. Lochen moved closer and tried to help him sit upright, but he was waved away as the old Navedi choked and sucked in air.

"He needs help," said Solveig. "We need to get him help."

They all began to move, heading for the entryway. Nevarnik waved, trying to stop them.

Quest of Eight Part Five: Release of the Demons

Richard Reda

"No," he gasped in little more than a whisper.

He reached out and grabbed Lochen's arm. Contrary to his frail appearance, his grip was incredibly strong. Lochen felt the bony hand on his arm and a wave of heat passed through him. He looked from the sentinel and then to his friends who were running for help. At first glance he thought they had stopped. But then he could see that they were moving, but extremely slowly.

He looked around the dimly lit chamber. He could see everything with unbelievable clarity. He saw dust motes floating through the air, inching across his field of vision. In spite of the low lighting, he could see with surprising detail the stones in the floor and the walls; the tiny cracks that had developed over the centuries; the dust that remained unswept in the corners of the room.

He turned to look at the skeletal hand clutching his arm. He could see the veins beneath the paper thin skin, the tiny hairs on the arm, and the slight discoloration of the skin that came with aging. He looked into the eyes of the Nevarnik. He was instantly overwhelmed by the intense fear and despair he saw in them.

"Please," rasped the sentinel, "don't...leave me."

"Of course not," said Lochen.

He spoke as soothingly as he could, patting the hand that was still tightly holding his arm. He moved closer, sitting on the edge of the old man's pallet.

"I have done...terrible things," the Nevarnik continued, his breathing becoming much more difficult. "I have seen...terrible things. I have...atoned for...my deeds. Please...forgive me."

"It is not for me to forgive you," Lochen said in a subdued voice. "You have done nothing to me that requires forgiveness."

"I have...done more...than you can...understand. You must..."

The old man's words were cut off by a spasm of coughing. He gasped for air. Lochen looked in vain for some water. The sentinel had dropped back onto the pallet. He still held Lochen's arm but his grip had relaxed. His breath was so thin it looked like he wasn't breathing at all. His skin color had already been ashen. Now it looked even worse. Lochen was torn between staying and soothing the old man's passage to the next life, and joining the others to seek help.

He turned to find Stella, thinking that perhaps she knew some kind of a healing spell that would give Nevarnik the air he urgently needed. When he looked back to where they had been only seconds ago, he could see that she was already outside with the others. He was about to get up, when he saw the sentinel's eyes flutter and slowly open. He tightened his hold on Lochen's arm, but by now he was so weakened that his grip felt as light as cobwebs.

"No," he gasped and coughed.   "...split...stop them...you are...connection...go to...homes."

"I don't understand," said Lochen. "I didn't hear everything. What did you say?"

The old man fumbled under his covering with his free hand. The exertion was taking its toll on his strength. He seemed to fade for a few seconds and then, with a last burst of what little energy he had, he pulled an old, tattered book from under his covers. He forced his eyes open and tried to push the book to Lochen. With his free hand, Lochen took the book.

"Do you want me to read something to you?" Lochen asked.

"You...keep...help to...defeat them."

Quest of Eight Part Five: Release of the Demons

Richard Reda

He fell to another spasm of coughing, his eyes closed and he let out a gasp of breath. Desperate to save the old man, Lochen gently pulled his arm free and jumped up to run out of the chamber.

"Help," he shouted. "Come quickly."

He was at the top of the steps when he was met by the others who were returning with the Navedi who had led them here. He turned around, leading them back inside.

"He revived for a second," Lochen said, panting. "He said something. I couldn't hear it all."

They all ran back into the chamber, to the pallet where Nevarnik was lying. Nothing was there. Nothing but a pile of white dust.

"He's gone," said Solveig. "Just like the others."

"That's probably what he meant about being released," said Stella.

Liam turned to the Navedi.

"We're sorry for your loss. Was he a chief or some kind of hero?" he asked.

"Hero?" the Navedi asked. "No. He was Nevarnik."

"Yes," said Liam. "We know that. He told us his name."

"No," said the Navedi. "His name was not Nevarnik. He <u>was</u> a Nevarnik – a traitor."

"That can't be right," said Lochen. "He was a sentinel. He was chosen by the Alchemist."

"How old was he," asked Natalie. "Do you know?"

"No one knows," answered the Navedi. "As long as anyone knows he has been here. Generations have come and gone, but he has remained."

"Here in this village?" asked Summer.

"Village? No. Here in this cell."

"Cell?" they all asked in unison.

"This is a cell?" asked Quinn. "You mean a prison cell or like a prayer cell?"

"No. Yes," was the answer. "Not a prayer cell. A prison cell. He was a traitor, but we were not permitted to deal with him in our own way, as we would have with any traitor."

"What do you mean?" asked Summer.

"Like the hobgoblin. We will deal with him our way."

"What way is that," Sean asked, not sure he wanted to know the answer.

"He will appease the creatures of the soil."

"And what does that mean?" Natalie asked.

"He has been staked out over a nest of fire ants. He will be covered with honey. They will be attracted to the honey and then he will be gone. They will eat and clean him completely and we will wear his bones and his teeth."

"I knew you shouldn't have been making them mad," Sean whispered to Summer.

"But you said you weren't permitted to do this with Nevarnik – with the traitor," said Lochen. "And it's apparent that you didn't. Why not?"

"It was forbidden. We were told to save him."

"Save him for what?" asked Lochen.

"Not what," said the Navedi. "Who. To save him for you."

"Us?" asked Liam. "Why us?"

"We were not told. It was explained to us that the Nevarnik would know, but not us. The only purpose for him to live was to meet you. We were only told to save him. We have watched him one generation to the next until now – now that you have come."

"And now he's gone, and we don't know what he was supposed to tell us," said Lochen, forgetting the book he was holding in his hand. "Who told you to do this? Who told you to save him for us?"

The Navedi looked strangely at him and then the others. It was as if he wondered if he was being tested, or if this was some kind of a joke. When he determined their question was for real, he turned and pointed at Stella.

"She did," he said.

Chapter five

Stella looked completely stunned, and shouted, "Me?" when all eyes were turned towards her. "Me? You must be mistaken. That's impossible. I've never been here before. I never saw that...that...sentinel, that Nevarnik person; not ever. You said he's been here for...how long? Just how old do you think I am?"

The Navedi was startled by her reaction. He regained his composure after everyone shifted their stare from Stella to him.

"You are Enchantress," he said defensively and a bit indignantly. "You have the Enchantress stone. It is in our history. It was you!"

"I don't know anything about your history," Stella shot back.

She took a few steps towards him. Even though he was much taller than her, he backed away until he ran out of room, bumping into the wall. He was staggered by her vehemence. He looked to the others for help, but all he saw were their blank stares, waiting for some kind of response.

He looked for his tribesmen. Three were standing in the entryway, purposely looking at anything but him. They did not want to do anything to incur the wrath of this diminutive Enchantress. At the same time, they were uncomfortable for not coming to his aide. The best thing they could think of doing was to ignore it all.

Seeing the tension had mounted quickly, Liam intervened.

"Why don't we start from the beginning," he suggested, turning to the Navedi. "Tell us about what happened with Nevarnik."

The Navedi looked around the room, and then nodded. He told them that the stories that had been passed down by their ancestors told of a time when their forest was green and vibrant. Their people lived on the other side of the river from the people of the Pathfinder – before the Swamp became poisonous; when the two communities were at peace and were allies with each other.

At some point a very powerful person – a Kelpie – rose up among the Pathfinder's people. He had magical skills, but no conscience to guide him. He joined with others like him – these were the Kelpies. United, they were too strong for any one group of people to defeat. The Pathfinder's people tried to stand up to them, but the Kelpie poisoned the land and the water. In the centuries that followed, the land became the Swamp, and the people died out.

"The Navedi saw what was happening to the Pathfinder's people," he continued. "They were much stronger than we were. If they could not stop the Kelpie, we knew we would not be able to, either. Providing help to the Pathfinder's people had to be done in secret.

"We made hiding places, and sneaked families out of the Swamp to safety. We moved our village every day, hiding ourselves deep in the forest. But the Kelpie captured one of us – the Nevarnik. He turned him against his own people. The Nevarnik told the Kelpie where we were hiding and where we were protecting the Pathfinder's people.

The Kelpie cast a spell on our forest. It is still our home, but it is a dead home – a place where only the Grackles will stay. It shames me, but the Navedi were forced to turn over those they had saved. The Pathfinder's people felt betrayed."

The Navedi lowered his head in silence before continuing. "They <u>were</u> betrayed. From that time on, they never forgave us. We had thought they fled the Swamp, forever our enemies."

He looked at Liam.

"Until today we thought they had moved. Until today, we never knew they ceased to be."

He paused for a few seconds to collect himself.

"Before the Kelpie could take his vengeance against the Navedi, the Alchemist and the Enchantress overpowered him. They could not kill him, though. He was, instead, cast into a prison near here. The Navedi wanted to avenge themselves on the Nevarnik, but the Enchantress said it was forbidden.

"The Alchemist cast a spell on him and left him with us. The Enchantress told us that a time would come when strangers would seek him out. We were tasked with tending to him."

"But why do you think I'm that Enchantress?" asked Stella.

"You wear the stone she wore," he answered. "It is broken, but it is the same."

"But you weren't alive that long ago," said Natalie. "How do you know it's the same stone?"

"The Nevarnik spoke of it," he answered.

"What did he say?" asked Lochen.

"He described it in detail. He claimed to have touched it," the Navedi answered. "He said that after that time, she returned once or twice, but it was not with her then. He said she told him she was keeping it in a safe place. He said the Kelpies would rise again and he would be freed. He said the Alchemist had cursed him and that when the Kelpies rose again, he would have his revenge on the Alchemist."

"Did he tell anyone what he was supposed to tell us or give us?" Lochen asked.

"No," the Navedi answered. "He only said the spell the Alchemist cast would make him last until you came, and that he would be forced to do as the Alchemist had instructed until you were gone."

"But that didn't happen," said Solveig. "He died before he told us anything, and we never left him."

"We did," corrected Lochen. "I stayed with him when you all ran for help, but he began choking again before you came back. I was afraid he would die, so I, too, ran for help. In that instant, he was left alone – we...I left him alone."

"This wasn't your fault," said Summer. "We all ran out. It doesn't matter that we were all trying to get him help. None of us knew what would happen to him once we left him. That explains what happened to the other sentinels."

"Did he say anything to you when you were alone with him?" asked Natalie.

"Yes," answered Lochen, "but it didn't make much sense."

"What was it?" asked Natalie.

"He said something about splitting and stopping them. I assume he meant the Kelpies. And something about us being a connection to our homes."

"You're right," said Quinn. "That doesn't make a lot of sense."

"Oh," Lochen added. "And he gave me this book. I don't know for what purpose. I haven't had time to look at it. He said something about needing this to help defeat them."

"So what do we do now?" asked Sean.

"I need to think about all this," said Lochen. "And to see what this book has to offer."

"Some food and some rest would be nice," said Solveig. "While you're thinking," she added.

Liam asked the Navedi, who made all the arrangements. They moved from the old sentinel's prison cell and were provided one of the half sunken huts where they found bedding and food. While the others dug in – most of them happy to be eating something they could identify, and not something Sean had whipped up – Lochen only picked at his food. It was clear he was deep in thought.

"So," Sean repeated his earlier question, "what do we do now?"

"Before answering that," said Lochen, "I think it would be prudent to identify exactly what we know and what we either don't know, or about which we can only speculate. Is that agreeable?"

"Yes," they all answered.

"All right, then," he began. "First, I initially thought that our earlier encounters with Ena Ray and that other individual, who is now trapped in a tomb at the base of a volcano, were unrelated to our recent adventures. Now I am not so certain. We know that the Alchemist and the Enchantress lived at the same time and knew each other quite well.

"It seems that the Enchantress may have had some protégés she was training. I believe those protégés were Ena Ray and that other ghastly creature."

"Why do you think that?" asked Solveig.

"Because Ena Ray had that band," said Stella. "The one that Summer took away from him and which we used to be transported...wherever that was."

"I don't see what that band has to do with any of this," said Natalie.

"The band had symbols on it," explained Lochen. "As best I can recall, those symbols were exactly the same as the ones Quinn showed us in the Ice Kingdom."

"That just shows how that band is connected to us," said Sean.

"That's what we thought at the time," said Lochen. "But I believe the symbols were not at all connected to us. They were connected, rather, to the Kelpies."

"The Kelpies?" said Quinn. "That can't be right. That's not what I learned. And what I learned came from the Sage. You better not be trying to tell me the Sage is wrong."

"Duly noted," said Lochen. "For the time being, let's put any possible connection between the symbols and us aside. We can come back to that later. For now, though, I believe there is a connection between the symbols and the Kelpies."

"I agree," said Stella. "The vision I have of the map has those same markings. The markings designate the places where the Kelpies are being hidden."

She turned to Quinn and added, "I know that's hard to accept, but maybe the symbols are connected to both us and the Kelpies."

"That's too weird to even think about," said Summer.

"It certainly does result in a shift of our paradigm," said Lochen.

"Our who?" asked Quinn.

"Our view," he said. "Our perspective. It may be difficult to consider this, but we must. Furthermore, there appear to be eight Kelpies and there are eight symbols."

"All right," said Liam. "Even if we agree that Ena Ray is a part of all this, how does that other guy fit in?"

Lochen continued. "The Rebbercand that took Natalie there did so to entice Stella – an Enchantress. He also had a piece of the pendant. I think it's safe to say the band and the piece of the pendant belonged to the Alchemist's partner – the Enchantress. The fact that these items were in some way associated with these two other individuals makes it reasonable to conclude they were associated with her.

They are not Kelpies and there's no indication that they were involved with the Alchemist. Therefore, I believe they were under the tutelage of the Enchantress."

"The Rebbercand was called Bacham," said Natalie. "I heard the others call him by that name. The creature he intended to free was named Tebaga. I kept mispronouncing it to make him mad, hoping he'd make a mistake and I could escape."

"How do you know they — Ena Ray and this...Tebaga monster...or whatever he is — how do you know they aren't Kelpies?" asked Solveig.

"There's no indicator for them on the map that appeared to me," explained Stella.

"OK," said Sean. "I'm convinced, at least about that part of it. Keep going."

"The second thing is the pendant," Lochen continued, "which seems to have belonged to this ancient Enchantress, was broken into four parts. I'm only guessing, but I'm fairly confident in my guess, that those four parts were scattered to the far corners and lost for hundreds of years. The Alchemist found two of them — the one he hid at Virkio and the other that he hid in the Thumper's fortress.

"The other two were found by different people and passed from one person to another over time. One ended up with Sean, who gave it to Summer, who gave it to Stella. The other was found by the Rebbercand we left behind in the crypt in the volcano."

"Why do you think there were only four pieces?" asked Liam.

"From the shape of the two that are now with Stella," Lochen said. "The center piece was a triskelion, which leads me to believe the other three pieces are virtually identical. And, the other two pieces are now in the possession of someone else."

"How do you know that?" asked Solveig.

"I know," said Stella. "I could tell the moment the last piece was found. It attached itself to the other missing piece, and the map appeared. I'm convinced the map that appeared to me also appeared to the person – the Rebbercand who appeared in the tattoos on the troll. I think he has the other two parts of the pendant."

"And that brings us to the third thing," said Lochen. "And the fourth thing. I think they go together. Whoever is ahead of us is releasing the Kelpies. I'm not sure how or why, but the Nevarnik said we were too late; that the Kelpie had already been released. Also, the troll said that whoever had arrived at the Thumper's village was headed for the Swamp to find a Kelpie.

"And from the markings on the troll's body, it appears that this Rebbercand has others with him. I don't think those others are also Rebbercands, but some other creatures; that is, if the images can be trusted."

"Could they be gargoyles?" asked Sean.

"They didn't look like gargoyles to me," said Liam. "They were close, but they looked too big. But, as Lochen said, that's only if the images can be trusted. They were only tattoos, after all."

"Where do these sentinels fit in?" asked Summer.

"Ah, yes," said Lochen. "That's the fifth thing. From what many of them have told us, I have pieced together that the Alchemist anticipated that we, or others like us, would be seeking the Kelpies to either destroy them or to keep them hidden. He selected them to serve as guides – sentinels – to help us along the way. He cast a spell on them to slow down their aging process, but the spell is broken once they've made contact with us."

"That explains why they all shrivel up and disappear," said Stella.

"Yes," Lochen continued. "And they were all given a piece of information or something to help us in our endeavors."

"This is all wonderful," said Quinn. "But why us?"

"That I don't know," answered Lochen. "Unless, of course, your insistence that the symbols in the Ice Kingdom, do, in fact, connect to us. If that's true, then we, as well as the Kelpies, are in some way connected to one another. I simply don't understand at this moment what that connection is."

"What about the book Nevarnik gave you?" asked Natalie.

"It's very old," said Lochen. "And the writing in it is in a language I'm not familiar with. There are a few words I can make out. It's possible it's some kind of spell that would further secure the Kelpies in whatever prisons they're held, but that's only conjecture at this point. I'll need to spend more time translating it."

"You talked about what we know," said Summer. "I know this is going to sound stupid, but what don't we know?"

"That's not stupid at all," answered Lochen. "It's important to identify what we don't know. We don't know much about the wars that resulted in the banishment of the Kelpies. We don't know where they each came from. We don't know precisely who is releasing them or why. And, we don't know much about each other's ancestral history."

"Why is our history important?" asked Quinn.

"If there's a link between us," answered Lochen, "and between us and the Kelpies, it must be deep in our respective histories. Besides, knowing more about where we all came from will help us understand where we need to go."

"History, shmistory," said Sean. "When are we going to get to the part about what we do next?"

"Actually," answered Lochen, temporarily distracted from the subject of the connection between each of them and the Kelpies, "right now would be appropriate. I thought it important to clarify where we are and what brought us here."

"Arrgggh!" groaned Sean, cutting him off. "I know where we are. We're in a freaking forest with a bunch of carnivals."

"Cannibals," corrected Summer.

"Whatever," he responded. "And I know what brought us here. A freaking dragon and then we walked until the carnivals or the carnivores or the cannibals dropped us in their village. What I want to know is where are we going next? If we're chasing a Rebbercand, I want to hurry up and catch him and send him to join his ancestors!"

"I'm with Sean," said Liam. "These Rebbercands have been nothing but bad news. We need to catch this one and put a stop to whatever he's up to."

"I agree," said Lochen. "The dilemma is that we don't know for certain where he's going next."

"There are two markers that are close to the same distance from here – or, I mean, from where the Kelpie in the Swamp is...was located," said Stella. "I can see the symbol, but not clearly enough to tell exactly what it is. They all sort of fade in and out until we get close. Then the picture gets clearer and clearer."

"That's how we'll know the precise location, isn't it?" asked Natalie.

"That sounds reasonable," said Liam. "But right now the other two – the ones that are closest – they're both blurred?"

"Yes," answered Stella. "They're clearer than the rest, but neither of them is as distinct as the one in the Swamp was."

"Can you tell anything at all about where they are?" asked Liam.

"Oh, yeah," she answered. "That part's easy."

"Where are they?" asked Quinn.

"One is in a desert," Stella said, "and the other is located among some mountains."

"I know where both of those are," said Liam. "The desert is east and slightly south of here, and the mountains..."

"Are near our home," Solveig finished the sentence. "Lochen, they're going to be invading our home!"

"No," said Stella. "I think these mountains are further to the west. I know that's not very comforting."

"How can you be sure?" Solveig asked.

"The mountain range runs from the Cerulean Sea to the Viridian Ocean," said Liam. "There are valleys in between the various peaks, and it's really all the same range, but there are distinct parts."

"Yes," said Stella. "The map, the one I see with the Kelpie locations, shows it's the middle part of the range."

"Still," said Solveig, refusing to be consoled, "that's too close. What are we going to do?"

"How do we decide which way to go?" asked Sean.

"We split up," answered Lochen.

"What? NO!" they all objected at once.

"We can't split up," persisted Summer. "That would be a disaster-piece."

"I don't see how splitting up is going to help," objected Natalie. "We're not sure what we're supposed to do when we find these Kelpies. What if the stone Stella has is the key? Then whichever group she's not in will be helpless."

"I'm sure the pendant has some power associated with it that will help," said Lochen. "But I don't believe that's the only weapon we have. The Alchemist was too clever to leave only one method to keep them imprisoned or defeated. There must be others. I'm certain that once I can translate this book, those alternatives will be revealed."

"So for now," said Liam, "you're suggesting that we split up and take our chances."

"I agree that it's not the optimal approach," said Lochen, "but I don't see how we can be in two places at once otherwise. And without knowing where they're going next, it's essential that we travel to both places as quickly as we can. That can't be done as a single group. I'm open to alternative suggestions, if there are any."

No one spoke immediately. They were all wracking their brains for another solution. Nothing was forthcoming. Eventually, they all had to agree that splitting up might be the only way to stop what was happening.

"How do we decide who goes where?" asked Sean.

"I suggest the following," said Lochen, who had already given this much thought. "Since we are fairly certain that the Rebbercand ahead of us is likely to head towards the closest location, we should divide into two groups. One will head to the desert, and the other will head to the mountains."

"What happens if one group runs into the Rebbercand, or misses him and is too late?" asked Natalie.

"Then," explained Lochen, "the two groups should go to secondary targets. Stella, what are the nearest locations to those two sites?"

Stella closed her eyes for a few seconds, concentrating on the map and the other markers.

"The location closest to the mountains would be further north and west to a volcano," she said. "The location closest to the desert would be on the other side of the Swamp at the edge of the Ice Kingdom."

"Oh, poop," moaned Quinn. "You mean there's one of those Kelpies in the Ice Kingdom, too?"

"It gets worse," said Stella. "It looks like there's one in that forest where Solveig got lost and then turned blue, another one not far from Nohkmar Cambin, and one more that seems to be somewhere in the Viridian Ocean."

"This just keeps getting better and better," moaned Sean.

"Then the desert team should try to get to the Ice Kingdom, and the mountain team should go to the volcano," said Lochen. "On the other hand, if either team is successful in their first location, and stops the Rebbercand, we should all meet at Solveig's palace. It will be the closest safe location."

"What if we're not successful after going to both places," asked Liam. "I hate to sound negative, but we should have a contingency plan."

"You are quite correct," said Lochen. "If the worst should happen, and both teams fail to intercept the Rebbercand after two attempts, it would be wise to regroup. Judging from the locations identified by Stella, it might be most prudent for the team in the Ice Kingdom to stay put and the team coming from the volcano to join them."

"Why wouldn't we just go on to other locations, instead of meeting in the Ice Kingdom?" asked Sean. "That seems to make more sense."

"Because," explained Lochen. "If we haven't been successful after two attempts, then our strategy is flawed and we need to reconsider our approach. We can't do that still separated."

There was some discussion about the pro and cons of Lochen's plan, but they all knew time was growing short. The longer they debated the more of a lead the Rebbercand and his party had on them. Finally, they concluded this seemed the best approach.

"So, who goes where?" Natalie asked.

"Once more," said Lochen, "I would suggest the following: Liam lead the team going to the desert and Quinn lead the team going to the mountains."

"Me?" asked Quinn. "I'm not a guide. I don't know where to go."

"I think you know more than you believe you do," said Lochen.

"Liam's the Pathfinder," he continued to object. "He knows how to get to places when no one knows where they are."

"And so do you," Lochen persisted.

"No, I don't," Quinn moaned. "Before I met you guys, I had never left the Ice Kingdom. How can I find some Kelpie in a mountain?"

"The same way you find your way around uncharted areas of your own world," answered Lochen. "The same way you left the Ice Kingdom, crossed the sea into the Venomous Swamp and found Liam."

"I...I..." stammered Quinn. "I didn't find Liam. He found me."

"Yes," said Liam. "But I found you in the Swamp. You made it that far on your own. You can do this. I know it."

Quinn was stymied. While he was trying to come up with some other rebuttal, Lochen went on.

"Natalie should go with Quinn to the mountains, and Solveig should go with Liam to the desert."

Quest of Eight Part Five: Release of the Demons

Richard Reda

"The mountains?" asked Natalie. "Really? I'm not all that comfortable with heights."

"And why should I go to the desert?" asked Solveig. "I'd be better in the mountains."

Lochen took a deep breath. He had expected some disagreement, but he hadn't thought every suggestion would be challenged.

"Natalie," he explained. "I appreciate your dislike of high places, but you would suffer more in the desert. You are a water creature. The desert air would weaken you immeasurably. And Solveig, I know you would prefer the mountains, but I am afraid being so close to your home, you would be distracted."

Natalie and Solveig sighed deeply. They wanted to be supportive, but were not comfortable with their assignments. Before they could object further, Lochen continued.

"Summer, you will join Quinn and Natalie, while Sean will join Liam and Solveig," he said. Before either of them could begin a recitation of objections, he finished, "Stella will go with the desert team and I will go with the mountain team. This divides our respective talents and abilities about as equally as possible.

"We can debate the strengths and weaknesses of these placements, but there are advantages and disadvantages to all of the possible alternatives. In the end we will not likely establish a division significantly more rational than this one, and we will have lost valuable time doing so."

In fact, during the time between the departing of the sentinel, Nevarnik, and this discussion, he had contemplated a number of different options. The one he settled on gave each team a guide – someone who was able to find his way even when he didn't know the terrain. Liam was by nature a Pathfinder, and although Quinn lacked the confidence, Lochen was convinced he shared many of Liam's capabilities.

Each team had someone who was proven to be resourceful and fierce in a battle. Sean was unmatched in his courage and his accuracy with a slingshot. And Natalie had managed to survive being kidnapped by a very dangerous Rebbercand. Not only had she survived, she had been key to his defeat.

Each team had someone who brought unusual and special talents to their group. Summer could make herself nearly invisible and, being as small as she was and able to fly, could go places where the others couldn't. Solveig had studied warfare and combat strategies of every known civilization and could anticipate danger.

Finally, each team had a member well practiced in magic. Stella's and his own abilities to cast spells and mix potions were about equal. And because of this, he believed that Stella could transmit her vision of the map to him.

Lochen knew that splitting up had its disadvantages, too. It divided their collective power. However, if they were wrong about the next location, they could be chasing after this Rebbercand and now at least one of the Kelpies, from one end of the continent to the other. He only hoped this strategy worked.

Liam gathered his team and told the others that he knew where they were in the Forest and thought it might be better if he lead his team into the Swamp to one of his closest supply stores. He had created several of these all over the Swamp in case he needed a place of refuge away from his home base. He knew that in the one he was thinking of, he had stored one of his transportation contraptions. If he could get to this, it would make getting to the desert faster.

Before Liam headed out with his team, though, Lochen said he needed a few words with Stella.

"You want me to transmit the map, don't you?" she asked.

"That would be very helpful, if you could," he answered.

"I don't know if I can, but it's worth a try."

She closed her eyes to bring the image forward in her mind. Then she placed one hand on Lochen's head and concentrated. She knew she'd never be able to provide him with the same image or even all of the locations. He would need the pendant pieces in her possession to do that. However, she thought that if she focused on the image in the mountains, this just might work.

Lochen could feel a surge of heat move through Stella's hand into his head. He couldn't see anything at first, and hoped she was using the right spell. He didn't want his brain cooked. After a few seconds, he closed his eyes. He didn't see a map of any kind, but he had a sensation that he knew right where the Kelpie was buried.

"I hope that works," said Stella.

"I believe it did," Lochen answered.

He was about to leave to join his own team when he felt a chill pass through him. He wasn't sure what it was, but the first thing that came to his mind was the stone in Stella's headband. He turned back towards her.

"I can't tell you why I'm asking this," he said. "But I think you should take the stone out of your headband."

Stella looked at him oddly.

"Why?"

"I really don't know," he answered. "Just a feeling I have."

He waved his hand and conjured a strip of rawhide with thin netting at one end. The netting looked like nothing more than a spider's web. He handed it to Stella.

"I think you'll find the amulet will fit perfectly in this cradle," he told her. "I know the netting looks delicate, but I can assure you, it is as strong as steel. It's Sorcerer's thread."

She held the leather necklace in her hand, studying it, and then looked up at him. He only smiled and turned away. She knew better than to dismiss his premonitions. She removed her headband and took the stone from its setting. She then slipped the stone into the thread. He was right. It not only fit perfectly, the thread wrapped itself tightly around the stone as if it were a part of it.

She returned her headband, and then placed the rawhide around her neck. It, too, had been enchanted. The rawhide constricted so that the stone rested in the space at the base of her throat between the inner parts of her collar bone. Now there was no way for the necklace to slip over her head.

She then went off to join Liam, Sean and Solveig. Once the farewells were said, they moved east out of the village and followed the edge of the cliff that overlooked the river separating them from the Swamp. It would take a day to get to the supply hideout that Liam was headed for, but after that, they would make better time on their way to the desert.

"I sure hate to see them go," said Quinn. "They're going to have one of Liam's boat things. They'll be able to get to the desert pretty fast. How are we going to catch up to the Rebbercand if he's gone to the mountains?"

"It's funny that you should ask," said Lochen. "While I was divining the strategy of separate teams, I assumed Liam would be resourceful enough to take steps to close the gap his team might face. I then thought about options for our team."

"I have a bad feeling about this," said Natalie.

"Your apprehensions are probably well placed," Lochen responded. "And I must apologize for not raising this sooner."

"Raising what?" asked Quinn.

"I spoke with the Navedi who brought us here and explained our situation. I asked if the sentinel had given any instructions about help that was to be provided to us. Unfortunately, he hadn't. He was so reviled by his kinsmen that they seldom spoke to him at all. However, our host indicated that he could furnish us with some assistance."

"You're taking too long to tell us," said Summer. "It must really be bad."

"Well," said Lochen, "the word bad is open to interpretation. I prefer to describe it as an unusual opportunity."

"Spill it," demanded Natalie.

"Grackles," answered Lochen.

"What about them?" asked Natalie.

"They can carry us."

"They can what?" asked Quinn.

"Carry us," said Lochen. "Actually, it sounds quite reasonable. You may not be aware, they fly in very tight formations, almost like a swarm. And their talons are very strong. They can carry more than their own weight."

"Wait a minute," said Natalie, shaking her head. "You mean to tell me a bunch of those scruffy, squawking birds are going to pick us up in their claws and fly us into the mountains?"

"I'm not sure scruffy is an apt descriptor. They're quite clean and well groomed. In fact, they often tend to each other..."

"I don't care about their grooming habits," Natalie cut him off. "You expect them to lift us up...into the air? The air??? After what I went through being carried on those horrible beasts by that horrible Rebbercand?"

"I can appreciate your reticence," said Lochen, "but this time you won't be held prisoner."

"Stop," she said. "Just stop. There's no way you can make this sound good. Let's just get it over with."

As she and Lochen exchanged comments, Quinn stood by with his mouth in a perfect "O." He was too shocked to speak. The last, and only time, he had ever left the ground was in the Wedgamaroon, and he still hadn't gotten over how that had ended. He snapped his mouth closed and kept his fears to himself when Summer spoke.

"Sounds all right to me, as long as they don't think I'm a snack. Let's get going."

With Quinn frightened into silence, and Natalie grumbling to herself, the four moved to a clearing near the edge of the village where their Navedi guide was waiting for them. When they were ready, he whistled, and thousands of Grackles began to squawk.

Dozens of them dropped down out of the trees and clutched Lochen's robes along his shoulders. They started dragging him forward and other Grackles swooped down towards his waist and back, picking up more of his clothing in their claws. Finally, another group took his pants and shoes into their grip and he was airborne.

They descended on Natalie next. Her body went rigid as soon as she left the ground. Her arms were being pulled along by part of the formation, preventing her from covering her eyes with her hands. In seconds, she was pulled into the air and alongside Lochen where they flew in a haphazard holding pattern waiting for the others.

A few flew down to grab Summer, but she took flight on her own, evading their grasp.

"Thanks," she said, "but I'll do this myself."

It took nearly a hundred of them to raise Quinn off the ground. Try as he might, he couldn't close his eyes and he had to instruct himself to breath. As soon as he joined the others, the Grackles tightened their formation and darted away, changing direction instantly – moving right and then left – in no particular order and for no particular reason.

When the visitors had been carried away, the tribe of Navedi silently came together in the center of the village. Gradually, their bodies began to shift and transform. Their arms extended and became forelegs. Their faces stretched forward into muzzles and fur sprung out all over their bodies. In a matter of seconds they had returned to their original shapes and the pack of jackals that guarded the sentinel returned to the forest.

Chapter six

As soon as Pantano Izaki rose from his crypt, the plants that had been attacking B'nair and the hobgoblins, and the animals and reptiles that they hadn't yet seen, but were on their way, all stopped. They had heard their master's voice – a voice that had been dormant for centuries. Still, it was recognized and no creature, plant or animal, would act without a command from that master.

The green eyes were fixed on B'nair, glowing like fire. The outstretched hand, pointing the long thin finger at the Rebbercand held fast, not wavering. When no one answered, Pantano Izaki's voice didn't boom. He didn't scream and he didn't threaten. Instead he

116

leaned down closer towards B'nair and spoke in little more than a whisper.

"I asked you a question," he demanded.

B'nair straightened up and held his head erect, but for only a second. He thought better of being confrontational. He lowered his head and spoke.

"Forgive me," he said. "I am B'nair of the Rebbercands. It was I who freed you from your prison."

Pantano Izaki breathed in deeply and looked at the hobgoblins huddled around and behind the Rebbercand.

"And who are your friends?" he asked.

"Hobgoblins," B'nair answered, his head still lowered. "They have assisted me in my search."

"Have you found the others?"

"The other Kelpies? No. Not yet. You are the first."

"Where are the witch and the sorcerer?" Pantano Izaki asked.

"Who?" B'nair asked.

"The Enchantress and the Alchemist."

"I don't know," B'nair answered. "I know very little of these two."

"And the pendant? What of that?"

At the mention of the pendant B'nair's body went rigid. He thought for a minute of denying that he had part of it, but quickly reconsidered. He knew very little of the power of these Kelpies. In spite of his reservations, he knew this was not the time to get off on the wrong foot.

"You have it," Pantano Izaki said. "I can sense it in your reaction. Or you have at least part of it. Don't you."

"Yes. A part of it," B'nair admitted. "I don't know who has the other part, but that person is not far behind us."

"Show me," Pantano Izaki demanded.

His initial reaction was to demand that it be given to him, but he knew the Rebbercand would not part with it. He could have taken it from him forcefully, he knew; but he suspected that the stone carried with it the knowledge of the location of his fellow Kelpies. He also knew the trickery of the Enchantress, Meri Hocto. If the location of his brethren was connected to the pendant, he didn't want to interfere with that information. The Enchantress would have put spells within spells on that stone.

Even if she had died when the pendant was shattered, she would have cast a spell on it. Such a spell would likely cause the knowledge connected with the stone to evaporate like a mist if ownership was taken instead of yielded. Better to leave it with the Rebbercand – for now, at any rate.

B'nair reached into his inside pocket and removed the stone. He held it tightly in his hand and reluctantly opened it, keeping it close to his body. He kept his eyes focused on the Kelpie, unsure of what his intentions were.

"The power of that pendant in the hands of the witch," Pantano Izaki said, "stole my kingdom from me, and cast me into a prison worse than death. Let me hold it."

"You should know," countered B'nair, "that upon finding these two pieces, they merged and then revealed to me a map with the locations of your brethren. I believe the continued existence of that map is directly related to the possession of this stone. That information could be lost the instant I hand you this trinket."

He was making this up, and hoping that the Kelpie wouldn't detect the lie. Or, if he did, that he'd be uncertain of the extent of the lie. B'nair had his hand still close to his body with the stone tight in his grip. The Kelpie had his hand still extended, waiting to have the stone passed to him. They held those poses for several seconds.

"That would be a terrible loss," Pantano Izaki finally said, slowly lowering his hand. "Still. I would like to see it."

B'nair watched the Kelpie's arm return to his side and then extended his hand only slightly, opening it so that the stone was exposed on the flat of his palm. When B'nair's fingers released their grip, the stone was positioned so that the open section – the part where the pieces Stella had would fit – was facing the Kelpie.

In a split second, the stone spun around so that the opening was facing B'nair. The large partial circle of the outer edge now faced the Kelpie. In that same instant, a flash of light burst from the edges, slicing horizontally from right to left. He had never seen that happen before. He was mesmerized by the inexplicable beam of light.

The thin beam swiped across the face and eyes of the Kelpie. He buried his face behind his arm and screeched. It was an example of the Enchantress' reach. A reach from beyond the grave, the Kelpie could only hope.

"Cover it," he shouted in a piercing scream. "It is blinding me."

B'nair closed his hand and quickly lowered his head, to cover the smile that had broken across his face. He had no fear now that the Kelpie would try to take the stone from him. Something about it was lethal to the ancient sorcerer. He put it back in his pocket.

"Forgive me," he said, not really meaning it.

"It was the doing of that cursed Enchantress," gasped Pantano Izaki. "She, or that Alchemist. I will have my vengeance on both of them."

"You said your kingdom had been stolen from you," said B'nair. "I don't understand. What kingdom was that?"

The Kelpie was still shielding his eyes. The burning sensation had stopped, but he was not sure whether or not some other spell would unfold. He slowly lowered his hands and straightened up. He resumed his regal posture.

"These lands here," he responded, his arms outstretched to encompass the Swamp.

"This Swamp?" B'nair asked, not understanding why anyone would want to live here, let alone claim it as a kingdom.

"It was not a swamp when I ruled it," Pantano Izaki answered.

A cruel smile stretched the skin across his face.

"That was my parting gift to those who opposed me," he continued. "This area – from these rivers to the Cerulean Sea and the bay to the north– was a garden paradise. It was my home. The people of the Swamp at that time were led by Ketua. He was not a king or a ruler, but a wise man – or so they thought. He was nothing. I was the Mengassi – the king. He should have paid deference to me. But he did not.

"When I...how shall I say...disagreed with him? There was a revolt. It had to be put down. They had to know their place. Ketua made a plea for help, and I called on my brothers. But the Alchemist and his witch singled us out to divide us and conquer us through their trickery. They enticed my own people – the inhabitants of this paradise – to side against me. Some did not, but most of them did.

"They aided the Alchemist and the Enchantress, helping to deceive me; to trap me; and to imprison me. But before I was rendered powerless, I cast a spell that not even the Alchemist could counter. I poisoned the land, the waters and the people. I was held in this crypt, so I made sure they were equally imprisoned. If I was to lose my home, I made certain that they would lose theirs.

"No matter how toxic their environment became, they would not be able to leave it. I cursed them into eternity until they became extinct. They would know this land and all the ways out of it. They would be born with this knowledge and they would die with it, but they would never be able to use it to free themselves. Only the last of their kind would be able to escape, and only to tell all he met of his fate."

B'nair listened without comment. He didn't know how much of this was fact or fiction. He had a strange feeling, though, that he might have encountered the last of the inhabitants of this dreadful place. His memory of dangling from his own whip off the side of a bridge came unbidden to his mind. It was just a flicker, but enough to make him wonder if the one who had cut that whip was from this land. For the time being he decided to keep that suspicion to himself.

"And now it is your turn," the Kelpie said. "Tell me what you know."

B'nair explained how he came to be with the small band of hobgoblins. He omitted the part about being in the mines of the Trepans, and the rebellion, vaguely describing an unfortunate accident from which the hobgoblins had rescued him. At this point he didn't know enough about whomever it was that had helped the Trepans. He was only certain that someone had.

He told of what the hobgoblins had shared with him about their ancestor and the pendant. He described capturing one of the stones at the fortress of Virkio, and of finding the second stone in the village of the Thumpers. He didn't bother to explain how the map originally appeared to him. It sounded implausible to himself when he thought about it. Instead he only indicated that the map was revealed to him as a vision once the two stones were joined together. He had chosen this site first because it was the closest.

He knew others were following him, but he admitted he didn't know who they were (although his suspicions were growing) or exactly how close behind they were. He described in general terms where the other markers were, not admitting that the vision itself was vague about this until he physically got closer.

"Let them follow us," said Pantano Izaki. "The Swamp will swallow them all."

B'nair was not as convinced of that as the Kelpie was. After all, the Kelpie had been dormant for two thousand years. It was he, B'nair, who had dealt with these pursuers.

"Do you have a plan?" Pantano Izaki asked. "We must release the other Kelpies. Where is the closest?"

"There are two other places that are nearly equal distances from here," answered B'nair. "One is to the south and east – in a desert; and the other is to the south in the mountains. After that, the locations are spread out far and wide."

He didn't want to reveal too much information. He was certain that once he was no longer of use, this Kelpie or the others would quickly dispose of him and fight over the stone. He needed to make himself invaluable to them.

"If you have no objections, I would suggest we travel to the desert and then decide at that time which place would be most advantageous to reach."

"I have no objections, of course, but I'm curious. Why did you choose the desert first?"

"It will reduce the amount of back tracking in reaching the other locations," answered B'nair. "Some is inevitable, but this way seems to be the fastest path to reach each site."

"A very wise course of action," Pantano Izaki said.

"It will be a long journey. We should leave soon, even if we won't have a full day of travel."

"I will need the rest of this day and the night to regain my strength," the Kelpie responded. "We can leave tomorrow at first light."

"But we may lose whatever advantage we have by waiting," B'nair objected, although not too vehemently.

"Our travel will not be a problem. I will take care of that in the morning."

B'nair realized the Kelpie wasn't revealing all he knew, either. He would have to be very careful with this one. He turned to Vardelos and told him to have the rest of the hobgoblins make camp on the rafts – and to make sure the Banchu leaves covered the flooring. He also instructed that guards be posted.

"You will have no need of guards," said Pantano Izaki. "Nothing in this Swamp will bring harm to you. I have returned."

Vardelos gave B'nair a knowing look. Without exchanging any words, Vardelos let it be known that guards would be posted, as B'nair had instructed. For the time being, B'nair thought, the hobgoblins were still his allies. He wondered how much longer that would last.

The posting of guards proved to be unnecessary. No one slept. All through the night the Kelpie paced along the edge of the river, chanting in some unknown language. The chanting was broken only when he would snatch some nearby plant or passing reptile and devour it greedily. It was as if they were drawn to the chanting. The plants moved – B'nair had only heard of such things. And the reptiles crawled or slithered. It was as if they were all answering the Kelpie's call.

With every one of the Kelpie's movements, the smell of death and decay permeated the air. The only change from this was the smell of the blood and guts of whatever unsuspecting creature heeded the spell of the incantation by coming too close, only to be ripped apart by the Kelpie's jaws.

The arrival of the dawn revealed the same steel gray skies of the last several days. It also revealed a pile of bones, skins and parts of snakes, lizards and river creatures on which the Kelpie had fed during the night. None of this did anything to improve the foul nature of his breath. However, there was something about him that had changed.

He looked less frail. That was the only way B'nair could describe it. His eyes burned with a fire that the day before hadn't been as strong. His movements were quicker and more assured. Physically there was nothing significantly different, but there was an aura of strength and power that seemed to flow from him. B'nair's first thought was that the Kelpie was now more dangerous than he had been before. He was beginning to wonder if releasing the rest of them was such a good idea. It was too late, though, to now turn back.

He also noticed that Pantano Izaki had what looked like a large snake in his hand. It was not moving. In fact, it was fully extended and quite stiff. The head was bent perpendicular to the rest of its body with its mouth frozen open, exposing its fangs. The Kelpie appeared to be using it as a walking stick or, more specifically, a staff, since the snake was almost as long as he was tall.

"We can leave now," the Kelpie announced, planting the tail of the snake in the ground. "We must find my brethren. You can lead the way."

"We are several days from the desert," B'nair answered. "Can your powers transport us there?"

"No," Pantano Izaki answered. "That skill is not mine. However, the one we will find in the desert will make all our later travels much simpler."

"In that case, we will have to travel by river for part of the way," B'nair began to explain. "None of us has been this way before, and we don't know what dangers lay ahead."

"No harm will come to you in this Swamp," the Kelpie assured them.

He waved his arm and a prism of air encircled the rafts, the hobgoblins and B'nair. It started as a wavering ball and then opened up into a circle and flowed over, under and around them, closing back to a ball and disappearing once it had passed.

"I created this Swamp," he continued. "I will protect you from its dangers."

His words did little to instill confidence in B'nair or the hobgoblins. Vardelos looked at the Rebbercand and exchanged the same look that went between them regarding the posting of a guard during the night — they would remain vigilant regardless of the assurances the Kelpie gave them.

B'nair closed his eyes in order to focus his thoughts on the location of the next sorcerer to be released. He could see that the river would carry them much of the way. Eventually, they would have to cross the desert to get to their location. In spite of his extensive travels, this was another location that B'nair and the other Rebbercands had avoided. It was too inhospitable even for them.

"I will be in the lead raft with the Kelpie," B'nair told Vardelos. "I need you to control the other one. You must be my eyes and ears to protect us from behind."

"Yes, sir," the hobgoblin replied. "I will not disappoint you."

"Stay close," B'nair told him. "And stay alert. I don't trust this wizard."

Vardelos only nodded and then boarded the second raft. In a few minutes the two crafts had been pushed from the shore and were now flowing with the current. The Cerulean Sea was hundreds of miles in front of them, and the desert to which they were headed was hundreds of miles to the south.

---------------- *** ----------------

Liam, Sean, Solveig and Stella left the encampment of the Navedi, reluctantly leaving the others behind. They soon were traveling along the ridge overlooking the river that separated the Navedis Forest from the Swamp. The skies overhead were still gray and the mist that seemed to enshroud the Forest slowly began to evaporate. The view of the river was becoming clearer and clearer.

They were thirty or forty feet above the river, and the trees they were passing were changing from the dead black ones of the Forest to thicker and greener varieties. Liam was concentrating on getting back into the Swamp, about the best place to cross over, and how they would safely get to the nearest storage location when Stella reached up and grabbed his shirt, jerking him backwards and down to the ground.

"What are you doing?" he called out.

"Shhh," she whispered.

He looked back at her and saw that she, Sean and Solveig were all crouching behind a line of shrubs. She was motioning for him to duck down and to be quiet, at the same time she was pointing towards the river.

He got down as low as he could and moved one of the branches in front of him, opening his view of the river. Below him he could see two rafts floating several hundred yards down the river, moving away from them. The one in back was laden with about a half dozen gruesome looking bodies. He recognized them as being the same as those who had launched the attack on the bridge to Tower Five.

"Hobgoblins," he whispered.

"Worse," said Stella. "Look at the raft in front."

He could see more hobgoblins and two other figures. One was larger than the hobgoblins and heavier. He had a large double bladed axe in one hand. They were too far away for Sean to clearly see who it was. The other was tall and thin and covered with clothing that looked like moss and vines.

"A Rebbercand," said Liam. "And someone else."

A shudder ran through Liam. He had grown up on stories about an ancient evil sorcerer – a Mengassi who had slain the ancient leader of his people: the Ketua. He had dismissed those stories as myths, but the figure that was quickly moving away from him resembled the descriptions.

"A Kelpie" whispered Stella. "The Rebbercand has the other pieces of the stone. He's the one. That's the Kelpie he released. They're heading to the next one. The sentinel was right. We were too late."

"If they're going in that direction," said Solveig, "they must be going to find the one that's in the desert. Shouldn't we go back and tell Lochen and the others? Wouldn't it be better if we were all together, especially since we now know where the Rebbercand is headed?"

"No," said Stella. "We would be wasting time by going back for them. In doing that, even together we won't get to the desert location first. This way, maybe the others can find the Kelpie in the mountains before it's released and destroy it. If we get to the desert in time, we should be able to stop or at least delay the Rebbercand and the hobgoblins."

"Why don't we attack while they're on the river?" asked Sean.

"They're moving too fast and they're already too far away," said Stella.

She reached to the pendant at her throat and held it tightly. She could feel a gentle pulsating and a slightly warm sensation emanating from the stone. It had come alive, sensing the close proximity of the other half. She wondered if the Rebbercand could feel the same thing. And if he did, would he realize what was causing it?

At that very instant the Rebbercand jerked around and faced their direction. They all instinctively ducked down as he seemed to scan the shore line. He was too far away to be clearly distinguishable, and for them to tell exactly what he was looking at. In a few seconds later both rafts disappeared around a bend in the river and the Kelpie, the Rebbercand and the hobgoblins were out of sight.

"Come on," Liam said as he stood up. "We need to get moving."

He had been silent the whole time they watched the procession below them. The more he thought about it, the less he was certain that the one identified as the Kelpie looked like the Mengassi — the personification of evil; the creature about which he had been told from his earliest childhood. He couldn't bring himself to believe those stories were true. He shrugged off the feeling, trying to dismiss it from his mind.

They ran down the remainder of the incline to the shore line, but there was no place to cross. There were places where the river narrowed considerably, but in those locations, the current was much swifter and the opposite shoreline was less appealing. It was also difficult to know how deep the water was. In the wider portions, even where it was likely to be shallower, the water was so murky the bottom was hidden from view.

Liam didn't have to tell them – they already knew – it was not wise to try to wade across to the other side. No part of this waterway was safe. Eventually they came to a narrow stretch where there were a number of tall trees on their side of the water, and what looked like fairly solid ground on the opposite side.

"This looks like a good place to cross," said Liam. "We need to find a log or something that will stretch across."

"Let me help," said Stella.

She pointed her finger at one of the trees closest to the water's edge and then slowly shifted towards the far shore. The tree creaked as it bent and twisted, extending over the river and dropping to touch the ground on the opposite side.

The four walked carefully over and once they were on the ground, Stella pointed back at the tree. It reversed its earlier motion and returned to its original position as if nothing had happened. On the Swamp side of the river, she spun her hand in a circle and pieces of fallen trees and driftwood sprang upright. The pieces moved as if they were walking and lined up before her.

With her other hand, she charmed some vines from the brush and wove them in and around the trunks assembled before her. When she was finished, she flipped her hand forward and the raft she had created dropped into the marsh.

"That should make getting through the Swamp a little easier," she said with a smile.

"Easier," agreed Liam, "but not necessarily safer. Too bad you can't make us fly."

"That one's not in my bag of tricks," answered Stella.

Solveig climbed onto the raft and said, "I think we'll manage."

The others followed and Stella waved her hand again, propelling the craft forward. Liam pointed out the direction and they glided across the water and the reeds effortlessly.

"How far do we have to go?" asked Sean.

Even though the marsh wasn't deep, it was still water, and Sean was as uncomfortable in the shallows of the swamp as he was on the depths of the ocean.

"There's a supply station close to here," said Liam. "But it doesn't have the vehicle I think we need. We'll stop there, though, to pick up a few items I think will come in handy."

In about an hour they arrived at a large mound of rocks. On the face of the rocks was a huge wooden door, complete with a large lock. The door showed signs of prior attacks, but seemed solid enough. Liam jumped off the raft and gave the area a quick scan. When he was sure no one was around, he moved some of the rocks off to the side of the door and dug out a key for the lock.

"That doesn't seem to be the most secure method of keeping your hiding place safe," said Solveig.

"The only ones in the Swamp besides me who would be able to use this key are the gargoyles," he answered. "They have a hard time understanding how to do simple tasks. Knowing they should look for a key, figuring out where the key was hidden, and then knowing what to do with the key on the off chance they even found it, are all beyond their capabilities. How do you think I've been able to live here as long as I have all by myself with so many of them?"

Quest of Eight Part Five: Release of the Demons

Richard Reda

Sean was more than happy to be on solid ground, despite any other possible dangers. He followed Liam into the storeroom. Inside, Liam struck a flint and lit a small oil lamp. The walls were covered with shelves and each shelf was filled with all sorts of supplies: food, clothing, weapons and tools.

Liam pulled several daggers and short swords from one of the shelves and handed a few to Sean. Then he filled his arms with small bundles. He handed those to Solveig and Stella, and took one more look around. Rope, he thought to himself. I need to make sure to put a supply of rope in these places.

"All set," he said when he could think of nothing else to draw from the supply room.

They left the vault. Liam reset the lock and returned the key to its hiding place. Back on the raft, he directed Stella to guide it to the next location.

"What did we get?" asked Solveig.

She had seen the weapons that Sean was carrying. She assumed the small bundles contained food, but she was curious what kind of food would keep indefinitely in a storeroom.

"Some of it is…" Liam started to answer. "Let's just say that some of it is better left undefined. There's some…it's…it's like jerky."

"You're really making it sound appetizing," Solveig answered, uncertain that she would be interested in trying it, no matter how hungry she got.

"Anything besides food?" asked Sean.

"There are some roots, leaves, and plants," he answered. "They can be used to make potions and poultices, in case we need them."

"Good thinking," said Stella. "Although I hope we never have to use them."

For a few more hours they wound their way through the marshes, deeper and deeper into the Swamp. They ran into several nests of insects, which Stella was able to fend off. Liam kept expecting to see some larger and more threatening predators, and was a bit surprised when none appeared. He knew they were going out of their way, but hoped to make up the lost time once they reached their destination.

Eventually they arrived at what looked like a long dock. The raft glided to a stop. Liam got off first and secured the raft to the pier. He told the others to stay put until he made sure everything was safe. He approached the opposite end of the dock and vanished from sight. A few seconds later he reappeared and waved them all to join him.

They hustled down the pier and around a large fern, coming face to face with a much larger storeroom than the first one they had visited. Liam pushed aside an even larger door and they all walked into a small living space.

"This one," he explained, "was designed to keep me safe for several days. It's still quite a distance from my home base. When I came out here to explore or to map the area, I usually couldn't get back before nightfall, and there's a nest of gargoyles not far from here. There were times I was holed up here for as long as a week."

"I think I'd go nuts," said Sean.

"Too late," said Solveig, good naturedly.

"Funny," answered Sean. "What now? Do we head for the desert?"

"No," said Liam. "We need to stay here for the night."

"But it's not night, yet," said Stella.

"No," responded Liam. "It's not. But it will be before we are able to get back to the river. It'll be safer for us to stay here."

"But we didn't run into anything too hard to handle coming in here," argued Sean. "Why can't we just keep going until we get to the river?"

"Because the predators at night are much more dangerous, and most of them we won't see coming until it's too late. I know we stand to lose some time, but if we try going out in the night, we may not make it to the desert at all. Trust me. We'll make up some of that lost time tomorrow."

This was his home territory, and they all knew his judgment in this matter was probably the soundest. They had been traveling the entire day and could use the rest. They each found a comfortable spot and hunkered down for the night. In a few hours each of them was in a deep sleep.

Sometime during the middle of the night, their rest came to an abrupt halt. They were awakened instantly by a loud screeching sound and then an earth shaking crash against the door. The first crash was followed by repeated banging.

"What was that?" shouted Sean.

He had jumped to his feet and pulled out his slingshot. He was spinning back and forth scanning the dimly lit chamber for an unseen attacker.

"Relax," said Liam, who had barely changed his position. "It's the gargoyles. They discovered the raft and realized someone had slipped past them. That made them angry, so they picked it up and smashed it against the door."

"The raft?" asked Sean. "They picked up the raft?"

"Yeah," said Liam. "They're dumb, but they're pretty strong. They'll rant and rave for a little while longer, and then they'll forget what they were angry about and leave. They'll be gone by morning. Go back to sleep."

There were several more crashing sounds, accompanied by snarling and shrieking. Eventually, the noises faded away and everything returned to normal – or what passed for normal in the Swamp. Regardless, only Liam was able to fall back to sleep. The others kept their eyes glued to the door; certain something was going to break through.

Although none of them could tell from inside the keep that it was morning, they all knew it was time to leave. Liam pushed aside a panel next to the wall and revealed one of his unusual home-made contraptions.

This one was a small boat with wheels. The wheels had large, wide cogs along the outer rims to facilitate traveling through mud or sand. There was no sail. Instead, between the pairs of wheels were small blades the extended the length of each of the axels. Both axels had four sets of these short, wide extensions that served as paddles to propel the vehicle through the water.

"How do you come up with these things?" asked Solveig as she marveled at the construction.

"Too much time on my hands," Liam quipped. "That or they're the result of my misspent youth."

He loaded the supplies he had gathered from the first storage room and added some more from the current one. He also grabbed a few cross bows and a large supply of arrows.

"You have enough weaponry for an army," said Stella.

"I just want to be prepared for the unexpected," he answered.

"Hey," Sean laughed. "Wouldn't that make it expected?"

The others only looked at him without comment.

"Well, wouldn't it?" he asked.

When everything was ready, he opened the large door and wheeled their transport out of the chamber. There were broken pieces of their raft all over the place, and a few more gouges in the face of the door. Other than that, though, there was no sign of the gargoyles.

"We're going to have to move fast," said Liam. "This boat doesn't have a cover. If we run into an attack of any kind, the only protection we're going to have is the edging around the deck. It's not much, though. I wasn't expecting to have any passengers when I built this one."

Stella could cast a spell or two, if needed, and Solveig could flash lightning bolts. Liam loaded the crossbows and handed one to Sean.

"Thanks," he said, "but I'm more comfortable with my slingshot. Probably more accurate, too."

"OK," said Liam. "I hope you're right."

Once the storeroom door was locked tight, he pushed the boat off the dock into the marshy water. He held to the edge of the craft while the others boarded, and then hopped on, pushing off from the pier. He got behind the steering wheel and positioned his feet in the pedals and began pumping.

Because the boat was smaller than his usual constructions, it picked up speed quickly and moved through the reeds. He didn't have to warn his passengers to keep away from the sides of the ship and to keep alert. Sean moved to the front to keep watch. Stella moved to the port side and Solveig went to the starboard. Liam pumped the pedals and they were off.

135

Chapter seven

B'nair and his hobgoblins spent three days on the river. They never stopped. The Kelpie told them he had slept for nearly two thousand years. He needed no rest and all of them could rest when they were dead. The hobgoblins relieved each other in shifts and B'nair had to rely on Vardelos more than he wanted to, but he could not go without sleep.

By day four they had left the rafts on the shore and set out on foot into the desert. At first the ground was solid. The land within a mile of the river benefited from the moisture that seeped through the soil. After that, however, it quickly dried out and became hard as stone.

136

None of them were suited for long marches on such a hard surface. After a full day, their feet, ankles and legs were burning in pain. To make matters worse, the heat was beginning to climb. The sky was still filled with dull gray clouds, blocking out the sun. But the dryness of the desert generated its own heat, and that was held close to the ground by the low cloud cover. It was like a sauna.

"How can this be?" Vardelos finally asked B'nair. "The ground is completely devoid of moisture, but the air is thick with it."

"Nothing I've seen since learning of this Alchemist, his Enchantress and these Kelpies has made any sense to me," he answered.

As soon as the words were out of his mouth, he regretted them.

"Then why do this?" the hobgoblin asked.

B'nair thought a minute, trying to choose his words carefully. If he appeared to falter, he may lose the support of the hobgoblins. He wasn't sure how loyal they were, but they were all he had. He was certain that if they abandoned him, the Kelpie would do whatever he wanted to take the stone. In spite of his reaction to it, B'nair was sure that the Kelpie would find some way of handling and using it.

"My people," he started, and then corrected, "our people were pawns in the battles between the Alchemist, the Enchantress and the Kelpies. I'm not sure how or why, just that we were. I believe an opportunity awaits us to even the score."

"Even it with whom?" the hobgoblin asked.

"Whoever wins," B'nair said as he gave the hobgoblin a knowing wink.

In spite of the Kelpie's objections, B'nair convinced him that they would have to stop for the night. There was no way they would be able to keep this pace without rest. Since Pantano Izaki did not know the location of the next Kelpie, he had no choice but to agree. While the others slept, he paced around the campsite, going as far as he could without losing sight of the campfire.

Early the next day, the ground beneath them softened. It became sand, and was even more difficult to walk on. All they could see in every direction was the bleached white sand. It rose in mounds and dropped into long, low valleys. They walked high along the crest for miles and then wound through hundreds of ravines.

"I'm afraid to ask, sir," Vardelos ventured. "How much further is it?"

B'nair wiped the sweat from his one good eye. His heavy leather armor was baking him. The axe that had become a part of him had gotten so heavy, that he was dragging it in the sand.

"Enough," he shouted, not answering the question.

He stopped walking and turned to the hobgoblins.

"We've gone far enough today," he announced. "We'll stop here and rest."

"What?" demanded Pantano Izaki. "There are several hours of daylight left. We can go much further. Who are you to decide when and where we stop?"

"I'm the one with the map," B'nair growled back. "We are less than a full day away. We can't make it there before tomorrow, so we might as well rest here. You're free to continue if you like."

The Kelpie glared at the Rebbercand, but held his tongue. A time would come when this fat, one-eyed brute would no longer be necessary, thought Pantano Izaki. When that time came, he would take great pleasure in dispatching him.

"You're right," he said, although he didn't mean it and B'nair knew this. "I forget myself. Tomorrow will be soon enough."

Quest of Eight Part Five: Release of the Demons

Richard Reda

"Thank you, sir," mumbled Vardelos once the Kelpie was out of earshot. "We were not made for this kind of traveling."

"Did your friends dig any tunnels under all this sand?" B'nair asked, wondering what the extent of the hobgoblin's subterranean work had been.

"No, sir," he answered. "We made it to the far western edge of this desert, but even a hundred feet down, the sand kept caving in. We had never seen anything like it. This entire area was cursed."

B'nair was beginning to think this entire venture was cursed. He had reservations now about releasing a second Kelpie, but feared that they had gone too far to turn back. He considered he might have to wait for the right moment and separate Pantano Izaki's head from his body. He'd wait for the time being to see how things developed over the next day.

The Kelpie said nothing more about the sudden and unexpected stop. Sensing a possible rebellion by his guide and the hobgoblins, he walked a few yards away from the encampment to the lowest point in the sand. There he waved his hand in a circle several times, murmuring an incantation. Then he drove the tail of his snake-staff into the sand, twisted it back and forth a few times, and removed it.

In a few seconds, a stream of water sprung up. The water would not only satisfy their thirst, but make them more pliable. He had cast a spell on the spring before creating it. The water wasn't real, but to the others it would taste and feel real. This should keep them in line, he thought.

B'nair and the hobgoblins drank heartily. All the time, though, B'nair wondered. If the Kelpie had such power as to bring water from beneath the desert, why hadn't he done this sooner? He drank his fill and felt refreshed – no longer thirsty; but he believed deep down that the water was just an illusion.

Quest of Eight Part Five: Release of the Demons

Richard Reda

The next morning the Kelpie waited patiently until B'nair indicated everyone was ready to begin again, and pointed out the direction. By midday, they stopped again. This time Pantano Izaki controlled his temper and waited for an explanation.

"This is it," said B'nair. "I don't see anything, but according to the map, we've arrived."

The Kelpie only smiled. He motioned for the others to stand behind him, and then he spread his arms and began an incantation in a language none of them had ever heard and one that none of them understood.

As the incantation was ending, the sand began to shift. Immediately in front of the Kelpie, a large round stone broke through the surface of the desert and climbed upward into the air. It was a pillar of some kind.

The Kelpie backed away as several other pillars emerged. They formed a large circle, about thirty feet across. They were very old. Some were cracked and some were broken at the tops. At one time they each stood ten feet high and three feet in diameter. They were made from individual segments about two and a half feet high and stacked on top of each other.

The carvings that ran from top to bottom were intricate, looking like vines and leaves that had wrapped around the trunks. The stone from which the pillars were carved was a softer white than the surrounding sand – almost a cream color. Inside the pillars was a wall. The wall was an inner circle to the circle of pillars and extended two-thirds of the way around.

It was made from interlocking blocks, some of which had broken and fallen away. All of this stood on a base of large closely cut stones. In the center of the circle was a rectangular stone box that stood about three feet high, four feet long and less than two feet wide. The box had a large slab lid with carving on the surface. The carving looked like letters, but from a long dead language.

"It's a crypt," said B'nair. "Your brother must be inside. Should we remove the lid?"

"No," said Pantano Izaki. "I would suggest that you not touch it. Who knows what traps the Alchemist left behind. Stay behind me."

He was about to step onto the stone base when one of the hobgoblins shouted.

"Look, someone's coming."

"Impossible," shouted B'nair.

All eyes turned towards the direction they had been traveling. Sure enough, they could see a strange looking object rising over the crests of the sand dunes and disappearing into the valleys, only to rise above the next crest.

"What is it?" one of the hobgoblins asked.

"It looks like a boat," said another.

Liam, Solveig, Stella and Sean had all taken shifts to pedal the craft, and were able to travel while their adversaries had to rest. As a result, they had been able to catch up to them and were rapidly approaching.

Pantano Izaki stepped back from the structure and examined the approaching ship. The hobgoblins unsheathed their swords and readied their bows and arrows. Vardelos deployed them in defensive positions, and readied them to quickly switch to an offensive attack.

When the ship was about a dozen yards away, the Kelpie waved his arm. A large sand dune rose up like a great wave of the ocean and swept across the bow of the ship. The small craft was not built to withstand such turbulence. It rolled perilously onto one side as the wheels continued to propel it forward. It hung like that for several feet before capsizing completely.

At the time the Kelpie swung his arm to create the wave of sand, his spell struck three of the pillars closest to him. They toppled and the separate segments crashed into the sand, rolling in several directions. Some of them nearly collided with the capsizing boat as it slid across the sand coming to a halt.

"Take care of them," he ordered, and he returned to the crypt.

Liam had stayed behind the tiller, trying to hold on tight when the ship rolled over. Stella had lost her grip on the side, careened across the deck and flipped over the railing on the opposite side of the ship. She was hanging on, but was outside the boat. Solveig had tried to stop her momentum, but had missed and was now attempting to pull her back on board, but fighting the shifting of the floor beneath her feet.

Sean had been standing in the front, and when the boat began to roll onto its side, he had scampered onto the railing in an effort to stay on top. One of the pillar segments rolled into the ship's path and gave it a final nudge. The nose of the boat dug into the sand and dropped onto its side, pinning Stella underneath.

She was dragged a few feet until the ship came to a stop, resting on top of her, covering her from her feet to her ribs. Her upper body and face were half buried in sand. She was on her side with her right arm stuck deep beneath her.

Liam was tossed off the back, and managed to grab a quiver of arrows and a cross bow before he was catapulted away from the protection of the boat. He rolled a few feet and scrambled behind a nearby piece of one of the pillars as he watched his ship grind to a halt. When the ship came to a sudden stop, Sean was thrown in the opposite direction and rolled across the sand to another one of the pieces of the fallen pillars to shelter on the far side of the ship from Liam.

142

At the same instant arrows began to rain from the sky. The hobgoblins had let loose a volley to pin the intruders down. Sean popped his head up from behind the stone and fired his sling shot. As soon as B'nair saw him and saw the small rock he had fired thwack against the body of a nearby hobgoblin, he knew who it was.

"The Dozor," he said in a low voice.

B'nair's rage burst to the surface. The Dozor — the one he thought had dropped into the river of lava; the one that had caused him to fall and nearly meet the same fate; the one who was the reason he had one good eye and one good hand. He began to lunge forward until the Kelpie called to him.

At the other end of the ship, behind another one of the fallen pieces of stone, Liam was shooting cross bow arrows at Pantano Izaki. He was only able to catch glimpses of this figure. He knew it was the Kelpie, but a nearly uncontrollable fear crept into him. Could this Kelpie be the Mengassi? How was that possible?

He pushed his fear down to focus on the important matter at hand. He needed to do whatever he could to stop the release of another Kelpie. The Kelpie, in the mean time, was raising segments of the fallen pillars and dropping them on the ship, trying to crush it. He tried to drop them on Liam, but Liam's accuracy with the cross bow was making the Kelpie miss.

Solveig was still trying to pull Stella free. Stella had been stunned when the ship rolled over on her and was unable to free herself. Solveig was throwing bolts of lightning haphazardly, but with little effect.

"Can't you move this boat," Solveig shouted to her.

"No," she shouted back.

Quest of Eight Part Five: Release of the Demons

Richard Reda

She had been able to scrap some of the sand away from her face with her left hand, and she was still spitting grains out of her mouth, trying to clear her airway. She was barely able to move at all.

"My right arm is stuck in the sand under me," she said, "and I can't get enough of an angle on the ship with my left hand. I'm afraid I'll only push it and if I do that, it's liable to take my legs with it. I don't have a cure for no legs."

Sean fired another volley and then ran further away from the ship to another piece of pillar. He was trying to get a better shot at the Kelpie and to maybe get the hobgoblins in a cross fire between him and Liam.

"What is it?" demanded B'nair when he retreated into the structure, behind the wall in response to the Kelpie's call.

"I've opened the crypt," said Pantano Izaki, "but there was nothing in it. Nothing but a swirl of dust. Are you sure this is the right place?"

"Yes, I'm sure," B'nair responded, ducking one of Sean's stones. "Could the Kelpie be buried in something else?"

The swirl of dust that Pantano Izaki mentioned was still spinning around like a tiny tornado. It blew past them and then in between them, buzzing them like a pesky mosquito. The Kelpie swiped at it to no avail.

"No," he answered. "The markings on the surface were clear. This is the location of Angin Topan. She must be here."

"Maybe someone got here before us," said B'nair. "Maybe we need to get out of here and find the next one."

"NO!" insisted Pantano Izaki. "Angin Topan is one of the triumvirate. She is essential."

Quest of Eight Part Five: Release of the Demons

Richard Reda

The swirl of dust brushed past B'nair, who had been squatting down to avoid the assault of stone and arrows. The brush by pushed him over onto his butt. He caught himself with his good hand, and in anger, swung his axe through the small whirlwind.

As he did so, the swirling stopped and the particles of dust and sand peeled back. A swarm of insects emerged. Pantano Izaki immediately raised his hand and the swarm divided around him. B'nair felt the same electrical charge he had felt when the Swamp Kelpie had been released from his tomb.

The insects dispersed, but not before stinging the closest hobgoblin. They descended on him, attacking him repeatedly. In seconds he was covered with small bites, which swelled up and festered. His airways closed and he began to choke. The sand opened up immediately beneath him and then, as quickly, covered him completely.

A small figure dropped to the ground as this was happening. It was less than a foot tall, had short, close cropped hair and three pairs of long, narrow wings on its back. And it was pale blue from the top to the bottom of its frail, diminutive body.

"Master," said Pantano Izaki, and he bowed his head.

"Master?" questioned B'nair.

The small figure looked up at B'nair and then at Pantano Izaki. The Kelpie had referred to this person as "she," and then called it "master," but B'nair found it impossible to determine a specific gender. He or she – whatever it was – looked weak and uncertain.

"What has happened?" she asked.

"You have been freed," Pantano Izaki told her. "This Rebbercand has the power. And he has part of the pendant."

"Who is this?" both the Kelpie and B'nair said of each other.

Quest of Eight Part Five: Release of the Demons

Richard Reda

At that moment a cross bow arrow ricocheted off a nearby block and narrowly missed the smaller Kelpie.

"Introductions will have to wait," said Pantano Izaki. "We need to rid ourselves of these intruders."

"I recognize one of them," said B'nair. "His friends are not to be underestimated. They are all quite treacherous and devious."

"As am I," Pantano Izaki replied.

He turned away from the Kelpie he had called "master," and popped his head over the stone wall to see where the attacks were coming from. He could see Liam to their right, behind a part of a pillar, firing a cross bow. Liam was watching the hobgoblins and missed seeing him. He next saw the ship on its side and could see flashes of lightning bursting forth, but striking nothing. Then he looked to the left and saw several yards away from the ship some small creature behind another section of pillar firing stones from a sling shot.

"A cross bow and a sling shot," shouted Pantano Izaki. "That's all they are armed with? You have allowed them to continue this attack with those paltry weapons?"

At that moment, B'nair felt a wave of heat rise from inside his vest. He pressed his hand against his side and felt the stone of the pendant beneath. He reached in and removed it. He could see the colors inside the stone shifting and he knew the other pieces were close by.

"That's not all they have," he told the Kelpie. "They have the rest of the pendant."

"One of them?" asked Pantano Izaki, incredulously, motioning towards Sean and Liam.

"No," answered B'nair. "One on the other side of the ship – where the flashes are coming from. It's an Enchantress. I can feel it."

All of a sudden, Pantano Izaki was not as brave as he had been a few seconds before. He looked back at Angin Topan, and considered that this might be an opportunity for him to impress one of the Kelpie leaders. He began to formulate a plan.

"Assemble your hobgoblins," he directed B'nair. "Focus their attack to the right. Have them kill or at the very least distract whoever is shooting that cross bow. We've been lucky so far, but he is far too accurate and he needs to be eliminated."

"What about the Dozor?" argued B'nair.

"The what?" asked Pantano Izaki.

"The one with the slingshot," he explained.

"Him I leave to you. That is, if you can handle him."

B'nair was filled with rage. The thought of carving the Dozor into hundreds of little pieces and scattering them across this desert appealed to him.

"It will be my extreme pleasure. What will you be doing?" he challenged the Kelpie.

"I will move between the one with the slingshot and the front of the ship and dispose of the Enchantress."

B'nair started to say something, but the Kelpie cut him off.

"You may claim the stone from her dead body. It will be my gift to you."

"In that case, you will have my unconditional support," B'nair replied.

He understood the implications of the agreement that had been reached between them. This may not be as bad as I had thought earlier, he said to himself.

"Vardelos," he called, his eyes still on the Kelpie.

"Yes, sir," Vardelos answered, as he scurried over.

"Reform your men," B'nair told him. "Focus their attack – their total attack – on the one with the cross bow."

"What about the other one?" he asked.

"I'll take care of him. You make sure your target is destroyed. Is that clear?"

"Perfectly, sir."

Vardelos moved off and began repositioning his men. Sean was creating havoc with them, his strikes never missing their targets. However, as powerful as his slingshot was, he was unable to do any significant harm. He was only a distraction.

Once the forces of the hobgoblins were all directed at Liam, he had to shift his efforts completely to his own defense. As soon as that happened, B'nair began moving towards Sean. Once or twice Liam was able to get a shot off in B'nair's direction, but the distance was getting too great, as the Rebbercand got closer to Sean.

Sean could sense before he saw the approach of the Rebbercand. He popped his head up to fire off a shot. When he did, B'nair was barely ten feet in front of him. For the first time he could recall, his shot missed. He was so stunned by who he saw, his concentration broke.

"You!" he shouted.

"Yes, me," answered B'nair, leering at him. "I still like Dozors. But I still can't eat one all by myself. In your case, though, I'll make an exception. And I'll take my time."

Sean reached in his pocket and pulled out the remainder of his ammunition. He had a half dozen stones left. Right now he was wishing he had taken one of those cross bows from Liam. He only hoped he could hold the Rebbercand off long enough for Liam or Stella or Solveig to come to his rescue.

He popped his head up and fired a shot. B'nair flicked his axe up and deflected the stone. He kept walking almost casually towards Sean. Sean popped up again and this time he fired a shot at the Rebbercand's knee. Once more B'nair flicked his axe and deflected the shot.

He's not even looking, thought Sean. Four stones left. He needed to make them count. He popped up again. This time he shot at the hand holding the axe. B'nair moved his good hand with lightning speed and caught the stone in midair. He tossed it up in the air and caught it again and threw it back to Sean.

"Here," he said taunting Sean. "You're probably running out of stones. You many need this one."

By now he was a few short steps away from the large stone behind which Sean was hiding. He decided to wait no longer. He took one quick long step and closed the distance. Then with his other foot, he pushed hard against the section of pillar, tipping it over right on top of Sean.

The movement had happened so quickly and so unexpectedly that Sean found himself flattened and pinned underneath the large stone. It covered the entire width of his body and from his feet to just under his chin. He struggled to move the stone, but it wouldn't budge. B'nair was holding it in place with his foot.

149

Quest of Eight Part Five: Release of the Demons

Richard Reda

The Rebbercand put more of his weight onto the rock and peered over the top to look into Sean's eyes. Sean looked up to see the scarred face with one eye covered by a patch. The face stared back and grimaced. Sean supposed the Rebbercand was trying to smile, but it only made him look worse.

"I can't tell you what it means to me to finally get to meet you," said B'nair. "Eye to eye, so to speak."

"I'll close one of mine, if it'll make you feel better," Sean shot back.

B'nair pushed the stone a little harder. The wind was pressed out of Sean's lungs and he had difficulty catching his breath.

"That won't be necessary," said B'nair. "Maybe when I pick you apart, I'll start with the eyes."

"Well," gasped Sean, "if you're going to pick me apart...you're going to have to stop picking your nose."

It wasn't much of an insult, but it was all he could think of. He could see that it had no real affect on the Rebbercand. He decided his time had come and he waited for the final blow. The pressure of the stone on his chest had pushed the air from his lungs. He was already getting light-headed and his vision was fading. He knew it wouldn't be much longer now.

Shortly after B'nair began his advance on Sean, and while Liam was preoccupied fending off the hobgoblins, Pantano Izaki snuck between Sean's location and the nose of the ship. He rounded the corner and saw two figures a few feet ahead of them.

One of them was digging in the sand with one hand while blindly thrusting her other arm upward, casting bolts of lightning. Her back was to him. It was the other one – the one pinned under the ship and half buried in the sand – that saw him when he came around the bow of the ship.

150

"Solveig," she gasped. "Behind you."

Solveig jumped up and started to shoot a blast at the Kelpie, but he was too fast. He swept his arm sideways and she was flung back against the deck of the ship. The force was so strong that the wind was knocked out of her. She hit the deck and slid down in a slump to the sand, stunned.

Pantano Izaki saw the one in the sand raise her free hand and begin to cast some kind of spell. A wave of rippling air came towards him and he waved his other hand, pushing it aside easily.

"It will take more than that," he said.

He took a few quick steps towards Stella. When he was standing over her, he pressed his foot down on her arm, preventing her from moving it.

"Let's have no more of that, shall we?" he said, applying pressure on her.

Stella struggled but was unable to free her arm. The other one was still buried beneath her in the sand. She looked up at the strange face staring down at her. The Kelpie moved his snake-staff. With the pointed end he flicked the pendant that was hanging from her neck.

"My associate," he said, "– the one disposing of your friend with the slingshot – will be very happy to possess this trinket."

He was careful not to touch the stone himself. He recalled what happened when he touched the portion that B'nair had shown him. He could feel Stella trying to wiggle her arm free, and he put more of his weight onto her.

"You're an Enchantress, I see," he said. "Probably a descendant of the witch who imprisoned me for nearly two millennia. Where is your consort? Aren't you always paired with someone? Is one of those two out there your Alchemist? Is she your princess?"

He motioned over his back towards Solveig.

"It matters not," he said when Stella refused to talk. "Your connection will be terminated soon."

He lifted the end of his staff and moved the point over her eye. He began to lower it as slowly as he could. He was enjoying the torment. Then he stopped. A look of shock came over his face, and his body began to writhe.

After she had been slammed against the deck, Solveig had blanked out for a few seconds. Her senses slowly returned and she became aware of the Kelpie standing over Stella. She could hear him ask about Stella's consort and then saying her connection would be terminated. She needed to do something.

She looked around for a sword or a knife. Liam had brought so many of them on board. Where were they now? She couldn't see any of them. Frantic, she struggled to her feet, still scanning the ship and the sand nearby, looking for something. As she stood up, the weight of something in her pocket brushed against her leg.

She reached inside and felt the dragon's tooth. It was better than nothing, she thought. She pulled it from her pocket and leaped at the Kelpie, driving it deep into his back. At first he didn't seem to move at all. Then his body jerked, and a wave of energy burst, radiating outward.

Stella watched from below as his spasms and twitching increased and his skin began to crawl. His face and then his body transformed into dozens of snakes, all intertwined together, forming his shape. From behind, Solveig, who had jumped up onto his back to deliver the fatal blow, could feel a change in the body under her. It was slithering. She slid off and moved away from him.

The snakes fell in a heap, scattering over the ground and onto Stella.

"Get them off of me," she shouted.

She pushed them away with her free hand and Solveig dropped to her knees, flinging them away with the dragon's tooth. Gradually, they all began to melt into pieces and were absorbed in the sand, disappearing from sight.

At the moment of the burst of energy, Angin Topan knew that Pantano Izaki had been destroyed. These attackers were more powerful than the Swamp Kelpie had expected. She, herself, was too weak to intervene. She knew that she had to escape.

"Rebbercand," she shouted.

Her voice was frail and wispy. It took more strength than she could afford to use, just to call to him. At the sound of her voice, B'nair turned back in her direction. He had felt the blast, but was unaware of its source or meaning. He thought that, perhaps, the Swamp Kelpie had unleashed a power that he had kept hidden until now.

He saw the small winged Kelpie motioning to him. She was gesturing for him to move back to her location. He looked down at Sean, who was lying beneath him, motionless. The shock and damage done to him by the large segment of pillar B'nair had thrown on him had caused him to black out. Thinking him dead, B'nair raised his axe, and in a final fit of rage at having been deprived of killing the Dozor slowly and painfully, drove the blade into the stone pillar, splitting it in half.

He strode back to the stone temple where Angin Topan sat in a heap behind cover. He noted that the ineffectual blasts of lightning had stopped. He looked to where Liam was pinned down behind another segment of pillar, under attack by the hobgoblins. That battle appeared to be a stalemate.

"Why did you call me back?" he demanded of the small Kelpie.

153

"We must escape," she said. "Pantano Izaki is destroyed."

"I can defeat this enemy," he said to her.

"No," she said. "You can't. Trust me. They possess a power you don't have. They used it to destroy Pantano Izaki. They will use it to destroy you. If that happens, then I am lost, too; and if I am lost, all is lost."

"Surely you can defeat them," he said.

"Another time, yes," she answered. "I have been dead for two thousand years. I need time to rebuild my strength. Until then, I have no power to battle them. We are wasting time with this discussion. We need to leave."

B'nair looked at her for a few seconds, recalling the insistence of the Swamp Kelpie to wait a day before traveling, and the change in his appearance the next day. What will this one need, he wondered, to return her power.

He quickly debated the options before him. Ultimately, he considered that she might be right. If the other Kelpie had been destroyed, the ones hidden behind the ship must possess something more powerful. He knew the rest of the pendant was only a few yards away. He also knew that the pieces he held gave him no special powers.

If the one holding the other parts was an Enchantress, then he was clearly outmatched. But if the other parts were held by someone else... He left the thought unfinished. There was too much at risk for him to gamble that this Kelpie was wrong.

"Vardelos," he shouted over his shoulder.

The hobgoblin broke away from the others who maintained the attack on Liam. B'nair stepped carefully closer to him, avoiding the all too accurate shots coming from Liam.

"Pull back," he said. "Order your men to assemble as close to me as possible – and as quickly as possible."

"Yes, sir," Vardelos answered without question.

"What do you plan?" B'nair asked the Kelpie.

"I believe I have enough strength to move all of us, but not very far," she answered.

"It better be far enough," responded B'nair.

The hobgoblins began an orderly retreat with Vardelos covering them as they moved. When the others were safe, he started to withdraw. Liam jumped up enough to fire off an arrow, hitting the hobgoblin in the thigh.

B'nair saw him drop and against his better judgment, ran over to him, shielding them both with his axe. He jerked Vardelos into the air, threw him over his shoulder and rushed back to the others.

Once he was back and the hobgoblins were gathered as closely to the Kelpie as possible, she waved her arms and the sands around them began to swirl. Liam came from behind his cover, firing arrow after arrow at the growing tower of sand and dust. But the Kelpie's magic was too strong. The arrows merely glanced off the whirlwind, as if ricocheting off rocks.

Inside the dust storm, B'nair was hoping the Kelpie had enough strength to get them away. In seconds, he felt the stone floor beneath his feet fall away and he could feel himself being lifted into the air. A few seconds later, he landed with a thud in the sand. His first thought was that it hadn't worked. They hadn't gone anywhere. When the dust settled, though, all he could see was desert. They escaped, but to where?

Quest of Eight Part Five: Release of the Demons

Richard Reda

Liam watched as the cyclone of sand deflected his arrows and then disappeared in the blink of an eye. Once it disappeared, the large circular floor, the wall, the crypt and the pillars all turned to sand and fell into a heap, mixing with the rest of the desert sand. In seconds, it was as if none of it was ever there.

Liam ran over to look at Sean. Seeing him nearly buried in the sand under the broken pieces of the pillar that had now evaporated, he was certain his friend was dead. He ran around the ship to see what had happened to Stella and Solveig.

"You're all right," he said with relief.

"What happened?" asked Stella.

Liam described what he had seen.

"What about Sean?" asked Solveig.

"I think that Rebbercand killed him," Liam said with immense sadness. "He's not moving."

Solveig jumped up and ran past Liam. As she approached Sean's prone body, she slowed down, hoping against hope that Liam was wrong. She knelt down next to him and brushed the sand from his face. His eyes fluttered and then opened.

"What happened?" he asked. "It was the same one...the Rebbercand...the one in the mines. It was him. Where is he?"

"Forget about him," said Solveig. "Are you all right?"

"I'm alive," answered Sean. "But I think some of my ribs are broken. I can't move, and it hurts to breathe."

"Stay relaxed," she ordered. "Liam and I will get Stella freed and she can help."

Quest of Eight Part Five: Release of the Demons

Richard Reda

She ran back to the others and reported on Sean's condition. She and Liam began to dig around Stella and under the ship. In a few minutes, they had cleared enough of the sand so that she could climb out. Aside from a few scrapes and bruises, she was fine.

She went over to Sean and knelt down next to him. She placed her hands on his injured ribs and began a low incantation. He couldn't understand her words, but he could feel a tingling inside of him. After a few seconds she pulled her hands away.

"They're going to be tender," she said. "But you can get up. Don't do anything strenuous for a few days. Maybe we'll come across some herbs and I can make a potion to speed the healing process. If I can't, you'll need to be careful for a while."

"Thanks," he told her.

He sat up, took a few deep breaths and then got to his feet. Together they re-joined Liam and Solveig.

"I'm glad you remembered that dragon's tooth," Stella said.

"I'm glad I picked it up," she answered. "I had forgotten all about it. I had no idea what it would do. I wasn't sure it was sharp enough to stab him. I never thought it would make him vanish."

They explained to Liam and Sean what had happened.

"Did you get a good look at the Kelpie?" Liam asked.

"Only for an instant," said Solveig.

"More than I wanted," said Stella.

"Describe him, please," asked Liam.

"Really ugly and creepy," said Stella.

"A walking pile of weeds," said Solveig.

"No," said Liam. "More than that. Describe his face; his body."

It had happened too fast. They were unable to give him a clear picture of the creature they had encountered. In fact, their recollections didn't seem to match up at all.

"Why is it so important?" asked Solveig.

"I guess it doesn't matter," said Liam. "Forget about it."

He was frustrated that he hadn't gotten a better look and that neither Stella nor Solveig could give him any more information. Even if the Kelpie had been the Mengassi, he was gone now. It no longer made any difference. He then turned his attention to the condition of his small craft, walking from one end to the other and assessing the damage.

"Can you straighten this up?" he asked Stella.

"Sure," she answered.

She reached forward and put her hand on the side. With no apparent effort, she lifted the ship from its side and righted it. Liam looked it over and saw no damage to the hull.

"We need to get moving," he said.

"You mean to chase after them?" asked Sean. "We don't know where they went."

"No," he answered. "We didn't stop them. We can only assume they're headed to the mountains. Maybe Lochen and the others will have better luck than we did. Fortunately, they still have only one Kelpie to deal with, and not two. Still, we need to get to the Ice Kingdom."

"Right," said Stella. "We need to find that Kelpie."

"Or, if nothing else," added Solveig, "meet up with the others."

"Oooohhhh noooo," groaned Sean.

"Are you all right?" asked Solveig.

"Did you re-injure your ribs?" asked Stella.

"No," said Sean. "To get to the Ice Kingdom we're probably going to have to go by water."

Chapter eight

Shortly after Liam and his team departed, and the Grackles lifted Quinn, Lochen and Natalie into the air, Quinn was beginning to wonder if this mode of transportation was such a good idea. There must have been more than fifty of the black birds digging their talons into his clothing and struggling to keep him aloft.

Summer was equally unsure. She had opted to fly by her own power. Within minutes of leaving the Navedis Forest, she had fluttered over to say something to Lochen and one of the Grackles nipped at her. After that, she kept her distance, flying slightly above and behind the other three, keeping a close watch on the nasty birds.

Quest of Eight Part Five: Release of the Demons

Richard Reda

Lochen had tried to use the flying time to study the book the sentinel had given him but the way he was being held by the Grackles made it impossible to hold the pages close enough to be read. It was all he could do to force his arm inward to stick the book beneath his robe under his belt.

Natalie kept reminding herself that she wasn't afraid of heights, but was not being very successful. Her experience in being bound and hauled over the back of an Yder, flying high over the open sea, had scarred her. For most of the time, she shut her eyes and tried to ignore the wind blowing in her face.

The birds carrying Quinn were having difficulty keeping him in the air. They would raise him up until his weight became too much, and then they would spread their wings widely and coast. When this happened, he glided downward, but the birds were able to rest. That was fine for them, but it caused no end of anxiety for him. He was diving headlong towards the ground, and could only hope they would pull up in time.

By the end of the day they had reached the foothills of the central range of the mountains. The Grackles deposited them and departed, flying back to the Forest, leaving their passengers in the middle of no-place.

"I thought they would take us into the mountains to where the Kelpie is hidden," said Natalie.

"Either we were too much of a burden to them," answered Lochen, "or they have no indication of where the Kelpie is. I suspect both were factors in our being dropped here."

"I'm just as glad either way," said Quinn. "I was getting sea sick with all the up and down motion. Can you get sea sick in the air?"

"I can't say I'm sorry to see them leave," said Summer. "They were simply rude."

Quest of Eight Part Five: Release of the Demons

Richard Reda

"What's the plan now?" asked Natalie.

"I suggest we make camp here," said Lochen. "It's as good a place as any. We can get some rest. I will use the time to try to translate this book and we'll get a fresh start in the morning."

They gathered some sticks and fallen branches to make a fire. Lochen twirled his finger and conjured a pot and four bowls. Then he snapped his fingers and the pot filled with a thick stew. The aroma rose up and filled the air.

"You mean you could have done this all the time?" asked Summer.

"I suppose," Lochen answered. "I hadn't really thought about it."

"What's in the pot?" asked Quinn. "Something gross?"

"It's a vegetable stew," Lochen told him.

"Stew?" asked Natalie. "We could have had stew instead of whatever it was that Sean tried to feed us?"

"I can replicate Sean's recipe, if you would prefer," said Lochen. "Personally, though, I didn't find it particularly appealing."

"NO!" they all answered.

"Stew is fine," said Quinn. "Why didn't you do this before – I mean, aside from the fact that you hadn't thought about it?"

"I don't need to eat as often as the rest of you," he said. "Consequently, the need for food never crosses my mind. I assumed you all were satisfied with the nuts and berries that Solveig discovered or the concoction Sean created."

"Trust me," said Natalie. "You assumed wrong. The nuts and berries were fine – although not very filling – but the...whatever...that Sean cooked up...I wouldn't use it for bait."

As they had been talking, Lochen was scooping out the stew and passing the bowls around. As an afterthought, he snapped his fingers once more and produced spoons.

"That should make dining a bit easier," he said as he passed the spoons around.

They wolfed down the dinner and were soon asleep around the fire. As the others rested, Lochen studied the book the sentinel had given to him. He had never seen the kind of writing that filled the pages. It was a combination of characters and symbols completely foreign to him.

He tried looking for repeated letters – or whatever they were – in an effort to decode the text. Nothing appeared to be repeated, though. How could that be, he wondered. Maybe it was a map – a drawing, rather than a description. But nothing looked like topographical markings. He was still pouring over the pages when dawn broke, barely lightening the gray sky, and the others awakened.

"Any luck with that?" Natalie asked, pointing to the book.

"I'm afraid not," Lochen answered. "Except for one thing. The symbols that were engraved in the Ice Kingdom, and which I believe are also on the band that held the pendant, appear at seemingly random locations on some of the pages."

"What do you think it means?"

"I have no idea, other than that the symbols appear to relate to the text – or whatever it is these markings represent. It's possible the surrounding information addresses a manner in which the Kelpies can be destroyed; or it could equally represent how they can be released. There's no way to tell."

"What happens if and when we find this Kelpie, then," she asked.

"I don't know the answer to that either, I'm sorry to say. I'm sure something will come to us. For now, though, I think it's safe to say that we have some climbing ahead of us."

"How do we know which way to go?" asked Quinn. "There are a lot of mountains here. Which one do we choose?"

"This one," said Lochen, pointing to the base of the peak nearest to them.

"How do you know it's this one?" asked Summer.

"Because this is where the Grackles left us," he answered.

"And you trust a bunch of nasty birds?" she asked.

"No, but in the absence of any other or better method of selection, that's as good as anything."

"Wonderful," said Natalie. "We're going to climb a mountain at random, going someplace where we don't know is the right place to go, searching for something that we don't know where it is, looking for someone we don't know what they look like, taking on something we don't know how to take on – all based on where some crabby birds got tired of carrying us and just dropped us."

"I think that sums it up about perfectly," replied Lochen. "Is everyone ready?"

He tucked the book back into his belt. Not waiting for an answer, he flicked his hand, making the campfire disappear and began his approach to the mountain. The others followed in silence, Summer flying up to the front to scout the way.

In the beginning they followed a path that someone long ago had started. It wound back and forth around the base of the mountain. The incline was moderately steep, but the path was wide and even. Soon though it started to narrow and the incline increased. And it began to rain.

At first the rain was not much more than a mist. It was enough to eventually penetrate everyone's clothing and make it cling, cold and wet, to their bodies. Everyone's hair was plastered to their heads, and the moisture seeped down into their faces.

There were a few trees along the way that periodically provided some degree of shelter from the mist, but not enough to help. Eventually, the path extended beyond the tree line and the leaves and needles that had covered it disappeared to be replaced by mud.

This continued for several hours. They had to stop and rest frequently, at which time they tried to scrap the accumulating muck from the bottoms of their feet. There was no shelter from the mist and no way for them to dry off. The air was cooling down and the wind was picking up, adding to the difficulty.

"Summer," Lochen called. "You might as well ride in my hood. There's no sense in you suffering this inclement weather."

"Thanks," she said. "But I'd be of more use scouting the way ahead to spot any problems before you get there."

"Suit yourself," he answered, "but I don't anticipate any significant obstacles until much later."

"Did you anticipate rain?" asked Natalie.

"Good point," Lochen conceded.

Quest of Eight Part Five: Release of the Demons

Richard Reda

The sky had become so overcast, that it was hard to tell how close they were to nightfall. It didn't matter, though. The path had narrowed further and the rise had gotten steeper. By now they were climbing more than they were walking, and it was tiring them out. They all agreed to stop for the time being, even though there was probably enough light to continue for another hour or two.

There was no cave or any other kind of opening for them to seek shelter. They found a small niche in the rocks that was wide enough to allow them to stretch out to sleep. Natalie created a small bubble that kept the rain off of them. Lochen picked up a rock the size of a melon and pressed it tightly in both hands.

It began to glow and he dropped it on the ground. It was soon generating enough heat to provide a little bit of warmth and take some of the dampness out of their clothes.

"Aren't you worried about someone seeing the light from that rock?" asked Quinn.

"Not really," Lochen answered. "I don't believe our presence here is a secret to anyone. Whoever has the other piece of the pendant, by now knows for certain that he is being followed. Chances are he's already encountered our friends. If they've been successful, then our venture is merely insurance. If they haven't been successful, then our enemies are already forewarned. We might as well be as comfortable as we can get."

"Sounds good to me," said Natalie, shivering slightly.

"Can you make more of that stew?" asked Summer.

"I was thinking perhaps a gumbo," Lochen answered, conjuring up the necessary ingredients.

As the others slept, he continued to try to crack the code of the book he'd been given, but was no more successful than he had been previously. The next morning it was evident that the rain hadn't stopped, but had actually gotten heavier. The day was so dark, that it was hard to believe it was morning.

Before long, there was no longer any sign of a path. The good news was that there was no more mud. The bad news was that they were now climbing from one pile of rocks and series of ledges to another. Following the least difficult passage, they seemed to be making their way around a very large and very wide spire. Just as they thought they would complete a circle, the mountain curved out in the opposite direction.

They were climbing along a ledge that had been more than a foot deep, but was gradually narrowing, when Summer flew back.

"This ledge ends about twenty feet ahead," she told them.

Her wings were covered with water; her hair hung limply down her back and sides. She was exhausted and it wasn't even midday yet. Three faces as wet as hers stared back at her. Lochen thought a minute and then told her to show him. Natalie and Quinn began to sidestep after him.

"You might as well stay put," he said to them. "We may have to go back."

"I don't want to think about that," said Natalie, "and I don't want to sit here and just get wet."

They crept forward until Lochen stopped and saw what Summer had discovered. The narrow ledge faded into the mountainside to nothing. However, a wider ledge appeared about fifteen feet later on. Lochen pulled his sleeve back and pointed his finger at the stone. Bits of rock broke away, and an extension to the ledge was chipped out.

"That should do it," he said when he had connected one overhang to the other.

Quest of Eight Part Five: Release of the Demons

Richard Reda

He continued moving carefully across. His face was pressed to the mountain and his feet were spread outward so that he could keep as much of them on the ledge as possible. Natalie followed right behind him. Quinn was struggling. He was walking nearly on tip toes, pushing himself against the wall, his arms stretched out for balance. He had his face turned toward Lochen, his cheek rubbing the stone of the mountain, unable to look down and see where he was stepping.

Lochen made it across to the wider outcropping and stopped. He turned back and extended his hand to Natalie, pulling her across. Once she was safe, he reached for Quinn. As Quinn moved to take Lochen's hand, the ledge beneath him broke off. He could feel his weight shifting, pushing him to his right, but he had nothing to grab to stop his fall.

He looked like a tree that had been chopped near the bottom of its trunk, getting ready to fall – almost like it was in slow motion. His right foot, after breaking through the ledge, lifted up in search of something solid. His right hand slapped back against the mountainside, trying to slow his fall. Instead, it merely skidded across the wet rock.

His left hand slid up and down searching for a niche or a branch or even just a crease in the rock to hang onto. There was nothing. His face, still pressed against the wall, slid along the same smooth surface on which his hands could find nothing to grab.

Lochen, Natalie and Summer looked on in horror as he tipped over – unable to do anything to stop him. At the last second, while Quinn's right leg was raised, still hoping to find a solid step, Lochen dove forward, extending his body from the wider overhang. He reached out and wrapped his hands around Quinn's left foot.

Quinn brought his right foot down, landing on Lochen, breaking his fall. The only problem was that he could move no further since

Lochen was gripping his left foot. If Lochen let go to release the foot so Quinn could take a final step to safety, then Lochen would fall.

"Thanks," stammered Quinn. "But I don't think this helps."

"You may be right," Lochen answered. "We do seem to be in somewhat of a dilemma."

"What were you thinking?" shouted Natalie. "You could have missed and fallen down the mountain."

"It seemed like a good idea at the time," answered Lochen. "However, in retrospect, admittedly it appears that it was not particularly well thought out."

"What now?" asked Summer.

"I'm thinking," grunted Lochen.

The strain of keeping his body extended, even without Quinn's weight, was quickly getting to be more than he could withstand. Without waiting for anyone, Natalie stepped out onto the backs of Lochen's legs.

"That's not helping," he groaned.

"Just hold on a little longer," she snapped at him. "And quit complaining. This was all your doing."

She reached up and took Quinn's hand, pealing it away from the side of the mountain. His eyes were as big as saucers as he watched her step back to the ledge and pull his hand with her.

"Easy now," she said to him. "Step as far forward with your right foot as you can. NO! Your <u>right</u> foot!" she shouted when she saw him begin to lift his left foot.

"Sorry," he said, barely whispering. "I forgot which was which."

He skittered his right foot forward until he was spread-eagled as far as he could reach. His right foot wedged itself between Lochen's legs.

"Now," Natalie continued. "Slowly lift your left leg. Lochen, hold on tight to his foot and arch your back when he steps up."

Lochen's body was too stiff to bend backwards very far, and Quinn was afraid that if he tried to bring his legs together, he'd either break Lochen in half or force him to lose his grip. So, he maintained his spread-eagle pose and started to lower his right arm, as if he was doing a cartwheel.

"Now is not the time for carnival tricks," said Summer.

"I know what I'm doing," said Quinn. "At least I think I do."

Before he had to go very far, Lochen was able to turn himself around and sit upright. He let go of Quinn's foot and Quinn was able to bring it down to stay upright. When both feet were on the wider ledge, he shuffled a few steps forward to give Lochen room to get up.

"Well," said Lochen. "That wasn't so bad, after all."

"Can we try not to do that again?" asked Natalie.

"That would be fine with me," said Quinn. "Or I can let someone else do it."

After a short rest, they continued. Although the climbing was somewhat easier, the rain had gotten heavier. Now it was like someone was pouring buckets of water on them. They were making very little progress, and finally reached a point where the only way left to them was straight up.

"We can't do this in this rain," said Natalie. "It's too dangerous."

"I agree," said Lochen. "We might as well stop here and see if things improve tomorrow."

They made an early camp under another bubble, and the burning rock and warm dinner helped them rest. Lochen used the time to once more try cracking the mysterious markings. The next day wasn't much brighter. The sky was still a dull gray, but at least it had stopped raining.

Summer flew ahead, spotting places for hand and foot holds while the other three climbed step by grueling step towards the top. There were few places to stop, so the going was slow. Lochen maintained the lead, with Natalie in the middle and Quinn at the rear. Summer kept shuttling up and down, scouting the immediate next few yards, and then offering encouragement to each of them. Eventually they reached a point where the way before them seemed to disappear.

"Summer," said Lochen. "Can you fly a little further this time? It appears that either the angle of our climb changes dramatically, or the mountain ends."

She looked above her at what Lochen was describing. He was right. There were several cracks in the side that had served as supports, but the top edge of the mountain seemed to round off and bend inward. She flew up, close to the side and up over the top. A gust of wind blew her out and away from the mountain.

It hadn't been that strong. It just took her by surprise. She gave herself some space and rose over the top once more. They had arrived. Where, she wasn't sure, but they had reached the top. It was a large plateau. Now what, she wondered. She dropped back down and reported.

"The rest of the way doesn't look any different or harder than what you've already climbed," she said. "After that, it's level."

"Level?" asked Lochen. "Don't you mean the incline decreases?"

"No," she said. "It's level. Flat. Like someone chopped the top off. That kind of level."

His curiosity overcame his fatigue. He scrambled the last several yards and pulled himself over the edge onto the surface of the plateau. Natalie and Quinn came up behind him at their normal pace. By the time they reached the top, he had moved from the edge and was looking at the view before him.

The plateau extended several hundred yards in a large oval. Where he was standing was the outer lip of a giant caldera. The lip circled the outer edge and was fifteen to twenty feet wide. In the center of the elliptical opening were several natural stone obelisks – nine in all. They had been shaped by the wind and rain over centuries and rose hundreds or even thousands of feet upward, but were all on the same level as the lip of the caldera.

"I've seen this," exclaimed Lochen. "I've seen this before."

He pulled the tattered book from his belt and flipped through the pages. He stopped when he found what he was looking for.

"I thought it was a symbol of some kind. It's a map. Sort of. Here, look."

He held it open for the others to see. The page to which he had turned had other symbols and markings on it, but in the top left corner taking about a quarter of the page was an oval with nine circles inside of it, each spaced nearly equally apart and at equal intervals from one another.

"I suppose it looks like the same thing," said Quinn. "But what do all those squiggles and scribbling around it mean?"

"I'm sure it has something to do with whichever Kelpie is held here and how to destroy him," he answered excitedly.

"Or release him," added Natalie.

"Yes," agreed Lochen. "Or release him."

"How do you know this is where the Kelpie is?" asked Summer. "The drawing in that book could mean something else."

"No," Lochen disagreed. "Look closely at the circle in the center. There's a square in the middle of that circle. And look more closely at that square. There is a triangle and the same markings as those in the Ice Kingdom that designated..."

"Someone of high rank from the mountains," finished Quinn. "That's supposed to be Solveig! Not some Kelpie! Maybe this book means something else. Maybe this isn't where the Kelpie is!"

"We'll find out shortly," said Lochen.

"What do you mean?" asked Natalie.

"We have to get to the center obelisk," answered Lochen.

"Are you crazy?" asked Quinn. "Look how high we are. Look how far apart those things are. Do you expect we can fly there?"

They all turned to Summer.

"No," she said, anticipating their question. "I can't generate enough faerie dust. It's not strong enough to do that."

"But it can give us a needed boost," countered Lochen.

"Oh, no," said Natalie, understanding his comment.

"Oh, yes," he said. "It will be simple."

Quest of Eight Part Five: Release of the Demons

Richard Reda

"What will be simple?" asked Quinn, not really wanting to know the answer to his question.

"You can't be serious," said Summer.

"Sure I can," said Lochen. "I'm confident it will work."

"What will work?" asked Quinn, not really wanting to know the answer to this question, either.

"It's too far. We won't make it," objected Natalie.

"What's too far," pleaded Quinn. "We won't make what? SOMEBODY ANSWER ME!!!!"

All eyes turned to him.

"He thinks we can jump across to the other plateaus," said Natalie.

"Oh, NO!" shouted Quinn. "You can't be serious. It won't work. It's too far."

"That's what we've been telling him," said Summer. "Haven't you been listening?"

"I'll go first," said Lochen. "I am confident of this, believe me."

He walked to the side furthest away from the next spire.

"As I'm running to the edge, Summer, sprinkle your dust on me. I'll jump and then should be lifted enough to span the gap and land safely on the next obelisk."

"And what if that doesn't work?" asked Summer.

"Then I would suggest that no one else try it," he answered. "Get ready because I'm going to start running."

Quest of Eight Part Five: Release of the Demons

Richard Reda

Before anyone could object or stop him, he started a gawky, lumbering run to the other edge of the caldera's rim.   Summer swooped around and lined up immediately above him, sprinkling him as much as she could.

As soon as he reached the opposite edge, he leapt into the air, his arms waving and his legs kicking as if this would help propel him. He was still aloft when the near edge of the next obelisk passed under him. He stopped flailing and tried to drop down. He landed in the center of the plateau and discovered that the top was solid granite: smooth as glass and as slippery as ice.

He crashed down, landing on his back-side and began to skid across the slick surface. There was nothing to stop him. He kicked his feet downward trying to create some friction. At the same time, he turned over onto his stomach. He began to slow down, but not before his feet and his legs slid over the other side.

His arms were outstretched, his face was pressed to the stone, and he was bent at the waist with his legs dangling over the far edge. He had closed his eyes, fearing that he would overshoot the landing. Now that he had stopped, he opened his eyes to see Summer fluttering above him – her hands to her face, and a look of horror on her face. This immediately changed. Her hands went to her hips, and her look transformed to one of anger.

"You are certifiable," she said. "You could have at least let me check out the landing area before you jumped."

"Yes," he said. "That might have been a wiser course of action."

He wiggled his elbow, pulling himself up and dragging his legs and feet from over the edge.

"Let's try a little less dust with Natalie, shall we?" he told her. "I'll stand at the other edge to break her landing."

"You think you're going to <u>catch</u> her?" Summer asked incredulously.

"Catch might not be the exact word I would choose," he answered. "Perhaps, I'll just manage to get in her way and slow her down."

Summer merely shook her head, flew back to the caldera lip and delivered the bad news to Natalie. Lochen chose not to hear her complaints, satisfied to watch her reaction. When she had apparently ceased objecting, she stomped to the far side of the lip and began running towards Lochen. Along the way, Summer sprinkled dust over her.

She leapt into the air, a look of panic on her face when she saw how high she had jumped. Lochen watched her closely, trying to gauge where she would land. He moved back a few steps, and then forward a few, nearly stepping over the rim of the plateau until Summer shouted to him to be careful.

Natalie landed a few feet across the edge and slid into Lochen's waiting arms. The force knocked him over, and he fell on top of her, further slowing her down. They spun in small slow circles, coming to a stop in the middle of the plateau.

"Perfect," Lochen announced. "Now let's get ready for Quinn. Summer — about the same amount of dust you gave me, if you please."

Summer did as he asked. Quinn started running, but at the last minute came to a screeching stop. He shook his head, turned around and went back to the beginning. He shook himself and started again. Summer once more flew overhead, sprinkling. Once more he stopped suddenly, failing to make the jump.

Before he started the third time, Lochen shouted to her, "No more dust. He probably has too much already."

"Quinn," she said, "you need to just do it. I don't know if I've given you too much and I don't know how long it will last. You can't keep doing this."

"I know," he said. "But when I get to the edge, all I can see is how far down it is and how far across the landing is."

This time Summer flew as close behind his right ear as she could without him knowing it. He began his approach and at the moment when he got to the place he had stopped twice before, she shouted in his ear.

"JUMP!" she screamed.

He was so startled by her yell that he forgot everything else and rocketed off the ledge. He was halfway across when he realized what he had done and he now fixated on landing. He was certain he was going to squash both Natalie and Lochen. Instead, he landed flat on his face. Lochen grabbed his arm as it flew past, and sent Quinn into a spin, stopping several feet from the opposite edge.

"There," he said. "Simple – as I said it would be. We only have three more to go."

"Yeah," said Quinn. "And then we have to come back."

"Thanks," said Natalie. "I was trying to forget about that part."

The next jump was better. Lochen avoided sliding over the far edge. Natalie was as uncomfortable the second time as she was the first time, but kept her grumbling to herself. Quinn was able to make the jump on the first try and without the additional unsolicited support from Summer.

After the third jump Summer asked, "Couldn't you have simply conjured a bridge? Wouldn't that have been easier?"

"Where's the fun in that?" Lochen responded.

"WHAT?" shouted Natalie. "You mean you could have conjured a bridge?"

"No," he answered. "This area is very similar to the Towers at Virkio. There are spells cast on it – not to the extent of Virkio, and not as strong, but enough to affect my abilities."

"Does that mean no more stew?" asked Quinn.

"I think I can still do that," Lochen told him. "But as we've gotten closer to the center, I've felt my powers lessening. Right now I'm more concerned about our being able to defend ourselves."

"Now's a fine time to think of that," said Summer.

"Oh, I thought of it sooner than this," he said as he prepared himself for the next jump. "But there was nothing I could do about it at the time, and we still need to get to the Kelpie. I'm sure the problem will resolve itself when necessary."

The last obelisk before the center one was further away than the others had been and the surface was smaller. Lochen told Summer to cut back a little on the faerie dust so he didn't overshoot his landing. The slipperiness of the surfaces hadn't reduced any from one spire to the next.

Lochen misjudged the end of his take off and jumped a step or two too soon. Summer could see that he was going to miss the landing and tried sprinkling more dust on him, but it was too late. He tried to pull his arms in close to his side and straighten his legs to make himself more aerodynamic, but it wasn't enough.

The top of the pinnacle rose above his eye-level and he was still several feet away. He slammed into the side of the spire, grasping at small breaks and protuberances to keep from falling. Somehow he managed to cling to the side like an insect, but he was unable to climb upward. There was nothing for him to hold on to.

Without thinking or waiting for Summer's dust, Quinn made a running leap and flew across the gap. He hit the edge with his shin and skidded across the surface on his face. Even before he stopped sliding, he scrambled back to the side where Lochen was hanging and reached over the edge. He was too far away. His hands couldn't quite reach Lochen's.

"Can you climb up at all?" asked Quinn.

It was all Lochen could do to turn his head and look up to Quinn. That simple motion shifted his weight enough to dislodge one of the handholds he was clutching. It broke away. Luckily, Lochen let it go and stuck his hand into the vacated niche.

"I think I'm at my limit," he said. "Any other suggestions?"

Natalie called Summer back to her and made the leap, joining Quinn.

"Here," she said as she crawled next to him. "Grab my ankles and hang me over the side. I'll get Lochen's hands, and you pull us both back."

"Are you sure?" asked Quinn. "That's a long way down."

"No, I'm not sure," she snapped, "and quit pointing out how far up we are or how far down everything else is. I can see that for myself. Now do this before I lose what little nerve I have left."

"Yes, ma'am," he mumbled.

He got a tight grasp on her ankles and slowly pushed her over the side. An almost overwhelming sense of vertigo passed through her. She closed her eyes for a second and reminded herself to breathe. Then she opened her eyes and forced herself to look only at Lochen.

Quest of Eight Part Five: Release of the Demons

Richard Reda

"Give me your right hand," she said. "NO. I mean your left hand. I was thinking of my right hand, but my right hand is above your left hand, so I need you to give me your left hand, because I'm going to hold it in my left hand; then you can give me your right hand and I'll hold it in my left hand; oh, I hope this works."

She was so nervous, she couldn't stop talking. Lochen was momentarily distracted from his own situation trying to figure out what she was talking about. He tried looking up at her without moving his head, but her outstretched hand was as far as he could get. He swallowed hard, let go and thrust his hand upward, reaching for hers.

"Got it!" she said. "I have it. I'm holding on tightly. So far, so good. OK, now let's do the same thing with the other hand – your right one. As quick as you can, grab my hand – my left one. Of course it would be my left hand. You're already holding my right hand. I couldn't grab your right hand with my left hand because your left hand is already in my right hand..."

"What are you two talking about down there?" asked Quinn. "Can't you save it for later?"

"Yes," said Natalie. "Of course we can. We're just making sure we have each other..."

Before she could finish, Lochen quickly turned his head to see where her empty hand was and at the same time, shot it upward and grabbed it. He could feel his movement push him away from the wall. He was losing his balance. He hoped Natalie had a good grip on his hands.

Natalie stopped talking. The sudden wrenching on her arms made her speechless. She hadn't been prepared to start pulling, but when Lochen released his hold with his right hand, all his weight was now supported by his feet. The small bulge on which he was standing was insufficient to hold him and both feet slipped out from under him.

Lochen's shift made Natalie constrict her muscles in reaction, and Quinn felt the change. Not waiting for any other signal, he yanked her upward. She cleared the edge of the plateau, dragging Lochen behind.

"That was exhilarating," he said. "But I don't recommend it."

Without further discussion, they each made the final jump to the center obelisk. This one was much larger than the others, and the surface was marred only by a large cube in the center. As they all jumped, they slid across the surface, coming to a stop against the cube.

Once everyone was over, they all crowded around the sides of the cube. Engraved in the center was a symbol they all recognized: a triangle centered over jagged lines representing mountains. Quinn looked devastated, but no one commented.

"How do we open it?" asked Summer.

"<u>Should</u> we open it?" asked Natalie. "Can't we destroy it without opening it?"

"I don't know the answers to any of those questions," said Lochen.

He moved a few steps away, sat on the floor and pulled the book from his waistband. It was clear he had nothing more to say.

"Well what do we do now?" asked Quinn. "Can you at least answer that question?"

"Yes," Lochen answered. "I <u>can</u> answer that question. We wait."

Chapter nine

B'nair looked around. In every direction, as far as he could see, there was nothing but sand. There was no sign of the river along which they had traveled. There was no sign of the stone sepulcher from which the Kelpie had been released. There was no sign of the intruders he and his hobgoblins had battled. He had no idea where they were. He looked at the others. The hobgoblins had all been transported, including Vardelos with the arrow still in his thigh.

The Kelpie was sitting in the sand, leaning on one hand. Her coloring seemed to have an ashy hue to it. Her wings hung limply behind her. She was exhausted, it was plain to see. B'nair was getting angrier and angrier. This was not the way things were supposed to happen. He was forced to flee from a fight, and for what? He had never fled from a fight. He had never run like a scared dog.

"We need to get that arrow out," he said to Vardelos. "If we don't it will get infected and you will become a burden."

"Yes, sir," he answered, understanding.

He wasn't really all that concerned about Vardelos' wound, but he was so angry that he was afraid he would explode. He needed another source to vent his frustration. B'nair reached down and without warning, yanked the arrow from the hobgoblin's leg. He knew how painful that was, but Vardelos didn't make a sound. Instead, he tore a piece of cloth from his shirt and bound the wound himself.

"Thank you, sir," he said when he was done.

"For what?" snarled B'nair. "Pulling that arrow out?"

"For not leaving me behind," he answered. "I will not forget it."

B'nair didn't know what to say. His anger seemed to evaporate. He had never experienced gratitude from any of his own people. Such words coming from the hobgoblin made him uncomfortable, although they did, somehow, manage to diffuse his anger. He turned his attention to the Kelpie.

"Where are we?" he asked.

"Safe," she said. "For the time being."

"What does that mean?"

"It means that in spite of the fact that you see nothing around you, this is not a safe place to stay very long," she answered. "It is safe enough for now. I must regain my strength before we can move again, and explaining things to you will not do that."

183

B'nair bristled at the curt answer, but held his tongue. He wasn't used to being spoken to like that. He stood next to the Kelpie, towering over her. She was supposed to be some powerful sorcerer. Instead, she looked weak and vulnerable. I could remove her head right here, he thought, and be done with all this.

"And if you did," said Angin Topan, "you would never leave this desert."

She could read his thoughts, B'nair realized. He stepped back from her, startled. He felt invaded and didn't like that at all. He wondered how long she had been doing this and if his thoughts were at all safe.

"It's only because you are standing so close to me," she said, once more reading his mind.

She smiled at the look of shock on his face.

"Don't worry," she continued. "It's not something I do all the time. It's a defense mechanism that is strong only when my other powers are weak. After having nothing to do for two thousand years but to contemplate my fate, my powers have atrophied. I spent the time wisely, though, honing my ability to read minds. Of course I had only my own mind to read, so I'm not sure that counts. It will take some time for my powers to be restored, at which time my mind reading ability will diminish. Or so I believe."

B'nair considered what she was telling him, trying to be careful about what he was thinking. He didn't know if he could believe her or not, and then realized it didn't matter. He would believe she could read his thoughts whenever she wanted. She had planted the seed, and now it would grow of its own accord.

"What can I do to help?" he asked in an effort to divert the conversation.

"Help what?" she asked. "Read your mind?"

"No," he shot back. "Help you restore your powers, so we can get out of here."

"I need sustenance," she answered. "But not the kind that you and your army need. It must be food from the desert."

"And what food would that be?" he asked, looking all around him. "I see nothing growing anywhere near here. Do you eat sand?"

"You have the pendant, don't you?" she asked.

"A piece of it," he replied warily.

"Don't worry," she said. "I don't want to take it from you. I'm sure it's been cursed. Put it in your fist and press it tightly. Then drive it into the sand as deeply as you can. Do it over here, near me."

He moved closer, standing so that his body was between her and his free hand. In spite of her claim that she didn't want the stone, he didn't trust her. He removed it from his vest, knelt down and pushed his hand into the sand, holding the stone tightly. He twisted and turned his arm, forcing it as deep as he could.

He felt the pendant vibrate and begin to heat. He held it in place until the motion and the heat reached a point he could no longer tolerate. Then he yanked his arm from the sand. At first nothing happened, other than that the vibration and heat stopped. The sand looked the same. In a few seconds, however, three or four sand worms crawled to the surface.

B'nair had never seen anything like them. They were six inches long and about an inch in diameter. They had long thin pincers extending from both ends of their bodies, but no indication of any eyes, mouths or feet. They were the same tan color as the sand from which they crawled, but had a sticky looking coating on them. The Kelpie quickly scooped them up and shoved them into her mouth.

Quest of Eight Part Five: Release of the Demons

Richard Reda

"These will have to do for now," she said between sucking sounds as she seemed to swallow them whole. "Scarab beetles would be better, but they don't seem to have a nest nearby."

He had eaten some strange things in his time, but nothing like this. He got to his feet and stepped back slightly. The Kelpie sat up a little straighter, the blue hue in her skin deepening slightly. Her wings seemed to perk up as well, and fluttered slightly. She closed her eyes momentarily and breathed deeply and slowly. When they opened again, her eyes were a much deeper blue, and were more piercing.

"Gather your men," she told him. "I can move us once more. It still won't be far enough, but it should be closer to what I need."

"Where are we going?" he asked.

"It won't matter to you," she said. "You will not see any difference in the surroundings, but I will know the difference."

B'nair did as she directed him. He watched as Vardelos stood. He was in obvious pain, but said nothing. If he didn't heal quickly, B'nair wondered if he would have to leave the hobgoblin behind. It was one of those difficult decisions he had told the hobgoblin about. He limped over to the rest of the group and, when they were all gathered, the Kelpie whirled her hand, enveloping them in a cloud of sand.

No one felt like they had moved, but in seconds the small storm subsided. It looked like nothing changed. The desert sands around them were identical.

"We've moved," Angin Topan told them, "regardless of what your eyes tell you."

She could sense the doubt and uncertainty in their minds. Even their leader wasn't sure, but he was shifting his focus from one topic to another trying unsuccessfully to keep her from reading his thoughts.

She smiled to herself at his failed attempts. But she decided to let him believe this would work.

"Over here," she called to him and she pointed a few steps away. "Place your fist and the stone into the sand here, but be careful. A large nest of scarabs is close. It wouldn't do for you to lose another hand."

B'nair looked to where she had motioned. He stepped slowly over, removed the stone again and held it in his hand. He bent down and dug it into the sand. The tingling and the heat came much faster this time. When he pulled his hand out it was immediately followed by a swarm of beetles. Several of them were snapping at his fist. He had removed it within seconds of being bitten.

He bolted upright and stepped back. The Kelpie dove at the creatures, scooping them up and shoveling them into her mouth. At the same time she looked back over her shoulder at B'nair, glaring at him like a dog protecting its food. She didn't have to say anything. He moved away and motioned for the hobgoblins to do the same. He looked at his hand to make sure the fangs of the beetles hadn't pierced his glove.

Each of them carried a pouch that contained a kind of jerky with which they had to satisfy themselves while the Kelpie gorged herself on the beetles. Her appetite seemed to be insatiable. B'nair's had vanished within seconds after the eruption of the beetles from their nest. He was slightly shaken at how close he had come to having no useful hands.

He could only watch as the Kelpie fed herself. She was so ravenous that she often stuffed sand as well as the scarabs into her mouth. After a while, the crunching sound became irritating, and B'nair and the hobgoblins moved even further away. B'nair stopped looking altogether.

Quest of Eight Part Five: Release of the Demons

Richard Reda

The feasting went on for over an hour. The scarabs kept pouring forth from the indentation in the sand that B'nair had created with his fist. She had been right. The nest was large. Every once in a while one of the beetles would veer off to one side or the other, but escape was impossible. The Kelpie's hands darted out, grabbing any stragglers and shoving them into her jaws.

The sand around her was soon littered with bits of wings and legs from the pieces that dropped from her mouth. B'nair almost expected her to scoop those up, too, but they remained where they fell.

Finally, the source seemed to have dried up, and her gorging slowed to a stop. She wiped her mouth with the back of her hand and glanced over to the Rebbercand. He could see an increased intensity in her eyes. He could also see the color of her skin deepen and almost sparkle. She was still a pale blue, but it seemed to be more iridescent.

"My powers are returning," she said. "I can feel it. But I must rest for a while. We can speak, though."

He took that as an invitation and moved closer to her. She was sitting on the sand and, although she said nothing, he could tell by the look she gave him that she didn't like him towering over her. He looked around to make sure there were no more beetles around, and then sat down beside her. Still, he was more than two feet higher than she was. She would have to deal with that, he said to himself, and then instantly regretted the thought.

He looked at her in a sideways glance, but she gave no sign that she was offended. He wondered if, with the restoration of her other powers, her ability to read his mind was diminishing. Unless she revealed herself, he considered, he would never know.

"How did you discover the pendant," she asked.

He told her an abbreviated version of the events and included the fact that he knew that the rest of the pendant was in the possession of one of their earlier attackers. He told her of the map that had appeared to him and how the locations of the Kelpies had been displayed.

"We must find the other masters," she said. "They will know what to do now that Pantano Izaki has been destroyed."

"The other Kelpie – Pantano Izaki – called you master. Was he a servant to you?" B'nair asked.

"No," Angin Topan laughed. "It's not that kind of master. It's similar to masters and apprentices, except that Pantano was not an apprentice. It only means the powers of the masters are greater."

"You said we must find the other masters," B'nair said. "How many are there?"

"Three," she explained. "I am one. Akmen Milzu, the Mountain Kelpie is another, and Ollos Foscos, Kelpie of the Sea, is the third. Do you see these on your map?"

"The Mountain Kelpie is clear to me," answered B'nair. "Because he is the closest."

"She," corrected Angin Topan. "The three masters are all women. Does that surprise you?"

B'nair thought before he answered.

"No. In my world, it is not much different. The Mountain Kelpie is the nearest to us. The Sea Kelpie, though, is far away. The visions of their locations become clearer the closer we are to them. When I obtained the second piece of the pendant, and the map was given to me, the Swamp was closest. We went there first. After that, the desert and the mountains were the same distance. Our choice was random."

"I'm glad you chose as you did," she said. "Who is it that attacked us? Do you know of them?"

189

"Not at first," he answered. "I knew we were being followed. I could sense that before I possessed the first stone. I didn't know who they were until recently. I had met the Dozor before and thought him dead."

"Apparently you were wrong."

"So it seems. But that has been corrected. I crushed him before we fled."

"Will they follow now that one of them is gone?"

"Yes," he answered. "There are others."

"How do you know?"

"When I met the Dozor before, there was another with him – a giant. The giant wasn't in the desert. I don't know how many of them there are, but it's unlikely that the giant would go off by himself. Their group must have divided. Some of them went to the desert. The others must have gone to the mountains."

"How would they know where to go?" asked the Kelpie.

"I'm sure the one who has the other half of the pendant has the same map as I. I assume they tried to reach the Swamp before me, but failed. I have to think that they then divided, since the next nearest locations – the desert and the mountains – were equally distant. They are trying to prevent the release of you and your brethren."

"Then they must be stopped," said Angin Topan. "They must be destroyed. We must obtain the rest of the pendant. What of the band?"

"What band?" asked B'nair.

"The pendant belonged to the witch," explained the Kelpie. "It was made of the stone and a band of gold that held it. Where is the band?"

"I don't know where it is," said B'nair. "I know nothing of a band."

"It's not important," said the Kelpie.

She had assumed the Rebbercand knew about the band as well as the stone. It was clear to her now that he had no understanding of the power of the pendant, or that the band was more important than the stone. They needed to get to the other masters before something happened to them. They needed to get all of the other Kelpies freed. Then they could decide what to do about replacing Pantano Izaki. Without all eight Kelpies, the full power of the pendant would escape their grasp. Of course, they would need to obtain the other half and to locate the band. First things first, though.

"I need to rest now," she said, dismissing him. "We will leave in the morning for the mountains. Prepare the others."

------------------ *** ------------------

Liam helped Sean into the ship, careful not to jar his tender ribs. Stella had suffered several bruises from the ship landing on her, but had to endure them. In spite of her powers, she could not heal herself. Solveig volunteered to take the first shift pedaling the small craft. It was clear that Sean would not be able to take a shift, and she wasn't sure Stella had the strength, either.

"Just point the way," she said to Liam.

He looked around at the dunes of sand and then up to the sky. Finally he pointed to the right and Solveig turned the craft in that direction. While she was pedaling, Stella asked Liam if he could remove some of the side railing – not much, just a couple of pieces.

"I suppose," he answered. "Why?"

"I might be able to help get us where we're going a little faster," she answered.

He looked from one side to the other and decided upon a piece from the transom and another from the decking behind the helmsman's seat. The second piece left an opening on the deck that exposed the hold beneath, but not by much. When he was done, he moved them to the center of the ship.

"Here you are," he said. "What are you going to do with them?"

Without speaking, Stella pointed at the longer of the two pieces and mumbled an incantation. She rubbed her hands together – palm to palm. The beam stood up on end and then began to stretch, twisting back and forth in time with Stella's hands as it grew taller and taller. It rose to a height of fifteen feet and then rose up a few inches.

Stella moved her hand to center the beam in the middle of the deck, front to back and left to right. Then with her other hand she tapered the bottom part of the shaft and created a hole in the deck. She lowered her hand and fit the mast into place. After that, she waved to the other piece, stretching it to six feet in length, and motioned it upward to within two feet of the top of the mast.

With her other hand, she notched the mast and the cross beam, fitting them tightly together and drove some of the chips in to nail the pieces together. When she was done, the small craft had a mast and spar.

"You'd make an excellent carpenter," said Liam. "But we don't have a sail."

"I think we do," said Stella.

She turned to Solveig and asked for the cloak that had been given to her by Beebee. Solveig patted the pockets to make sure they were empty. She took the dragon's tooth out of one of them, some nuts and a few dried up berries out of another and a handful of leaves out of a third.

"Where did these come from?" she asked aloud when she discovered the leaves.

She handed the cloak to Stella, who merely waved her hand and flung it up to the spar. The cloak moved as if it had a mind of its own, wrapping its edges along the spar and stretching itself to a point towards the bottom of the mast. When it was secured, Stella thrust her hand forward, and the sail was filled with wind.

"I think you can stop pedaling now," she told Solveig. "All you need to do is steer."

The ship sailed across the sand and shortly before nightfall, they reached the end of the desert and arrived at the delta where the river that separated the desert from the Swamp emptied into the Cerulean Sea. From there they followed the coast line, eventually passing the place Summer, Solveig and Liam had been once before.

Even if they had thought about it, though, they wouldn't have seen it. By then it was the dead of night. Sean was steering the ship and the others were sleeping. He agreed to take the night shift only because he couldn't see how much water surrounded them in the dark. He knew it was there, but somehow it was better for him not to see it. He had mixed feelings about the lack of light from the moon and the stars – still hidden by the gray clouds.

He was glad that the light was blocked, since it kept the sea in blackness, but he also knew that those clouds could be a sign of an approaching storm. Being on the water was bad enough. Being on the water in a storm reminded him of things that he tried hard to forget. He decided to pedal. Pedaling while the sails were pulling the ship would help get them where they were going faster.

Quest of Eight Part Five: Release of the Demons

Richard Reda

Late in the night, a fog settled in and Sean lost sight of land that had been off to his left. He wasn't sure exactly when that happened, but as soon as he noticed he thought he should probably wake Liam up to make sure they were still on course. Liam was curled up near the front of the boat, deep in sleep.

Sean started to call to him, but stopped. He was afraid he'd awaken Stella and Solveig. Then he decided to get up and shake Liam, but he was afraid to let go of the tiller. He was undecided as to what to do. He looked towards the shore, straining his eyes to cut through the fog.

"How far away could the coast be?" he muttered to himself. "There's fog over there. Doesn't there have to be land to have fog? As long as I can see the fog, I can assume that the land is right behind it. Right?"

"I don't know," he answered himself. "I don't like being on the water, so how would I know?"

He realized he was talking to himself and, worse than that, he was carrying on both sides of the conversation. He stopped.

"How can you have fog on top of water?" he continued after a few minutes. "Isn't fog part water? If it is, then how can there be fog on top of it? Wouldn't that be water on top of water?"

"You're talking to yourself again."

"I know, but there's no one else to talk to."

"Well, stop it. You're starting to freak me out."

So he did.

"But what if there can be fog on water?" he started again. "There are sand storms on sand. Why can't there be water on water? I think there can. I mean look around. The fog is all around us. There isn't land all around us. If there was, then we'd be in a lake, or a pond, or something. There must be fog on water."

"But what do you know? You hate the water. You never go near the water."

"What do you mean I never go near the water? What about that time with Lochen when he almost drowned me?"

Solveig mumbled something in her sleep and Sean stopped talking.

"Did you say something?" he whispered.

"Of course she didn't say something," he said when she didn't answer. "You're imagining things."

"Like the fog? Am I imagining that?"

"No. I suppose not."

"And don't forget that garbage scow."

"What are you talking about now?"

"I'm talking about the other time I was on water, so don't tell me I never go near the water."

"I think you're losing your mind."

"Oh, yeah? Well it's your mind, too, you know."

The night was so black by now that Sean couldn't see the shore, even if it hadn't been blocked by fog. He had been able to hear the waves on the shore at the time they first moved from the desert to the sea. Now, though, he couldn't, and he couldn't recall when that change had occurred.

Quest of Eight Part Five: Release of the Demons

Richard Reda

He began to feel dizzy. He couldn't see a horizon line and had no point of reference to maintain his balance. The sea was unusually calm, and the ship was moving only slightly from side to side. Each little movement was exaggerated in his mind. He had to close his eyes to settle himself.

"You're going to fall asleep if you do that," he mumbled after his eyes had been closed for a few seconds.

"But if I don't close them, I'm going to be sick. My head is spinning and I feel like I'm going to throw up."

"What's worse? Throwing up or falling asleep?"

"I hate throwing up. You know that."

"But it's better than falling..."

He didn't finish the sentence. He had started drifting off.

"Wake up," he told himself as he jerked his head up.

His eyes were dry and itching; his head was buzzing; his stomach was rumbling. All this felt better when he closed his eyes. It was so easy to close them – the lids were getting so heavy.

"Wake up," he mumbled out loud, jerking awake again.

"Just steer the boat. That's all you have to do."

"But I can't see where I'm going."

"If you don't move the tiller, then you can't change directions. Just keep the tiller in the same..."

His eyelids slowly dropped until they were closed. His head slowly sank and his body slowly relaxed. His grip on the tiller loosened and he tipped to the side.

"I'm awake," he said out loud again.

He stretched his eyelids as wide as he could, and took in several deep breaths.

"Maybe you should wake one of the others to take over for you," he told himself.

"What if I haven't done my full shift, though?"

"How would they know?"

"That's not the point. I need to do my fair share."

"Even if it means...even...if...e'en...fff...beans...no, not beans...what word was I thinking...beans, deans, leans...that's...not...right...I mean tight...no, light...night light...good night..."

He could fight it no longer. Sleep descended on him like a heavy blanket. He wobbled back and forth a few times in time with the movement of the sea, but even that didn't waken him. Instead, he let go of the tiller and slumped to the deck where he curled up and stayed throughout the night.

He awoke shivering. The air had gotten decidedly colder, but the sky was as bleak as it had been for the last several days. He rubbed the sleep from his face and then realized that he had never woken anyone up to relieve him. He sat bolt upright and saw Liam at the tiller.

"I fell asleep," he said.

"So I see," answered Liam.

"I didn't mean to. It just happened."

He looked over the side and saw nothing but water. Then he looked in the opposite direction only to find the same view. He spun towards the front and then towards the back. It was all the same. There was no sight of land in any direction.

"Oh, no," he wailed. "I got us lost. I'm sorry, really. I can't believe I did that. What are we going to do?"

"We're not lost," said Liam.

"We're not? How could that be?"

"We're off course," Liam clarified. "But we're not lost."

"How far off course are we?" Sean asked, afraid to hear the answer.

"That's hard to say," answered Liam. "Probably a few hundred miles."

"Ooohhhhh," groaned Sean. "I'm sorry. You should just throw me overboard."

"If we did that," said Stella, "we wouldn't have anyone to pick on."

She had been sitting on the deck on the opposite side of the boat watching the exchange. During the night, she had sensed something internally – a shift in the map in her mind, or perhaps a change in the feeling of power in the stone around her neck. Whatever it was, it woke her up.

She saw Sean sound asleep on the deck and nothing visible more than a few feet around the ship in any direction. She woke Liam up to let him know. He was surprised they had managed to stay on course as long as they had. The fog had gotten so thick there was no way anyone could have maintained the direction.

He took over at the tiller and let his internal guidance system take over. They were still heading north. That much was evident by the drop in temperature. The tides had carried them to the east, but not past the large land mass that made up the Ice Kingdom.

He adjusted course and Stella increased the wind in the sail. Then she roused Solveig, allowing Sean to catch up on some apparently well-needed sleep. As the night sky faded away, revealing the familiar gray skies, Solveig declared it a truly dismal day.

"Let me make it up to everybody," he said. "I can probably catch some fish or something and make my uncle's famous cold fish soup."

"NO!" they all shouted in unison.

"That won't be necessary," said Stella, trying to soften the rejection. "You spent far too much time at the tiller last night trying to guide us through the darkness."

"That's right," added Liam. "You really have no reason to feel like you need to make up for anything. We aren't that far off course."

"Besides," said Solveig, "we don't have...there's nothing to...I'm not hungry."

She hadn't been able to think of anything better to say. Sean looked at each of them, unsure of what was going on, but decided not to pursue it.

"But it would be nice," she continued, trying to change the subject as she turned to Stella, "if there was a way we could get warmer. The air has really gotten cold, and my cloak...is serving another purpose."

She glanced up at the make-shift sail. Stella had thought about creating a small bubble over the ship, but in doing so, she would cover the sail and the ship would stop. They'd be back to pedaling it. She had increased the wind strength so that they would make faster time.

Solveig was right. The air was getting colder much more quickly, and the wind was making it even colder. She looked around, but there was nothing on board she could heat up, like a rock.

"I think we're going to have to endure this for a while," Stella said.

"What happens when we get to the Ice Kingdom?" asked Liam. "We should have thought about that when we were back in the Swamp. I could have packed some additional clothing."

"I can help with that," Sean announced proudly. "Quinn showed me where he set up caches like you have in the Swamp. He put them all over the Ice Kingdom. I'm sure I can find one once we make land."

"That won't be as long as we thought," said Liam.

He pointed to the horizon in front of them. Off in the distance they could see a line of bluish-white begin to rise into the air. Their attention was focused forward as the line grew higher and higher. Several minutes later they could see the vast edge of a giant glacier taking shape. They also began to hear the rumble of thunder.

"Where's that coming from?" asked Sean. "It doesn't look like rain."

His gaze was fixed to the dull gray sky above. Everyone glanced upward at his comment. There were no firm cloud formations; no signs of lightning; and no indication of rain. While they were all searching the sky for signs of a storm, the small ship began to react to a significant shift in the surface of the sea.

"What just happened?" asked Solveig. "Where did that wave come from?"

"I don't know," said Liam.

It seemed as if a single rogue wave had appeared from nowhere and lifted the boat high into the air and then down again. In a few seconds, the movement stopped and the water was still again. By now they could see more distinctly the wall of ice that was getting closer to them. It stretched as far as they could see from right to left. There didn't seem to be any way around it.

Then there was another rumble. Their eyes immediately went to the sky, and again, nothing provided a clue or even a hint at an approaching storm. And once again, a few seconds later, the boat was elevated on another large wave.

"Maybe it's coming from something beneath the sea," said Solveig.

"Nothing that I'm familiar with," said Stella. "Any sea creatures that could make a noise like that would have to be on or above the surface."

Liam scanned the approaching horizon. Far to his left he saw a large section of the glacier break away and drop into the water. Shortly after, the sound of the calving of an iceberg reached their ears, to be followed by the wave created when the berg dropped into the water.

"We need to steer clear of that section of the wall," he told the others. "Those things are a lot bigger than this boat. If we get too close, we can get swamped."

"How can you tell where they're going to break off?" asked Sean.

"Good question," he answered. "I don't know."

"Wonderful," Sean said. "And just how do you plan to avoid them?"

"OK," admitted Liam. "I guess we can't. Hope you're prepared to get wet."

"Sorry I asked," said Sean.

Quest of Eight Part Five: Release of the Demons

Richard Reda

Liam kept one eye on the wall, searching for possible breaks in the ice, and the other on steering the boat. When they were about twenty or thirty yards away, he told Stella to take down the sail. He'd make the rest of the approach by pedaling.

A few minutes later, he brought the craft around so that one side rested against the glacier's edge. The wall of ice rose above them more than a hundred feet. Liam looked to the right and back to the left, but saw nothing that indicated where or when it dropped down to a level where they could more easily dock.

"Any suggestions?" he asked.

"If I had a rope, I could climb to the top," said Sean. "Then I could pull the rest of you up."

"I have some rope below deck," said Liam. "But nothing that long."

"I think I can help with that," said Stella. "If Solveig doesn't mind giving up her cloak again."

"I've gotten sort of attached to it," she said. "But, sure, whatever you need, although I don't think it's near long enough."

Stella spun her index finger around the bottom edge of the cloak. It began to unravel. She took the end of the rope and tied it securely to the threads of the cloak. She waved her hand over the cloak, placed it on the deck and then handed the rope to Sean.

"As you climb, the cloak will continue to unravel and will expand as much as you need," she told him.

He looked at the threads of the cloak a bit skeptically.

"Are you sure that's going to hold?" he asked.

"Those threads will be stronger than that rope," she assured him.

"If you say so," he commented and turned to begin his climb.

"Oh, and one more thing," she said.

She turned to the glacier. She flicked the same index finger and small sparks flew out, cutting chips into the ice.

"Hand and foot holds," she explained.

"Wait," said Solveig.

She bent down to the cloak and felt around. She pulled out the dragon's tooth and handed it to Sean.

"You may be able to use this," she said. "In case the holes Stella made aren't deep enough...or if you run into something...well, you know...once you get to the top."

He took it from her, smiled, tucked it into the cord tied around his waist and began to climb.

Chapter ten

Angin Topan rested briefly, but didn't sleep. The recuperation of her powers didn't require that she sleep, only that she rest. As she rested, she watched B'nair and the hobgoblins. The one that was wounded would slow them down, she believed. Unless he could keep up, he may be left behind. She waited until all but the Rebbercand were asleep, and then she motioned to him to join her.

"Please tell me, how a Rebbercand came to be in the company of hobgoblins?" she asked.

He told her of the mining operation in the caves and the rebellion of the Trepans. He had suspected that they were not capable of mounting such a revolt on their own, and had discovered some of those who had aided them.

Quest of Eight Part Five: Release of the Demons

Richard Reda

He explained the incident with the Dozor and the giant that had saved him, and his belief that the two of them had fallen into the river of lava. He described his salvation and rehabilitation by the hobgoblins and the story of their common ancestry, as well as the lore behind the axe. He wasn't sure why, but he felt less guarded about telling her this much than he had felt sharing with Pantano Izaki. He expected her to ask about the stone, but she didn't, which surprised him even more.

"And now it's my turn to ask a question," he said.

"Of course," she answered. "Ask what you like."

"How did a pixie end up in the desert?" he asked. "I thought your people liked the forests and hated wide open spaces."

"Imp," she corrected. "I am an imp, not a pixie. They are much smaller – and red."

"My apologies. We Rebbercands have only heard about both imps and pixies. We...I've never encountered one."

"I understand," she said with a hint of a smile. "No apology is necessary. Very few people ever see us. At one time we all lived together – imps, pixies and even the faeries. And you are correct. We all prefer forests. As a blue imp, I was what you probably would call a queen. Our word was Malkia – it's less...regal, I suppose.

"I ruled the imps, pixies and faeries. Until the Alchemist and his Enchantress felt threatened by the powers of the Kelpies. We had formed an alliance to...how should I describe it? To better serve our collective needs. We had grown tired of the restrictions the Alchemist was forcing on us, and he and his witch resented our challenge.

"They knew they were no match against our collective power, so they began to separate us from one another and trap us. Pantano Izaki and I were among the last to be taken prisoners. Our parting gifts to the

Alchemist and the Enchantress, and those who supported them were the creation of the Swamp and the desert."

"Izaki said he poisoned his own land," said B'nair. "Is that what you did to your forest?"

"Oh, I find 'poison' such a distasteful word," she answered. "I prefer to say we made some ecological adjustments."

"I see," said B'nair. "Him turning his land into a toxic waste, and you completely defoliating yours – ecological adjustments? Very interesting."

"Do you object?" she asked.

"Not at all," he said. "I find the phrasing innovative, that's all."

She smiled. It wasn't a warm or inviting smile. B'nair wasn't sure she was capable of that. He supposed her smile was a lot like he imagined his was – a facial reaction, and nothing deeper than that. It did not instill trust, not that he would ever trust her. But she was clearly different than the other Kelpie – not so puffed up with her own importance.

He looked around. The night sky was still clouded over, and he could see no more of the desert surroundings than were illuminated by the campfire. He wondered what sort of dangers lurked beyond that glow, and how long he and his compatriots would last without whatever spells the Kelpie had cast to keep them safe.

He realized she had not commented on his thoughts about her smile or about the dangers beyond the campfire. He wondered if her other powers had returned sufficiently that her ability to read his thoughts no longer existed. Then he wondered if that was all just a lie to keep him guessing. Time would tell, he thought.

"Will you transport us to the next location tomorrow?" he asked when she still hadn't commented on his thoughts.

"Yes," she answered. "But not in one move. My powers are still regenerating. Besides, there are too many of you for me to do that, even if my powers were at full strength. And I'm sure you don't want to leave any of them behind. Do you? What kind of repayment for their hospitality would that be?"

Was this an option she was suggesting, he wondered.

"Not just yet," he answered, not waiting for her to expand on the idea.

The next morning, the twin suns had done little to brighten the day. Their light barely penetrated the overcast sky, but it was enough to dispel the shadows of the night. Vardelos was slow in rising. It was clear to B'nair that the hobgoblin's wound was bothering him. He wondered if it was healing properly. He looked like he hadn't gotten any rest at all. Hobgoblins might be cousins to Rebbercands, but B'nair never thought any of them looked appealing. Vardelos looked even worse, if that was possible.

Vardelos slowly limped over to join the others as Angin Topan spread her arms and gathered them up in a whirlwind of sand. He was barely ready when he was swooped up into the small cyclone. They seemed to be in the air for only a few seconds and then dropped to the ground.

When they landed, the suddenness of the stop jarred Vardelos and he fell to the ground. He rolled to his side, and stayed there trying to catch his breath. He was in too much pain to notice that they were in a large grassy field. The others, though, were perfectly aware that there was no sign of the desert in any direction.

"We will stop here for a few minutes," said the Kelpie

Quest of Eight Part Five: Release of the Demons

Richard Reda

The hobgoblins stood around unsure of what to do; Vardelos rolled over onto his back and stayed where he was in the grass, too weak to stand. B'nair watched as Angin Topan walked off a little ways, apparently in search of something. It was odd to watch someone with wings walking. It came to him that her powers were probably restored to a lesser degree that she was admitting.

Was she threatened by him, he wondered. He watched where she was walking. She seemed to have a specific destination in mind. She came upon a nearby stream, bent down and took a drink of the water. Then she turned around and walked back. You're starting to imagine things, he told himself.

When she noticed him watching her, she gave him that same cold smile she had before. It was enough to make him wonder if she was still reading his thoughts. She looked at him as if she knew he had been watching her. The uncertainty was infuriating.

"I am ready," she announced when she returned. "I only needed some water. Tell the others to gather together."

Before everyone got close enough to be encompassed in her whirlwind, she reached up towards B'nair.

"I must touch your head," she told him. "I must know where we are going so I can move us in the right direction."

She had reached up to place her hand on his head. Even though her hand only rose as high as his chest, he jerked his head back instinctively. She didn't lower her hand. It was as if she expected his reaction and was waiting for him to get over it. He eyed her closely, but didn't immediately respond. What kind of trick was this, he wondered. Her arm was still extended upward, waiting for him to bend down to it. Finally, he lowered himself to one knee and bent his head forward. Her hand felt gritty – like the sand itself – and cold. He felt the cold of her touch move through him like a dull knife.

Quest of Eight Part Five: Release of the Demons

Richard Reda

He closed his eyes and could see the map in his mental vision. A shadow crept across the image. It was her touch, probing into the map, seeking the location. When the shadow reached the symbol in the mountain, a small flash appeared. Then the shadow moved on to the next location. He jerked his head back, breaking her connection.

Her eyes flew open and stared at him without expression. He held her gaze, waiting for her to say something. She slowly lowered her hand, still looking back at him, that same cold smile on her face. Eventually, she stepped away and looked at the hobgoblins.

"We can go now," she declared, her voice flat. "Gather close."

The others did as she instructed. B'nair was the last to move. He hadn't stopped watching her, but she didn't react to his stare. Finally, he stepped forward and at the same instant, she swept her arms in a circle. Sand and wind swirled around them and they disappeared from the grassy plain.

In an instant the wind stopped and the sand died down. They made another jarring landing at the base of a mountain. Vardelos fell to the ground. His injured leg could not support his weight. B'nair began to think she was doing this on purpose, but couldn't figure out why. He bent down and jerked Vardelos to his feet.

"Thank you, sir," the hobgoblin said, his breath coming in gasps. "I wasn't expecting such a sudden stop."

He was covered in sweat. His wound was probably infected, thought B'nair. He wondered how much longer the hobgoblin would last — how many more sudden stops before he couldn't get up again.

"From here," said Angin Topan, "we will have to go in two stages. We must go to the top. After that I will be able to see exactly where to go."

She said nothing else, but watched Vardelos. Was she waiting for him, wondered B'nair. Before anyone could say anything, Vardelos got to his feet and limped to the cluster of hobgoblins. He knew he was dragging the others down. He hoped they would find the next Kelpie soon. If the first two were any indication, they would need to rest at least a day before moving to the next one. One more day of rest should help.

Before she swept them up in another storm, B'nair backed away from the group and looked up at the wall of stone in front of them. He could barely make out the top of the mountain and was studying the narrow cracks and ledges along the side.

"Where do you expect to stop on the way up?" asked B'nair. "I don't see anything big enough to hold all of us. Or are you going to take us to the top in smaller groups?"

He was looking up the side of the mountain. He had no idea that it was close to the same place that Lochen, Quinn, Natalie and Summer had climbed. He saw no ledges or outcroppings anywhere large enough for all of them to land on – safely or otherwise. Angin Topan cocked her head slightly to one side and a smirk broke across her face as she looked at B'nair.

"There will be sufficient space," she responded vaguely.

He looked doubtful.

"Do you fear I will strand you," she purred like a cat, "or endanger you? I feel you do not trust me. I am disappointed."

He wasn't sure if he was being goaded or not. He wasn't sure how to answer her comment, or if she even expected an answer. The silence hung between them for a few seconds.

"I trust no one," he finally said, defiantly.

Quest of Eight Part Five: Release of the Demons

Richard Reda

The smirk widened, but she didn't respond to his comment. Instead, she spread her wings and without taking her eyes off of him, began to rise up into the air. She fluttered slowly, her wings making an irritating buzzing, whining sound. She continued to climb, all the while her eyes fixed on his.

When she had shrunk to little more than a dot, B'nair assumed she was about half way up the mountain. He thought she had stopped rising, but couldn't tell what she was doing. There was a flash of light and a quick crack of thunder. A few seconds later, bits of rock dropped down on them.

The hobgoblins scattered to avoid the downpour of stones. B'nair stood his ground, raising the axe over his head, his gaze still fixed on the Kelpie. Shortly after the rocks, he could see her floating back down. She was still staring at him. What kind of game was she playing, he wondered.

"Did you think I left you?" she asked when she landed.

He kept his silence, refusing to be drawn in to whatever she was trying to do. She continued without waiting for a response from him.

"You must learn to trust me," she said. "Our fates are sealed to one another. I thought by now you surely would understand that. I am indebted to you for my freedom. I would never repay that debt with treachery."

He didn't like the idea that she felt indebted to him. He didn't believe she actually felt that, but her voicing that sentiment only disturbed him.

"I will learn to trust you," he lied.

She smiled at him once again, knowing he was lying.

"There is now an alcove where you will all be safe," she said after a few seconds. "I would not want your fears to dampen your bravery. You will need to be brave. There are others who have gone this way before us. I am sure they are waiting for our arrival."

B'nair tried not to let his surprise show. How could they have gotten here so fast, he wondered. Did they bury the Dozor? He wished he had followed Pantano Izaki to the other side of the ship and seen who was there. How many more had been hidden back there out of his sight? And who were they?

"These are not the same," said the Kelpie.

She could no longer read his thoughts. She had only made an educated guess, but she could tell by his reaction that she had guessed his thoughts. She knew for certain, however, that their earlier assailants included an Enchantress who possessed the rest of the pendant. There were no traces of that in the clues these others had left behind. What she couldn't tell, though, was if the earlier assailants were friends or foes of those who were now waiting. She imagined they would be foes, but she knew she would find out soon.

"Who are they?" B'nair asked.

"I assume by your question that whoever they are, they are not your allies."

"That's a safe assumption," he told her.

"Then we must be careful," she said.

She motioned for B'nair and the hobgoblins to gather together, and then she swept them up in another whirlwind of sand and dust. In the blink of an eye, the wind evaporated and they found themselves high up on the side of the mountain in the niche she had carved out for them. She had carved an alcove, all right, but it was still very narrow. Some of the hobgoblins were teetering on the edge.

"Prepare your weapons," she instructed.

The hobgoblins unsheathed swords, armed crossbows, and notched arrows. When she was satisfied that they were ready, she swept them up once more. The swirl of sand reappeared and then vanished from the alcove.

- - - - - - - - - - - - - - - - - *** - - - - - - - - - - - - - - - - -

Lochen had been pouring over his book, while Summer and Quinn made various unsuccessful attempts to open the cube. Summer had sprinkled faerie dust all over it, trying to raise it into the air. Quinn had knocked on the top, kicked the sides, and pushed against it with all his weight. Nothing they did had any effect.

Natalie had watched them for a while, more intrigued by the engraving on the top of the cube. It is exactly the same as the mountain and triangle markings Quinn had shown them – how long ago? She pointed this out to him and was somewhat surprised by his reaction.

"Those symbols don't have anything to do with these Kelpies," he argued. "I don't care what Lochen says. He can't be right."

"Then how do you explain the fact that they're repeated here on this stone?" she asked.

"Maybe it just means that's who locked this Kelpie away."

He knew it was a feeble argument, but he refused to believe the symbols could represent such dark forces.

"Maybe it means that Solveig should be here. This is her sign," he added. "Maybe it means...I don't know!" he shouted.

He turned his attention back to the cube, clearly not intending to answer any more of Natalie's questions. He kicked the sides again, and tried lifting the edge. It was immovable. He began to look along the top edges, searching for seams of some kind. Seeing that he was not receptive to any challenges to his view of the markings, she turned to Lochen for support.

Lochen, however, was sitting cross-legged on the far side of the plateau, his head buried in that book. Natalie walked over to him. He failed to notice her approach. Even when she sat down next to him, he stayed glued to the pages. She waited for a few minutes, hoping he'd reach a point where he could stop.

"Lochen?" she said, interrupting his thoughts when it was clear he wouldn't be stopping soon.

"Hmmm?" he mumbled.

"Do you really think those symbols refer to the Kelpies and not to...and not what Quinn thinks they refer to?"

"Here," he said, apparently not hearing her question. "Look at this."

He moved the book closer to her so she could see.

"Those symbols appear in several places in these pages."

She leaned over to look as he flipped through. The writings or drawings or whatever they were, were incomprehensible to her. The symbols, more often than not, were lost in the mix. She had to take his word.

"Have you been able to decipher any of the text?" she asked.

"I'm afraid I have been quite unsuccessful," he answered. "I've read every page several times looking for some kind of pattern. Certain letters or symbols appear more frequently than others in most languages. While I've seen some characters repeated, the regularity of those repetitions is inconclusive."

"Do Quinn's symbols...the ones he showed us in the Ice Kingdom...are they all in that book?"

"Yes," he said. "Every one of them, and several times."

He seemed pleased with this discovery. Natalie wasn't sure if that was good or bad. They sat in silence for a while, each lost in thought.

"What do you know of your history?" he finally asked.

"Mine?" she responded. "Uh...well...my parents were..."

"No," he interrupted. "I didn't mean your personal history. I meant that of your people – the Sea Sprites. What can you tell me of the history of the Sea Sprites?"

"How far back do you want me to go?"

"Tell me the folk lore of your origins," he explained.

She looked at him for a few seconds collecting her thoughts. She had grown up on stories about the first Sprites, but hadn't thought about them in years. They were more like children's tales and she never really took them seriously.

"Well," she started tentatively. "No one is absolutely sure when or where the first Sea Sprites came from. The earliest stories go back a few thousand years. The Sprites lived in the waters close to the shores. I don't remember hearing anything about wars or disputes with any other people or tribes. I think they lived in harmony with everyone.

"There was no real leader, but there was a figure called the Liderra who everyone looked to as...I don't know...a village elder, maybe? The Liderra was wise and fair, and made sure everyone's needs were met. He maintained a balance among the Sea Sprites and the other sea and land people and creatures. That's the best way I can describe it."

"Was he a Sea Sprite?"

"Yes, he was," said Natalie. "But at this time, the Sprites lived with all the other creatures of the seas. They didn't make distinctions between each other and they didn't live by themselves like they do now. There were different groups or tribes I suppose you could call them, but none of that made any difference. Everyone lived together."

"I thought you said they lived with people from the land," Lochen asked.

"They did," she answered. "They lived with both. I mean they didn't live among the people of the land. They got along with them. They lived in the sea. The Liderra was like a common figure among all the sea people. I think."

"You don't seem to know a lot about this person," said Lochen.

"None of this was written down," she explained. "It was all handed down from one generation to another by word of mouth. There were some writings over the centuries, but they were either lost or the stories began to change, everyone adding their own emphasis on things. But the basics always remained the same."

"What happened to this Liderra?"

"That's pretty sketchy, too. There was some kind of conflict," Natalie said. "I don't remember who all was involved, but there was some sort of division within the sea people. Things began to get out of hand."

"How?" Lochen asked.

"The wisdom of the Liderra was challenged. People were threatened. They were made to take sides. Although the Liderra never forced his

216

beliefs or opinions on anyone, those who began to oppose him did. War broke out."

"Was there a leader among his opponents?"

"Yes. That much of our history is pretty clear. The Banrian represented all that was evil to the Sea Sprites. It still is a term that means the same thing to this day."

"Who was he?" Lochen asked.

"She," Natalie corrected. "She was the one who rose up against the Liderra. She forced him into some kind of exile. He wanted to avoid the war and the violence, but the Banrian pursued him, trying to hunt him down. No one is really sure what happened to him, but our history tells of someone from the land who helped him."

"Who was that?"

Natalie let out a slight chuckle.

"If you think my knowledge of my people's history is vague, you're going to be even further disappointed. I have no idea. He was a real mystery. I don't think anyone knows who he actually was or where he came from. Some valiant champion from another place – something like that, I suppose.

"All I can recall is that he had been a friend from a distant land. He intervened in some way and the Banrian disappeared, never to be heard from again. Her influence didn't go away, though. To this day, the different people of the sea still remain separate from one another. In spite of the centuries that have passed, the trust was never restored. The Sea Sprites settled in the Cerulean Sea, and I think anyone who supported the Banrian ended up establishing communities in the Viridian Ocean.

"What does all that have to do with your book?"

"I'm not sure," he said. "Nothing, maybe – or everything.

She waited for him to explain, but in his typical fashion, he didn't.

"How did you become princess of the Sea Sprites," he asked.

She was surprised by the sudden change in the topic.

"Umm...do you mean my coronation or inheritance?" she asked.

"I mean how far back in your lineage does your title go," he explained.

She laughed a bit nervously.

"I don't know," she said. "As far back as I can recall. Why?"

"All your ancestors, then," he persisted, "have been the leaders of the Sea Sprites. Is that correct?"

"I guess," she said. "We're not really in charge, though. It's not like a monarchy or dictatorship, if that's what you mean."

"Not at all," he said. "And I didn't mean to sound critical. I was merely attempting to understand the role your ancestors played in the lives of the Sea Sprites."

"They were...I don't know...problem solvers...arbiters...village elders. That kind of thing. Why is that important?"

"Could you be descended from this Liderra?"

"Could I what???" she asked, rising to her feet.

He looked up at her, somewhat startled by her reaction.

"Did I say something wrong?" he asked.

"No," she said. "Not wrong – just preposterous. What would make you think that I was descended from the Liderra?"

"The Liderra was...please sit down," he asked her. "It is somewhat difficult to talk with you standing over me like that, and I am quite comfortable sitting."

She had her hands on her hips and was staring at him. She looked away for a second, over to where Summer and Quinn were still banging, kicking and pushing the stone cube. She shook her head and sat down.

"Better?" she asked.

"Much," he answered. "I know how much my hypotheses have alarmed Quinn – the ones about the symbols perhaps pertaining more to the Kelpies than to us. I haven't any solid evidence at this point and don't want to unsettle him any further."

"Evidence of what?" Natalie asked.

Lochen looked her in the eyes and debated. He seldom liked to explain things when he was uncertain of all the facts. In this case very uncertain of the facts. In truth, he was uncertain of much more than of what he was certain. Even rolling that thought around in his head was confusing.

"Well?" Natalie asked again when he failed to respond.

"Keep in mind this is just a theory," he said. "It's probably not even a theory, yet – more of an option that needs further exploring; perhaps a postulate."

"A what?"

"A postulate," he said. "An assumption – something much less than a theory."

"I don't care what you call it," she cut him off. "And that's not what I meant. Out with it!"

"All right," he said. "Let's assume for the sake of argument that you are descended from this Liderra person. Assume!" he emphasized when he saw her start to object again. "Just assume – for the sake of argument."

"OK," she agreed. "Assume."

"Let's make another assumption," he continued. "This Banrian character, this personification of evil – let's assume this person was a Kelpie. It might be possible then that the symbol that Quinn believes represents you…"

"The squiggly lines that look like waves with the triangle on top of them?"

"Yes," he said. "Those lines and the triangle. It might be possible that this symbol represents both the good and the evil connected with the Sea Sprites – it could represent the Kelpie – this Banrian, and it could represent the Liderra."

"Where do I fit in?" she asked.

"I'm getting to that," he said motioning for her to be patient. "If…and I emphasize 'if'…if you are descended from the Liderra, then this symbol would represent you as well."

"That's a big 'if'," she said.

"I'll admit, there are several leaps in this assumption," he conceded.

"Leaps?" she asked. "More like…I don't know…what's greater than leaps?"

"Bounds, perhaps," said Lochen.

220

"What?"

"Bounds," he repeated. "You asked what was greater than leaps. I believe bounds are greater than leaps – as in 'leaps and bounds.'"

"Never mind."

"Regardless," he continued. "My assumption would make sense of the apparent dual reference of the symbols – to us and to the Kelpies. That would explain, or at least address, Quinn's very strong belief that those symbols represent us, while also explaining why those symbols – the very same symbols – appear in conjunction with the Kelpies."

"I suppose," she admitted grudgingly.

"I admit, though, that I may be forcing facts to fit a hypothetical conclusion."

"Whatever," responded Natalie. "Supposing you're right – and I'm not saying you are – but supposing; then what does that mean?"

"I don't know," he said. "I haven't developed that part of my theory."

"You don't know? That's all you've got? I'm not buying that. You've obviously given this a lot of thought..."

"Not that much, really," he interrupted.

"You've given it more thought than any of us, so, as far as I'm concerned, you've given it a lot of thought."

"If you say so," he started to argue, but conceded when she began to stand up again. "All right; all right. If my theory is correct, then Quinn's original belief that we are special would seem to be accurate. I'm not sure what being 'special' means or entails, but it might explain why we have been drawn together."

"What do you mean?" she asked, sitting back down and lowering her voice.

"I don't believe that our discovery of each other and our repeated association was random. Our first encounter certainly appeared that way, but now I'm not so sure."

"Have you discussed this with any of the others?" asked Natalie.

"No," Lochen said. "Only you, so far."

"Then you haven't really tested your theory, have you?"

"Which part?" he asked.

She rolled her eyes and said, "Any of it – either part: the symbols part or the 'we weren't drawn together by random chance' part. Take your pick. You haven't tested either of these theories, have you?"

"Not extensively," he admitted.

"What about your history?" she asked.

"Mine?"

"Yes. If what you believe is true..."

"What I theorize," he corrected. "I can't quite say I believe it, just yet."

"You know, you can be a real tool sometimes. If what you 'theorize' is true, then it should be true for you, too. So spill it. What about the history of your people?"

"I'm not sure it would parallel your history," he said. "Solveig is my sister, but I am also her sorcerer. I am connected to Solveig, much the same way Stella is connected to you. But Stella is not exactly a Sea Sprite, although that's all she's known."

"That's not true," countered Natalie. "Stella is a Sea Sprite – as much as I am. She was born an Enchantress, though, which gave an additional aspect to her ancestry. Still, she's a Sea Sprite."

"What would that be?"

"What would what be?" asked Natalie.

"The additional aspect to her ancestry," said Lochen. "What do you mean by an additional aspect?"

"You'd have to ask her," said Natalie. "I don't know enough about it. But you're avoiding the question. What about you?"

"Like Solveig," he started to say, "I am of the mountain people, but being a sorcerer, I am somewhat different from them."

"That's putting it mildly," she said. "What makes your situation different than Stella's?"

"On reflection, maybe our situations are not all that different," he mused.

Before he could explain any further, there was a brief flash of light, followed by a distant crack of thunder. Summer and Quinn looked up to the sky, searching for a sign of an approaching storm. Natalie did the same. Lochen, however, looked to the edge of the mountain over which they had climbed earlier that day. They both slowly got to their feet. Natalie's eyes were still fixed on the skies, and Lochen's still fixed on the far side of the mountaintop.

"Where did that come from?" asked Quinn. "I don't see any signs of a storm."

He scanned the sky in every direction. When he noticed that no one had answered his question, he turned back to look at Lochen and Natalie. He could see that Natalie was looking skyward as he and Summer had been doing. But then he noticed that Lochen was looking someplace else. He turned around to see where that was, but saw nothing.

"What?" he said.

He started moving away from the cube and closer to Lochen and Natalie. As he walked he shifted his gaze from the far edge of the mountain to Lochen and back. Lochen hadn't changed what he was looking at – or for.

"What is it?" he asked again. "What do you see?"

"Summer," Lochen called.

"What?" she asked, still looking at the sky for a sign of a storm.

"You need to move over here with the rest of us," he told her. "Quinn, you, too."

Quinn had already started moving towards Lochen and Natalie. Now he moved faster, looking back over his shoulder for – what, he didn't know.

"Why?" asked Summer. "It was just a little thunder and some lightning. I don't see any signs of rain. What's the problem?"

She turned towards Lochen. By now Natalie had sensed the urgency in his voice and was no longer looking at the clouds. She had shifted her gaze from the sky, to Lochen, and then to the far edge of the mountain. Summer saw the look on Lochen's face and noticed that Quinn had moved closer to him. She looked back over her shoulder to the edge of the mountain, but didn't see anything.

"What?" she repeated. "Somebody tell me. What's going on?"

"Summer," shouted Natalie. "Get over here fast."

"But why?" she persisted, even though she started to fly in their direction.

"I think we're about to have company," said Lochen.

Chapter eleven

The landing onto which they reappeared after leaving the alcove was much gentler, although when the sand cleared Vardelos discovered he was standing extremely close to the edge. He shifted his weight to move away, putting unexpected stress on his wounded leg. His knee buckled and he grabbed his closest compatriot to keep from falling. B'nair wondered if the Kelpie had done that purposely.

Before anyone could react, she ordered them to stay close and swept them up again. A second later they were at the top – on the same slick ledge Lochen, Natalie, Quinn and Summer had reached not long before.

Quest of Eight Part Five: Release of the Demons

Richard Reda

The Kelpie stepped away from the circling dust and walked to the inner edge of the mountain lip. She surveyed the line of obelisks and the large cube in the middle of the center one. The cube blocked her view of those who were sitting in wait, but she could sense the presence of the others.

On the center spire, Quinn and Summer had moved to the far edge and were huddled close to Lochen and Natalie, watching and waiting. The cube blocked their view of the arrival of the Kelpie, the Rebbercand and the hobgoblins, but the churning sand and dust was visible over the top.

"What's that?" whispered Quinn.

He pointed at the cloud of dust as it dissipated in the air. Summer was hovering low to the ground when he asked his question. No one answered. No one had an answer for him. She hadn't seen anything and didn't know what he was asking about. She decided to elevate herself to get a better view. Staying behind Quinn, she slowly fluttered upward. Gradually, she was high enough to see over the top of the cube.

At the moment she rose over his shoulder and the distant rim and intervening obelisks came into view, Angin Topan had once again swept her companions up into another cyclone to move them closer to their goal. Summer saw the puff of sand as it vanished from the lip and reappeared on the first spire.

As soon as the cloud landed on the tower, the figures inside became visible. The Kelpie stepped forward, spread her wings and fluttered a few feet upward. In that instant, Summer saw who it was. In that same instant, the Kelpie saw her. Their eyes were locked on one another. Summer felt her blood turn to ice.

"NO!" Summer screamed in horror.

She dropped down behind Quinn as fast as she could, knowing it was too late.

"It's...it's...a...a...it's the Malkia!" she stammered.

The fear in her voice sent chills down the spine of her friends.

"That can't be," she wailed. "This isn't happening. We need to hide. We can't stay here. We need to get away."

"What is it?" asked Quinn.

His voice began to tremble. He hadn't understood what she had said, but he could hear the panic in her voice. He took a step back, coming close to the edge. Natalie reached up and held his arm to keep him from going over the edge. He seemed to have forgotten where he was standing, focusing only on the fear in Summer's voice.

"We need to hide," Summer kept crying. "We need to get out of here. It's the Malkia. Don't you understand? It's the Malkia!"

"There's no place to go!" Lochen said, sternly.

"What are we going to do?" Summer wailed. "We have to do something. We can't stay here. You don't understand."

"Quinn," said Lochen. "Get behind Natalie and me."

"What is it?" he kept repeating.

He was oblivious to Lochen's instructions. He was looking at Summer, then at Lochen, and then at Natalie, but no one was answering his question. His head swiveled from one to the other and then to the other, and back again. Summer kept shouting it was the "Malkia," but he had no idea what that meant. The fear in her voice was warning enough. Whatever it was, he knew it was bad.

"Natalie," Lochen said. "Move forward a little with me."

She did as he asked. Summer flew up immediately behind him, hovering over his shoulder. She was tugging on his ear.

"No," she whispered urgently. "Don't move forward. We have to move back. We have to get out of here."

Quinn had taken another step back and was now perilously close to the edge. Lochen turned around to speak to Summer, and saw where Quinn was. He reached back, grabbed Quinn's clothing and pulled him forward. At the same time he tried as gently as he could to get Summer to stop pulling on his ear.

"No," Quinn objected. "We have to leave."

He reached up and put his hand on Quinn's shoulder, speaking to him as calmly as he could.

"Look at me," he directed. "Don't look ahead, and don't look at Summer. Look at me."

Once he had Quinn's attention, he continued in a calm voice. He kept motioning, his index finger raised, his hand moving back and forth between Quinn's eyes and his.

"There's no place for us to go. Natalie and I will use our powers to protect you. Do you understand? But you have to stop stepping backwards. You're going to fall off the edge. If that happens, we won't be able to help. Do you hear me?"

Quinn stared at Lochen, taking in his words. It took a second or two for them to sink in. When they did, he looked back over his shoulder and saw how close he was to the edge. He took two quick steps away, pushing into Lochen.

"Easy," said Lochen. "That's far enough. Now kneel down and stay behind me."

Quinn did as he was instructed. Summer was still in a state of panic.

"No," she said to Quinn. "Don't get down. We have to leave. It's the Malkia. Don't you understand? We have to hide."

Lochen reached out and grabbed her in his hand, turned her around and moved her close to his face.

"Stop," he commanded.

He waved a hand in front of her face and then snapped his fingers. She stopped talking immediately. Her eyes widened, but seemed to glaze over. Her face went slack. The look on her face was just like Quinn's.

"Did you just cast a spell on them?" Natalie whispered, as if Quinn and Summer weren't close enough to hear.

"I'm sorry I had to do that," he said, and then turned back to Summer. "Now listen to me. There is no place to go. Natalie and I will do everything we can to keep you safe. I know you're afraid, but we need you to be calm. Can you do that?"

She nodded her head silently.

"I'm going to let go now," he continued. "You need to be brave. I know you can be brave. Natalie and I will not let the...the..."

"Malkia," offered Natalie.

"Thank you," Lochen said to her, and then continued with Summer. "We will not let the Malkia harm you, but you cannot panic. Not now. Is that clear?"

She nodded again, and he released his grip. She spread her wings and fluttered over to Quinn, dropping down onto the floor.

"I'm sorry," she said, regaining her awareness. "It was just the sight of the Malkia that...that..."

"I understand," said Lochen. "Stay with Quinn and the two of you stay close to us."

Back on the second spire, the Kelpie lowered down to the floor of the obelisk.

"There are three more spires to reach," she said, "and then we'll be where we need to be. But we are not alone."

"The Enchantress?" asked B'nair, incredulously. "How can that be? How could they have gotten here before us?"

"No," said Angin Topan. "Not the Enchantress. These must be different friends of yours. One of them – a faerie – belongs to me. Another is a giant."

"Him?" growled B'nair. "Could it be the one who saved the Dozor?"

"That I don't know," said the Kelpie. "You can answer that question yourself in a few seconds. I'm sure you will be able to extract whatever information you like."

She spun her arms again and the sand whirled around them, moving them to the second spire. She wasted little time. The instant they landed, she swept them up again and moved them to the third spire. She had taken note of the slick surface when they landed on the rim. She knew she could have moved to the center obelisk in a single motion, but in doing so she would have generated too much speed to ensure they wouldn't skid across the surface.

They could have easily slid into their welcome party, or worse – over the edge. Moving one spire at a time would only take a few seconds, and allowed for more accurate landings. It also allowed her to savor the moment when she would deal with one of those traitorous faeries. She knew the anticipation of her arrival would be escalating the fear in the faerie.

One after the other, she sprung from one spire to the next until they landed on the center one on the opposite side of the cube from their adversaries. As soon as the whirlwind subsided, Angin Topan moved close to the cube. She hugged the side farthest from the others and turned back towards the Rebbercand.

"Deploy your men," she ordered B'nair.

He, too, was behind the protection of the cube. He turned around towards the hobgoblins, and directed them to spread out on either side of the cube. The swordsmen were in front, with the crossbows right behind them. An archer with a long bow was in the back. They all waited for the command to attack.

On the other side of the plateau, Lochen and Natalie watched as the Kelpie disappeared behind the cube. They saw the Rebbercand for a fleeting moment. His movements looked familiar, but the damage to his arm and face made him unrecognizable. Then he, too, disappeared behind the cube. All that was visible were the eight or so heavily armed hobgoblins, prepared to launch an attack.

"More hobgoblins," said Natalie. "Do you suppose they were with the others at the Tower?"

"Yes," said Lochen. "I imagine so. And I also imagine the Rebbercand was there as well. He may be the one we saw on the tattoos on the troll – the one now in possession of the other half of the pendant."

"He has the stone?" wailed Quinn. "Oooohhhh! We don't have a chance."

"It's not him I'm worried about," said Lochen. "It's the Kelpie with him. That's who is likely to be more dangerous. Natalie, can you defend against the hobgoblins? I don't believe they will advance against us, at least not immediately. I assume they will try to disable us with their arrows first."

"Yes," she said.

"The Rebbercand appears only to have an axe," Lochen continued. "He, too, is unlikely to engage in a hand-to-hand assault."

"But what about the power of the pendant?" she asked. "Won't he use that?"

"If it bestowed any magical power in him," said Lochen, "I have to believe he would have used it immediately. But if you look closely, he's deployed the hobgoblins in an offensive posture. He's going to launch an attack with them. Why would he do that if he had powers from the pendant?"

"I hope you're right," answered Natalie.

"Mmm...me, too," stammered Quinn.

Summer was covering her eyes and hiding behind Quinn, afraid the Kelpie would see her again. Lochen and Natalie inched forward to move away from the edge of the plateau. Quinn duck-walked right behind them, and Summer, holding on to his pant leg, was dragged along right behind him.

"I can probably fend off the Rebbercand, too," said Natalie, "or at least throw enough at him to keep him occupied. Would that help? Can you deal with the Kelpie?"

"We shall see," answered Lochen. "I suggest, however, that we not wait until we are attacked. We should..."

Before he could finish his sentence, Natalie jumped forward a few steps and swept her arms from left to right. A wave of energy blasted from her towards the enemy. B'nair ducked behind the cube, next to the Kelpie. The hobgoblins were knocked over; some of them perilously close to the edge of the plateau.

"What were you saying?" Natalie asked.

"I was about to say that we should take the offensive," answered Lochen, "rather than assume a defensive posture. However..."

He interrupted his response by sending a ball of wind and ice towards the Kelpie.

"...it seems my suggestion was unnecessary," he finished saying, flicking his wrist once more as an afterthought.

The ball bounced across the floor of the spire, increasing in size as it went. It struck the cube and flew up into the air, coming down immediately above the Kelpie. She saw it at the last minute and waved it aside. What she didn't see was the blast of freezing water he had curled around the opposite side of the cube at almost the same time. The second blast was the result of the afterthought – a one-two punch Lochen hoped would catch their opponents off guard.

The blast of water struck both the Kelpie and B'nair, pushing them from behind the protection of the cube. As soon as they were exposed, Lochen let loose. He shot balls of fire, rocks and a gush of oil at them. Lochen hoped to increase the slipperiness of the stone with the flood of oil. If it worked, another blast of wind or energy might be enough to push them all over the side of the plateau.

Angin Topan was fooled the first time, but she would not be fooled again. She flew up into the air and thrust her arm downward, creating a wall that blocked the oncoming attack. At the same time she sent her own barrage. Hundreds of arrows filled the sky and rained down on Lochen and the others.

Lochen waved his hand and the arrows turned into feathers and then dissolved into nothing. As he was doing this, the Kelpie shot hundreds of shards of glass along the plateau floor towards their feet. These were immediately followed by a hail of rocks from above. She was alternating between aerial assaults and ground attacks. At the same time, the barrage of arrows continued from the hobgoblins.

The Kelpie was waving one arm after the other, firing one spell on top of another. It was becoming more than Lochen could keep up with. At the same time, the hobgoblins were firing arrows and crossbows. Natalie was deflecting these as best she could, but the Kelpie had cast a spell on the hobgoblin's armaments. As Natalie tried to defend against the missiles, they changed shape and direction and continued on their path.

It was all too much. More was coming at them than they could defend against. They had not been prepared for such an attack. In an act of desperation, Natalie swirled her hand and created a bubble around the four of them.

"Stop casting spells," she shouted to Lochen. "They won't penetrate the bubble. They'll only bounce back on us."

They stood on the inside as assault after assault struck the dome and fell away ineffectually.

"That's certainly a relief," said Lochen. "However, it prevents us from fighting back or doing anything to keep them from opening that cube."

"I'm sorry," said Natalie. "I hadn't expected spells on the hobgoblins' arrows. It got to be too much for me to defend against."

"Is this thing going to hold?" asked Quinn.

He slowly stood up, still ducking reflexively as the arrows, rocks, glass and all sorts of other things struck the dome. The bubble was slightly higher than the top of his head and slightly wider around than the reach of both of his arms. He stepped forward and pressed against it. It felt soft, but it moved only slightly at his touch.

Then he turned around to look at the back of the bubble to see how far it extended. It wasn't very big, he thought. Summer slid to the back of the bubble, and was the only one to notice that the fabric of the protective sphere stretched beneath them as well as above them. They were completely enclosed.

"Yes," Natalie assured Quinn. "It will hold."

Once B'nair could see that the spells from the Kelpie could not penetrate the bubble, and that nothing could come from inside the bubble directed at him and the others, he stepped defiantly away from the cube. He waited for some kind of opening to appear in the clear dome that sheltered his attackers. He presented himself as an appealing target, but it was not appealing enough for them to break their cover.

That was when he saw Quinn stand up to touch the inside, and then turn around to look at the back of it. That was when he recognized the giant who had slid across the collapsing bridge; the giant who had rescued the Dozor; the giant who had been instrumental in his disfigurement. The images of that event flooded his memory. The rage that filled him burst to the surface.

He glared at the giant's back as he began to storm towards the bubble. He was blind to the looks on the faces of the Sorcerer and the Sea Sprite. The faerie was hidden from his view, but even if she wasn't, he would have been blind to her as well. All he could see was the giant. He raised his axe in both hands as he strode menacingly ahead.

"What's he doing?" Natalie said, her voice edged in panic.

Lochen looked at the approaching Rebbercand. There was something familiar about him. He tried to look past the scarred face and the burned arm. He studied the eyes that were coming closer and closer.

The axe wielding threat wasn't looking at him, or at Natalie, Lochen realized. He turned to see what the Rebbercand was looking at. It was Quinn. Then the pieces fell into place.

"I believe he thinks he's going to attack us," said Lochen. "He seems to be fixated on Quinn. I think he's one of the Rebbercands from the Trepan mines. In fact, if I'm not mistaken, that was the leader of the mining operation."

At the sound of his name Quinn turned around and looked down at Lochen. But Lochen wasn't looking at him. Lochen was looking at something on the outside of the bubble. Quinn raised his head to see where Lochen was looking, having momentarily forgotten about the attack. That was when he saw this very large and very angry Rebbercand bearing down on him with a very large axe in his hands, raised high above his head.

B'nair reached the front edge of the bubble immediately after Quinn turned to face him. He brought his axe down with all his strength, aiming to split the giant's head like a melon. The blade of the axe struck the dome. The substance of which it was made immediately thickened around the blade, slowing and finally stopping it.

On the inside of the bubble, there was no indication of any penetration by the axe blade. It was as if the leading edge had disappeared. The clear wall of the sphere shook slightly with the impact, but didn't break or part. Quinn was frozen, staring at the large blade suspended inches above his face. On the inside, the portion of the blade that looked as if it had pierced the sphere was merely a mass of glittering air.

B'nair couldn't understand what had happened. His axe had cut stone. It should have burst this bubble without stopping. He pulled it free and swung again. This time Quinn saw it coming and raised his arms unnecessarily in defense.

The second strike was no different than the first. It sunk into the bubble, moving it little, and breaking it not at all. As before, on the outside, it appeared as if the leading edge of the blade had disappeared, but on the inside, once again, it was nothing but a series of miniscule flashes of light.

"What's he doing?" shouted Quinn, ignoring the fact that the blade had not penetrated the bubble. "He could have killed me."

"I presume that's exactly what he was trying to do," said Lochen. "You seem to be the source of his irritation. I wasn't aware that you even knew him. What exactly did you do to incur such wrath?"

"This isn't funny," Quinn shouted again. "He could have killed me."

"You said that already," said Lochen. "And I was not making an attempt at humor. He seems to be particularly annoyed with you. Is he the one that you saved Sean from? Is he the one that you dropped into the lava river?"

"I don't know," shouted Quinn. "I don't care. He could have killed me!"

"You don't have to shout," said Natalie.

"I'm not shouting," shouted Quinn. "He could have killed me!"

"Yes," said Lochen. "We know. Trust me. If he could, he'd kill all of us. He wouldn't limit his mayhem to you."

"What do we do now?" asked Summer.

She was still crouched down behind Quinn, but was fighting to overcome the sudden shock of seeing an ancient omen of evil.

238

Richard Reda

"There's not much we <u>can</u> do," said Lochen. "Our exchange of spells is at a stalemate. They can't reach us and we can't reach them. It looks like all we can do at this point is to wait and watch."

"Is the thing going to hold?" shouted Quinn.

Finally able to gather his wits, he had moved as far back as he could. B'nair had stopped trying to cut into the bubble, but was seething – glaring at Quinn.

"Yes," repeated Natalie. "I've already told you. It will hold. It held back thousands of tons of pressure under the water. There's nothing they can throw at us or do to us that can penetrate these things. Trust me. We're safe in here."

"And, unfortunately," said Lochen, "they're safe out there."

While B'nair was unsuccessfully trying to split Quinn's head, Angin Topan was fluttering around the cube, looking for a way to break it open. The hobgoblins had fired several volleys of arrows at the bubble, but seeing that they had no effect, they stopped. Vardelos, seeing that no attack would be launched, gratefully dropped to the ground to ease the pain in his leg. The exertion had wrung him out.

"Rebbercand," the Kelpie shouted. "Forget about them. They aren't going anywhere. Come here and open this tomb. We can deal with them later, and I promise you, aside from the faerie, they are all yours to do with as you please."

B'nair was breathing heavily from both the exertion of his attack and from the anger still burning inside him. His ears were filled with a roaring sound. It was the blood in his body that was coursing through his veins, but it might as well have been a raging storm. He heard nothing else, including Angin Topan.

The Kelpie flew over next to him, hovering beside his face.

"You will have time to deal with them later," she said in a low voice.

Those words he heard. He slowly shifted his gaze from Quinn to her. It took a few seconds for him to realize that she had been speaking to him and what she had said. He looked back at the cube and the hobgoblins that were gathered on the other side of it, and then back at the four figures protected by the mysterious bubble.

"Aside from the faerie," Angin Topan told him, "you can have the others – all of them – and do what you like with them."

She turned her head and looked down at Summer. Summer was once again frozen with fear. The Kelpie revealed a reptilian smile, lowered herself closer to the bottom of the bubble, and then, her eyes still glued on Summer and with the same smirk on her face, blew her a kiss. Summer ducked her head, looking away. The Kelpie rose back up to B'nair's eye level and made a sound that B'nair thought was meant to be a chuckle. Then they both turned back to the cube.

"Can you move this bubble forward any?" Lochen asked Natalie once the two attackers had turned away.

"Sure, but why?" she asked.

"If you can move it forward far enough, can you encompass the cube as well?"

"I'm not sure about that," she said. "I don't think I can expand it without including the two of them."

She gestured to B'nair and the Kelpie.

"If you enclose them, can you envelope them in a separate bubble inside this bubble?"

"No," she said. "I don't know. Maybe. But I'd have to do it fast enough to keep them from hurting one of us. I don't think I can do that. I'd probably have to open this bubble. I don't think I should try doing that."

Lochen looked at Quinn and Summer. He agreed that the risk was too great.

"If we don't do something," he said, "we'll be sitting her uselessly while they release another one of the Kelpies."

"I don't see any alternative," said Natalie. "Even if we stay back here and I open the bubble so that one of us can cast a spell, that won't get us any further than we are now. It will only delay the inevitable."

"You CAN'T open the bubble," wailed Quinn.

He had been listening to their conversation with utter horror. He couldn't imagine that they were even considering opening the bubble.

"What if you aren't able to close it fast enough?" he added. "What if that guy with the axe gets inside?"

"He won't get inside," said Lochen. "We won't be opening the bubble."

He watched helplessly as B'nair and Angin Topan reached the cube. B'nair walked all the way around it, taking his time, glancing back every so often at the sphere. He seemed to know the four could do nothing to stop him and he was savoring the moment. Finally, he stopped at the side of the cube, raised his axe, took one more look back at his observers, and then cut into the stone box with all his strength.

Unlike with the bubble, his axe cut into the granite crypt and cracked it open. The outer shell split and then began to fragment. The initial crack spread across the cube to the ground and then zig-zagged the entire width of the plateau, causing B'nair to step back. The strike of his axe on the cube spider-webbed in every direction across the top and down the sides. It continued to create thousands of tiny particles along the surface, and then it fell apart, dropping away in pieces no thicker than an egg shell.

The particles skittered across the smooth surface of the plateau. The hobgoblins had seen enough of the curses placed on these tombs, and were able to avoid the fragments as they crystallized, cracked and then disappeared harmlessly. Once more, B'nair felt the charge emitted by the stone, and wondered what would have happened if his comrades had failed to be careful.

Underneath was what looked like a large figure, carved of stone and curled on its side. At first nothing happened. The debris from the shattered covering coated the figure in a layer of dust. A look of doubt became visible on B'nair's face, but the Kelpie merely looked on expectantly. Then the figure began to move.

Slowly it uncurled its legs, stretching them out. The dust from the demolished outer layer of the cube rolled off the legs to the ground. One arm extended upward, and then the other reached out across the floor of the plateau. Finally, its head emerged. The figure rolled over onto its stomach, brought one knee underneath and pushed itself up to a standing position. As its torso rose and its back straightened, it seemed to climb forever.

Fully upright, the creature stood ten and a half feet into the air. It was gray from head to toe – the gray of the granite in which it had been entombed. Its clothing was gray, its hair was gray, and its skin was gray. When it opened its large eyes, they were gray. It shook off the last remnants of the covering under which it had been locked away, but nothing altered the gray coloring from head to foot.

The figure wore a long multi-layered cloak. The material looked like stone, but moved like silk. It fluttered in the slight breeze and swayed with the creature's movement. It dragged along the ground, keeping in contact with the earth from which the Kelpie sprung. The sleeves were long and billowing. It had long hair that faded into the folds of the clothing. Its face was squared as if chipped in stone.

It took a step forward, staggered slightly, but caught itself. It looked around, first at B'nair, who had freed it, then to the hobgoblins who were staring in awe. It took a tentative step towards them, but then stopped and turned to Angin Topan. When it spotted the Kelpie, its chiseled lips broadened into a smile.

"Angin Topan," it said.

The voice rumbled like an avalanche. It was deep and gravely, but oddly feminine.

"My old friend."

The smaller Kelpie fluttered upward to nearly eye level.

"Akmen Milzu," she replied. "It's good to see you once again."

They studied each other in silence for a few seconds.

"You've brought some new friends, I see," said Akmen Milzu.

The stone giant gestured to the others standing nearby watching the two Kelpies.

"Yes," she answered. Gesturing to B'nair, she added, "The Rebbercand is the one with the power that freed you. The hobgoblins are his associates."

It was not lost on B'nair that neither he nor the hobgoblins were referred to as partners in any way. It was more as if they were servants, or a necessary bother – an afterthought. The mountain Kelpie nodded her head in understanding. She then turned to look at the place in which she had been held for two thousand years. Then she turned towards the bubble and the figures held within.

243

"And who are they?" she asked. "More friends?"

"No," answered Angin Topan. "They are intruders – minions of the Alchemist and the witch. Those you see, however, are not alone. Others are out there somewhere, and one of them has a piece of the pendant."

The reference to the pendant captured Akmen Milzu's attention.

"A piece?" she asked. "Not all of it?"

"No," answered Angin Topan, as she pointed to B'nair. "Half is with one of them. The Rebbercand has the other half."

The larger Kelpie shifted her gaze to B'nair. It was right about this time he was beginning to think less attention to him would be better. He held his ground, but felt slightly intimidated by her stare. He wasn't sure if he should continue to hold her gaze or bow his head. He wisely decided to say nothing, though.

"Are any of them important to us?" Akmen Milzu asked.

She gestured to the four in the bubble without bothering to look in their direction.

"No," answered Angin Topan. "Not at all."

She buzzed her wings and turned towards the bubble, giving one more look towards Summer. Then she turned back to her friend.

"There is a faerie among them that I would enjoy toying with," she continued. "And the Rebbercand has a special interest in the large one among them. But none of them is really significant to our needs."

"We need waste no time with them," declared Akmen Milzu.

She gave a swipe of her left hand while she was still facing the smaller Kelpie. Without warning an invisible wave washed across the bubble and it was pushed over the edge of the plateau into the chasm below. Then the mountain Kelpie looked at the crack that stretched across the obelisk immediately beneath their feet. She slowly raised her left leg and brought it back down with a thunderous stomp.

The crack that had run under the cube, which had been created by B'nair's axe, began to widen. As it opened up, the Kelpie stepped to the side where B'nair and the hobgoblins were standing and then gave the other half a push with her foot.

The broken half of the enormous spire teetered for a second and then began to drop away towards the line of other pillars. It struck the nearest spire with a crash. The impact caused that one to shift and fall, crashing into the next one. Like dominos, one after the other, the stone towers fell into and on top of one another, down into the abyss, following the bubble carrying Lochen, Quinn, Summer and Natalie.

The Kelpie staggered again, surprised and dismayed that the slight exertion had weakened her as much as it did. Angin Topan fluttered closer.

"You will be weak after such a long exile," she said to her friend. "You will need to replenish your strength."

The giant Kelpie sat down with a thump and looked around. Angin Topan turned to B'nair.

"She needs food," she announced, as if he could provide whatever was needed.

"And what does this one eat?" he asked the smaller Kelpie.

He was at a loss as to what he was expected to do. There was no sign of any kind of vegetation. There were only rocks in every direction.

He wondered if that would whet the Kelpies appetite. The mountain Kelpie looked at him, and then at the hobgoblins.

"One of them will do," Akmen Milzu said to him, swiping her hand in the direction of the line of hobgoblins. "You can choose which one."

The response had stunned B'nair to silence. At first he thought he was being tested. He looked at the stone Kelpie and then at Angin Topan, waiting for some kind of clarification or explanation. They were serious, he realized. It then dawned on him that unless he offered one of the hobgoblins, he might be the one to replenish the Kelpie's powers.

He turned to the small group of hobgoblins. They had all been standing nearby and had heard the statement from the Kelpie. Some of them looked behind them, seeking a place to escape. There was nowhere to go. Vardelos was unable to move. Even if he had been, he wouldn't. He stood his ground looking at the other hobgoblins.

"You can have him," B'nair said, gesturing to Vardelos.

Vardelos hadn't been looking at B'nair, and was unaware of who had been offered until the Kelpie reached forward and snatched him up. She opened her mouth widely. Her jaws extended – unhinging like a snake's. As she was lifting him into the air and towards her open mouth, he looked back at the Rebbercand.

"But, sir," he said, pleading. "Why me? I've served you faithfully. I trusted you. Why would you do this?"

B'nair looked at the hobgoblin as the Kelpie began to chew on his feet and legs. Over the screaming, and before Vardelos lost consciousness, he answered.

"Because it's my nature."

Chapter twelve

ochen and Natalie were standing at the front of the bubble watching as the Mountain Kelpie unfolded from her mausoleum. Quinn had been watching from behind, looking over Lochen's shoulder, and Summer, still trying to hide on the floor, was watching from around Quinn's feet. It was taking everything she had to overcome her fear of the Malkia. They were all taken unawares when the gray Kelpie swiped her hand, and their sphere slid off the plateau.

"Oh, my," said Lochen in reaction to the sudden weightlessness as the bubble dropped into the abyss. "I hadn't anticipated that."

"Do something!" shouted Quinn. "Do something. We're falling."

Natalie had been thrown to the part of the bubble that was now at the front. She had a clear view of the quickly approaching bottom of the chasm. She knew that the bubble would hold, but, in spite of that, it wouldn't cushion their fall. It would also not prevent them from colliding with one another as they were thrown about in the small space. She needed to do something quickly or they'd be in real trouble.

She immediately waved her hand and enveloped Quinn in his own bubble. He looked stunned at being enclosed so closely. Before he could comment, she then did the same thing for Lochen. Summer was ricocheting off the sides and it was difficult for her to capture her. She missed twice, and then decided to put another bubble or two around Quinn and Lochen. They'd all need the extra padding.

The triple bubbles around the other two also reduced the space in which Summer could bounce, making her an easier target. One, two, three – three bubbles around Summer and then she covered herself. The plummeting sphere was now filled with bubbles inside of bubbles inside of other bubbles. She hoped it would be enough to protect them. It had to be; it was the best she could do.

Just as she finished the third one around herself, the sphere caromed off the sides and then hit bottom. It bounced up once and then again before settling on the bottom. Natalie was about to reverse the spells when she saw through the distorted layers an avalanche of rocks and boulders following after them.

"Hold on," she yelled.

Her warning was simply a reflex. There was nothing to hold on to. By the time the sphere had reached bottom, Natalie was off to one side, Summer had been jostled to the bottom, Lochen was in the middle and Quinn was at the top – face up. He looked up at her warning and saw all that was bearing down on them. He began to scream as he watched the tons of boulders crashed towards their small shell.

"Hold on to what?" he shouted. "Get us out of here. This thing isn't going to hold. We're going to be pummelized."

Lochen, who had been turned in the opposite direction, had no idea of what was headed their way.

"I think you mean pulverized," he corrected. "I'm not sure, but I believe pummelized is not a real word. Regardless. I don't understand your concern. We've already landed. We're safe now. There should be no cause for..."

He had been wiggling his body like a worm, trying to twist himself around. As he made the comment about being safe now, he finally managed to turn himself sufficiently to see what Quinn had been watching. Before he could finish his last sentence, he was just in time to see the boulders about to land on them.

"Oh, my," he said. "I hadn't anticipated that either. I see what you mean."

"It will hold," promised Natalie.

"I'm sure it will," said Lochen. "The question is will it flatten? It may hold, but if yields under the pressure of those rocks, we'll be ground to powder."

"That's not something I need to hear right now," mumbled Summer from the bottom.

She couldn't see what they were talking about, but the anxiety in their voices was enough for her.

"That's what I said," shouted Quinn in response to Lochen's comment about being ground to powder. "Pummelized."

Before Lochen or anyone else could say another word, the boulders began landing. They pounded down on the small sphere, battering and burying it, but not breaking or flattening it. The closest ones were inches from Quinn's face. He was too frightened to close his eyes, and could only hang there, immobilized in the layers Natalie had spun around him.

"THIS IS NOT FUN!" he gasped.

He had been holding his breath, waiting for the rocks to crush him. Once he realized he hadn't been squashed, his relief immediately turned to anger.

"Who does something like that? We need to get out of here and go home. Why are they doing this?"

He shouted one question after another, not waiting or expecting an answer. In fact, he was merely shouting to shout; venting his fear and anger. He really had no idea what he was saying. When he stopped shouting, he was panting to catch his breath. In the momentary silence, Lochen made his own observation.

"That was very quick thinking, Natalie," he said. "Thank you."

"You're welcome," she said. "I think. I probably should have thought of something else. Maybe we could have avoided being buried alive, but this was the first thing that came to mind."

She began to slowly and carefully reverse the process, starting with herself. The outer layer surrounding her popped and then sizzled as it dissolved into nothing.

"Whoa," said Summer. "What was that?"

She had slipped to the bottom and was face down. She heard the popping noise and could feel the slight shift as Natalie freed herself from one layer after the other.

"Don't worry," said Natalie. "I'm just giving us some room."

"What about air?" shouted Quinn. "Is there enough air in here?"

"There's enough air," said Natalie. "The bubble generates oxygen on its own. How do you think we lived under the ocean for years?"

"I don't know," said Quinn, still shouting, but slowly running out of steam. "I wasn't there."

She popped the second one, shifted herself more to the side and popped the third one. Then she started on Lochen.

"You can take care of the others first," he told her. "I'm actually enjoying the floating sensation."

"No," she answered. "I have to get you out next. Even though the outer bubble held, it did get a little misshapen. I'll need your help when I release Quinn. We'll have to get him resituated to a more upright position. I'll undo Summer last. Sorry Summer."

"That's all right," Summer answered.

"I'm just afraid that there won't be enough room for her to maneuver if I get her out earlier, and, if one of us slips wrong, she could get hurt."

In a few seconds, after more popping and sizzling sounds, Lochen was freed. Then Natalie started to unpeel Quinn. When she removed the first layer, his weight shifted; he spun backwards and then forwards, and he began to panic again.

"Wait," he shouted. "What if those rocks cave in? What if they move? Shouldn't you leave these things in place?"

"I believe the rocks have settled," said Lochen. "They seem to be wedged against one another. I'm assuming the Kelpie toppled the spires between him and us. If that's correct, then there are several hundred tons of stone on top of us. I doubt that anything we do in here would be sufficient to disturb that much mass."

"What?" shouted Quinn again. "Several hundred? Tons? How do we get out of here? What are we going to do?"

"We're going to start by getting everyone out of their cocoons," said Natalie. "Then we'll figure out what to do."

She continued to remove the bubble layers from Quinn. When she disposed of the last one, neither she nor Lochen were ready for him. They had expected him to stand upright and only need some minor steadying. Instead, he stepped backwards onto the bubble in which Summer was covered. She was oblivious, being completely protected in several coverings, but Quinn was startled.

He tried to overcompensate, but the interior of the sphere was too small. He knocked his arms into Lochen and Natalie, pushing them away. His feet flew into the air and he landed on his butt, right on top of Summer. She still didn't feel any undue pressure, but her multiple bubbles were pressed against the bottom of the outer shell.

At that same instant the rock against which the sphere was pinned, slid back and was replaced by a face. The face was round with large circular cheeks. Between the cheeks was a large, wide nose with a huge wart on the right side. Above the cheeks on either side of the nose were two large brown eyes under a single, very bushy eyebrow that extended over both eyes. Beneath the nose was a wide mouth with sliver thin lips over a broad, square chin. On the chin, as if to balance the wart on the nose, was a nearly identical wart on the opposite side.

Summer let out an ear piercing scream. The face staring at her was looking at her eye to eye, separated only by the layers of bubble. She screamed again, as one of the eyes rotated, taking in the entire sphere, while the other eye remained fixed on her.

Quest of Eight Part Five: Release of the Demons

Richard Reda

Natalie immediately peeled the remaining layers off Summer, and she shot like an arrow as far away as she could get. Once she was out of the way, the others were able to see the source of her shock. The face was pressed up against the bubble, distorting it even further, as if that were even possible.

On either side of the face was a pair of hands, also pressed up against the bubble. The hands were thick and wide, the fingers short and stubby. On top of the face was a covering of thick, curly, dark hair with flecks of gray. The hair was covered with a long, pointed hat.

"It appears to be a gnome," said Lochen.

"I don't care what it is," said Summer. "It scared the life out of me."

"Is it dangerous?" asked Quinn.

He was hopping from one foot to the other, trying to get even further away from it than Summer was, which was impossible. He was also bumping his head against the rocks that had buried the bubble.

"I don't know," said Lochen. "They have always kept to themselves, tending to be quite anti-social. I've never known them to be outright hostile, although given that we are so close to the place of detention of one of the Kelpies, I couldn't guarantee that they would be friendly."

"We'll be all right for the time being," said Natalie. "At least he can't get inside with us."

The gnome turned its head from side to side, its face still pressed against the bubble. Its one eye remained fixed on one or another of the occupants while the other continued to scan the entire bubble. Then it knocked on the bubble with one of its hands. Hearing nothing, it pressed its lips against the outer coating and appeared to be blowing against it.

Instead of blowing another bubble inside the bubble, the gnome's cheeks filled with air, distorting the face even further. Then the face backed away. Its right hand began to move around the bottom portion of the sphere, feeling it.

The gnome started prodding the bubble with its index finger. In a few seconds, the finger broke through into the interior. Summer let out another scream.

"How did he do that?" she shouted. "I thought you said this bubble couldn't be penetrated."

"It can't," said Natalie. "At least I thought it couldn't. I don't know how this is happening. I've never seen anything like this."

The stubby little finger wiggled back and forth, and then began to move in a circle. The circle got wider and wider, slowly enlarging the opening. The occupants could feel a shift in the air flow, although the bubble's structure never weakened. The rocks all around it remained unmoved.

After a few moments, the hole was almost a foot in diameter. The finger withdrew and the gnome popped his head inside. Summer screamed again.

"What's he doing?" she shouted. "What does he want?"

"She," said the gnome in a high pitched voice.

"She?" asked Quinn. "Summer? You want Summer? Well, you can't have her. We won't let you have her."

"What's a Summer?" asked the gnome.

"That's me," Summer answered. "But you can't have me."

"I don't want you," said the gnome.

"Then why did you say 'she?'" asked Lochen.

"Because the little one with the wings – the Summer – said 'what does he want?' I'm not a he. I'm a she. Don't worry. I'm not offended. It happens all the time. Well not any more, I suppose; but it used to."

The gnome pulled her head out of the opening and disappeared into the rocks. A few seconds later, she popped her head back in.

"Are you all going to stay here?" she asked. "Or do you want to get out?"

The gnome didn't wait for an answer. She removed her head and disappeared once more. Lochen began to follow, but Natalie pulled him back.

"What are you doing?" she asked. "We don't know if he...she...is friendly or not. You could be going into a trap."

Lochen moved back inside and looked around the bubble. He motioned to the surrounding rocks.

"Unless you have a way to dig us out in that direction," he said, "I don't see an abundance of alternative options."

He, like the gnome, didn't wait for an answer. He ducked through the opening and disappeared. Natalie took a deep breath, groaned something about this being against her better judgment, and then followed after him. Quinn looked at Summer and then at the rocks above him, and decided he'd take his chances with the gnome. He didn't wait for Summer. He bent over and pushed his head first through the opening.

He was certain his body was going to get stuck. He hadn't thought about that until his head went through. But to his surprise the hole seemed to expand enough for him to fit. Once he was through, Summer debated for only a second. As frightened as she was, she was more frightened to be left alone. She shot through the opening seconds before it closed up, sealing tightly immediately after her exit.

The hole from the bubble led to a short gap in the rocks, which led to a large, arched hallway. The hall was about ten feet long with a ceiling that rose higher and higher as they walked forward. From there, the hall opened to a cavernous underground hall. It was at least thirty feet in diameter. The ceiling was high above them and covered with stalactites. Some of them stretched all the way to the floor like giant pillars. The floor was as black as coal, which Lochen quickly discovered it was. There were lanterns hanging from several places, providing enough light for them to see. They stopped at the end of the passageway, not crossing into the hall. They looked around them. As far as they could tell, they were alone. The gnome was nowhere to be seen.

"Over here," came a shout.

They looked around in all directions, since the voice echoed off the walls and ceiling. They took a few steps forward through a large archway into the main part of the hall. There were several chairs arranged in a circle. There was no other furniture around, and there was no apparent reason for the chairs to be there, but there they were. And there was the gnome. Sitting regally in one of the chairs.

The seats of the chairs were very low to the ground, but probably not too low for a gnome. They were elaborately carved out of coal, but rubbed and polished to a hard, dust-free finish. The feet of the chairs were carved in the shape of skulls, which did not give any of the visitors a good feeling.

There were low, narrow arms on either side of the seat and backs that rose four to five feet in the air. Each chair was similar, but not the same. The carvings, all elaborate, were unique, representing trees, leaves and small woodland animals hidden in the branches. Lochen noticed that aside from the one occupied by the gnome, there were eight chairs. It was as if they had been expected – all eight of them.

"Are you them?" asked the gnome. "Although, I suppose if you're not, I'm in really big trouble. In that case, I hope you're them. Are you them?"

"We've been asked that before," said Lochen. "While we're not entirely sure what it means, I believe you are correct. We are 'them.'"

The gnome hopped off her chair and waddled up to Lochen. She was barely two feet tall, and almost as wide as she was high. She wore a bright yellow shirt with full sleeves under a brown leather vest that was cinched by a wide brown leather belt. She had on baggy brown pants that were tucked into the tops of brown boots, covering feet that were very wide and very long.

The boots had large gold buckles on the top and squared toes. Lochen estimated that the gnome's feet were about a third as long as the gnome was high. Her legs were shorter than her feet and she wobbled from side to side as she walked. The long pointed hat on her head – also brown – added another foot to her height.

She came up to him and stood within inches, running her eyes up and down him. Lochen tried to look into her eyes, but one was moving upward while the other was moving downward. He wasn't sure which one to look into. She moved next to Natalie and did the same thing.

Natalie, who also tried to look into her eyes, had to look away. The separately moving eyes of the gnome were making her dizzy. The gnome didn't seem to notice.

Then she moved to Quinn and nearly toppled over as she bent back to see his head.

"Hummph!" was all she said, holding on to her hat to keep it from falling off.

257

Then she waddled over to where Summer was hovering and immediately took a step backwards. She seemed to be as uncertain of Summer as Summer was of her. When she completed her inspection, she returned to Lochen and gave him the once over again.

"Where's the rest of you?" she asked.

Lochen looked puzzled. He ran his hands over his body and looked down at his legs.

"The rest of me?" he asked. "I believe I'm all here."

"Not you," said the gnome. "You."

"I'm sorry," said Lochen. "Were you speaking to me or someone else?"

"I'm speaking to you," she said. "Where's the rest of you?"

"As I said, madam," he responded, pointing to himself. "Here."

"No," she said. "I didn't mean you. I meant you."

Lochen looked back at the others for some help. Natalie shrugged her shoulders. Quinn shook his head, and Summer made a motion indicating she thought the gnome was crazy. He moved a bit sideways to look at her head on and bent closer to look into her eyes, trying to make sure both of them were fixed on him, and that one of them was not rotating wildly.

"I'm all here," he said slowly and a bit more loudly.

"I'm not deaf," she said equally as loud, taking a step back from him. "And I'm not blind. I can see that you are all here. I want to know where's the rest of you?"

Lochen smacked his hand against his forehead. He was clearly missing something. He decided on another approach.

"Do you mean, 'where are the others?'" he asked.

The gnome crouched down as if ducking out of sight and stretched out both arms. She looked up towards the ceiling and then around the great hall. She turned slowly in a circle, examining the depths of the hall, and then turned back to Lochen.

"Are the others here?" she asked in a whisper. "Where?"

"Let's start again," suggested Lochen. "There are four of us, not including you, of course. All of us are here. There are, however, four more in our group, but they are not here."

"That's all I asked," grumbled the gnome as if she had been insulted. "You might as well sit down."

She motioned to the chairs and took a seat herself. When they were all settled, she jumped up.

"No," she said, insisting they were sitting in the wrong seats.

She grabbed them by the sleeve one at a time and rearranged them. Then she sat back down.

"No," she said again. "That's still not right."

She jumped up, grabbed them one by one, moving them once more. She sat down, but immediately jumped up again, deciding that the new arrangement was still wrong. She moved them again. No sooner were they seated than she jumped up, waving her arms, once more telling them that it was still wrong. This went on three more times before she was satisfied. When she was done, they were all in the seats they had originally taken.

"So," she said when it was clear they would not be exchanging seats again. "You're them. I've been waiting a long time. Do you have any idea how long?"

"Two thousand years?" asked Natalie, having heard this from earlier sentinels.

"No!" said the gnome. "Wrong! It's been two thousand years."

The gnome folded her arms across her chest. Natalie looked at Summer and mouthed the words, "that's what I said." Summer again made a motion indicating that the gnome was crazy. Quinn only squirmed in his seat.

"What can I do for you?" the gnome asked.

"I don't know," said Lochen. "Are you a sentinel?"

"No!" said the gnome. "I'm a gnome. Oryxx is my name. That's Oryxx with two zekkas."

"Two what?" asked Quinn.

"Zekkas," said the gnome, holding up two stubby fingers. "Two of them."

They all looked at her blankly. She jumped up off her chair and walked back and forth in front of them as if she was lecturing a class of dull witted students.

"Oryxx! Sapphquoise, pinarett, ninnius, zekka, zekka. Two zekkas, like I said."

She counted the letters out on her extended fingers as if she was counting numbers.

"I'm sorry," said Natalie, waving her hand to get the gnome's attention. "I didn't understand a word of that – except for the end part."

"The two zekkas part?" asked the gnome.

"No," answered Natalie. "The, 'like I said' part. That's all I understood."

"I think I understand," said Lochen in an attempt to avoid another spelling lesson. "Your name is Oryxx and it's spelled with two zekkas – on the end. Is that correct?"

"Well, yeah," said the gnome as if it was obvious. "That's what I've been saying. None of you seems to be particularly bright."

She waddled back to her chair and hopped back onto the seat.

"I'm supposed to help you," she declared. "Do you need help? I can't make you smarter, so don't ask me to do that. I'm not sure there's enough magic in the universe to do that. I know I can't do it."

"Are you a sentinel," Lochen asked again.

"NO!" she shouted. "I already told you. I'm a gnome."

"Then why do you think you're supposed to help us?" Natalie asked as patiently as she could.

"Because that Alchemist guy made me a sentinel," the gnome answered waving her head back and forth, as if she had been asked the most stupid question possible.

"But he just asked you..." Summer started to object.

"Never mind," Lochen said to Summer out of the side of his mouth. "It's not worth trying to sort out."

He turned to the gnome.

"How are you supposed to help us?" he asked.

"I don't know," she replied. "What do you need?"

Lochen thought for a second. There were so many things they needed he didn't know where to begin. Then a thought struck him. He pulled from his belt the book that the Navedi sentinel had given him. He showed it to the gnome.

"Can you read this?" he asked.

The gnome leaned over to look at the book and then jumped out of her seat, ran around behind her chair and poked her head out around the far side.

"Where did you get that?" she asked in a loud whisper.

Before Lochen could respond, she added, "Never mind. I don't want to know. Put that thing away. You shouldn't have it. That's how I got in trouble in the first place – reading something I wasn't supposed to read. I'll never do that again. Look where it got me? Here. Waiting for you, and you're not all here. What's <u>that</u> all about?"

"I can assure you," said Lochen, "there's nothing wrong with my having this book"

He was still holding it in his hand, extending it towards the gnome. She had her hand up, blocking it from her view, with her other hand over her lowered face in an attempt to shield herself. She was torn between hiding behind the chair and pushing it, and Lochen's hand, out of sight.

"PUT...IT...AWAY!" she demanded. "If the Alchemist finds out you have it, there's no telling what he'll do. All I did was read it and look what happened to me. I don't even want to be around when he finds out you stole it."

"I didn't steal it," said Lochen. And then in a flash of inspiration he said, "The Alchemist <u>gave</u> it to me. Unfortunately, we were unexpectedly separated before he could explain to me how to read it. He said you could probably do that. He said you could explain to me how to read it."

The gnome's head jerked up. She slowly came from behind the chair.

"The Alchemist said <u>that</u>? Wow."

"Most certainly," said Lochen. "So, here. Can you tell me what it says?"

He extended the book towards the gnome once again.

"No," said the gnome, shielding her eyes from the pages.

"But I just told you that the Alchemist said it was all right."

"That's not what you said," she insisted. "You said the Alchemist told you I could explain to you how to read it. He didn't say that I could read it. That's an entirely different matter. I won't be trapped like that. Not again."

Lochen realized the mistake he'd made in not being perfectly specific. He also knew he couldn't change his story now. The gnome would realize it was all fabrication. He wondered what the gnome meant by being trapped like that again, but he knew that now was not the time to pursue that matter.

"Yes," he said. "That's right. I'm sorry. I did not mean to trap you. I was mistaken in my request. Please. Explain to me how I can read it."

The gnome eyed him suspiciously. She slowly came from around the chair, her eyes still on the book. Lochen made an exaggerated display of putting it back inside his cloak, beneath his belt. Then he placed his empty hands in his lap where she could see.

"Simple," declared the gnome, satisfied with the apology. "I'll teach you the letters and symbols in which the book is written."

"That would be perfect," said Lochen.

"It's written in a language familiar to the Alchemist, and not much different than the written language of the gnomes."

"Ah," said Lochen. "Complete with sapphquioses, ninniuses, and zekkas?"

"Don't forget the pinaretts," laughed the gnome. "No. That's my language. What you need to learn is the Alchemist's. But don't worry. It'll be easy. There are only six hundred and ninety-two letters and three hundred and twenty-seven symbols."

"Six hundred and ninety-two letters?" Lochen echoed.

"And three hundred and twenty-seven symbols," added the gnome. "Don't forget those."

"Of course not," said Lochen. "I'm looking forward to it. But we're in a bit of a hurry. Could you write all that out for me?"

"Already done," the gnome replied with a wide grin. "You don't think I've been sitting here all this time doing nothing, do you?"

"Not at all," Lochen answered.

She reached into her vest and pulled a small scroll which she handed to Lochen. He unrolled it and peered at the tiny printing.

Quest of Eight Part Five: Release of the Demons

Richard Reda

"The lettering is awfully small," he muttered.

He looked up to see a scowl on the gnome's face.

"But very neat and precise," he added. "I'm sure this will do just fine."

"Good," said the gnome, slightly mollified. "Will there be anything else?"

"Actually," said Natalie. "Now that you mention it. We do have quite a ways to go to get to our next destination. I don't suppose you could help us with some mode of transportation."

"Well I'm not going to carry you," laughed the gnome. "I can't do that. No. That's one thing I can't do. Well, actually, there are a lot of things I can't do. But that's certainly one of them – carrying you, that is."

"What can you do?" asked Quinn. "I mean about helping us get where we need to go?"

"How about one of these?" she asked.

She reached into the other side of her vest and whipped her hand out. In her fist was an opalescent piece of rock. She opened her hand to expose the magical transporter stone. She looked from one to the other with a wide smile on her face. Natalie noticed, perhaps for the first time, that the gnome had only three teeth in her mouth. It was so noticeable, that she wondered why she hadn't seen this before.

She turned to Summer and saw that she, too, had noticed the gaping smile. She got up from her chair and approached the gnome. As she reached for the transporter stone, she looked closely at the gnome's features. Strands of silver and gray were in her hair that hadn't been there before. Her hands looked thinner and the knuckles were more pronounced. They were covered with age spots. There were lines and wrinkles in her face that Natalie was certain had only recently appeared.

"We can't thank you enough," Natalie said.

She was trying to not show her realization that the gnome was aging rapidly before their eyes. She took the stone from the gnome's hand and backed away. The gnome looked into Natalie's eyes. In spite of Natalie's efforts at hiding her understanding of what was happening, the gnome could see that awareness. She had felt the changes in her body from the moment her visitors had arrived. She knew her long wait was finally over.

"No," the gnome responded. "I can't thank you enough."

"We will never forget you," Natalie told her.

Natalie moved closer and gave the gnome a hug. At first the gnome was startled, not sure what was happening. Then she slowly raised her arms, extended them around Natalie's back and patted her gratefully.

"Oryxx," said the gnome proudly.

"Sapphquoise, pinarett, ninnius, zekka, zekka," said Natalie, stepping back. "I won't forget."

The gnome smiled again, but the brightness was fading from her eyes. She yawned widely.

"Oh," she said. "I'm sorry. It's just that suddenly, I'm very tired. Please pardon me if I don't see you off. Feel free to stay as long as you like. I'm just going to sit here for a moment to rest. Don't mind me."

Lochen rolled the scroll back up and placed it in an inside pocket. He patted the book to make sure it was secure, and then he rose from his chair. He took a few steps towards the center of the great hall, and motioned the others towards him.

"Your offer is most generous," he said to the gnome. "But I'm afraid we have a previous engagement to attend to. We must be leaving."

"I understand," replied the gnome.

She yawned once more. Her eyelids were getting heavy and she had started to slump over to one side in her chair. Lochen waved everyone closer.

"It might be best if I hold the stone," he said to Natalie. "Thank you for thinking to ask for it. It never occurred to me that she might have one."

At the sound of his voice, the gnome opened her eyes again, trying hard to focus.

"Safe journey," she said in barely more than a whisper, waving her hand goodbye.

"Thank you," Summer called back to her.

"Oh," the gnome added, fighting to stay awake just a little longer. "Give my regards to the Alchemist, should you see him. Tell him we are even now."

"I will," said Lochen.

"If we see him," Natalie added under her breath.

Quinn looked over at the gnome. It looked as if she had already fallen asleep. He could barely see her breathing. She looked so peaceful. The features he had first thought as being harsh and manly seemed to have softened.

"Is she going to turn to dust, too?" he whispered.

"It's already started," answered Natalie.

"Why is this happening?" asked Quinn. "Why do they have to...to...you know...whenever we come along?"

No one had an answer for him. Instead, Lochen closed his eyes and focused on the next nearest location on the map that Stella had shared with him. As he concentrated on the symbol he took a moment to think about the others, and hoped they were safe. He hoped he – they: Quinn, Natalie, Summer and he – would see them soon.

"Summer," he said. "It might be better for you to take your usual seat."

She flew up to his shoulder and settled into the folds of his hood. Natalie took his free hand in hers, and with her other one she grabbed hold of Quinn. With the transporter stone in Lochen's other hand, he gave a silent command. In a flash they were gone. Within seconds afterwards, the gnome completed her journey. All that remained was a pile of dust.

Chapter thirteen

As the gnome was quickly returning to dust, Lochen, Natalie, Summer and Quinn were thrown hundreds of miles away. The flash of the transporter stone snatched them from the hall under the mountain hiding place of Akmen Milzu to another mountain. They arrived on the outer rim, similar to, but also quite different from, the rim of the mountain from which they had left.

The outer covering of this one was coated in ice and snow. Winds circled around the top, whipping the vapor that rose from inside the crater that formed the circumference of the peak. Those vapors were generated by the heat from the active volcano inside the mountain.

"This is not better than where we just came from," moaned Quinn.

"Of course it is," answered Lochen. "The only Kelpie here is locked away, and there are no Rebbercands or hobgoblins."

"Not yet," he countered. "But I'll bet they'll be here soon, and then it won't be any better than before."

"I still disagree," Lochen responded. "This time we'll be better prepared."

He stuffed the transporter stone into a pocket on top of the scroll the gnome had given him with the letters and symbols needed to translate the book he had been given earlier. He motioned the others to a small niche on the inside of the ledge where they were standing.

"We need to get out of that wind," he said. "Before we do anything, we should study the terrain. Summer, can you carefully fly around the inner edge and then tell us what you see?"

"Sure," she answered.

"Camouflage yourself," Natalie added. "Just in case. We can't be too sure of anything around here."

"Good point," Lochen added. "Better safe than sorry. Off you go, now."

She took a second to blend into the background and then flew off in a counterclockwise direction along the interior of the mouth of the volcano. As she surveyed the area, Lochen was studying the cuts and depressions in the walls around the central crater. Natalie took a few steps off to one side and was looking at the view below, while Quinn sat down and waited.

Where they waited for Summer was away from the icy winds that blew up and around the outer area, but also avoided the waves of heat that rose up through cracks in the dried and cooled volcanic rock that coated the inside of the crater. After a few minutes Summer returned.

"I've looked it all over," she reported. "Is there anything specific you want to know about? I can't see anything that looks like that cube on the last mountain."

"I would expect that the Kelpie secured here is in some different kind of prison," said Lochen. "I don't believe we'll see the exact same thing as before. Describe everything, just as you saw it."

"OK," she said. "The whole crater is sort of round, but with places that look squished in."

"What does that mean?" asked Quinn.

"I don't know how else to describe it," Summer answered. "The edges wind back and forth, but all end up in a big circle. There are parts that are closer to the center and parts that are farther from the center. And the sides are all different heights. "

"You're doing fine," said Lochen, encouraging her. "The sides will have been formed by hundreds of years of volcanic eruptions. Rocks and lava that spewed forth will have shaped the interior of the cone. It makes perfect sense."

"If you say so," said Quinn.

"What else?" asked Lochen.

"There's something like a floor," Summer continued. "You can see it from here."

She pointed downward from the ledge on which they were standing. Before them was a rugged and somewhat hilly crust of ash that stretched out towards the opposite side.

"That covers about a third of the inside of the crater," she explained. "But there's a hole in the middle and cracks that lead out from the hole. It's like someone or something threw a big rock through it and broke it open. There are bigger cracks on two sides of the floor. They cross from one side of the crater to the other and join together like a 'T.' And someone's been here before us."

"How can you tell?" asked Natalie.

"Because there's a bridge that crosses the bigger crack," Summer told her.

"A bridge?" asked Quinn. "What would a bridge be doing here? Why would someone build a bridge in a volcano?"

"To reach a Kelpie," said Lochen. "Is there more?"

"Yes," said Summer. "The bridge leads to a narrower area – a lot narrower than the floor with the hole in it. It's like a cove, except there's no water in it. On the right side is a cliff. It's pretty big and flat, and there are a lot of deep recesses in the wall from the top of the cliff to the top of the mountain.

"On the other side there's a much bigger cliff that goes all the way up to the top of the mountain. The difference is that this one is covered with broken rocks and boulders. It looks pretty dangerous. That stuff could slide very easily – like an avalanche.

"There's not much to our left. There are a lot of edges and outcroppings. They all extend over a smaller section that looks like the floor below us. But this floor looks different."

"Different how?" asked Lochen.

"The floor below us is mostly black. It gets grayer the closer to the hole. The other floor, though, is gray all over, and nearly white near the middle. But both of them are really rocky and sparkly."

"I've seen those sparkling rocks under the ocean," said Natalie. "They're from the volcanic ash."

"Yes," said Lochen. "This is a caldera volcano. That explains the formation. The lighter colored covering probably means the crust is thinner in those places. We should probably avoid them. How large do you estimate the opening to be?"

"I'd have to guess," Summer told him. "I think it's about a mile wide and a mile and a half to two miles across from where we are to the opposite side. Is that good or bad?"

"It's not so much that it's good or bad," said Lochen. "It just is. We're standing on the ring fault. It's the edge of the volcanic chamber. Those cracks are secondary volcanic vents, which is why this cloud coverage exists around the top of the mountain. It's from the heat below. The sparkly rocks, as you called them, indicates that the magma that formed them is rich in silica. Unfortunately, silica-rich magma is very thick and doesn't flow easily."

"So who cares about how it flows?" asked Quinn. "And what does that have to do with us and with finding the Kelpie?"

"Lava that doesn't flow easily," explained Lochen, "tends to have gases trapped within and under immense pressure. When the lava gets closer to the surface – especially this surface with its much colder air – the gases decompress rapidly, triggering an explosion."

"Oh," said Quinn. "How big of an explosion?"

"How do you think this mountain was created?" Lochen asked by way of explanation.

"We need to get out of here," Quinn said.

273

His voice started to rise. He began to pace back and forth in the small space. It was clear he was beginning to panic.

"We will," insisted Lochen, trying to calm him down. "We will. As soon as we've done what we came to do."

"How do we find where the Kelpie is hidden?" asked Natalie.

"There's a cave," said Summer.

Everyone looked at her, momentarily distracted from Quinn's impending panic attack.

"I wasn't finished," she said defensively. "I was going to tell you about the cave. I just hadn't gotten that far."

"Where is this cave?" asked Natalie.

"It's on the other side of the bridge – at the end of that narrower section between the two cliffs.

"That's where the Kelpie is buried, isn't it?" said Quinn, his anxiety level slowly coming under control.

"That would be a safe assumption," answered Lochen. "It would have been helpful to know what the crypts for the other Kelpies looked like. All we have to go on is the last one, which was fairly obvious. However, I don't believe there is another place in this crater in which to have secured a hiding place, so I have to agree. The Kelpie is most likely in the cave."

"You couldn't have just said, 'yes?'" asked Quinn. "Whatever. Let's get there right away and bury it even more or push it into the lava or whatever, so we can get out of here. Let's use that transporter stone thing. It'll be faster that way."

"Summer," said Lochen, ignoring Quinn. "Is there an easy way down from here to the floor below?"

"It was easy for me," she said. "I just flew."

"Yes," said Lochen. "Thank you for that keen observation. What about a way for the rest of us? Is there an easy way for <u>us</u>?"

"Oh. Yeah. Sort of," she answered. "You'd have to do some climbing, but it didn't look too bad. Why? Why wouldn't you transport yourselves there?"

"Because," explained Lochen. "By walking to the other side, we will be able to explore more of the caldera. The cave you discovered may be the obvious place to have hidden the Kelpie, but it might not be the correct place. And besides that, this will give me an opportunity to identify places to hide or to retreat to, or to even launch an assault, should we have the time."

"Launch an assault?" asked Quinn. "On who?"

"Whom," said Lochen.

"What?"

"On whom," he explained. "Launch an assault on whom."

"Whatever," responded Quinn. "Whom are you planning to launch an assault on?"

Lochen was about to once more correct his grammar, but then thought better of it.

"If we can't leave here before our adversaries arrive," he said. "Then we have to be prepared to defend ourselves. The bubble Natalie

275

created was suitable for the last encounter, but we saw what could happen with that. If we are cast aside here, it would be into a very intense inferno. I doubt we would be saved by anyone living in a cave below the lava."

"You can't know that," argued Quinn.

"In this case, I can," Lochen shot back. "Furthermore," he continued before Quinn could argue any further, "if we are fortunate enough to have sufficient time, we should take advantage of that and mount our own attack."

"I agree," said Natalie. "If we have a chance to send those creeps to the dark side of the moon, I say we take it."

"Oh, I don't think we could send them..." Lochen started to say, and then realized Natalie was speaking metaphorically. "Um...yes...I see."

"I'm with you two," said Summer. "We need to end this once and for all."

They all looked from one another and then to Quinn. He had a pained look on his face. He wished he was just about any place else but here. Finally, he resigned himself to his fate, breathed a deep sigh and stood up.

"I suppose," he said. "But can we get started? The sooner we get this over with, the better."

Summer led the way. Flying ahead of them, she scouted out the safest route. The others began a slow and careful descent. They climbed in and around columns of sparkling black rock.

"Be careful," Lochen cautioned. "The edges of this rock can be exceedingly sharp."

Quest of Eight Part Five: Release of the Demons

Richard Reda

As they traveled down to the floor of the caldera, they all kept an eye on the sky above them and the surrounding ledges, anticipating the arrival of the Rebbercand, his hobgoblins and the Kelpies. After a while, they reached the base.

"I suggest we avoid crossing near the hole," said Lochen. "And we should stay away from areas of ground that are gray. We should be safe traveling along the crater wall until we reach the large crevasse that Summer mentioned."

No one argued for taking the shorter approach and they soon fell into a single file, hugging the side. Summer flew slightly ahead, followed by Lochen, then Natalie, and finally Quinn.

"Summer," Lochen called.

She fluttered back and hovered a few feet away at eye level.

"Tell me what happened back there," he said.

"Back where?" she asked. "On the ledge when I was describing what I had seen?"

"No," he answered. "Back on the obelisk when you first saw the Kelpie. It seemed to have had a more profound effect on you than it did to any of us."

"Oh," she said, lowering her head. "I'm sorry. I don't know what got into me. I'll do my best not to let you down again."

"You didn't let us down," Lochen said, turning to face her. "Not in the least. You have never let us down. I didn't mean for my question to cause you to believe otherwise. I am merely curious as to why you had such a significant reaction to seeing that Kelpie. Knowing why may help us in the future. Had you seen that creature before?"

"No," she said immediately. "Yes. Well, sort of. I've heard descriptions ever since I was a child. It was the Malkia. I mean, it looked like the Malkia."

"Who is this Malkia?" he asked.

"She is evil," Summer answered. "She is the source of all that is evil."

"A figure from your ancestral stories?"

"Yes," she said. "How did you know?"

"An educated guess," he answered without further explanation. "Tell me about her."

"She drove my ancestors from their home," Summer explained.

"I thought the forest was your home," said Lochen.

"It is," she answered. "But not the forest where we live now. A very long time ago, we lived in another forest. In fact we lived with pixies, imps, and other small people. Our leader was the Wakuu. He was very wise and was like a father to all of us, including the pixies. I know. That's hard to believe, but it's true. Of course we had some disagreements, but nothing serious – nothing the Wakuu couldn't help us resolve.

"Then the leader of the imps – this Malkia – started trying to take over everything. She gained tremendous power. No one really knows where it came from, but it was enough to wage a war. She turned the imps, the pixies and the faeries all against one another. The Wakuu tried to keep us all together. I'm not sure how or what happened. I think he tried to get some help from the forest creatures."

"Your people were friendly with the forest creatures?" Lochen asked, somewhat surprised.

"Yeah," she said, matter-of-factly. "We were friendly with everyone. It was like everything was in balance – until the Malkia tipped it all over."

"That's an interesting description," noted Lochen. "She tipped things over."

"She didn't really tip anything over," clarified Summer. "But that's what it felt like. Being an imp, she was able to easily convince the imps to follow her. She must have promised the pixies something, because they joined her revolt. It was horrible. Then she disappeared.

"The history of the faeries doesn't explain what happened to her; only that she disappeared. But not before turning our forest into a desert. Somehow she destroyed everything. My ancestors were forced to flee and find another home. At first we settled with the forest creatures, but then something happened.

"I don't think anyone really knows for sure what it was, but everything bad that ever happened to the faeries after being forced from the forest was blamed on the Malkia. The Malkia took the Wakuu away from us. The Malkia threw us from our home and then destroyed it. The Malkia turned the forest creatures against us. The Malkia stole our little ones. The Malkia will get you if you're not good. You get the picture."

"Yes, I do," said Lochen. "Very clearly. How did you come to believe that what you saw, though, was this Malkia?"

"From the description," said Summer. "From as long as I can remember, she's been described to us. There are even drawings that have been carved into rocks or trees, displaying her image. They're all the same. And they're all what I saw. I was certain she had come for me."

"I have to admit," said Lochen. "That creature did seem to have a certain attraction to you."

"Thanks," said Summer. "That makes me feel real good."

"I'm sorry," he said. "I didn't mean to frighten you any further. It was merely an observation."

"Then I wasn't imagining it?" she asked.

"I don't believe you were," he answered. "She clearly made eye contact with you and seemed to be directing her attention towards you – more so than to any of the rest of us. I wonder if Solveig, Stella, Liam and Sean were able to reach the location where she was imprisoned before she escaped."

"Why?" asked Summer. "What difference would it make?"

"I'm curious to know if there was any type of symbol or marking associated with that location or the actual enclosure in which she was held."

"Is that important?"

"I don't know, yet," he said. "Just a theory I'm considering."

"Look," she said, swinging around to face him directly – hovering immediately before his face. "I know I reacted badly back there. I panicked. But I promise it won't happen again. I won't let her scare me that way again."

"I am certain that you won't panic again," he said. "Should you encounter her again, it won't have the same degree of shock as it did the first time. However, you would be wise to remain frightened of her. I believe you are right in that she is the personification of evil. She will do us all the most egregious harm and think nothing of it. Her primary goal is to ensure the release the others like her, and she will let nothing stand in her way – least of all us."

"Now you're starting to make me worry," she said.

"Good," he answered. "You <u>should</u> be worried. We all should be worried. I haven't been able to sort out everything quite yet, but from what I <u>have</u> sorted, I understand enough to know that all of us – and all we know and hold dear to us – all of it is lost if we fail and these Kelpies are freed."

"But why us?" she asked.

"That's the question Quinn has asked more than once," he said. "Again, I don't have the answer, but I do have a theory."

"And what exactly is that theory?"

"Something to be continued at another time," he said. "We've reached the large crack. At least I hope this is the large crack. I'd hate to think there's one bigger than this."

Summer turned to look over her shoulder. He was right. They had reached the point where the larger of the two huge gashes in the crust touched on the outer edges of the caldera. From here they followed along the crack for several hundred yards until they reached the bridge.

It was like none they had seen before. It was comprised of slabs of what appeared to be granite. Each slab was six inches wide and about three feet long. Imbedded on the sides of the slabs at each end were eyebolts to which a chain was attached. Each length of chain was comprised of four very thick links. The links and the eyebolts connected one slab to the next, extending across the chasm. There was no hand rail or other line to hold when crossing.

The distance between each slab, created by the length of the links and the bolts, was about the same as the width of the slabs themselves – six inches. The links attached to the first slab were also attached to what appeared to be a long spike planted into the rock at the edge of the caldera floor.

"How long do you think this bridge has been here?" asked Natalie.

"I assume as long as the Kelpie," said Lochen. "Of course, also assuming the Kelpie is in the cave on the other side and not hidden someplace else. This bridge could be merely a diversion."

"Are you sure we're in the right place to begin with?" asked Summer. "I mean here in this volcano?"

"Yes," said Lochen. "The vision Stella implanted in my memory is quite clear. We are where we are supposed to be."

"Is that thing going to hold?" asked Quinn. "It looks pretty long. Maybe I should stay here and stand guard."

"Are you sure you want to stay here by yourself?" asked Natalie.

Quinn looked around. The sky above, though still gray and foreboding, was shielded from sight by the layers of steam that rose from the fissures in the caldera floor. He looked at the crater in which he was standing – completely devoid of color or any signs of life.

"I suppose not," he mumbled. "But I don't want to go first – not over a bridge that's two thousand years old and has been stretched out over a field of lava that whole time."

Lochen knelt down to get a closer look at the bridge and the chain. He reached out and touched the stone. It was cold – apparently impervious to the heat from below. It was smooth, but not slippery. It was the same black as the ash that surrounded them. He touched

282

the chain. It, too, was cold to the touch. It also looked as if it was new.

"I don't think we have to worry about the strength of this bridge," he said. "And I will be glad to take the lead."

Without waiting for any objections, he stepped out onto the bridge. It barely moved as he put his full weight on it. He began to walk. At first he was watching his steps to make sure he didn't step into one of the gaps. But then he realized that he was able to walk at his normal pace and gait, and his feet landed naturally in the center of each slab. He gradually relaxed and shifted his focus to the far side.

Natalie followed and, like Lochen, after a few steps noticed the same thing. Her pace and gait landed her naturally in the center of each slab. How can that be, she wondered. Lochen's legs were longer than hers. She should have had to compensate. Before she was even midway across, she had relaxed and moved her eyes ahead to the other side.

Quinn watched both of them. He saw their first tentative steps and then the change in how they walked. It was as if they were taking a leisurely stroll along a path in the woods – as if walking across this crazy stone bridge, that moved imperceptibly, was the most natural thing in the world.

He extended one foot and put it down on the nearest slab. Gradually he shifted his weight, ready at the least sign to jump back. The next foot followed. Instead of taking a full step, he brought his second foot up to the same slab as his first foot and then stepped forward again. Taking these half steps, he inched his way across, all the time waiting for the bridge to collapse. He was all the way across before he realized it. He looked up to see the others waiting patiently, but none of them said anything.

They had arrived in what Summer had described as a cove. It was an accurate description. With the bridge behind them, the mouth of the cave gaped before them about a hundred feet ahead. To their right was the series of ledges that climbed up to the rim of the caldera. To their left was a larger, sheerer cliff, covered with large rocks imbedded into the side. Summer was right about that, too. It looked like an avalanche waiting to fall.

The ground they were on was fairly flat and covered with volcanic ash. It was like walking on a beach. This beach, though, slanted downward towards the cave. The open area was as first observed, about a hundred feet from the bridge to the cave and little more than thirty feet from cliff wall to cliff wall.

"An excellent place for a trap," observed Lochen.

"I hope it's not us that gets trapped," said Natalie.

They moved quickly, but cautiously towards the cave. The shape of the rocks that formed the opening gave each of them a chill. It bore an uncomfortable resemblance to a gaping mouth filled with long, sharp teeth. They stepped across the opening and into the darkness.

"Can you generate a light?" Summer asked Lochen.

"Yes," he said. "But let's wait for the time being. I'd like not to draw attention in here unless we have to."

"Oh, wow," said Quinn – the last of them to enter the cave. "It stinks in here. What kind of place is this?"

"You're right," said Lochen. "There is a rather pungent odor. I haven't yet determined its source, though."

"Keep sniffing," said Quinn. "I'm sure it will come to you. It's poop! I've smelled enough poop to know this stuff is poop."

"Please keep your voice down," said Lochen.

They were creeping forward, all huddled closely together, slowly moving deeper and deeper into the darkness. Soon their only source of light – the cave opening – was several feet behind them. They were more than twenty feet into the cave when they heard motion.

"What's that?" whispered Summer.

"You heard it, too," moaned Quinn.

"Keep your voice down," Lochen hissed.

He was scanning the black walls and ceiling that had closed in on them, trying to see through the darkness. He snapped his fingers and the sound echoed off the stone.

"Why did you do that?" whispered Natalie.

"I'm trying to gauge the size of the cavern."

"Well, did you?"

"Yes," he said. "I believe so. It seems rather large, and I don't sense any obstacles."

"What does that mean?" she whispered again.

"That there's nothing for a large animal to hide behind. I hope."

"I think it's time for some light."

"I agree," he answered. "But something small."

Quest of Eight Part Five: Release of the Demons

Richard Reda

He rubbed his hands together and a static charge formed. He rolled it between the palms of his hands, shaping it into a ball. When it was the size of a plum, he opened his hand and raised his palm in the air. The small ball of light began to brighten as it floated from his hand upward into the air. It climbed higher to about ten feet up when it struck the ceiling. At the same time the light increased, poking into the blackness.

As soon as that happened, the air was filled with thousands of ear piercing screeches and the flutter of thousands of wings.

"Bats!" shouted Summer. "Bats!"

She dove into the folds of Lochen's hood, burying herself for protection. Quinn dropped down to the ground and covered his head. Natalie readied herself to enclose them all in another bubble, but stopped when she saw Lochen's hand raised in her direction.

"I don't believe they will harm us," he said. "I think they are merely frightened."

"They're frightened?" mumbled Summer from beneath the hood. "They're frightened? Are you serious? I nearly wet my pants, and I'm not even wearing pants."

"What?" exclaimed Lochen. "You...in my hood?"

"Relax," she snapped at him. "It was only a figure of speech, but I think you get the point."

The bats flew out of the cave, zooming close, but never hitting any of the intruders. They circled the outer rim of the volcano and then disappeared from sight.

"I think it's safe to come out," he said to Summer. "And for you to get up from the ground, Quinn."

Quinn lifted his head and then realized where he was.

"Awww, poop," he said. "I was right. I smelled poop, and now I've fallen down in it. I'm going to stink. I hate this place."

Lochen helped him to his feet as Natalie tapped his shoulder. She turned him around and pointed to the wall at the deepest part of the cave. They were standing less than ten feet from it. In the center of the wall was an oval. It was part of the black stone, but it was glowing a deep, dark red. Natalie extended her hand closer to the wall, but didn't touch it.

"It's hot," she said. "Really hot. It must be a vent for the lava."

"No," said Lochen. "Look."

He pointed to a carved symbol in the center of the red oval. It was the symbol of the flame that Quinn had identified as representing Stella.

"That doesn't mean anything," said Quinn before anyone could comment. "It doesn't mean those symbols represent the Kelpies. It could mean something else."

"Of course it could," said Lochen.

"Don't say, 'of course it could,' like you mean, 'of course it couldn't,'" he nearly shouted.

"I didn't mean it that way," said Lochen. "I agree with you. It's very possible that this mark was made by whomever imprisoned this Kelpie and that whoever that was may have been represented by this symbol. Regardless, though, I think it's safe to say we've discovered the location of another Kelpie."

"Great," said Summer, poking her head out from the hood. "What do we do now?"

"I think it's time we take the offensive," Lochen answered.

"What do you propose?" asked Natalie.

"Whatever it is," said Quinn. "Can you propose it outside this stinking cave?"

They moved out of the cave and onto the small cove. Lochen looked around, searching for strategic locations.

"Natalie," he asked, "how far away can you be to cast one of your bubbles?"

"I don't know for sure," she said. "I've never tried creating one over any distance. If I had to guess, I would say no more than thirty or forty feet. Why?"

"I'd like you to position yourself on the lower ledge next to this cove. Find a place to hide yourself until the appropriate time. My plan is to attempt to trap them – the Kelpies, the Rebbercand and the hobgoblins – all of them – inside the cave."

"With a bubble?" asked Summer

"They're pretty strong," said Natalie. "But I don't think they'll hold all of them inside the cave. They could just push it out."

"That's where Quinn comes in," said Lochen.

"Me?" he asked. "What am I supposed to do? Hold the bubble in place?"

"No," answered Lochen. "I want you to take a position up on top of this cliff on the opposite side. Once Natalie casts the bubble, I want you to start pushing some of those larger rocks down the cliff."

Quest of Eight Part Five: Release of the Demons

Richard Reda

"To create an avalanche," said Natalie. "Brilliant. I can cast another bubble over all those rocks."

"And Quinn can push more on top of that," finished Lochen.

"What do I do?" asked Summer.

"I'm afraid you have the most dangerous task of all," he said.

"What's that?" she asked with more than a little trepidation.

"I need you to once again camouflage yourself and hide inside the cave. You must stay there until all of them are deep inside, attempting to open the crypt. Once they are all in as far as they can go, you come out of the cave and make yourself visible. I'll be on a ledge on the opposite side. I can cast some spells to help keep them in and distracted while Natalie and Quinn block the passage. I will also be in a position visible to them and will be able to signal them at the most opportune time."

"This might just work," said Natalie.

As the pieces of the plan became clear to them, their mood improved considerably. For the first time in a long time, they felt in control and confident. They left Summer at the mouth of the cave as the rest of them began the return trip. There was no way for Quinn to get to the top of the cliff other than by going back the way they had come.

Summer hovered around the opening, close to the top, keeping an eye out for any of the bats that might return to the cave. She was as worried about them as she was about the Kelpies and the Rebbercand. She was certain that bats liked to snack on faeries. At least that's what she had been told.

Natalie separated from Quinn and Lochen and climbed up the shorter cliff. At the first level, which was about twenty feet above the cove, she found a cleft in the side of the mountain in which she could hide, but still have a view of the rest of the caldera. She could also better understand why it would be necessary for Lochen to be on the opposite side. From her hiding place, she couldn't see the mouth of the cave.

Quinn and Lochen crossed back over the bridge and made the walk around the crust back to where they started. Lochen continued on from there a few hundred yards further until he found an alcove very much like the one in which Natalie was hiding. It was in a perfect position to see the cave, Natalie's location and where Quinn would be hiding.

"All right, my friend," he said to Quinn. "You should be able to traverse the rim of this volcano all the way to the peak of the cliff. Be careful, though. Don't get too close to the edge. It wouldn't do to start the avalanche prematurely. And by all means, keep low. We don't want our foes to be alerted to our plans."

"Got it," said Quinn.

Lochen lowered himself into position while Quinn set off for the cliff. He watched Quinn as he walked along the ridge. Once he arrived at the cliff, Quinn looked around and found several large volcanic rocks. He moved a few of them nearer the edge and arranged them to provide something large enough to hide behind. He squatted down, and then popped his head up. He looked over towards Lochen and waved. Lochen waved back, and then motioned for him to get down.

"I hope this works," Lochen said out loud to no one. "If it doesn't, we may be overly exposed with no place to which to escape."

There was nothing more he could do at this point but wait. He removed the book from his cloak and began to leaf through the pages of indecipherable markings. He was looking forward to some free time so he could compare the book to the scroll of letters and symbols the gnome had given him.

He was more convinced than ever that the symbols they observed in the Ice Kingdom were the same symbols as on the band they had used to seal the portal of the gargoyles; and the same symbols they were seeing now, in conjunction with the Kelpies. They were all connected. We all seem to be connected, he thought.

"And this book holds the key," he said, once more aloud and to no one in particular.

Chapter fourteen

B'nair was pacing restlessly. He had watched the reaction of the other hobgoblins as they looked on, trying not very successfully to hide their horror as the Mountain Kelpie took her time devouring the leader B'nair had appointed and then, most recently, sacrificed to the Kelpie as dinner.

"Next time," he hissed at Angin Topan, "I'd like a little bit of warning about what's going to happen, if it's not too much to ask."

The desert Kelpie turned her head towards the Rebbercand, somewhat surprised by the tone of his voice.

"I'll take your 'request' under consideration," she answered. "But I strongly suggest you re-evaluate your importance to us."

Her voice was low and controlled, but there was no mistaking the undercurrent of malevolence. At this point in time, though, B'nair no longer cared. He knew that he was no more indispensible – no less disposable – than any of the hobgoblins. His only salvation was his possession of the piece of the pendant, still in his inside pocket, and the map contained in his memory.

Possession of the stone was tenuous at best. The Kelpies seemed to have some kind of adverse reaction to it, although they had all, so far, expressed a somewhat intense interest in it. He figured it would only be a matter of time before they would either be able to counter the reaction, or find a way around it. When that time came, he had no doubt they would easily relieve him of ownership.

The map was another matter. It seemed they had no clue as to the location of the other Kelpies. He was beginning to think that strange. The Swamp Kelpie was buried in the Swamp; the desert Kelpie in the desert; and the mountain Kelpie in the mountains. Of course, these were all very large areas, and the specific locations could have been anywhere, but he wasn't altogether confident that they were as clueless as they let on.

He would have to keep his senses alert for an opportune time to part ways with these creatures. For the time being, he realized he needed to be more subservient and to make himself invaluable.

"Forgive me," he said. "I had not expected a request of that nature, and I was taken by surprise. I meant no disrespect."

The imp viewed him without a change in her expression. She was suspicious of his sudden remorse. After a few seconds, she thought that perhaps he had realized his error and she dismissed it.

"You chose wisely," she said. "He was weak and injured. He wouldn't have been able to keep up and would soon have become a liability."

He couldn't disagree with her assessment, but it still rankled him that he was the one singled out to make the choice – and without knowing what the ramifications of that choice were going to be. He thought about how he was going to more carefully word his next question.

"Do you expect we will be here for any length of time?" he asked.

"You mean so Akmen Milzu can restore her strength and power?"

"Yes," he answered. "But I also thought we should consider the best way off this mountain and to find the quickest way to the next destination."

"And where would that be?" she asked.

"The closest one is a volcano to the north and west of here. Even with your ability to move us, I think it will take two days – maybe a little more; maybe a little less."

"I see," she said. "It appears we will be searching for Neraka Ferr."

"Another master?" B'nair asked.

"No," answered Angin Topan. "But a powerful ally all the same. I will confer with Akmen Milzu."

She didn't have to say any more. It was clear to B'nair he was being dismissed – not that there was any place for him to go. He stepped away from her and turned towards the hobgoblins. He took a tentative step in their direction, and then thought better of it. He was not likely to receive a warm welcome from them.

He looked at the mountain Kelpie, who was standing at the edge of the plateau, gazing at the fallen spires. He knew better than to approach her. In the end, he found a corner of the obelisk where he could be by himself. He took the time to close his eyes and resurrect the image of the map so he could see exactly where they were going.

Quest of Eight Part Five: Release of the Demons

Richard Reda

The locations were getting farther and farther apart. Traveling would take longer and longer. He had arrived at the first location well ahead of his pursuers. They had caught up to him at the second location, and they were here before him this time. It was apparent they had divided up. What he didn't know was how many of them there were, and if any of their number was already at the volcano.

He would need to take stern measures with the remaining hobgoblins to keep them in line. After giving up Vardelos as easily as he did, he knew they would not trust him. He would need to be able to rely on them, though, since he was certain they would run into more and more resistance along the way. That is, unless they were able to defeat and destroy whoever was trying to stop them.

While B'nair was contemplating his next strategy, Angin Topan flew over to the mountain Kelpie and hovered close to her ear.

"When you have regained your strength," she said, "we will need to move quickly."

"Who were those intruders?" asked Akmen Milzu.

"I don't know. I assume they are allies of the Alchemist. Or his minions."

"After all this time? Do you think that's possible? Surely he must be long gone."

"Nothing about him is certain," said Angin Topan. "Least of all his demise."

The mountain Kelpie turned her head and looked into the eyes of her friend.

"Or the witch," the smaller Kelpie added.

"What was done to me," said the larger one, "was her doing."

"Yes, I know. Encasing you in Harridan's stone was typical of her – stone as thin as paper, but as hard as steel."

"I could see through it," added the mountain Kelpie. "I saw the changes of the seasons year after year, decade after decade, for centuries."

She spun around to face the imp head on.

"I will have my revenge," she nearly shouted. "I will have my revenge on her, on the Alchemist, and on all those who aided them."

"And you will not be alone. We must rescue the others, but we must be quick about it. Whoever it was that was here waiting for our arrival – they were not the same ones who attacked at my release."

"You were also set upon?"

"Yes, and nearly lost," said Angin Topan. "It would not be wise to underestimate these people."

"And this Rebbercand with his assembly of hobgoblins," asked Akmen Milzu. "They can be trusted?"

"Trusted may be too strong a word," the desert Kelpie added. "Necessary is a more appropriate description. They fought adequately, although ineffectively, against those who attacked me. The Rebbercand has led warriors before, and can be ruthless. However, his ruthlessness also makes him unpredictable."

"What do you mean?"

"The hobgoblin he gave up to you was one he had chosen as a leader of the other hobgoblins. The Rebbercand had saved his life as well. But then, without a moment's hesitation, he sacrificed him. I had not expected him to do that."

"Perhaps he merely doesn't want you to know his thoughts," Akmen Milzu said, making a subtle reference to the desert Kelpie's ability to read minds.

"I think it is more than that. It matters not. He is more necessary than the others. He has half of the pendant, and he has the map to tell us where our brethren are. The stone we can take from him when we feel like it, but the map is only in his mind."

"Then you are right. We must lose no time. I am ready to travel."

"That's good to hear. I can move us, but we will have to pass in short leaps. I do not think it advisable – at least not yet – to leave these hobgoblins behind. And we need the Rebbercand for the time being. There are too many of them, and you are too large, for me to transport great distances. Our next destination is the volcanoes."

"Neraka Ferr," said the mountain Kelpie.

"Yes. We will need her powers in the Ice Kingdom, which is where I am certain we will find Saldeti."

"So they buried us in our own lands."

"It seems that way," replied the imp. "It is where we believed we were the safest. We let our guard down. We must learn from that so it never happens again."

"You're right, then," said Akmen Milzu. "We can't afford any further delays. I know you mean well, but you can't transport all of us that distance without it taking too great a toll on you."

"It's a sacrifice I'm willing to make."

"But an unnecessary one. I will summon our wings."

The desert Kelpie had been hovering near the mountain Kelpie's shoulders. Now she backed away, a look of deep concern spread across her face.

"Harpies?" she asked.

During the revolt of the Kelpies, Harpies had played both sides against each other. They were unreliable and had been a main factor in the near eradication of the imps. Angin Topan doubted that their allegiance or their fondness for her people had changed in two thousand years.

"Better," answered Akmen Milzu. "Yokai."

"Are there any left?"

"Enough."

The Yokai were creatures related to the Harpies. However, unlike the Harpies, the Yokai were totally dedicated to one master, and that dedication was unshakable. They had large and muscular hind legs with hoofed feet. Their forelegs were more like arms, ending in long, sharp claws. They had long tails that extended ten feet behind their bodies, and had several dagger-like spikes on the end.

Their wings spread twenty feet across and were strong enough to support ten times their own weight. At the ends of their long necks were heads that resembled jackals. Their bodies were covered – not with feathers, but with a thick coarse fur. Before the end of the Kelpie rebellion, Akmen Milzu had amassed a large herd of these beasts.

"Where are they?" asked Angin Topan.

The mountain Kelpie smiled and spread her arms.

"All around us," she answered.

She took a deep breath, moved her hands up around her mouth and shouted.

"Yokai!"

The call echoed across the mountain tops and deep into the basin in which the obelisks stood.

"Yokai!" the Kelpie called again.

As the echoes died out, the sound was replaced by cracking and grinding that seemed to reverberate from every direction. The hobgoblins looked around, startled by the noise. B'nair stepped away from the edge and wondered what was happening.

The sides of the walls surrounding the central spire began to break apart. Bits of rock and stone fell away and dropped to the bottom. One by one, shapes began to appear. Creatures, dormant for as long as their master had been, came awake. Statues that seemed to have been carved into the face of the earth took shape – the same gray as the fabric of the mountain from which they were emerging; the same gray as their master.

They shook their massive heads and more rock and dust flew off. They pulled themselves free of their perches, peeling away layer after layer, and spread their vast wings. The air was filled with the roar of the beating of these wings and the growls and roars of the Yokai as they took flight.

Within minutes of being called forth, there were dozens of them circling the skies above. Akmen Milzu watched with pride, while the others, including Angin Topan, looked on in apprehension. One of the creatures, much larger than the others, lowered from the circling pattern and approached the edge of the obelisk. Everyone but the mountain Kelpie backed away.

The beast's wings slowed down and the hind legs landed first on the plateau, followed by the forelegs. Once it was down, the wings quickly folded into its sides and it walked up to the waiting Kelpie. It lowered its head and was greeted with a gentle stroke down its neck. The Kelpie turned back to the others.

"My pets will carry us where we need to go," she announced.

She approached the creature and climbed onto its back, tucking her feet behind the wings. She then turned back to Angin Topan.

"Please," she said, "Ride with me."

She motioned to the space immediately in front of her. The desert Kelpie hesitated only a second and then flew over and seated herself between her friends hands. Akmen Milzu grabbed the fur on the beast's back in each hand to hold on and then nudged it with her feet. The wings spread widely and began to beat.

As it was rising into the air, she motioned to the other Yokais and pointed down at the hobgoblins and Rebbercand. One of the other creatures landed and moved close to B'nair. He looked up at the Kelpies, and then at the Yokai, unsure of what to do. Taking a deep breath, he moved nearer, grabbed some fur in his free hand and flung his leg over the side.

It was difficult for him to hold on with only one hand, but he managed. As soon as he was lifted clear of the plateau, other Yokais landed and the hobgoblins followed their leaders, awkwardly climbing on and holding on for dear life. They were creatures of the underground. Climbing high towers and crossing lofty bridges was unsettling to them. Flying was unthinkable.

It took a few minutes for all of the hobgoblins to mount the Yokais. In the meantime, the Kelpies circled the obelisk, climbing higher and higher. B'nair moved with them, but the movement was not at his instruction. The beast on which he was mounted was following directions, not from him, but from Akmen Milzu. The thought of this did not please the Rebbercand.

He tried to pull the Yokai in a different direction, but nothing happened. He tried to keep his face impassive, but inside he was seething. He did not like the lack of control. In fact, he hated it. He tried to put his feelings behind him and focus on the location of the next Kelpie. He took some minor satisfaction when his ride moved up next to the Kelpies.

"There are several volcanoes in the northwest," said Akmen Milzu. "You will take us to the one that holds our friend."

It was more of a command than a request. B'nair fought to hold his tongue. Angin Topan watched him in silence. He looked from one to the other, and then bowed his head slightly and forced a smile.

"With pleasure," he said.

He gave a pull on the fur and discovered that now the Yokai was compliant with his lead. He knew that wouldn't last. He turned to the northwest. The sky hadn't changed from before. It was the same dull gray it had been for the last several days. The air was cold and would be getting colder. B'nair knew things would get worse before they would get better.

---------------- *** ----------------

In the opposite direction of where the Kelpies, the Rebbercand and the hobgoblins were traveling, Stella, Solveig and Liam watched as Sean climbed the face of the glacier. Their small boat bobbed gently in the water below him. His first few steps were awkward, but he eventually fell into a rhythm.

He drove the dragon's tooth into the ice with one hand, and pulled himself up so he could reach the next notch Stella had cut with his other hand. Then he moved one foot into the nearest cutout and

301

lifted himself upward. He put the tooth between his own teeth so he could switch hands and mirror the process for the next step up.

Up and up he went. Stella had done a good job of cutting the hand holds. They were spaced just the right distance and, for the most part, were deep enough. A few times Sean had to chip a little deeper or change the angle, but her efforts made his climb a lot easier. He only wished she could do something about the noise.

The soft sloshing of the water against the side of the glacier was often disrupted by a loud crack as part of the colossal ice shelf broke off and fell away from the main body. The sound came so suddenly it startled him.

There seemed to be no pattern to the calving, either. One could be followed immediately by another, or there could be several minutes between them. He couldn't tell how close or how far away the breaks were, either.

His friends in the boat could, though. Solveig noticed the increased wave activity after hearing the crashing of the broken parts into the water. Sometimes the jostling happened almost immediately, while other times it was several seconds or minutes later. She also noticed that sometimes the waves were much larger than other times. She assumed that this meant the pieces that broke off were also larger.

Sean had passed the halfway mark when he stopped to rest. He looked back down at his friends. They were about sixty feet beneath him. He had tied one end of the rope Liam had provided around his waist. The other end was tied to the unraveled piece of Solveig's cloak. He could see the strange fabric stretched out below, and the rest of the cloak at the bottom. He was surprised to see how much was still left.

"This might work after all," he said.

His arms and legs weren't all that tired, but his hands and feet were getting cold. The ice was having its affect on him. He took the dragon's tooth from between his teeth and jammed it into the wall. Then he heard another crack.

This one sounded much closer than all the others. His hand was still on the dragon's tooth, so he could feel that it was coming loose. He looked up to the point where he had driven it into the glacier. There was a jagged line extending upward and downward from the point of entry.

He followed the line upward as far as he could see. It faded into the lines and grooves of the glacier itself, but he was fairly certain it went all the way up. He then looked at the line that extended downward. He saw the same thing – the line followed the grooves in the wall down as far as he could see.

The only difference was that the line downward ran right between his feet. He needed to move, he thought. He pulled the tooth from the ice and the crack widened. He could hear a breaking sound and feel the vibrations in both hands and both feet.

Another iceberg was calving right in front of him. I've got to get out of here, he thought. But which way? He pressed himself as close to the ice as he could and still maintain his footing. He could hear the cracking sound grow as the fissure worked its way deep into the wall. He could feel the rumbling of it breaking away. But he still couldn't tell which side was staying put and which one was going to drop into the sea.

He looked down at the others. He wanted to warn them, but he was afraid to let go. He could see that Liam was the first to understand what was happening. He reached down to the deck of the boat and threw Solveig's cloak into the water. Then he took his seat and began pedaling the boat away from the wall.

"What are you doing?" Solveig asked when she saw that Liam had pitched her cloak overboard.

"It's breaking up," he shouted. "We need to get away."

"What about Sean?" asked Stella.

"Can you cast a spell to get him down here safely or push him up to the top?" Liam asked.

He was not really paying any attention to either of them. He was focused on getting them far enough away from the calving iceberg to survive. He knew there was nothing they could do for Sean.

"No," said Stella. "But we can't just leave him."

"If we don't there won't be anything left of us," he answered. "If he's lucky, he can ride the breaking part down to the water. He has a better chance than we do. Especially if we hang around here much longer."

Sean watched as the small boat moved away. He still couldn't tell which side was going to drop. The crack that extended between his feet and hands was growing wider. Which way, he thought frantically.

"One potato, two potato..." he started mumbling. "That's probably not the best way to decide. I need something faster. Eenie, meenie, minie...Ohhh, poop!"

The gap grew wider and wider, but still there was no indication as to which piece was going to fall. He knew that in seconds it wouldn't matter. The break would spread farther than he could reach.

"Go with your gut," he shouted to himself.

With that he let go with his right foot and right hand at the precise instant that this part of the glacier moved away and began to fall into the sea. He hung, swinging like an open door, hanging by his left foot and left hand, watching the enormous piece of ice drift further away and downward.

"Oh, Momma," he said. "That was too close for comfort."

Below him, Liam was pedaling as hard as he could. It was as if the giant berg was following them. It seemed to maintain the same distance from them, which was not far enough for Solveig, who was still standing in the bow, transfixed.

The falling section was dropping faster and faster. The three in the boat barely noticed that the water they were floating in was rising faster and faster along with the descent of the ice. Before they knew it, it was gone – completely submerged.

"Stella," shouted Liam. "Can you cast a spell to push us further away from the glacier?"

"I don't know," she answered. "Probably. Why?"

"Because...that thing...is going...to be coming...back up...very...quickly," he gasped.

He was pedaling so hard and fast that he was running out of breath. Stella immediately understood. However, by that time, it was too late. She no sooner turned back to the glacier and raised her hand than the iceberg shot back up through the surface of the water, directly underneath the boat.

It slammed into the tiny craft, shattering it completely and tossing the three of them into the air. Solveig flew forward and landed on the top of the broken ice shelf. Stella was thrown off the side. She struck the edge of the iceberg and bounced off into the frigid water. Liam was flung high into the air and dropped with the remnants of the boat into the sea.

As Sean watched the iceberg drop into the water, he began to feel like he was being pulled downward. He was unable to turn himself and get a better hold. His fingers and toes dug into the holds and began to cramp. What's going on, he wondered.

Solveig's cloak had gotten caught on a piece of the broken ice and was being pulled down with the sinking berg. It was still unraveling, but not as fast as it was sinking. It was pulling the rope that was tied around Sean's waist. He grabbed at it with his free hand.

Just when he was certain he'd be pulled off the face of the glacier, the pulling stopped and he nearly flew upward. The cloak had completely unraveled. He then watched as the iceberg broke the surface and destroyed the boat the others were in.

The best way to help them, he thought, was to get to the top as quickly as he could, secure the rope and climb back down. He jerked his body to turn himself around so he could dig out a hand hold for his right hand. One after the other, he cut notches, lifted himself, and climbed towards the top.

A few minutes later he crawled over the edge and saw the vast expanse of white in front of him. He looked around but found nothing to which to tie the rope. He took a few steps forward, moving away from the edge, and slammed the dragon's tooth as deeply into the ice as he could. He gave it an extra push and then stomped on it with his heel.

"That's going to have to be good enough," he said. "I hope nothing comes along to pull it free or eat the rope."

He tied the rope to the tooth and then began to climb down. When he got even with the top of the calved berg, he could see Solveig sprawled several feet away. She wasn't moving. The iceberg was still bobbing up and down, but the motion was gradually slowing. Sean swung back and forth until he was close enough to land on the surface.

Quest of Eight Part Five: Release of the Demons

Richard Reda

Careful not to let go of the rope, he dropped to his feet, and pulled the line with him as he ran over to Solveig. She was breathing and when he turned her over, her eyes fluttered briefly.

"I'm still sleepy," she mumbled. "Do I have to get up now? Just a few more minutes, please, and then I promise I'll get up."

Sean gently tapped her cheeks.

"You're not asleep," he said. "You're unconscionable. No, that's not right. You're uncognito. No, I don't think that's right either. You were knocked out," he finally shouted.

"What?" she muttered. "What happened? Where is everyone?"

He got her to her feet and quickly explained what happened. He pushed her to the edge of the iceberg and wrapped her hands around the rope. When she had it in her grip, she looked more closely at where she was.

"Whoa!" she shouted and backed up. "What are you trying to do?"

"You need to climb up to the top," he told her. "I'll hold the rope at this end to keep it from swaying. But you need to get to the other end to make sure it doesn't come loose. Once you get up there, I'll climb down and find Stella and Liam."

"OK," Solveig said, not sure she fully understood what was going on. "But you better not let go."

She started climbing up. Sean held the rope as tautly as he dared. He was afraid of pulling it loose from the dragon's tooth. If that happened, Solveig would have a long way to drop, and would probably be really mad at him. That is, he thought, if she survived.

It seemed to him that it took her forever to get to the top. When she did, she waved down to him. He wasn't sure if she was signaling that all was safe, or just waving hello. He opted for the former and slid down the rope.

Somewhere along the way, he passed the knot where the rope changed to the strings from Solveig's cloak, but he didn't remember when that happened. The far end was still in the water. That was all he was interested in. It needed to be long enough to get to the sea, and it looked like it was.

He was still several feet above the surface when he spotted Stella. She was floating face down in the water.

"Oh, no," he shouted.

He decided not to waste time shinnying down. He let go and dropped into the sea. He swam over to her and lifted her head. She was still breathing, but then he remembered that she was a Sea Sprite and was able to breathe in the water. There was a gash on her head from where she struck the iceberg after being thrown.

"It doesn't look like you're going anywhere," Sean said, not really expecting her to answer.

He pulled some of the strands from the water and looped them around Stella to make sure she didn't float away.

"You'll be all right," he said. "Just don't forget you can breathe under water."

He left her tied where she was and then went in search of Liam. He moved past pieces of the wreckage and eventually found him hanging on to one of the broken pieces of the boat. He seemed stunned, but all right.

"We weren't trying to leave you behind," he said when he saw Sean.

"Don't worry about it," Sean said. "If I had a free hand, I would have waved for you to get away."

"Where are Solveig and Stella?"

"They're safe. Well, Solveig's safe. I mean Stella's safe, too, but she's tied up at the end of the rope and still floating in the water. Solveig's up on top making sure the rope doesn't come loose. At least I hope she is. She wasn't making too much sense when I last talked to her."

They both swam back to where Stella was.

"You go first," said Sean.

"No," said Liam. "If you're right about the rope maybe coming loose, then you should go first. I weigh more than you. You can make it to the top faster than I can, too, so get up there and help keep it tied. Once you're on top, I'll come up. Then we can both pull Stella up."

Sean started to argue, but realized Liam was right. Their chances were better if he went first. He was worried about how much time Liam and Stella had been in the water. He was pretty certain Stella would be all right, but Liam wasn't used to temperatures this cold. He'd already been in the freezing sea too long.

Sean climbed as fast as he could. He didn't make a single stop on the way up. By the time he reached the top, his arms felt like rubber. He pulled the tooth from the ice, and without untying it, wrapped it around his waist and then drove the tooth back into the ice.

"Solveig," he said. "Do you know where you are?"

"With you?" she asked.

Still not all together here, thought Sean. It'll have to be enough.

309

"That's right," he said with a big smile. "Go over to the edge and wave hello to Liam."

"Liam's here?" she asked. "When did he arrive? Oh, yes, I have to say hello."

She ran over to the edge and leaned over the side.

"Oh, there he is," she said. "Hello, Liam," she shouted, waving her hand.

"OK," said Sean. "Now come back over here and sit behind me."

"All right," she said. "Are we playing a game?"

"Yes," he said. "Sort of. I want you to hold on tight to me. All right? Pretend we're riding that flying horse of yours, and you don't want to slip off."

"Oh, I'd never fall off my horse," she said. "Unless I fell off."

"Right. Hold on tight."

He could feel the pull on the rope and knew that Liam had understood the signal. He had started climbing up. Liam had been right. If he had gone first, it was likely the tooth would have come loose. His weight was pulling Sean across the ice. Sean dug his heels in and shouted for Solveig to hold on tight and to dig her heels in as well.

"Oh, wow," she squealed. "This is fun. We're going for a ride."

"Dig deeper," he yelled.

Fortunately, she did, and their skidding slowed down enough to give Liam enough time to reach the top. Once he was up, they began to pull Stella up to the top.

"I hope you tied this tightly," said Liam. "I didn't think to check the knot before I began climbing up."

"Knot?" asked Sean. "I just sort of looped it around her a few times, and maybe twisted it. I don't know how to tie any knots."

They stopped pulling for a second and looked at one another.

"Solveig," they both shouted.

"Go to the edge and see if Stella is still attached to the rope," Liam finished.

Solveig skipped to the edge and leaned over. She was leaning so far that Liam and Sean were certain she was going to topple over. Finally, she straightened and turned around to look at the both of them.

"Well?" asked Sean when she didn't say anything.

"Well, what" she asked.

"Is Stella still tied to the rope?"

"No," said Solveig.

They both could feel the weight still pulling on the cord and wondered if it wasn't Stella, what was it? Then Solveig spoke again.

"She's tied to the string from my cloak."

Sean rolled his eyes and Liam started to say something, but then decided it wasn't worth pursuing. They pulled quickly and efficiently, raising Stella up the side and over the top. Once she was safe with them, they untied the string. On its own, the cord began to move, reassembling itself into the cloak.

"Oh, good," said Solveig. "I wondered where that went."

She picked it up and put it on again while the other two tried to revive Stella. It was no use. She was completely unconscious. The cut on her head had stopped bleeding, but it had started to swell. Sean looked around at the seemingly limitless expanse of snow and ice.

"What now?" he asked.

"Do you know where to go?" asked Liam. "Because I have no clue."

"I think so," Sean answered. "I remember the last time I was here. We didn't get this close to the edge, but I think we need to go that way."

He pointed off in the distance.

"Looks as good as any other direction," said Liam.

He reached down and pulled Stella to a sitting position and then hoisted her onto his back, wrapping her arms around his shoulders and crossing her hands in front of his chest. He started walking, carrying her along.

"Let's get going," he said.

Chapter fifteen

he speed with which the Yokais carried their passengers was terrifying for all of the hobgoblins. B'nair was equally uncomfortable, but did his best to hide his fears. They flew without stopping. The sky darkened into night and they continued. The air got colder and the dawn that barely broke through the incessant cloud cover did little to warm the travelers.

The light that crept through the clouds was enough, though, to illuminate the one peak that rose high above all the others that surrounded it. B'nair had never been this far north. He had traveled to the southern edge of the Ice Kingdom in his frequent searches for new home lands for his people, but the ice and snow were far too inhospitable for their temperaments. It seemed now he was going to get more of a firsthand experience with the climate, although nothing so far led him to believe his earlier determinations were wrong.

The closer they got to the peak, the higher they had to fly, the colder the air became, and the stronger the winds blew. B'nair's hand was beginning to cramp up, and he was stiff. He had the axe cradled across his lap, but still had only the one hand with which to hold on. He looked over towards the other travelers. They were all exhausted. He turned in time to see one of the hobgoblins rubbing his arms to get warm. As he did this, the Yokai he was riding flapped its wings to surge a little higher.

The sudden motion caught the hobgoblin off guard and he lost his grip. He teetered backwards trying unsuccessfully to grasp the Yokais fur. Instead, he slipped down the back and off the beast. He must have known his fate was sealed. He fell in silence to the rocks below. B'nair watched, and seemed to be the only one to notice. More than ever, he had to do something to either change his status with the Kelpies, or find a way to escape.

"Escape," he thought to himself. An interesting way to describe his options. When had he changed his own perception of his involvement in all this from a willing participant – more: a driving force; to one who needed to escape?   He was beyond his depth and was quickly beginning to realize this. He would have to focus on making himself more of an asset to these sorcerers.

They finally rose higher than the top of the peak, crested the rim, and began their descent. Below them was the gaping hole of a giant, and hopefully dormant, volcano. B'nair scanned the area carefully. There was no sign of anyone else, but he could see hundreds of places where they could hide.

They were gliding down over the irregularly shaped circular opening. B'nair looked closely and could see a ridge that encompassed most of the outer edge. Off to one side he saw a stair-step of ledges opposite a long steep cliff littered with rocks and boulders. The two formations abutted a large, wide crack in the crusted inner surface, and a small cove in the triangle that was formed by the cliffs and the crack.

He wondered how strong that crust was. He could see another gash that intersected with the wider one. The largest area that was bordered by the two fractures had an immense hole in it and smaller fissures radiating out from the hole.

As they got closer, he saw a bridge that spanned the greater crack, leading from the area of the crust with the hole in it to the small cove resting between the two cliffs. It wasn't big enough for all of them and the Yokai's to land. With the wingspan of these creatures, there wasn't enough room for even one of them. They would have to take their chances on the crust.

Before they landed, B'nair spotted the cave. He knew instantly that this was where the Kelpie they were searching for was hidden. Just as he thought he would be touching down, the beast he was riding nosed up and circled around. It moved away so that the Yokai with the Kelpies could land first.

Angin Topan fluttered up into the air and off while Akmen Milzu dismounted. Once on the ground, the mountain Kelpie waved her hand and the Yokai rose up into the air and into the clouded sky. Only then did the second Yokai, carrying B'nai, land on the crust and allow him to dismount.

"I thought it better to have us land separately," said Akmen Milzu. "I was concerned that this crust would not hold the weight of all of us and the Yokai as well."

B'nair wondered if this was an attempt by the Kelpie to make up for the apparent snub of not allowing him to dismount first. He also wondered if he was making too much of it, and decided to simply nod his agreement. In the long run, he didn't really care. One by one the hobgoblins were lowered and deposited. No one commented on the absence of the hobgoblin who had fallen. It was as if he had never been with them.

They all stood, clustered around the bridge, each waiting for someone to take the lead. B'nair realized that the exact location of the buried Kelpie was known only to him. He had assumed the cave to be an obvious location, but then perhaps it was obvious only to him.

"It's in the cave," said B'nair.

He motioned across the bridge to the dark hole in the wall opposite the cove. He started to cross, but then remembered the landing. He stopped to wait for the Kelpies.

"She," corrected Akmen Milzu. "The Kelpie locked away here is a she, not an it."

B'nair turned towards the mountain Kelpie, bristling at being reprimanded like that. He fought back his anger and clarified.

"I meant the crypt," he said. "It – the crypt – is in the cave."

He motioned for the Kelpies to cross the bridge first, as if his hesitation immediately prior wasn't acknowledgement enough. He hoped that Angin Topan could no longer read his thoughts, because he was thinking how nice it would be if the bridge didn't hold her friend. If the desert Kelpie could read his mind, she gave no indication of this. She buzzed her wings and flew across in the company of the other one.

B'nair watched them cross, motioning for the hobgoblins to wait until Akmen Milzu was safely on the other side. He needn't have bothered. They all had enough experience with bridges to know they should wait. In spite of how strong it looked, any sort of spell could have weakened it. Once the Kelpies had crossed, B'nair motioned for them to follow. He stayed behind, surveying the rocks, the walls, the shelves, and every other place he thought might be a hideaway.

Quest of Eight Part Five: Release of the Demons

Richard Reda

Shortly after the last hobgoblin crossed, B'nair followed. He was paying more attention to the area behind him than he was to the cave he was entering. He was still outside as the others went ahead and entered. Immediately inside, though, everyone had stopped. They were all clustered close to the opening, not having ventured very far inside.

On the opposite side of the caldera, Lochen was crouched deep in an alcove. His reading – for the third time – of the book filled with the still undecipherable markings had been interrupted by the sounds of the beating of wings high above him. He closed the book, holding it tightly in his hand.

Peeking his head out from behind some rocks, he looked over to where Natalie was hiding. She had heard the same thing and had crawled behind cover. Lochen couldn't see any clue of her presence once she had moved. Good, he thought, hoping she'd be equally hidden from above. He looked up towards Quinn to find him standing up and staring at the creatures that had just flown over the crest of the volcano.

"What is he doing?" muttered Lochen.

He quickly stood up, keeping one eye on the arriving creatures and one on Quinn, and waved at Quinn, motioning for him to hide. Quinn looked over at Lochen and immediately dropped out of sight. Lochen ducked down and wedged himself into the narrow niche just as one of the giant winged creatures flew over head. He was hidden from view to the point that he missed seeing the familiar figure of the Rebbercand as he passed over.

Summer had seen the approaching beasts first and darted inside the cave. She immediately remembered the thousands of bats that called this place home and nearly darted back out into the open. Instead, she fought to overcome her fear, concentrated on blending into the background and making herself invisible, and, at the same, tried hard to ignore the stench. Please don't come back, she thought about the bats.

"Why do I get all the choice assignments?" she mumbled.

Natalie was able to crawl forward a few inches and peek around a pile of rocks once she saw that the Yokais had deposited their riders and flown up out of sight. She was able to get a fairly clear view of the cove and saw the Kelpies cross the bridge first, followed by the hobgoblins and then by the strange looking Rebbercand.

A shiver ran through her at the sight of him. She recalled her much too close encounter with another of his people – the one who had captured her and taken her to a far off island. Hopefully, that one was still stuck inside a distant tomb. This one, though, looked somewhat familiar.

High above her on the opposite side of the cove, Quinn had been trying to find the best way to start the avalanche Lochen expected him to deliver. He moved a few of the larger boulders to more strategic places, all the time mumbling that he hoped this was going to work. He tried to keep the arrangement looking natural, and, at the same time, provide him with cover.

"I hope he knows what he's doing," he said out loud. "I just want to get this over with and go home. We're no match for these Kelpie people. We're all just going to get killed. I could have been killed by that guy with the axe."

That was when he heard the flapping of wings in the distance. He stood up to get a better view and searched the skies for the source. Then he saw the enormous beasts swooping down on their location. He was mesmerized until something caught his eye. It was Lochen. He was waving. What did he want, Quinn wondered.

"Oh, poop," he said, realizing what was happening.

He dropped to the ground immediately and covered his head.

"This isn't happening," he said over and over again, crawling into a ball with his arms over his head. "If I can't see them, they can't see me."

A few minutes later, he could hear the noise from the Yokais rise into the air and disappear. He poked his head up just enough to sneak a peek down to the cove, hoping everyone had left. To his dismay, they were all on the ground. That Kelpie of stone was walking across the bridge with the really ugly, flying Kelpie right alongside.

Seven or eight hobgoblins followed after, and then came the Rebbercand. Quinn squinted, trying to get a better view of him. He looked familiar, but Quinn knew the only other time he had seen Rebbercands was in the mines of the Trepans.

"I don't remember seeing that one," he muttered, only able to see the scarred side of B'nair's face.

Seconds later, B'nair turned from the bridge towards the cave. When he did so, his head spun around in Quinn's direction. He paused for only a second. But it was long enough. Quinn could see the face full on.

"It's him," Quinn gasped.

In spite of the disfigurement, Quinn recognized him. He covered his mouth with his hands, afraid that the Rebbercand had heard him. He recognized the person who had nearly killed Sean, who had been dangling from the whip that was wrapped around Sean's ankle, and who had fallen to the river of lava below when Liam's knife cut through the whip.

How was that possible, he asked himself. He should be dead. Beads of sweat formed on Quinn's head. He had no idea that Rebbercands couldn't be killed. No one ever told him that. Why wouldn't someone say something about that? He was now in even greater dread. If

Rebbercands couldn't be killed, what did that say about the power of the Kelpies? He was frozen with fear.

The Kelpies, who had entered the cave first, seemed oblivious to the stench inside. The hobgoblins, however, were not. Akmen Milzu was the first to stop walking. The darkness had become pervasive. She was unable to see much more than a few feet before her. Whatever light was provided by the cave opening had been blocked by the small crowd of hobgoblins that had filled the entryway.

Angin Topan was having the same difficulty. While she did not find the smell offensive, she was able to identify it. It came from bats. Imps were a natural enemy of bats. Bats were one of their most feared predators. Even with her powers, she would not be able to overcome an entire colony. She scanned the ceiling, but couldn't see any indications of their presence. She strained to hear the subtle movement of their leather-like wings. Nothing. She fluttered closer to the mountain Kelpie for protection.

"We need some light in here," she whispered.

"I agree," said Akmen Milzu.

Having obtained her friend's concurrence, the imp immediately pointed her finger at a nearby stalactite. It slowly began to glow. It started as a deep red, gradually turned orange, then yellow and finally a soft white. The light it produced wasn't glaring, but it was sufficient to dispel the shadows.

"There it is," exclaimed the mountain Kelpie.

She was pointing to the large oval of deep red that was pulsating amid the black wall of stone. She started walking toward it. At the same time B'nair, who had been focused on what was behind all of them, finally turned and stepped inside the cave.

He looked at the luminescent stalactite and at the same moment detected the acrid smell inside the cave. He instinctively looked to the ceiling, expecting to see bats disturbed by the intruding light. There were none to be seen.

Something's not right, he thought. At this time of day, the ceiling should be covered with bats. That light should have startled them. They should have been screeching as they shot out of this cave.

Above him, almost pressed to the ceiling, Summer hovered as quietly as she could. Her wings flapped only enough to keep her stable. She hoped it would be dark enough, even with the light the Kelpie had generated, to hide the distortion in the air her moving wings created. She tried hard to watch the Rebbercand, the desert Kelpie and to be on the lookout for any returning bats, while at the same time, keep as silent and still as possible.

There was no way for her to be totally invisible. When she blended with her background it was more like looking through water. There was always some kind of ripple, especially when she had to flap her wings. Unbeknownst to her, her movements were lost in the flickering shadows cast on the ceiling by the hobgoblins moving below her.

She was too fixated on being discovered – by B'nair; by Angin Topan; by the bats – to have considered this. The Rebbercand was looking right up at her. She tried to stop moving and slowly began to drop. That was worse, she thought. The distortion would be coming right at him.

She took a chance and flapped twice to regain her altitude. He didn't react, so she held hope that she was still undetected. His gaze moved past her to the interior of the cave. He was searching the ceiling for something. Then she realized what.

"He's looking for the bats," she said to herself. "He knows they should be here. He knows something is wrong."

She began to get frantic. Would he figure out what was wrong before Lochen's plan could go into action? She was hoping he'd move a little further inside. He was too close to the opening. She'd barely have time to get out and pass the signal to Lochen. To do that, she'd have to show herself. At this close range, the Rebbercand would have to be blind not to see her.

"A little further," she pleaded mentally. "Just a little further."

By now the two Kelpies had moved closer to the tomb of their comrade. The hobgoblins were uncertain of what to do. Some of them had moved further into the cave, but others lingered near the entryway. They prevented B'nair from moving deeper himself. The Rebbercand and more than half the hobgoblins were still clustered too close to the opening.

"Come on," Summer thought. "Move it."

She tried willing the Kelpies to call the rest of them to come closer.

"Rebbercand," called the larger Kelpie. "Free our friend."

"Good," thought Summer. "Get him farther in there."

The hobgoblins still near the mouth of the cave moved further in and to the sides to make way for the Rebbercand. B'nair shifted his gaze from the ceiling as he heard Akmen Milzu call to him. He was momentarily distracted. The least she could do, he thought angrily, would be to learn my name. This slight diversion was enough. He had been concentrating too hard on what was wrong. The second he stopped thinking about it and focused on being summoned, it came to him.

He had turned to step further into the cave. He took two quick steps, and then, as his realization of what was wrong settled in, he slowed his pace and stopped. As soon as he had moved further into the cave, Summer darted from her hiding place out into the open right outside the entryway. She needed to signal to Lochen for the attack to begin. At the same moment, the realization of what was wrong struck B'nair like a thunderbolt.

"Bats!" he shouted. "There are no bats."

He turned back to the opening, looking at the ceiling of the cave and then again to the entryway.

"What are you talking about?" Akmen Milzu shouted back at him.

She was irritated that he hadn't come as she had instructed. She was talking to his back. He had turned away and was heading out of the cave. She became enraged by this demonstration of disrespect. Didn't he understand who she was? She turned to storm after him, brushing by Angin Topan.

"There should be bats inside the cave," B'nair answered back. "They're gone. Someone was here immediately before us."

He stopped abruptly just inside the entrance. He carefully stuck his head out and looked around. Only then did he step cautiously out of the cave, looking upward at the various places an enemy could hide. He suddenly realized how vulnerable they all were.

"How can you know that?" the mountain Kelpie continued, irritated at the delay. "The absence of bats proves nothing."

"It's a trap!" snapped B'nair.

Seconds before he moved to the mouth of the cave, Summer had shot out into the open and shed her invisibility. She was waving frantically at Lochen.

"Now!" she shouted. "Do it now!"

Her voice was lost in the wind. Lochen emerged from behind his hiding place and could see Summer reappear a few short feet from the opening of the cave. She needed to move. She was too close. He held off signaling Natalie and Quinn. When she didn't move, he stood up in plain view and waved his arms.

"Get away," he shouted to her.

As the words left his mouth, B'nair stepped out of the darkness. He saw Lochen and heard his caution. Who was he calling to, B'nair wondered. He shifted his focus to his immediate surroundings. He saw Summer who was only a few feet in front of him.

Summer saw Lochen stand up from behind his cover, wave his arms and shout to her to get away. She realized she was too close to the cave and started flying forward towards the bridge. She was unaware of the Rebbercand coming up behind her.

"Look out!" shouted Lochen.

He could tell that B'nair had seen Summer and was starting to come after her. His eyes were fixed on his target, and he had his axe poised for an attack. Summer was completely oblivious to the danger she was in. She was in a direct line between Lochen and B'nair. Any spell Lochen tried to cast to stop the Rebbercand would also strike her.

"Move!" he shouted to her.

She realized something wasn't going as planned. She stopped and hovered a few feet over the bridge and turned back to see what was wrong. That was when she found herself staring into the eye of the rapidly approaching B'nair. She was caught off guard, not only by how close he was, but by the figure of the mountain Kelpie marching immediately behind him.

B'nair increased his stride and raised his axe high behind his head. His eye was fixed on the faerie in front of him. For some reason she had stopped and turned back towards him. Without a moment's hesitation, he stepped onto the bridge and swung the axe.

Summer shifted her position, but not enough. She spun to one side, just as the giant blade came down. It quickly and neatly sliced through her wings, separating them from her body. She dropped through the space between one pair of the slats, down towards the chasm over which the bridge spanned.

B'nair had lunged forward to deliver the strike. The mountain Kelpie was immediately behind him. He felt no resistance to his cut and saw no evidence of its blow. He turned back towards the Kelpie to see her standing on the edge of the bridge where the faerie had disappeared, staring down into the abyss.

He looked up to see the wings fluttering like tiny leaves in the wind. He reached up with his free hand and snatched them out of the air. He looked down below towards the ribbon of lava deep inside the crevasse. There was no sign of the faerie.

"One less opponent," declared Akmen Milzu. "Well done, Rebbercand."

By now Angin Topan had flown up to join them. She looked from B'nair to the other Kelpie and then fluttered out over the edge of the bridge. There was no sign of Summer.

"She's gone," the desert Kelpie declared.

"I'm sorry to have robbed you of your toy," said B'nair. "Here. Take these as a souvenir."

He held out his hand and offered the severed wings. The imp looked at them for a second, taking in what she was seeing, and then took them from the Rebbercand's hand.

"Thank you," she said. "I'll keep them as a memento."

325

Quest of Eight Part Five: Release of the Demons

Richard Reda

Lochen had been watching all this as it unfolded. He was too shocked to react. In one instant Summer was there and in the next, she was gone. Before he could overcome what he was feeling, the mountain Kelpie had discovered him.

Akmen Milzu waved her hand at Lochen on the opposite side of the caldera. In less than a second, the ledge he was standing on collapsed. The ground beneath him dropped away. His arms shot up in the air. The book he had been holding in one of his hands the whole time flew up and away.

He fell more than twenty feet to the crust at the base of the cliff, falling face down. The book tumbled across the floor, teetered on the edge of the smaller of the two large gashes in the crust, and then dropped into the chasm. It burst into flames within seconds, and dissolved into ashes long before it reached the bottom.

Several rocks followed Lochen to the bottom of the ledge, striking him on the back and head. He was half buried in the debris and fell into unconsciousness. Angin Topan flew over to the sorcerer's body and hovered first on one side and then on the other, peering closely, but not coming within arm's reach.

"He appears to be dead," she called back to the others. "Or will soon be if he's not now."

Satisfied that he was no longer a threat, she flew back to B'nair and the mountain Kelpie. Quinn had heard her comment. A wave of deep sorrow swept over him, followed by an immense feeling of desolation. He sat on the ground with his head in his hands.

His fear and frustration grew quickly. He resented Lochen for putting them in this situation. He resented having been kept from his home for so long. He resented those below who had taken his friends from him. In a rage he turned over onto his hand and knees, and pushed several of the boulders that he had positioned for the avalanche. That done, he stretched out face down and began silently to weep.

Akmen Milzu mistook the advancing rockslide as the aftermath of the spell she had cast on Lochen. She saw the tumbling stones and waved her hand again. They all stopped in mid-slide and rose up into the air. She then shot her hand out towards them, and they were flung out over the rim of the volcano, over the side and to the bottom of the mountain.

Natalie, seeing two of her friends taken from her within seconds of one another, and Quinn's avalanche so easily thwarted, scurried back under cover. It was too late for her to cast a bubble blocking the cave. All she could do now was to stay hidden and wait for everyone else to leave. Then she'd see about Lochen and Quinn and try to make it back to the others.

"Stand guard in a perimeter outside of the cave," B'nair ordered the hobgoblins.

They spread out in a large arc stretching across the entire entryway, and took a defensive stance. B'nair then looked to the two Kelpies, and without a word, strode purposefully into the cave. The Kelpies followed wordlessly.

Once inside, Akmen Milzu caught up to B'nair and reached out to touch his shoulder. B'nair stopped and turned around.

"Rebbercand," she said. And then in a less demanding tone, "B'nair. I have underestimated you. It is a mistake I will not make again."

B'nair stared at the Kelpie, trying to discern if her comments were sincere or an attempt to pacify him. She was hard to read, but he decided to assume she meant what she said.

"Thank you," he finally responded. "Let's free your friend."

The three approached the deep red oval at the back of the cave. B'nair raised his free hand and felt the surface. The black stone surrounding the oval was cold, but as his hand moved to the dull glow

327

of the red, the heat became intense. In the center was an engraving that looked like the tip of a flame with beams of light emanating from the edges. He hesitated for a few seconds.

"What are you waiting for?" asked Angin Topan.

"Do you know what trick the Alchemist has placed behind this wall?" B'nair responded with his own question. "I'm certain that I do not."

The two Kelpies backed up slightly, but neither answered.

"The stone is hot to the touch," B'nair continued. "What manner of Kelpie is hidden here?"

"One of fire," answered Akmen Milzu.

B'nair looked behind him, ensuring that the few remaining hobgoblins were well clear of whatever spell or curse would be released with the freeing of this Kelpie. He thought about warning the two behind him, but then thought they, of all of them, should know what to expect.

He raised his axe and drove the blade into the stone. He had expected it to ring and reverberate, but instead it acted and sounded more like his blade had penetrated soft wood rather than granite. He pulled the axe free and at first nothing happened. Then a thick, blood-colored liquid began to ooze out of the opening.

The split widened, and the oozing became a gushing. The slime covered the floor of the cave. Angin Topan lifted herself into the air to keep from being covered, but Akmen Milzu stood her ground, letting the muck flow over her feet.

The material sizzled and began to smolder as it touched the Kelpie. It parted and flowed around B'nair who once again felt the protective power of the pendant inside his pocket. The cut in the face of the oval ripped further and with the last gush of slime, a figure emerged.

Quest of Eight Part Five: Release of the Demons

Richard Reda

He was deep red from head to foot. His skin was covered in what looked like burned flesh. Flakes of clothing hung over his body as if they had been burned to the torso. The body had fallen out of the opening and was crouched face downward, as if gasping for breath. The two Kelpies watched wordlessly.

The creature was kneeling, extended between B'nair, who was standing to one side, and the two Kelpies, who were on the other side. B'nair could only see the figure's back, legs and the back of its head. The legs appeared thin and muscular beneath the charred skin. The spine protruded with short nodules that grew larger and wider towards the head. The hair – what little there was – looked like burnt and twisted fibers emanating from a scarred scalp.

There was a sudden sucking in of air and the creature bucked, raising his head and finally standing up. The front of his body was covered with the same charred fabric as the back. Any skin that was exposed was the same burnt, scarred skin that was visible from behind. His face was short and wide, with ears that flared back like seashells, but curved up to points near the top of his head.

His eyes were like burning coals – completely red, except for glowing yellow centers were the pupils were. His nose was broad and very flat over a mouth that was wide. When he stood, he bent slightly forward as if crouched for an attack.

"Welcome back, Neraka Ferr," Akmen Milzu greeted the creature.

He looked silently from the mountain Kelpie to the desert Kelpie and then, finally to B'nair. He moved closer to the Rebbercand and looked him up and down. B'nair fought to control himself from reacting to the incredibly strong wave of sulfur that rose from the creature. He sniffed him and reacted visibly, moving away and covering her nose.

You don't smell like a garden yourself, thought B'nair. The odor was so strong it almost made his eyes water. He noticed, too, a sudden increase in the temperature when this Kelpie came close to him. It was clear that whatever the substance was that he was enclosed in was designed to counteract the tremendous heat he could generate.

"Who is this one?" he hissed in a voice that sounded like the striking of a match.

"He is with us," answered Angin Topan.

"I didn't ask who he was with," snapped the fire Kelpie, cutting Angin Topan off, but still facing the Rebbercand. "I asked who he was."

"You forget yourself," interjected Akmen Milzu. "You speak to a master."

The Fire Kelpie slowly turned and looked at the two as if seeing them clearly for the first time. He took a faltering step towards Akmen Milzu looking at her closely, and then turned his head towards Angin Topan. He looked the Desert Kelpie over and then turned back to the Mountain Kelpie.

"You are correct," he hissed. "My apologies."

"But to answer your question," Angin Topan continued. "He is a Rebbercand. He has half of the pendant and a map that discloses where the rest of our brethren are hidden. Does that clarify things for you?"

Neraka Ferr stared at the imp and then turned to the Rebbercand. He seemed to be assimilating this information. After a few seconds he turned back to the Kelpies.

"Have any others been freed, besides you?"

"Only Pantano Izaki," answered Angin Topan. "But he has been lost to us."

"He was a pompous fool," hissed Neraka Ferr. "Still, he was necessary. What are we to do without him?"

"We haven't discussed that," said Akmen Milzu.

B'nair had been listening to the discussion. He knew that for some reason, they needed all eight of the Kelpies. When the Swamp Kelpie had been destroyed, another image appeared on his map. It was not as distinct as the others, and didn't include a symbol like the others, but there was something that was revealed. At the time he hadn't paid much attention to it. Now he wondered if it was important.

"I may have some information that may be of use to you," he ventured.

The three Kelpies turned to him.

"Please share," asked Akmen Milzu.

B'nair explained about the indistinct image that appeared after the demise of the Swamp Kelpie. He said, based on the locations of the other Kelpies, this marking showed something hidden in the northern part of the Ice Kingdom. The next Kelpie was not far away from there – a location in the southern part of the Ice Kingdom.

"And the others after that?" hissed the Fire Kelpie.

"They are to the far south, except for one that is out to sea," B'nair answered.

"This may be one of the sorcerers the witch was mentoring," said Angin Topan.

"Could he be trusted?" asked Neraka Ferr.

"We may have no choice," answered Angin Topan.

"I suggest we seek this one out before moving south," said the Mountain Kelpie. "If he is of no value to us, he can be easily disposed of."

Those words did not fill B'nair with confidence about his own future.

"Do you need time to rest?" Akmen Milzu asked the Fire Kelpie.

"Help me out of this hole," he hissed. "I will do the rest."

The Mountain Kelpie offered her arm, which was taken, and the two walked slowly out of the cave. Once outside, the Fire Kelpie motioned to continue walking. They crept to the edge of the large crack. The Neraka Ferr released his escort's arm and stepped forward, dropping into the gap before anyone could stop him.

"What is he doing?" shouted B'nair.

They had risked a lot to get here, he thought. Too much for him to simply destroy himself. He turned back to the two other Kelpies and saw that they did not apparently have any concerns about their comrade's behavior.

A few seconds later, there was a rumbling sound from deep within the crack. The surrounding crust began to quake. B'nair and the hobgoblins backed away, clinging to the wall of the caldera. In a rush of hot air, the Fire Kelpie rose from a spew of lava. His body was still covered with burned and crusted skin and fabric, but seemed fuller and stronger.

The hobgoblins were relieved that it appeared he wouldn't need one of them to regain his power. At his return to the surface, the Mountain Kelpie once again called for the Yokais. They had been circling high above, out of sight. Now they returned, one by one, to gather their passengers.

As they climbed on, the creatures soared upward and disappeared in the gray skies. When quiet returned to the top of the volcano, Quinn raised his head and looked around. On the opposite side of the cove, he saw Natalie slowly emerge from her hiding place. He watched as she stood up, walked to the edge of the cliff and looked around.

Eventually her gaze turned towards Quinn. He climbed to his feet, wiped his eyes and waved to her. He turned around and began the trek around the rim to the place where he could climb down to the floor. She did the same, both of them heading for Lochen.

Chapter sixteen

iam had been carrying Stella on his back for several hours. Sean was leading the way, which was fine with him. He had no idea where they were going. Solveig seemed to have gotten her senses back, or at least he and Sean hoped so. Right now, though, he was worried about how much longer they could go without finding some shelter.

The first sun had set and the second one was not far behind. The cloud coverage hadn't changed, but the little bit of light that had broken through was better than the darkness that was approaching. He also noticed that the temperature, which was already low, was dropping even further.

334

Quest of Eight Part Five: Release of the Demons

Richard Reda

Ever since they had reached the top of the glacier and began their trek, the terrain had been pretty much the same: flat. Now they were beginning to see giant drifts of snow and ice and the outcroppings of rock. He had hoped this would provide some escape from the wind, but he was disappointed.

What on earth did Quinn like so much about this place, he wondered. He needed to stop. He was wearing out more often between rests, and they needed to consider finding a place to spend the night. He looked up and saw Solveig about ten or fifteen feet in front of him and Sean about the same distance in front of her.

"Solveig," he called. "I need to stop. Shout up to Sean to slow down for a few minutes."

She did as he asked, and Sean came back to join them. The cold was affecting him as well. He was shivering in spite of the pace he had been keeping. Only Solveig, who was wrapped in the strange cloak given to her by the old sentinel in the woods, was warm.

"I'm not going to be able to go on much longer," said Liam. "It's starting to get dark. We need to think about shelter."

"This is as good a place as any," said Sean.

Solveig and Liam looked around. All they saw were some drifts and a low rock formation. Sean could see by the looks on their faces that they were a bit skeptical.

"When I was here last time with Quinn," he explained, "he showed me what his dogs do to stay warm out in the open like this."

"Great," said Solveig. "But we're not dogs. We're not covered with fur."

"That doesn't matter," said Sean.

He asked Liam for one of the daggers he was carrying. Then he walked over to the rock mound and poked around a few times until he found the right spot. He began digging through the ice, chipping a hole. In a few minutes, he had carved out a long, narrow tunnel and disappeared inside.

Liam and Solveig watched, still not understanding what he was doing. Every so often he would reappear with an armload of chipped ice. He threw it out of the opening, scattering it on the ground. In about twenty or thirty minutes he poked his head out.

"All set," he said. "Solveig, if I could borrow your cloak, you can all come inside."

She reluctantly took off her cloak and stuffed it in to him through the opening. Uncertain, she looked at Liam, who only shrugged his shoulders.

"Go ahead," he said. "Crawl in and I'll slide Stella in to you and them come in after."

Solveig got down on her hands and knees. Her teeth began to chatter almost immediately. She inched her way forward into the darkened interior. After a foot or two, she could sense a larger opening and reached out to feel her way along.

"You can probably create a light ball," said Sean. "Or whatever those things are that you make light with."

Not bothering to explain, she rubbed her hands together. A static charge began to form and she thrust one arm forward. A popping sound was followed by an explosion of diffused light that attached itself to the walls of the interior and spread around, illuminating everything.

What she saw was like the inside of a large ball, but flat on the bottom, where her cloak was spread out. On the far side Sean was stretched out and smiling at her. Before she could react, she felt Stella being pushed in after her.

She turned around and grabbed Stella's shoulders, pulling her all the way in and stretching her out next to Sean. As soon as she was in, Liam entered. Once his head was through the opening, he stopped and looked all around.

"Interesting," he said. "Is this some kind of ice house?"

"Exactly," answered Sean. "Quinn showed me how to make these, except he made one cut out of blocks of ice. He called them unglues. Or maybe they were big goos. I don't remember. Anyway, we'll be nice and warm inside and the ice doesn't even melt. Go figure."

"What about this big hole I just crawled through?" asked Liam. "Won't cold air come in that way? And what about any stray animals?"

"Oh, yeah," said Sean. "I forgot. Go back outside and scoop up some of the ice I chipped out from here. Roll it into a ball and pull it to the opening. That should seal it up enough."

Liam did as he asked and returned to the inside. There wasn't much room, but it was beginning to warm up and that more than made up for the lack of space. He stretched out trying to get comfortable without sticking his feet into anyone's face.

"Just like home," he said.

"Really?" asked Sean, smiling broadly.

"No," said Liam. "Not really, but it'll do. It would be even nicer if we had some food. I'm so hungry I could eat dirt."

"Oh," said Solveig. "I may have something."

"I hope it's more than dirt," said Sean. "Liam's the one who said he'd eat dirt. Not me."

She felt around on the cloak until she found one of the pockets. She reached inside and pulled out some nuts and some fruit that had dried out.

"It's not much," she said, offering it to Liam and Sean.

"Keep some for yourself," said Liam.

He took only a portion of what she offered, and they ate their meager dinner in silence. The silence continued for several minutes. Each of them was lost in their own thoughts.

"I hope the others are all right," said Sean.

Solveig turned towards him, wishing he hadn't said anything. She had been afraid that saying anything would somehow bring bad luck. It was irrational, she knew. Their luck hadn't been very good at all, but at least they were all safe. Well, she thought, except for Stella, who was unconscious and had a nasty cut and bruise on her forehead.

She was still looking at Sean as these thoughts ran through her head. And then tears began to form and run down her cheeks.

"What?" asked Sean, feeling a little guilty. "What did I say? What happened? I'm sorry. What's wrong?"

"You didn't do anything wrong," she said. "Or say anything wrong."

"Then why are you crying?" asked Liam.

"I don't know," she said, wiping her face. "I wish we had never split up. I'm afraid something bad has happened to the others."

"What?" asked Sean. "What's happened? What do you know? Did you get some kind of vision?"

"Quit asking so many questions," said Liam. "Let her answer one before you throw three more at her."

"I don't know anything, for sure," she said. "Maybe I'm just tired. And worried. It's just that I always have some kind of connection with Lochen. I always sort of know he's all right. I haven't felt that connection for a while."

"Maybe there's some kind of spell near where the Kelpie he's looking for is," suggested Sean. "Maybe the spell sort of blocks that connection."

"I suppose," said Solveig.

"Come on," said Liam. "You know what Lochen's like. He always manages to get out of trouble. Besides, Quinn, Natalie and Summer won't let him get too crazy."

Solveig shrugged a little and gave a half-hearted laugh, but didn't say anything. She was worried about them, too. It was more than not feeling her connection with Lochen. She felt something awful had happened, but she couldn't put it into words. She didn't want to put it into words. That might make it real.

"I just need some rest," she said.

Dismissing any further discussion, she rolled over on her side and closed her eyes. After a few seconds, she raised her head and snapped her fingers. The light that emanated from the walls of the small enclosure dimmed, but did not go out altogether. In a few seconds Liam and Sean closed their eyes, and shortly they were all asleep.

Quest of Eight Part Five: Release of the Demons

Richard Reda

Outside the makeshift camp a large creature walked by. At first it almost missed the tiny cave, but then it caught a strange scent. Its head rose into the air, its nose searching for the source. There it was. The creature followed the unusual aroma to its source: a mound tucked against a small outcropping of rock.

The origin came from underneath. The creature could see where an opening had been carved out and then filled with a clump of chipped ice. It lowered its head and sniffed again. There were four inside. The beast moved away to the other side of the rock and settled in for the night. They would still be there in the morning.

When the dim glow inside the ice cave was matched by the dim glow of morning, still diffused by the gray skies, the campers began to awaken. Liam woke first, slightly stiff from having carried Stella the day before, and from sleeping on the hard, cold ground.

Sean woke next, but curled up tighter into a ball. In spite of how warm the interior had gotten, he was still chilled to the bone. All his life had been spent in the warm climate of the forest. During his unscheduled and unplanned visit with Quinn, he had never felt warm. Now was no different.

When Solveig rose, the sense of foreboding she had felt the night before was still with her. She decided, though, to keep her concerns to herself. She looked over at Stella and gave her a gentle shake. Stella did not respond. Solveig leaned close and could see that she was breathing, slowly and shallowly.

She touched the cut on her head and felt Stella's skin burning. She pressed her hand to Stella's forehead and could feel the fever raging in her.

"We need to find help," said Solveig. "Stella's really warm. In fact she's hot. I think she's got some kind of infection or something. If it were one of us, she'd have a potion or something to fix us; but it's not. And we don't know what to do to fix her."

340

"I don't think we're too far away," said Sean.

"Where exactly are we going?" asked Liam.

"Wherever the jackals are."

"What?" exclaimed Liam. "You're leading us <u>to</u> the jackals?"

"Well...yeah," said Sean somewhat uncertainly. "I just figured that nearly every time we found a sentinel, there were jackals around. I thought that, maybe, the jackals were, you know, like pets or something."

"Pets?" asked Solveig.

"Or something," added Sean.

"I don't believe it," said Liam. "What? Kelpies and Rebbercands weren't enough danger for you?"

"No," said Sean. "I mean, yes, they are plenty dangerous, but I didn't think that the jackals..."

"You didn't think?" Liam nearly shouted.

"Hold on, you two," interjected Solveig. "Give him a chance to explain. Go ahead, Sean."

"OK," he said. "Think about it. You ran into jackals in the woods, Solveig."

"Yes," she cut in, unable to heed her own advice. "And they were pretty scary, if you ask me – not something I look forward to."

"I know," Sean answered. "But nothing happened. I mean nothing happened with the jackals. You got turned blue, and that was something, but not because of the jackals. Right?"

"Go on," she said, not completely convinced.

"And then that Sarnanok guy...there were jackals there, too; and they were scary, but they didn't attack us. Remember? He told them to go away, and they did. Why would they do that just because he asked if they weren't his pets?"

"Or something," added Solveig.

"Right," said Sean. "Or something. When Quinn and Lochen and I were here in the Ice Kingdom, we ran into a pack of jackals. They cornered us, but they never hurt us. I bet there was a sentinel somewhere near, but we got away before he or she came out."

"So you think it was a good idea to go looking for jackals on the off chance that there might be a sentinel nearby?" asked Liam, outraged at the danger Sean had put them in.

"Yeah," said Sean. "It seemed like a good idea at the time."

"Really?" asked Liam.

"I agree," said Solveig.

"You what?" asked Liam, not believing what he was hearing.

"Yes," said Solveig. "I agree. Don't look so smug, Sean. You should have told us from the start. But, it makes sense. I was surrounded by them – well, not actually surrounded. They were on three sides, kind of like they were backing me towards the sentinel. They did the same thing with Sarnanok."

"I can't believe I'm hearing this," said Liam. "But I guess it's too late to do anything else. I sure hope you're right."

Me, too, Sean said to himself.

"We might as well get this over with," said Liam, resigning himself to their fate.

He kicked the ball of ice out of the opening and crawled to the outside. He then reached back in to grab Stella's shoulders and drag her out. Solveig followed and then came Sean. When Sean emerged, he pulled Solveig's cloak out and returned it to her. Then he discovered that he still had the dagger Liam had given him to chip out their shelter. He handed it back to his friend.

"Keep it," said Liam. "If you're wrong about all this, you're going to need it."

He reached down, took Stella's wrists in his hands, spun her around and lifted her onto his back.

"Lead the way," he said to Sean.

The trio, with Stella being carried on Liam's back, left the tiny shelter behind and continued around to the opposite side of the rock mound. Ahead of them was another expanse of open plain – nothing but white underneath the gray skies. The way ahead was so bleak, that Sean was losing confidence that he was heading the right way.

After a while the line spread out in the same pattern it had the day before. Sean was in the lead a few yards ahead of Solveig, with Liam and Stella a few yards behind her. The only sounds they heard were the crunching of their feet in the ice and the wind as it whipped across the frost.

In spite of this, Liam had the distinct impression they were not alone. He hadn't had this sensation immediately, but it seemed to have crept up on him suddenly. He looked to the left and then to the right. There was nothing to be seen in either direction. He wasn't sure if he wanted to see Sean's jackals or not.

Just as he was about to dismiss the feeling as basic paranoia, he heard a crunch almost immediately behind him. He spun around, dropped Stella and pulled a dagger from his belt. In that same instant, he knew the dagger would do him little good.

He found himself staring up into the face – the eyes and jaws were the most predominant features – of a giant arctic wolf. The wolf didn't appear ready to attack, but it took a more threatening position when it spotted the dagger.

Liam looked at the wolf, then at its eyes, and then at his dagger. He tried nudging Stella back across the ice and snow, away from the wolf, but she wasn't moving easily. He slowly stood straight up, raised his hands, and slowly put the dagger back in his belt.

"Take it easy, there, big guy," he said, trying to show no fear and that he was no threat.

"Hey, Sean," he called, trying not to raise his voice too much. "I think we've run into a little problem."

Solveig turned back first and let out a short scream at seeing the wolf. Sean, who hadn't heard Liam call to him, reacted to the scream. He spun around, pulling his slingshot from his belt and whipping out the dagger Liam had given him. He hadn't thought that he couldn't shoot the slingshot and hold the dagger at the same time. He ran up next to Solveig.

"Just stay calm," he said. "I'm going to..."

He looked down and saw the dagger in his right hand and the slingshot in his left hand. He looked from one to the other, and then handed the dagger to Solveig.

"I'm going to ease up next to Liam," he continued. "I'll try to get the wolf to back off..."

As soon as he said the word, something clicked. He looked up at the wolf, which was partially blocked by Liam. He took a few steps to the side to get a better angle. That was when he saw a crystal hanging around the animal's neck.

"It's wolfy," shouted Sean.

He ran towards Liam.

"Don't worry," shouted Sean. "He's a friend. He won't hurt us."

When he got up next to Liam, the wolf turned its enormous head towards Sean and growled menacingly. Sean skidded to a stop and fell backwards, his hand raised in a feeble attempt at defense.

"Whoa," he said. "It's me, wolfy. Remember?"

"He's a friend? Really?" asked Liam. "I'd hate to see how you're greeted by enemies."

"We didn't exactly get off on the right foot the first time we met," said Sean.

He put the slingshot away and slowly got to his feet. He raised his hands to show he was holding no weapons and slowly walked towards the wolf.

"Sean," cried Solveig. "Be careful."

"Trust me," said Sean, not fully convinced. "He won't hurt us." I hope, he added silently.

He had moved right in front of the wolf. Standing up as tall as he could, his head barely reached the bottom of the wolf's jaw. The wolf lowered its head and sniffed. He backed his head away for a second to fix his eyes on Sean, and then sniffed again. Then to everyone's surprise, it licked its huge tongue up Sean's face.

"See?" he said. "I told you."

The wolf moved around Liam to Stella and sniffed her. Then he took her arm in his jaw and, before any of them could react, he flipped her up onto his back. He lowered himself down to the ground and looked back at Sean and Liam.

"I think he wants us to climb on," said Sean.

Without waiting for any debate, Sean climbed on the wolf's back. Liam hesitated, but Solveig knew this had to be better than walking. She ran up, slowing down immediately once she got closer and then timidly climbed up behind Sean. Liam finally got on behind Solveig, and then the wolf rose and began to run.

Sean leaned forward to hold on to Stella and the wolf's fur, while Solveig held on to him and Liam on to her. At times it was like riding a rollercoaster as the wolf bounded over the plains, and the wind whipped across the ice. But no one was complaining. It was better, and much faster, than walking.

In a few hours a mountain began to rise on the horizon. As they got closer, they could see that the face of the mountain was a sheer cliff. Sean recognized it immediately.

"That's it," he shouted, pointing ahead. "That's where we were attacked by the jackals."

"I thought you said they didn't attack," Solveig shouted into his ear.

"Not so loud," he complained, ducking his head away and shielding his ear with his shoulder.

"Well?" Solveig pursued when Sean didn't answer.

"I never said these jackals didn't attack us," he said. "I only said the other ones – the ones all of us ran into – they didn't attack us."

Solveig reached up and smacked the back of his head.

"Don't ever do that again," she said. "You're just lucky Liam can't reach you."

"Cheeze," he whined. "You try to do somebody a favor…"

When they were a few hundred yards away, other figures began to appear. The ice jackals that had surrounded Sean, Quinn and Lochen reappeared. The wolf growled, barked and snapped at the growing herd. They threatened, but made no signs of advancing.

As they got closer to the cliff, it seemed as if a figure was taking shape inside the ice wall. Sean pointed him out and Solveig followed his finger towards the side of the mountain. Sure enough, in the center of the wall was a section that looked like a curtain of ice and inside was a man.

He appeared to be walking towards them. Solveig thought that perhaps the man was on the other side of the sheet of ice, but as she continued to stare, she saw him actually walk through it. Once he did, the jackals all turned their attention from the wolf and his passengers to the man.

He was very tall, and covered in silver and white fur. His white hair blended into the fur and bordered his wide face. His skin was dark and set with deep wrinkles. His nose was broad and separated high and distinctive cheek bones. His eyes were a piercing blue – the color of the sky that none of them had seen in a long time.

He stepped forward several feet and waved a hand in the direction of part of the herd of jackals. They howled as if in pain, dropped their tails and scurried away. He only had to look at the other half on the other side and they did the same. The wolf never slowed his pace, but ran right at the man.

Quest of Eight Part Five: Release of the Demons

Richard Reda

The man watched as the wolf approached, and then turned to walk back through the wall of ice as simply as if he was walking through a mild waterfall. The wolf gave no indications of slowing down. Sean braced himself for a sudden stop of some kind. Either the wolf would stop running or it would slam into the face of the cliff.

Solveig ducked her head, also waiting for the impact, shielding her face behind Sean's back. Liam tightened his grip around her waist and looked straight ahead. A few feet from the wall, the wolf bounded into the air as if he was leaping over a log and dove into the wall. He slipped through to the other side as if nothing was there.

Once inside the mountain, the wolf slowed to a halt, walked to where the old man was sitting and dropped to the ground. They were in the center of a cone shape cutout well inside the mountain. The cone rose high into the air and the top disappeared into the darkness. The old man was sitting cross-legged on a pile of furs comfortably arranged around a large fire.

Liam, Solveig and Sean climbed off the wolf's back and pulled the still unconscious Stella behind them. When he was freed of his burden, the wolf crawled closer to the old man and put his head in the man's lap. The man reached a broad, thick, but old hand, up and ran it over the wolf's head.

"So, Cara Lagun, I see you have brought guests," he said to the wolf.

His voice was deep and resonant, but couldn't hide the age of the speaker.

"Is that his name?" asked Sean. "Cara Lagun? We just called him wolfy."

The old man turned his piercing blue eyes on Sean.

"Cara Lagun is better," Sean said almost apologetically. "Wolfy isn't so good. Actually, it was Quinn who named him wolfy. I'm babbling now. Someone else talk. Please."

"What does it mean?" asked Solveig.

"Faithful friend," the old man answered.

He motioned for them to sit down and then looked at Stella.

"This one needs some attention," he said. "Bring her to me."

Sean and Liam lifted Stella and carried her over to him, placing her at his feet. He ran his hand over her forehead, smoothing back her hair. In spite of how large and powerful his old hands looked, his touch was surprisingly gentle.

"This one has the vision," he said.

He reached into his parka and pulled something from an inside pocket. Between his finger and thumb he held a pinch of what looked like a deep purple powder. He sprinkled it on the cut and brushed his thumb over it, softly pushing the powder into the wound. He reached behind him and picked up a small roll of pelts and tucked it under her head.

"She will sleep now, and will be better before you leave."

"Thank you," said Solveig. "Are you a sentinel?"

"My name is Afea. At one time I was a Protector of the Ice Kingdom. But that was long ago. Now I am a sentinel."

"Protector?" asked Liam. "Is that like a Guardian? One of our friends is a Guardian."

"No," Afea answered. "Guardian's are special. They are the chosen ones, descended from the Nelabas."

"I see," said Sean. "If you're a sentinel are you supposed to help us in some way? Can you tell us where our friends are? Are they safe?"

"The Alchemist knew you would split up. It was not a wise decision. They are coming, but they are not the same."

"What does that mean?" asked Solveig. "How are they not the same? What happened?"

"That is for another time. Not my time."

"But," Solveig persisted.

"No," said Liam. "Let him tell us what he has to tell us. Remember the others?"

Solveig recalled how the other sentinels had quickly passed away and turned to dust. As much as she wanted to know about Lochen and the others, she knew Liam was right.

"Life is not a separate event," Afea began. "Rocks, trees, mountains, and everything that is visible lives and is part of our lives. We are all connected."

"I see," said Sean when the sentinel paused as if waiting for some kind of response.

He didn't react to Sean's comment and continued.

"There are other worlds under this one and above this one, and they are like ours in everything, but they are different. Even in their difference, they are the same."

Once more he was silent. Once more Sean, feeling the need to fill the void, nodded and responded, "I see."

"The streams that come down from the mountains," continued the sentinel, "are the paths to the underworld, and the mountains are the stairways to the upperworld. Life comes from the north bringing the cold; its fingers creating the ice and snow. Until it changes and touches the land with its warm breath bringing new life."

He lowered his head. It almost looked as if he had fallen asleep. The three looked at one another and shrugged.

Sean again said, "I see."

The old man's head bobbed up and he continued as if there had been no pause in his speech.

"New life begins the cycle again. It is necessary. The suns bring warmth as the night brings the cold. Each one of us, from the smallest insect to the largest animal, we all touch each other."

He stopped again, but this time he didn't lower his head. He looked at Liam, then at Solveig and finally at Sean. He held Sean's gaze for several seconds.

"I see," repeated Sean, not sure what else to say.

"You tell me you see," the old man responded, "but you do not see. You are seeing with your eyes and not your mind."

Sean nodded as if he understood, and then shook his head left to right.

"You're right," he admitted. "I don't see what you're talking about at all."

The old man reached out and placed his hand on Sean's face, closing his eyes. His hand was so large it covered his face completely.

"See with your mind's eye," commanded the sentinel. "The mountains speak but are silent. They express their power and majesty by their presence. The sea is the source of life, but it cannot heal itself. The air nourishes us all, but takes its nourishment from us. We are all one. We have been chosen to be the stewards of the land, the sea and the air. We must not disturb the harmony, the balance, and the beauty of our gift."

He dropped his hand from Sean's face and looked deep into his eyes.

"You are eight because you must maintain the balance. Eight there were in the beginning. Eight in balance to face the others. The four corners of our world, matched with four corners to balance and compliment. All things must be in balance."

He stared into Sean's eyes, and Sean held his gaze. He could feel the old man's words boring into his mind, taking shape, taking meaning. Liam and Solveig watched him.

"Eight to fight the evil that grew unchecked. Even evil must be balanced. It cannot be allowed to rein free. Evil will destroy all if those who are good do nothing. Evil has risen again. It is your time now. My time has come to an end."

The old man turned back to Solveig and Liam. He looked down at Stella and placed his hand on her forehead once again.

"Her fever is gone," he said. "When she wakes she will know where you must go. Your challenge will be great. It will come from within as well as without."

He stood up, but motioned for them to stay where they were.

"You must rest. Your battle has just begun. You must not fail. I was one who had been given the gift of stewardship, but I squandered it. This is my atonement. I have now come full circle. I have completed the cycle and can return to my ancestors."

He turned and walked away from them towards the wall of ice through which they had passed earlier. The wolf, still on the ground nearby, raised its eyebrows, but didn't move. The sentinel kept walking, then stopped and came back.

"The jackals," he said. "They are protectors of the sentinels. But not these. They are ice jackals and are minions of the Kelpies. Do not trust them. Cara Lagun will guide you, but cannot take up your fight. Twice you have saved and protected him. He will give his life for you. The Alchemist has chosen wisely. Do not let him down."

With that he turned back and continued to walk. He walked through the wall of ice to the outside, and then disappeared from sight. The wolf whimpered, but didn't move. Sean got up to follow him, but the wolf sprung to his feet and cut him off.

"No," said Sean. "Back off, wolfy, or Cara Legume, or whatever your name is. We can't let him go out there by himself."

The wolf growled, but Sean wasn't threatened by the noise. When he tried to push his way around the creature, the wolf continued to block his way until, finally, it raised up on it hind legs, knocked Sean over and pinned him down.

"I guess he doesn't want you to leave," said Liam.

"It seems that way to me, too," said Solveig.

"But the sentinel," objected Sean. "He just said those jackals can't be trusted. He walked right out there. I'm sure they're still there waiting for him or for us."

"Sean," said Solveig. "Remember what happened with the other sentinels? When they meet us, their time is over. He knows that. I think he didn't want to simply collapse in front of us and turn to dust. Actually, I'm sort of glad he didn't."

She yawned widely as she finished talking. Liam had been yawning, too. The wolf gave Sean a lick with his tongue, but didn't let him up.

"All right," Sean said in resignation. "I won't go after him."

The wolf gave him one more lick and got off him, but still blocked the exit. Sean was suddenly very tired. He looked down at Stella, who was sleeping soundly, and then over at Liam and Solveig. They both had gradually dropped down to the fur covers, curled up and fallen asleep. Sean yawned, and decided he needed to close his eyes, if only for a few seconds. Before he finished the thought, he was sound asleep.

Outside, the ancient Protector, the long time sentinel walked away from the wall of ice. Sean had been right. The jackals were still there, waiting. His steps were slower suddenly, and his posture was less erect. The deep wrinkles on his face were even deeper, and his dark coloration had begun to turn ashen.

He sat on the ice, raised his head to the sky and told some unseen force that his task was done. He was ready to come home. As the pack of jackals leapt across the ice, he turned to dust and the wind carried off what remained.

Chapter seventeen

uinn turned behind him and looked for a way down to reach Lochen. The rim around the outer edge would take too long, he decided. He turned back towards the cove. The cliff face extending from where he stood to the bottom was steep, but angled. It would be risky, but he was sure he could slide down it. At this point he no longer cared about the risks. He walked around the few boulders that remained, looked down the slope, took a deep breath, and stepped out over the edge. He fell into a sitting position, half by accident and half on purpose, and began to slide.

Quest of Eight Part Five: Release of the Demons

Richard Reda

He dug his heels into the mixture of dirt, gravel and ash that coated the slope in an effort to slow himself down. It was enough to allow him to also shift his weight to swerve around larger, immovable rocks buried but not completely covered on the way down. In a few seconds he landed with a thump on the floor of the cove and slid across the smaller crust, rolling over onto his stomach as he spun around. When he stopped moving, he got up, brushed himself off and ran across the bridge.

At the same time Natalie was working her way off the shelf where she had been positioned in a more conventional, although slower, manner. She picked her way through the cracks and crevices to the bottom, managing not to fall, and reaching the cove shortly after Quinn had crossed the bridge.

He ran blindly across the granite slats, his feet pounding over the place where Summer had last been seen. The bridge swayed gently with his weight, but moved only slightly. As he ran, he glanced over the side in the slimmest of hope that she had survived the fall. There was no sign of her and he saw nothing that caused him to slow down.

He reached the opposite side of the bridge and ran along the edge of the smaller of the two gorges, near the thinner splits that emerged from the large hole like broken beams of sunlight. This was still taking too long, he thought. He changed his direction, moving too close to the sections of the large crusted area that were gray in color, instead of the black that covered most of the floor.

He was running so hard, that he almost didn't hear the cracking sound. Almost. At first he thought it was little more than the crunching of the ash and stone beneath his feet, but then there was a louder, single, wrenching noise that made him stop.

"That doesn't sound good," he said out loud.

Natalie heard the smaller cracks and stopped before she was even off the bridge. She looked up to where Quinn was and saw him trying to cut across the crust. He's too close to the hole, she thought. Before she could call out to him to warn him, she heard the grinding sound. She froze. And then she saw one of the thinner lines that ran from the hole to the smaller chasm suddenly split, growing wider and wider.

More thin lines began to appear, spreading like cracks in a pane of glass, zig-zagging in several directions. Quinn had stopped running and was now looking at the ground beneath his feet. It was still solid – or at least appeared to be. But the area behind him was littered with signs of broken crust. In spite of the pattern of fractures, it looked like it had stopped splitting. Even so, it didn't look sturdy enough to hold him.

He turned back to the ground ahead of him to see one of the lines from the hole had widened. It was too large for him to jump across. His path forward was now cut off. He turned around and debated about going back. There were dozens of cracks in the ground. He wasn't sure if any of it was safe. He looked up and saw Natalie looking at him. The expression on her face did nothing to lift his spirits.

"I think I'm stuck," he said. "I don't know which way to go and I don't think I can stay here much longer."

"Don't move," she called back to him. "I have an idea."

"Make it fast," he pleaded.

She rubbed her hands together, created a small bubble about the size of an orange, and threw it out onto the ground a few feet in front of Quinn. He looked down at it, and then back up at her with an expression of disbelief.

"That's it? That's your idea? I don't think that's big enough for me to fit in," he said, stating the obvious.

"You think?" she answered. "Just hang on. I'm not done."

She repeated the process over and over. Soon there was a layer of small bubbles spread out between Quinn and her. Some of them fell through the cracks and disappeared. She made larger ones to replace them that seemed to fill the opening. Once one layer was finished, she quickly generated more to make a second layer.

"I'm not sure if this is going to work," she told him. "Try to walk on the bubbles that are on the more solid parts."

"What if I step on the ones in the cracks?" he asked.

"I think you'll be all right. I tried to make them so they'd expand with pressure. Even so, try to avoid them. They may just push the crack wider and fall away."

"Great," he mumbled.

"You have a better idea?" she shot back.

"No," he grumbled.

Resigned, he put one tentative foot forward, leaning down to look more closely at the section he was stepping on. It seemed solid, so he put his foot down all the way and took the step. Nothing happened. So far, so good, he thought. He straightened up and tried to relax.

"What are you waiting for?" Natalie shouted, impatient with his deliberating.

"Hey!" he shouted back. "Who's the one doing this?"

Before she could respond, he took another careful step. This time there was another cracking sound. He closed his eyes and held his breath, waiting for the crust to give way. He felt the ground under his foot recede slightly, but then seemed to hold.

Quest of Eight Part Five: Release of the Demons

Richard Reda

"Closing your eyes and holding your breath aren't going to help," shouted Natalie. "Keep moving, but be careful."

"All right, all right" he said, gasping as he let out his breath and popped open his eyes. "No need to be pushy. Keep going. I can do that."

He took another step. This time he not only heard another crack, he saw the opening beneath him widen. Some of the bubbles to his immediate right dropped into the chasm and away from sight. At that moment, he forgot about being careful, about going slowly, and about the consequences. He bolted.

The ground dropped away piece by piece as one foot after another stomped down and pushed him forward. He ran straight for the bridge, the sound of the crumbling crust racing immediately behind him. He didn't slow down for an instant.

Natalie was still standing on the end of the bridge watching. Contrary to her own admonitions, she was holding her breath, although her eyes were as wide open as they could get. The shell that formed the floor of the center of the caldera was cascading like a wave crashing on the shore. It was folding away, dropping into the fiery abyss with Quinn running on the leading edge.

He and the crumbling floor were headed directly towards Natalie. Once she realized this, she turned back towards the cove, looking back over her shoulder as the disintegration and the runner came at her like a freight train. She began, almost too late, to start running herself, shifting her head towards the opposite end of the bridge and back again at the approaching disaster.

Within seconds, Quinn had caught up to her. She almost expected him to plow into her, but instead, he swept her up with one arm without breaking stride and leaped across the final feet of the bridge as the anchors on the opposite side dropped away with the rest of the section of crust to which it was attached.

The bridge dropped into the chasm, pulling away from the cove end and taking a few feet of the smaller shell with it. Quinn had dived to the end of the bridge and slid on his side, holding Natalie in his opposite arm, raising her in the air to keep her protected. As soon as he stopped sliding, he jumped up and headed for the step-like ledges where she had earlier been positioned, not waiting to see if the rest of the cove was going to hold or fall.

"I think...we're...all right...now," Natalie gasped as Quinn's arm squeezed her with each step. "I...think...you...can...stop...PLEASE!"

"I'm not taking any chances," he shouted.

He scrambled to the top before stopping and turning back. When he did, he saw that most of the cove was intact, but now nearly a third of the crust at the far end of where the bridge once had been was gone. The remains of the original hole looked like the letter "C" with jagged lines running from the top and bottom of the letter to what had previously been two large intersecting cracks.

There was no sign of the bridge, and, if Summer had somehow managed to grabbed a section of the slats or the chains when her wings were cut off, there was clearly no chance now that she survived. The thought left a pit in both Natalie's and Quinn's stomachs. Lochen was immobile on the far side of the caldera in the exact location and position in which he had fallen. The place where he had landed was still strewn with rocks, half of which were covering him.

"This is a nightmare," wailed Quinn as he sat down with a thump.

Natalie squirmed free and stood next to him. She couldn't argue with his assessment.

"Yes, it is," she said softly. "We need to get Lochen."

She put her hand on Quinn's shoulder, and then helped him to his feet. They slowly made their way around the outer edge to the place where they had first arrived. From there they cautiously climbed down to the remaining floor trying carefully not to disturb any more of the rocks that had fallen when the Kelpie had blasted the ledge on which Lochen had been standing. The earlier sense of urgency seemed to have left the both of them.

When they reached him, Quinn pushed the larger rocks off of Lochen while Natalie brushed the sand, gravel and ash from his face. She brushed his hair from his face, and then felt his throat for a pulse.

"He's alive," she nearly shouted.

Once he was unburied, they carefully checked him over for any signs of broken bones or cuts. Aside from a number of bumps and bruises on his head, they could detect nothing serious, at least on the outside of him.

"I hope he's not bleeding internally," said Natalie.

"That could happen?" asked Quinn, shocked at the thought. "He could bleed inside? Where would all the blood go?"

"It stays inside," said Natalie, "which is why it's called 'bleeding internally.'"

"But if his blood all stays inside," Quinn continued, "then he'll be all right, won't he? How could he be hurt if his blood all stays inside of him?"

"No. It could be worse. Especially if he's bleeding inside his head. We need to get him help. I just don't know where to go."

"Home," answered Quinn.

He said it with conviction as if it was the only logical answer. Without waiting for Natalie, he picked Lochen up and slung him over his shoulder. Then he started climbing back up to the top of the rim.

Richard Reda

"Home?" asked Natalie. "Your home?"

He didn't answer. He was on a mission. He walked back and forth on the rim, with Lochen hanging over him, looking for a safe way down the outside of the volcano. Natalie tried to talk to him again, but still got no response. Finally, she grabbed his arm and turned him around to face her.

"Answer me," she said, holding on to his sleeve. "Did you mean you're going to take him to your home?"

"I mean I'm going home!" he said with vehemence. "I'm going home, and I'm taking Lochen with me. I quit! I can't do this. You can come if you like, but I'm through. I'm not like the rest of you. I can't deal with all this – with the Kelpies and that Rebbercand who almost killed me; with hobgoblins and gargoyles; with jackals and sentinels; with all of it. I can't stand it anymore."

"So – what? You're going to haul Lochen to your home and do what?"

"Nothing," he shouted. "I'm going to do nothing but try to get him better and then he can do what he wants. As for me, I'm through."

"Through?" she asked, still not comprehending what he was saying. "You're just going to leave? Leave us? Is that it?"

"Yes," he answered. "No. You can stay with me if you like – in the Ice Kingdom – if you decide to come with me. But I'm not going to any swamp, or forest, or sea or anything. I'm going to stay put. I'm going to enjoy seeing my friends and family, and I'm going to play with my dogs."

"I don't understand how you can do that," Natalie said in dismay.

"Simple," he said defiantly. "I'll just do it."

"After all we've seen; after all we've been through. How can you turn away? These Kelpies are threatening everything. You can't quit now."

"Don't you understand? That's exactly why I'm quitting," he said. "We've all nearly been killed. And now we've lost Summer, and maybe Lochen. I can't go through that any more. I won't go through it. I QUIT!"

"But we need you," she pleaded.

"No you don't," he shot back. "You don't need me at all. You've never needed me. Not before; not now; and not later. I don't have any special powers. I don't have any special skills. I'm just a normal person. I used to have a normal life in a normal village with a normal family and normal...normal...stuff!"

"You're wrong," she said, speaking softly to him. "You have no idea how much you mean to us – how much we need you."

He shook his head, but said nothing. He turned and looked her in the eyes. She could see deep inside how defeated he was; how much pain he was in, and that his mind was made up. She knew nothing she could say would change it. She had never felt so alone before in her life. The feeling of desolation was overwhelming. A single tear formed in the corner of her eye and rolled down her cheek.

"I'm sorry," he said turning away, his throat tightening and his voice cracking. "I can't do this anymore. I'm going home."

Stella was the first to awaken. Her head was throbbing. She opened her eyes without moving, afraid her head would fall off. She scanned her surroundings, not recognizing anything. She remained as still as possible, listening for any signs of danger. All she could hear was the soft breathing of others sleeping.

Richard Reda

She slowly turned her head towards the sounds and a wave of pain flashed across her head. She reached up and felt the cut on her forehead, trying to recall what had happened. When she moved her fingers across the cut, she could feel some kind of powdery substance. She looked at her fingers and saw the purple residue on the tips.

"What's this stuff," she muttered.

She wasn't familiar with any poultice or potion that looked or felt like this. She hoped it was safe. She tried to recall what had happened. The last thing she remembered was watching Sean climb up the face of the glacier. Then it came back to her: the iceberg had broken off and dropped in the sea right next to them.

The next thing she recalled was the tiny boat she and the others were on – the one that Liam tried to move away from the glacier – was suddenly swept back towards that giant wall and then nothing. Everything went black.

She managed to roll onto her side and saw the person stretched out closest to her. She reached over and nudged Solveig.

"Wake up," she whispered.

When Solveig's eyes opened she smiled at Stella.

"He said you'd be all right once you woke up," she said.

"Who?" asked Stella.

"The sentinel," she answered. "Another sentinel. He's gone now."

"Where are we?" Stella asked.

She carefully turned her head to take in more of the strange surroundings. That was when she spotted the wolf. Its head was inches from the top of hers. She rolled over onto her stomach and

364

was face to face with it. She tensed up a bit, which must have been felt by the wolf. He opened his eyes without moving anything else, and stared back at her.

"I assume he's friendly," she said. "There's something familiar about him. What is it?"

"He looks like that wolf that we saw inside that volcano when we rescued Natalie," Solveig said. "Of course, I don't know about you, but I wouldn't be able to tell one from another. Except this one has a crystal around his neck. If I remember right, so did that one."

The wolf stretched its neck out, moving its face within inches of Stella's. Then, without warning, its long, pink tongue ran across her face, giving her a lick. Stella closed her eyes, wrinkled her face and then turned her head back to Solveig.

"Yes," she acknowledged. "He's friendly."

She managed to force herself to a sitting position, and rubbed the wolf's kiss from her face.

"How did he get here?" asked Stella motioning to the wolf. "Or there – or – I don't know; wherever we are."

"Beats me," said Solveig. "All I know is that he saved us yesterday. I'm pretty sure it was yesterday. It could have been longer. I don't know how long we've been asleep."

By now Sean and Liam had risen. They looked around the conical enclosure and found a bowl with strips of meat. They expected them to be as tough as jerky, but to their surprise the strips were very tender and very tasty. In truth, it wouldn't have mattered. They were all so hungry they would have eaten wood. They also found some fruit and a large canister of water.

"What happened?" asked Stella.

"Well," said Sean. "I was climbing up that wall of ice..."

"I remember that much," she said cutting him off. "I don't mean then, I mean, how did we get here – in this place – and what did the sentinel tell you?"

They explained the events from the time they reached the top of the glacier, their trek across the ice and their encounter with the wolf and the jackals. Then they told her about the sentinel – how he appeared to them, what he said and where he went. They tried to repeat verbatim what he had told them, but it was all a jumble

"What did he mean?" she asked Sean.

"I'm not sure," he said. "At first none of it made any sense – at least not to me. Then he put his hand on my face and kept talking. It still didn't make sense, but then...I don't know...it's hard to explain, but all of a sudden, it was like he pulled a curtain aside and I understood. But now I'm not so sure."

"And what did you understand?" she persisted.

"I'm still working it all out," he said.

"I thought you said you understood," she persisted.

"I said I understood," he answered, "not that I can explain."

"What about the rest of you?" asked Stella. "Didn't you hear the same thing? Do you understand?"

"He seemed to have some kind of connection with Sean," said Liam. "He didn't touch either of us – just him. I heard what he was saying, and it kind of made sense, but not completely. It was hard for me to put it all together."

"I felt the same way," said Solveig. "I felt like I was getting only part of what he was saying. I heard every word, but...I know this sounds nuts, but I felt like I only understood about every third or fourth word."

"That's right!" exclaimed Liam. "That's what I felt, too."

They looked at one another and then turned to Sean.

"Let's wait until we meet up with the others," he said. "I think we need to be all together. Maybe then all the pieces will fit. It makes my head spin trying to think about it."

"Yeah," said Solveig, nodding her head. "We need to be altogether."

"Fine," said Stella, who was far from satisfied with the answers, or the lack of them. "Did this sentinel give you any clue as to which way to go?"

"Can't you tell?" asked Solveig. "Can't you see your map anymore?"

"Oh, that's right," said Stella. "The map."

She closed her eyes for a few seconds. Her hand moved towards the stone which was still hanging from the Sorcerer's Thread around her neck. She furrowed her brow and placed her other hand on her forehead.

"Yes," she said. "It's not far from here."

"Let's go, then," said Liam. "The sooner the better. Maybe we'll reach it first this time."

"Wait," said Sean. "Let's see if the sentinel left us any warm clothing."

They moved to the dark edges of the enclosure and found a bundle of heavy cloaks. There were six of varying, but comparable sizes, and one that was much smaller.

"He made sure we had one for Summer," said Liam. "But he didn't get the right number. Does that mean something happened to one of the others?"

His voice had an edge of anxiety to it. His first thought was that the sentinel knew that one of the eight had been lost.

"I think he knew I wouldn't need one," said Solveig motioning to her deep purple cloak.

"This is too strange to think about," said Sean.

They wrapped up, gathered a few more food supplies and some water and then turned towards the clear opening. The wolf cut them off before they could cross, stopping them. Then he turned and led the way out.

"Is he going to be with us the whole way?" asked Stella.

"I don't know," said Liam. "You'll have to ask him."

They turned to Stella who had a look of surprise on her face.

"You mean he can talk?" she asked in shock.

Then they started to laugh at the joke. She just shook her head. They followed the wolf out, and seeing no signs of the ice jackals, they rounded the outcropping and headed north.

It was the time of year in the Ice Kingdom when the days were growing shorter and shorter. The sky was still covered with a blanket of gray, and the little bit of sunlight that was visible was shrinking each day.

They didn't get very far when they decided they had to camp for the night. They once more found a place where Sean could carve out an enclosure. Stella was less certain about being warm, since she had been unconscious the other time they had done this. She was pleasantly surprised.

"You've learned more than you shared," she said to them.

The wolf opted to stay outside for the night, and when morning came, he was gone. They all missed his presence, but none more than Sean. Although no one said anything, every one of them took his sudden departure as a bad omen.

Late in the afternoon of the next day, less than an hour before the second sun would disappear below the horizon, they arrived at a small frozen lake. The area around it was flat and bleak. The wind raced across the ice, making the air even colder than normal.

There were a number of low drifts along one side of the lake, but they didn't look inviting. They walked out to the center of the lake. Liam brushed aside the snow to reveal crystal clear ice that extended several yards downward.

Near the bottom was what appeared to be a block that was coated and filled with a strange mist. The ice around it was clear, but the block was not. It was a swirl of white and gray with a few flecks of black. The area of the frozen lake immediately above this block was much colder than the rest of the ice, if that was possible.

It was so cold that the four staring down at it could not stand there long. They backed away, moving to the edge of the lake. Stella didn't have to tell them they had arrived. They all knew it instinctively.

"I guess we found it," said Solveig.

Her throat was dry and her words came out in little more than a whisper.

"It looks that way," said Sean. "I suppose we should be glad, but I don't feel that way."

Like Solveig, his words came out in a soft, dry whisper.

"What do we do now?" asked Stella.

Liam looked at them and said, "We wait."

Quest of Eight Part Five: Release of the Demons

Richard Reda

ABOUT THE AUTHOR

Richard Reda spent most of his life working for various agencies and Departments in the Federal Government. He believes this gave him a solid foundation for writing fantasy and fiction, so much so that he was encouraged to return after retirement to write some more. He lives with his wife in Manassas, Virginia, where he retired – the first time.

The *Quest of Eight* series originated as bed time stories for his grandchildren. As the grandchildren got older and the bed time stories got longer, it was suggested to him that he write them down. So he did. One, however, was not enough. Follow the continuing saga in the next chapter - *Part Six: Loss of Hope.*

Quest of Eight Part Five: Release of the Demons

Richard Reda

www.ingramcontent.com/pod-product-compliance
Lightning Source LLC
Chambersburg PA
CBHW060154260626
47160CB00001B/269